COPYRIGHT © 2024 BY EMMA LUNA

All rights reserved. No part of this publication may be reproduced, stored or transmitted in any form or by any means, electronic, mechanical, photocopying, recording, scanning, or otherwise without written permission from the publisher. It is illegal to copy this book, post it to a website, or distribute it by any other means without permission.

This novel is entirely a work of fiction. The names, characters and incidents portrayed in it are the work of the author's imagination. Any resemblance to actual persons, living or dead, events or localities is entirely coincidental.

Emma Luna asserts the moral right to be identified as the author of this work.

Emma Luna has no responsibility for the persistence or accuracy of URLs for external or third-party Internet Websites referred to in this publication and does not guarantee that any content on such Websites is, or will remain, accurate or appropriate.

Designations used by companies to distinguish their products are often claimed as trademarks. All brand names and product names used in this book and on its cover are trade names, service marks, trademarks and registered trademarks of their respective owners. The publishers and the book are not associated with any product or vendor mentioned in this book. None of the companies referenced within the book have endorsed the book.

First Edition

Ebook ASIN: B0D7W1H4ZP

Model Cover Paperback ISBN: 9798343917543

Publisher: Luna Eclipse Publishing

Cover Designer: RJ Creatives

Editor: Amber Nicole

Proofreader: Abrianna Denae

Interior Graphics: Pretty Little Images

Formatting: Emma Luna

Contents

Author Note	v
Blurb	vi
Content Warning	vii
Dedication	ix
1. Marcus	1
2. Marcus	11
3. Chloe	19
4. Marcus	31
5. Marcus	45
6. Chloe	63
7. Marcus	73
8. Chloe	85
9. Chloe	103
10. Marcus	115
11. Marcus	129
12. Chloe	149
13. Chloe	159
14. Marcus	173
15. Chloe	195
16. Marcus	219
17. Chloe	233
18. Marcus	249
19. Chloe	261
20. Marcus	275
21. Chloe	293
22. Chloe	311
23. Marcus	329
24. Marcus	347
25. Chloe	359
26. Marcus	371
27. Chloe	391
Epilogue - Marcus	405

Acknowledgments	419
About Emma Luna	421
Follow Emma Luna	422
Also by Emma Luna	424

Author Note

Prized Possession is a dark mafia romance that is intended for mature readers. It may contain themes that are distressing for some people. Please see the content warnings page for more information, or contact me directly.

Emma Luna is a British author, and **The Rivals of Blackthorn Series** is set in England and Ireland. Therefore, UK English spelling, grammar, and phrases have been used. If you find any errors, please don't hesitate to email: emmalunaauthor@gmail.com

If you want to be the first to receive up to date information and giveaways, you can join my mailing list here:
https://www.emmalunaauthor.com

If you enjoyed the book, I'd love to hear about it. Please don't hesitate to put a post on any of my social media accounts, letting me know which characters you loved. If you can also leave a review on Amazon, that would be much appreciated too.

Thank you to everyone for taking the time to read this book, and for taking a chance on me. I really appreciate you!

Love, Em xx

Blurb

In the dark underbelly of Blackthorn, Marcus Morelli is a formidable leader, ruling alongside the rival Santoro family. When a high-stakes bet grants him possession of Chloe Santoro—his best friend's sister—everything changes. Chloe's meant to be off-limits, especially as she's engaged, pushed into an arranged marriage by her parents.

Stuck together for sixty days, Marcus peels back the layers of her carefully constructed facade and uncovers the trauma hidden beneath. He challenges her to embrace vulnerability, showing her that true power lies in surrendering control.

But as their connection deepens, the tension rises. With family loyalties on the line, and a fragile peace hanging by a thread, Marcus must decide: can he risk everything for a love that could shatter their worlds?

Content Warning

Prized Possession is only intended for mature readers, and features some scenes that may be triggering for people. This list features the main triggers in the book, but is not exhaustive. I acknowledge that some people have triggers that may not be triggers for others.

So, if you are worried, please reach out to me. I will respond quickly, and in the strictest of confidences, letting you know if your trigger features in the book or not. Please don't worry about getting in contact with me. Your mental health is important to me, and I don't ever want anyone to be triggered reading my books!

Please note - whilst the world the books are set in is dark, the relationship between the main characters is not. Ultimately, it is a love story.

TRIGGERS INCLUDE:

Torture
Violence
Murder
Historical Kidnapping
Historical Rape and Sexual Assault (With Forced Drugging)
Drug and Alcohol Addiction (Not MCs)
Coercive Control (Not Between MCs)
Gaslighting
Kidnapping
Sexual Torture of a Male (Not MC)
Mental Health Discussions
Edging
Praise Kink
Degredation

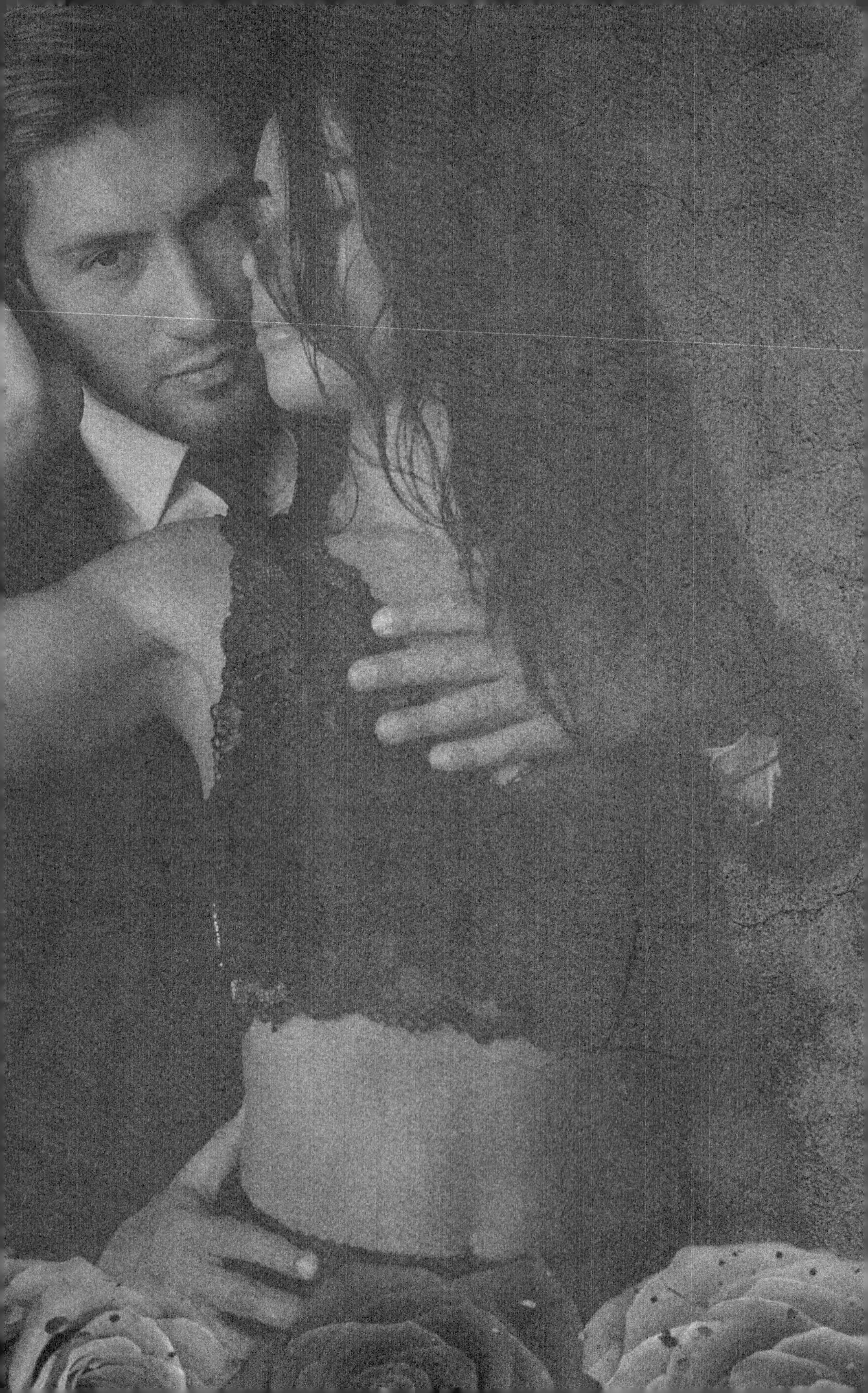

DEDICATION

*To anyone harbouring a secret crush
on your brother's best friend...*

This one is for you!

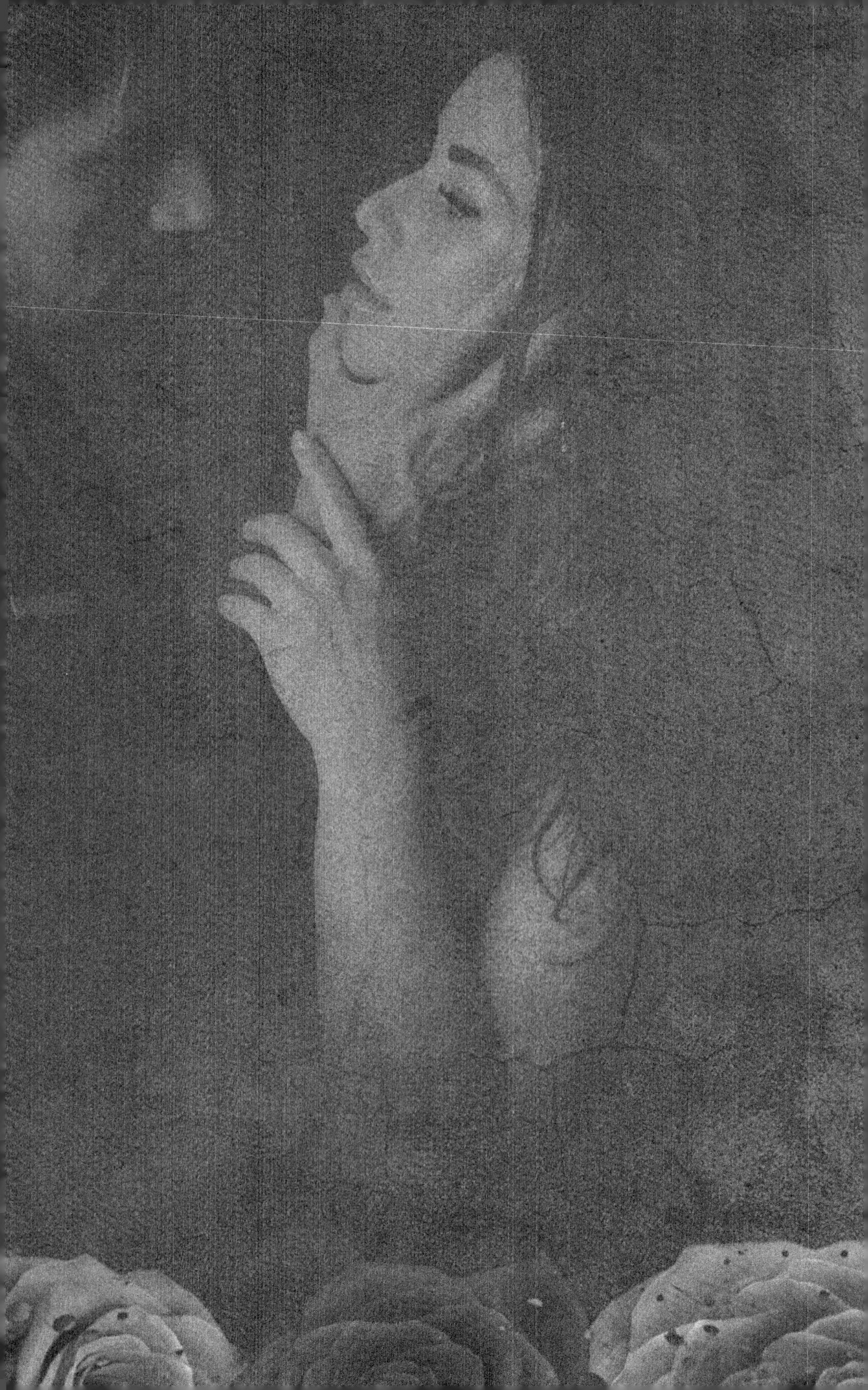

Prized Possession

RIVALS OF BLACKTHORN

USA TODAY BESTSELLING AUTHOR
EMMA LUNA

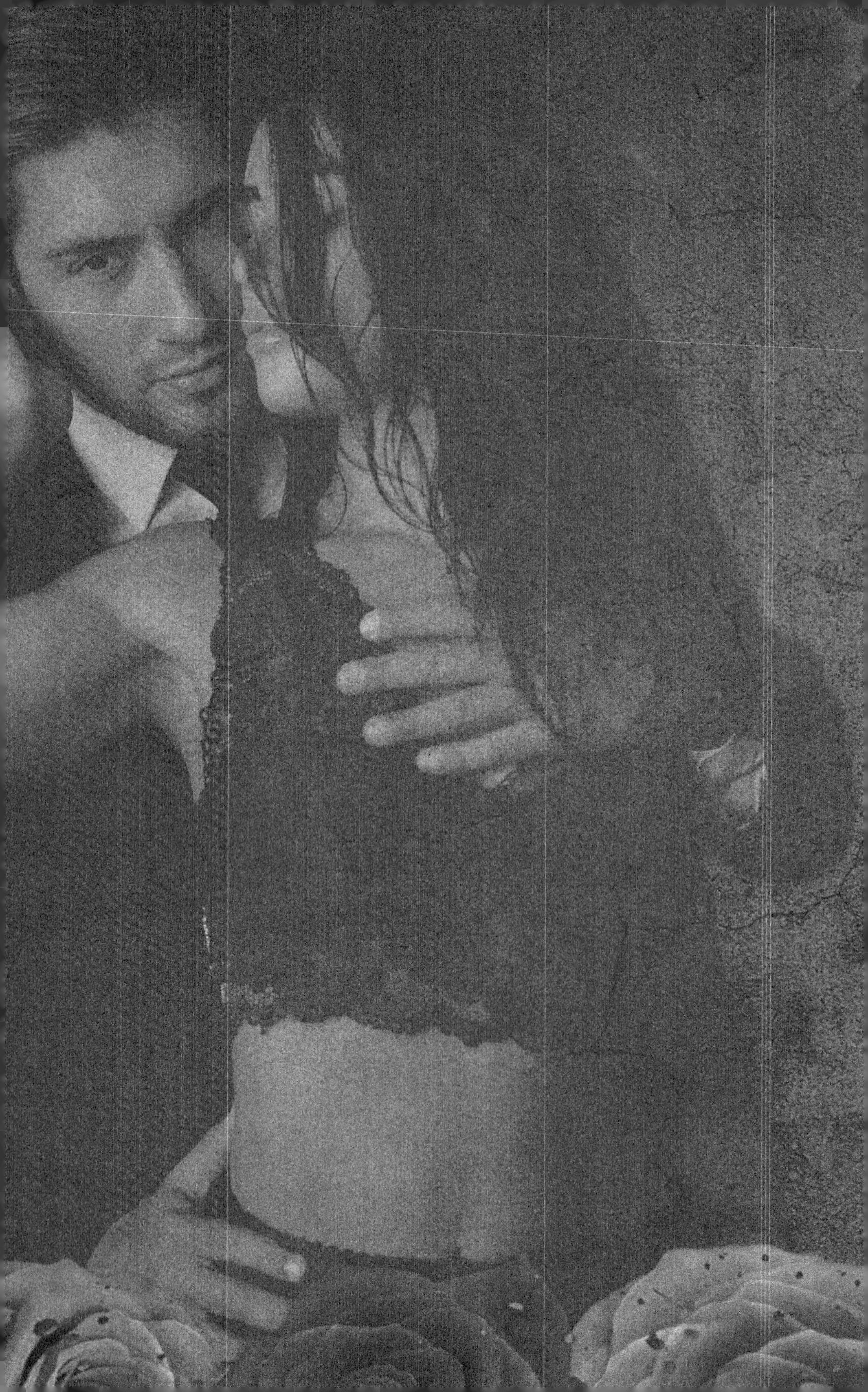

Chapter One
Marcus

"Your father will see you now," says the busty blonde secretary who looks to be even younger than me.

As I stand and walk toward my father's office, she throws a flirty wink my way, making sure to push her cleavage up. I shudder as I wonder if she does that to my father too.

He has a bad habit of fucking his staff, and she looks to be around the right age for him, though he seems serious about his current girlfriend, much to my disgust.

"Thanks," I mutter, keeping my gaze fixed on the door rather than at her.

Before I can let myself into the office, she calls out to me. "If I can be of any assistance to you, Mr Morelli, please don't hesitate to ask. It's my job to make sure you're well looked after." Her voice sounds far too fake, and it takes all my effort not to roll my eyes at her.

It's technically her job to answer the fucking phone and manage my father's schedule, not fuck his son, but I decide it's better not to point that little tidbit out.

"Thanks," I say again, turning away dismissively. I catch the shocked look that spreads across her face, like she's never been turned down before.

With my hand on the shiny doorknob, I take a deep breath as I clear my mind, pulling on the mask I wear in front of my father. As soon as I'm in control of my emotions, I turn the handle and open the door.

I quickly close it behind me before walking towards the desk in the middle of the room. My father is sitting behind the large mahogany desk, looking like a king ruling over his kingdom—which, I guess, in a way, he is.

As I lower myself into one of the two chairs on the opposite side of his desk, I take another moment to compose myself before we dive into the meeting.

My father is all business, dressed in his pressed black trousers and crisp white shirt. His dark hair has started to turn a little grey around the edges, but other than a few wrinkles across his brow and around his eyes, you wouldn't be able to tell his age.

At fifty-three, my father looks good for his age. He keeps in shape, using our home gym every day, though not as regularly as me. He was only twenty-five when he had me, and despite being thoroughly embedded in a world of danger and crime, he's aged well.

So much so that I'm regularly irritated when people comment on how much we look alike. Though it's true I inherited my father's strong jawline and jet black hair, my bright blue eyes very much come from my mother.

Even though she died when I was four, and I don't remember her, not only have I seen the resemblance in photographs, everyone who ever knew her makes a point of telling me.

You look just like your father, but you have your mother's eyes. Those words echo around my brain as I think of all the times I've heard that statement. The biggest problem, for most people, is that my personality seems to be a mixture of both my parents.

I have my father's ruthless, stubborn streak, along with the dangerous edge he's been teaching me since he told me I was destined to take over as the ruler of the Morelli crime family one day.

My mother had a wicked sense of humour, and a kindness that made her so well liked. I showed signs of inheriting those traits early on, and despite the training my father forced on me, he wasn't able to eradicate that side of me completely. Though it is only reserved for people I believe truly deserve it.

My best friend, Jacob, says that when I decide to really care about someone —to love them—I'd do anything for them, and it's true. I'm fiercely protective of the people I care about... It's just that I can count those people on one hand.

I've never been in love, so that cuts most women out of the mix. I have Jacob, who I've known my whole life, and my Head of Security and childhood friend, Miles, and I'd take a bullet for both. But other than my father, and a couple of members of his staff that helped raise me, I don't have many important people in my life.

In the world I'm part of, it's a weakness to have people who you care about, as they can be used against you. The last thing I want is for a girl to get killed because I let people think I was interested in more than just getting my dick wet, which is why I don't date.

I fuck women, when I'm in the mood, but they always know it's a one-time thing, and we go in with zero expectations, so nobody walks away heartbroken.

I know I sound like an arsehole, and I'm okay with that. Girls are a headache I just can't afford. Not when I'm trying to cement my new role as leader of the Morelli family.

Father clears his throat, grabbing my attention. He glares at me as he runs his gaze over my appearance. While he favours wearing smart trousers and a shirt, arguing that his appearance sets the tone for how he wants others to view him, I take a much more relaxed approach.

My dark wash jeans have rips across one of the knees, and the black biker boots I wear with them are more about comfort than image. Though the tight black T-shirt I wear that clings to my muscles in just the right way, and the leather jacket I always wear overtop, gives the air of danger that I'm going for.

While people look at my father and see a high-powered businessman, with me they see a dangerous bad boy, which is the image I prefer, though I wear a suit when my father forces me. Usually, during Council meetings and interacting with other important families.

"You're late," my father snaps, tutting at me when I roll my eyes at him.

I look at my watch and see that it's four minutes past nine, and if he hadn't kept me waiting out there, while his secretary perved on me, I would've been on time.

"Hardly. I was in your waiting room," I respond, trying to keep the irritation out of my voice, as that only winds him up more.

"I hope you're more punctual to official meetings," he drawls, before adding, "And more appropriately dressed."

It takes everything in me not to roll my eyes at him again, and instead I grip the arms on the chair tightly, reminding myself to control my breathing.

My father loves winding me up, and it's taken years of practice to remain aloof while he does.

"You know full well that I own a suit, and wear it when the occasion calls for it."

As much as I hate to admit it, I understand why my father views his suit as a uniform, and I can't deny that people show me a different level of respect when I'm dressed the way my father expects—even if I personally hate it.

He wrinkles his nose, his glare narrowing as he disapproves of the tone I used on him. I can tell he's about to start on another lecture about accountability and professionalism that I've heard a million times before, so I cut him off before he can begin.

"Was there anything in particular you needed to discuss when you called this meeting?" I ask, hoping it's enough of a distraction to prevent his lecture.

Although we meet regularly to discuss family business, this was very much a last minute, unplanned meeting, and it set me on edge from the moment Miles informed me it had been added to my schedule.

"Yes, as a matter of fact, I did have something important I'd like to discuss with you. But before I get into that, how's business? Everything going okay with Jacob? As I've made clear before, I'm worried about his recent behaviour," my father states, his gaze piercing into me as he tries to read my reaction to him bringing up my best friend.

Although I'm swearing and panicking inside my head, I make sure to keep my mask of indifference in place, so he can't see what's going on beneath the surface.

"As I explained at our last meeting, Jacob is going through a phase right now where he's partying a little more, blowing off steam, but that is all in his private life. Whilst he's at work, he's a complete professional, and we're working well together, just as we always have. I'm not worried, so you shouldn't be either."

I hold my breath, hoping my father is buying my lies.

The truth is, I am worried for my best friend. He's been slowly getting more reckless, engaging in activities that cast a doubt over him as a leader, and I know I'll only be able to protect him for so long.

"His father has also expressed some concern to me about his behaviour. If his own father is worried, then surely we should be too," he retorts, looking far too smug.

Fucking Jacob, I think to myself. I've been bailing his arse out of trouble since we were kids, but we're adults now, with massive responsibilities on our shoulders, and I'm not sure how much longer I'll be able to protect him.

"You know the relationship Jacob has with his father is complicated. I'm sure that's all it is."

Well, that's a massive fucking understatement. The relationship I have with my father is complicated. What Jacob and his father have going on is a whole fucking shit-show.

It's one of the reasons we've always got on so well together. We can both relate to the crippling expectations that come with being heir to a major crime family.

For generations, the Morelli and the Santoro family have been rivals, each battling for control over Blackthorn, the largest city in the North East of England. Whilst some of the bigger families were all fighting for dominance over London and the South, the Morellis and the Santoros set their sights further North.

With good transport links to all the major cities, as well as a port and airport for international imports, the Morellis quickly identified the benefits of this smaller, albeit just as profitable area. Sadly, the Santoros had the same idea, and for years our families were engaged in a turf war, each trying to take ownership for themselves.

When Maximus Morelli and Caleb Santoro came to power, they decided to call a truce between the warring families. For the past thirty years, our fathers have ensured a peace treaty remains in place, working together for the good of Blackthorn.

The Morellis, under my father Maximus' control, took ownership of the East, while the Santoros, led by Jacob's father, Caleb, ruled the West. They'd have regular Council meetings where they'd make decisions for the city together, whilst each retaining their own portion of power.

Me and Jacob were raised as our father's heirs, and we grew up together, knowing we'd be expected to rule as a team when we took over. Though it was drilled into us both that whilst it's important to maintain the peace treaty, we're still rivals, and should the time ever come, we'd need to take the other out in a heartbeat, or risk them doing the same to us.

Despite knowing this, Jacob still became my best friend. Although our friendship was initially forced on us as a result of familial obligation, it quickly turned into something so much more. We had a lot in common, and we bonded over the pressure we were under.

It wasn't long before I stopped seeing Jacob as just a friend who was forced on me, and instead he became like a brother to me.

So when he started going off the rails these last few months, of course I've been covering for him, hoping like hell too many people don't notice before I'm able to find out what his problem is and set him straight.

Unfortunately, the wrong people have taken notice before I can sort him out, so now I need to do everything I can to cover for him.

"I'm aware that Caleb and Jacob don't get on well, and he assures me that he's handling the issue, but I seem to be hearing new reports of his behaviour almost daily now," he responds, and I have to bite the inside of my lip to keep from cursing aloud.

With as much composure as I can muster, I ask, "Reports, like what?"

"This weekend, he was seen in our club—Caged—snorting cocaine out of one of the dancers belly button, before trying to fight three security guards who asked him to leave," he states, disgust dripping from each word.

Both my father and Caleb have always had strict rules, not just for us but all of their employees. The big one is that we're not supposed to sample the products we ship. Our job is to sell drugs to others, not get hooked on the stuff ourselves.

It was also drilled into us from an early age that the public's perception of us is everything. The only reason anyone should ever be talking about us is if they fear or respect us.

Airing our dirty laundry in public, or causing a spectacle the way Jacob has lately, has always been strictly prohibited. I'm actually a little surprised his father hasn't tried to stop him before now.

"I didn't know about that. Look, it's our monthly poker night on Saturday, so I'll talk to him about it then," I reply, cringing as my father's nose wrinkles in disgust once more. *It really is a wonder he doesn't have more frown lines.*

"You two still do that?"

He sounds like I just told him we take turns shitting on the table while the other watches, as opposed to the innocent gambling night it actually is.

When Jacob and I started taking more responsibilities from our fathers, and our roles as rulers grew, we knew we needed to find a way to work together, whilst still holding on to our friendship.

Although I see Jake as more like my brother, and we bonded over the commonalities we have in life, when it comes to our personalities, we couldn't be more different.

While he's funny, out-going, a relentless flirt, and a genuinely nice guy, I'm almost the opposite. I'm quiet, broody, and I have a 'stay the fuck away from me' aura that I give off at all times.

I'm the one who looks like I'll kill you in your sleep if you piss me off, when in actuality, Jacob's the hothead with the bad temper. I'm more likely to bide my time, plotting my revenge out thoroughly, before striking when you least expect it, and when I know I'll make the biggest impact.

Because of how different we are, we don't always agree on how to handle things. So to stop arguments from escalating, we created our monthly poker night.

During the event, we bring up any issues we have disagreed over, and we play for them. The winner gets to deal with the issue however they choose. Then when all the problems are sorted, we play for fun.

Our fathers hate the idea, but it's the best thing we could come up with to deal with our differences, without risking our friendship. And so far, it's been working well, but if Jake continues on like this, it won't be long before I can't protect him anymore, and his father will step in.

"You know we do," I reply, trying not to sound sarcastic.

"Well, clearly it's no longer working," he snaps, glaring at me.

Oops, guess he picked up on the sarcasm.

"I've told you, I'll sort it out this weekend," I respond through gritted teeth.

Father lets out a huff followed by a long sigh. "It might be too late for that. It brings us to the reason I called the meeting in the first place. I think Caleb might be putting things in place to replace Jacob as his heir."

My eyes snap open wide when I hear that, shock rippling through me like ice in my veins. "How?"

There are only a couple of ways that Jacob could be replaced, and I'd hate any of them. My heart races as my father sits there for a moment, looking like he's trying to find the right words.

"Caleb made the announcement earlier. In six weeks, Chloe will marry Scott Caprillo, uniting their two families together. I'm guessing he will be looking for Scott to take over from Jacob, if he doesn't get his shit together," my father growls.

My stomach flips and my heart sinks as he confirms my worst case scenario. I try to focus on my work, pushing all thoughts of *her* from my mind, the way I've been doing my whole life.

Chloe Santoro is the very definition of forbidden. She's my best friend's little sister, the girl I've been picking on since she was in pigtails, the daughter of our rival family. She's also the bane of my fucking existence—temptation at its finest—which is why I hate her so much.

"What the fuck is Caleb thinking? The Caprillos have been vying for power for years. If Scott and Chloe unite the two families, and that fucking prick, Scott, is made leader, it's only a matter of time before he tries to overthrow us," I grumble, trying to focus my anger on the business implications of this stupid fucking decision. Nothing more.

"I don't know what Caleb is thinking, but you need to sort this before it goes too far. Jacob has to remain as leader or our peace treaty will fly out of the window. It's on tentative ground as is," he replies, far more calmly than I feel.

"How the fuck do you expect me to sort this? If their marriage has been arranged and announced...it's final."

The words feel like ash on my tongue, but I know it's true. Very rarely in our world are the contracts of an arranged marriage nullified. Once you give your word and commit...there's no going back.

"I don't give a shit what you do, but you need to do something. I don't think there's much to be done about the arranged marriage. Like you said, usually when these things are announced, they're final. You're gonna have to work on fixing Jacob.

"Caleb would only ever hand over the reins to someone else if he was sure Jacob couldn't fulfil the role. He wants him to be his heir, so I suggest you focus on making Jacob aware of what he's going to lose."

As the words echo on repeat in my head, I know how tough this task will be. I may hate the pressure of being in the role I'm in, but I actually love my job, whereas Jacob has always hated it. The threat of him losing his status won't bother him one bit, but I need it to.

A million plans, all more elaborate than the last, run through my head. I have no idea what I'm going to do, but as I make my promise to my father, I know I mean it.

"I promise you, I'll sort this. The Caprillos will not get a single strand of power, if I have a say in it. No matter what I have to do, I'll ensure our peace treaty remains intact, and our family continues to reign with as much power and influence as we do now."

My fathers lips twist up into a smirk, a hint of pride visible that I rarely see. As I leave his office, my mind is whirling a million miles an hour.

Not only do I have to save my best friend from himself, I also have to do something to stop that arsehole Scott from gaining any power or influence.

My first thought is to find a way to stop the wedding before it happens, but I can't do that. If Chloe marries that wanker, she'll become his problem. I won't have to see her as much as I do now, which means she'll have less opportunities to drive me fucking crazy.

The part of me that's screaming to ruin her wedding needs to be silenced. I try to tell myself how much I'll enjoy her misery, watching her pretend to like the man her father is forcing on her.

I know she'll despise having her marriage arranged for her, and the sadistic side of me takes pleasure from her misery. So why is there a part of me that hates the idea of her marrying him?

I push the irrational thoughts to one side and focus on the assignment my father set for me. Talk about a fucking impossible task, and I have no idea where to start.

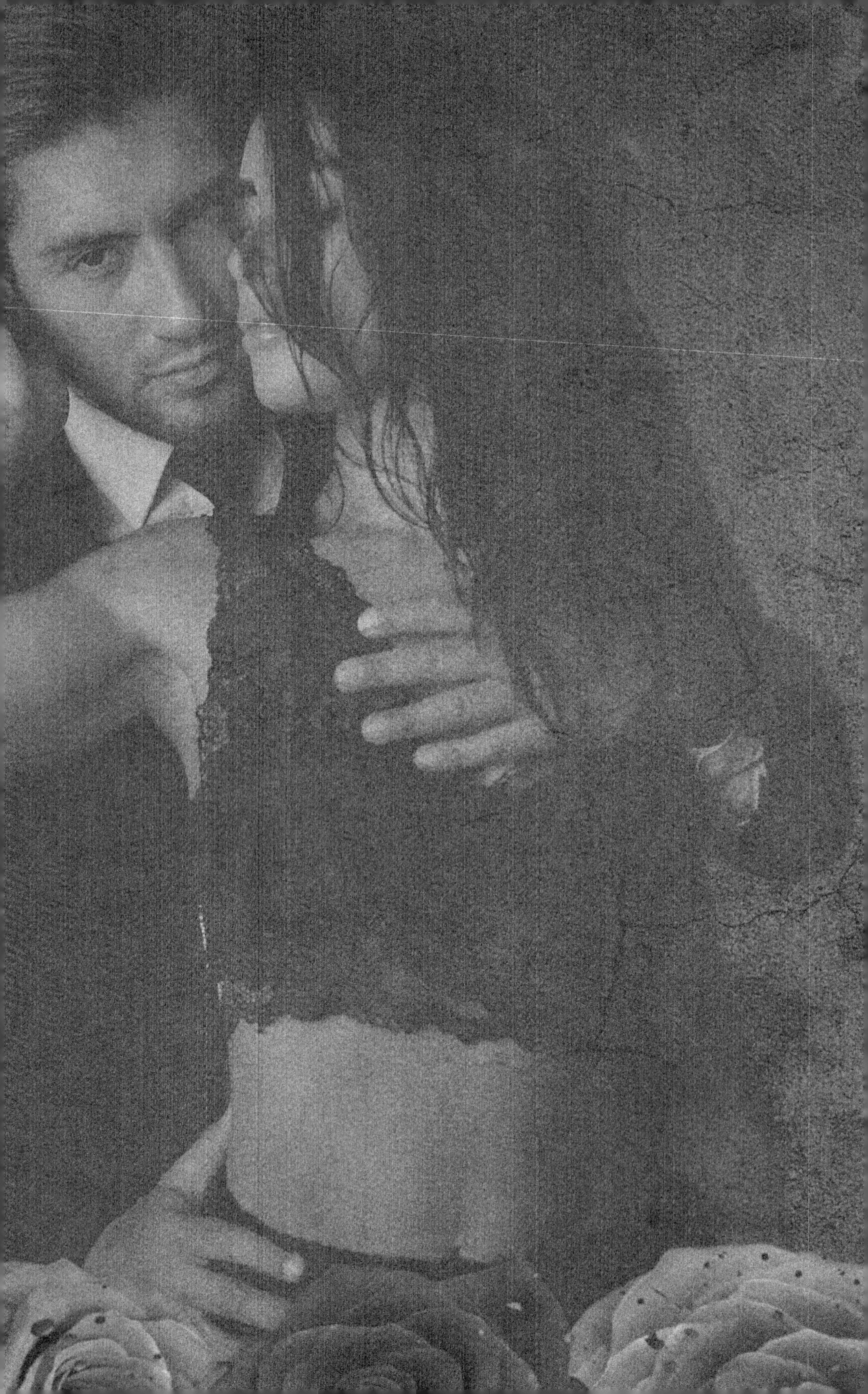

Chapter Two
Marcus

"Come on, Marcus. When did you start behaving like an old man?" Jacob whines to me down the phone.

I roll my eyes at his annoying tone, despite the fact he can't see me. "I'm not old, I just have responsibilities."

I resist the urge to remind him that he does also. But that's not how I'm going to sort Jacob out. He's already crippling under the pressure of said responsibilities, so highlighting that will only make things worse.

"Fuck responsibilities. We're only twenty-eight-years-old, Marcus. We should be going out on a Friday night. We should drink too much, blow off steam, and fuck pretty girls, whose names we can't remember the next day," he states, his voice raising in pitch as he no doubt becomes more animated on the other end of the phone.

I may not be able to see him, but I know Jacob well enough to be able to picture the way he's animatedly waving his hands around.

I want to remind him that we actually spent most of our late teens and early twenties doing exactly that. Though our fathers made the responsibilities we were born with clear, they also knew what the pressure of being an heir was like. They too had been pressured by their fathers before they were ready.

As a result, and a bit of pushing from our mothers when we were born, it was always agreed that we wouldn't be forced to work for the family business until we'd completed all of our education. And since we didn't really need the university degrees we were studying for, we made the most of being young, rich, single students while we could.

I threw myself into my role after I graduated, but Jacob has never really wanted to let go of the freedom we had as students. Hence, the night out he's trying to drag me along to.

I've been working all day, in and out of boring meeting after fucking boring meeting. And I didn't even get to hurt anyone, which meant the whole day dragged. I want nothing more than to go home, drink some good quality whiskey, and do fuck all. But that's not going to help with my assignment to straighten out Jake.

Oh, and taking him to a bar and getting fucked up alongside him will really help with the plan, I think to myself rather unhelpfully.

"I have an important meeting tomorrow, so I can't get shit-faced," I tell him with a sigh.

A loud whoop echoes through the phone, causing me to wince. *"Yes! It's been far too long since we had a proper good night out."*

I want to point out that we went to a bar just last week, and we meet up every month for our poker nights, that always end with us both consuming way too much alcohol. But I know that's not what he means, and I immediately set about fixing his expectations.

"Don't get too excited, Jake. I've agreed to come out, but this won't be a night out like when we were younger. I don't plan on drinking so much that we need to get our stomachs pumped. And your father will lose his fucking mind if you come home with a stolen, bright-orange traffic cone on your head again," I remind him.

The way my best friend chuckles tells me he doesn't look back on those incidents with the same feelings I do. *"He'd still prefer that than the time I was brought home in a cop car."*

I groan, remembering how furious both our fathers were about that. Jake was the one who got arrested for getting his dick out and pissing in an alleyway. I got into trouble for not stopping him.

"We were just lucky the cop who found you was on our fathers' payroll, or the outcome may have been really different."

Jacob snorts. *"Every cop is on their fucking payroll."*

He's not wrong. Sometimes, I think this is exactly the reason why Jake is as unruly as he is—there are no consequences for his actions. His father may yell and scream, or punish him in some way, but that's of no consequence to him. He knows the one real punishment would be to take away his role as heir...and that would be a prize for him, not a punishment.

"Even so, I don't want any trouble tonight. In fact, we'll go to Caged, so we can't cause any problems," I reply.

Jake's groan echoes loudly down the phone, sounding more like a petulant teenager than a guy who's not far off turning thirty. *"Do we have to go to your club? You'll just end up working. Plus, Maximus banned me from fucking any more of the girls who work there."*

I can't help but roll my eyes again. "That was me, not my father, and I did it because every time you fuck them and never call them, it causes issues for us. We've not had to replace as many girls since we put the rule in place."

"It wasn't that fucking bad," he grunts.

It really fucking was. "Mindy and Giselle tore fucking chunks out of each other's hair fighting over you, and neither of them realised you couldn't remember either of their names." I remind him, shuddering as I think of how truly brutal women can be towards each other when the green-eyed jealousy monster grabs hold of them.

"I still don't know who they are. But you should be thanking me for identifying your crazy staff members for you," he states casually, not caring how much he must have hurt the girls involved.

Don't get me wrong, I've been known to fuck a girl, not know her name, and not give a shit that I'll never see her again. But the difference is...I make my intentions very clear from the beginning. No names, no feelings, and no repeats. If she can't handle that from the off, I walk away. There will always be some woman who'll agree to my terms, and sticking by that means nobody has any expectations that can't or won't be met.

"Whatever," I reply dismissively. "I'll meet you at Caged at ten?"

"Fine," he grumbles.

"Oh, and Jake?" I say, grabbing his attention before he can hang up. "No fucking drugs."

"Fu—"

I hang up the phone before Jake goes into a full blown rant. I'm not sure agreeing to a night out is the best way to work on Jake's issues, but it's as good a place to start as any. Though I'm sure my father will disagree.

I need to make sure I come up with an actual plan and quick, as I know he'll ask me for the details soon. And right now, I have fuck all.

I arrive at the club by nine, even though I don't need to get there until ten. Honestly, even though this is supposed to be a night off, I can't help getting there early to check in with my staff.

Caged is just one of the legal establishments that we own, but it happens to be one of my favourites. It's the only one I've made sure remains completely free of any illegal activity, so when I choose to retire, I'll have a solid income. Not that I'll be able to retire until I have an heir to take my place, but thinking about the future is depressing.

Even just a fleeting thought of needing an heir sours my mood. I don't want kids. Why the hell would I want to bring a child into this world, and subject them to the same shit upbringing that I experienced?

If I were to ever have a child, I'd never want them to hate me the way I do my father, but that's an inevitable outcome if they're born with the same responsibilities on their shoulders.

Besides, to have an heir, I'd need to have a wife. The thought of a Morelli bastard would have all my relatives turning in their graves. No child with the Morelli name will ever be born out of wedlock, no matter how fucking archaic that might seem.

If I knock a girl up, I'll have to marry her for life. We don't do bastards or divorce. Which is why I always wear a condom, and no matter how much it pains me, I never come inside them. I pull out and take the condom with me.

After hearing horror stories growing up about how women could use my cum to trap me, the fear was enough to make sure I never allowed that to happen.

Why any woman would want to be tied to me, to this lifestyle, is a fucking mystery to me. Yes, I have a fuck load of money, and I'm not exactly bad looking, but there's a dark side to my life.

The dark, broody, bad boy image pulls women in, but that's all superficial. My life is full of danger and overwhelming expectations, and any woman by my side would be expected to fall in line with those. No matter how hot or rich I am, why would any self-respecting woman want that?

As I wander around my club, I take pride in how well the place runs, even without me there to keep an eye on things. The club is packed with people already, and everyone appears to be having a good time.

Everywhere I look, my staff appear to be doing their jobs. The guys behind the bar are making drinks with a smile on their faces as they chat to the customers. The DJ is playing a set that has the club pumped, and people are already grinding on the dance floor.

My security staff are blending into the background, like they're not really even present, but the lack of trouble lets me know they're doing exactly what I pay them to do.

Then there's the dancers. The reason the club is called Caged is because there are cages all around the room, each with a different dancer inside. Some of the cages are big enough to fit two people in them, and they're more for putting on a show.

There's even one large cage to the side of the mini stage with a pole inside it. Needless to say, there's always a lot of eyes on that cage in particular.

It's not just half naked women dancing in the cages either. There are men too, as I like to appeal to all of our audience members. Most like to see a man and a woman dancing together in the big cage. There's something very sexy about watching another couple lose themselves in each other during a sensual dance.

I didn't want Caged to be just another stripclub that only attracted certain types of people. I wanted it to be a club everyone would want to come to, and to do that, I had to try and appeal to everyone. It didn't take long for Caged to develop a reputation, and as a result, there's always a line around the corner of people desperate to get in.

Miles follows closely behind me, keeping an eye on our surroundings, doing his job at all times. With the amount of security staff I have in this place, I'm probably the safest I'll ever be, but that doesn't mean Miles will relax.

He's my Head of Security for a reason, and the only person I really trust to watch my back at all times, particularly when I have a few drinks and am more vulnerable.

I drop back a step until I'm in line with Miles, and he leans in closer to me, knowing I'm trying to talk to him over the noise of the club.

"Don't let me drink too much tonight. And make sure I'm home by one. We have that meeting in the morning."

A smile crosses his face and he chuckles. "You think Jake's going to try and get you pissed?"

I grimace. "I know he is. He'll probably try and talk you into it too."

Miles simply shakes his head. Although Miles is one of my best friends, his role as my security takes precedence over our friendship. If he were joining us as a friend, he'd make sure to have someone else take over as our security. But if there's no other security, he'd never abandon his role—no matter how much Jake might try.

"I'm here to work tonight. I'll make that clear to him, if he asks, but we both know he won't."

"If you wanna call another member of security in and take the night off with us, you can," I reply, cursing myself a little for not offering sooner.

I gloss over his comment about Jake not asking him to join us. I gave up trying to work out what is going on between them a long time ago.

We all used to be friends in school, then our final year of high school, something changed between them, and now they're cordial around me, and ignore each other when I'm not there.

Miles shakes his head to decline. "No, the meeting tomorrow is a big one, and you have your poker night too. I can't deal with all that if I have a hangover."

Miles is repeating everything I said to Jake, about how I want to be firing on all cylinders for the big day we have planned tomorrow. It's nice that Miles understands, as I know Jake will give me shit for saying things like that the minute he arrives. He enjoys shirking his responsibilities.

"That's exactly why I need you to make sure Jake doesn't try to lead me astray," I grumble, knowing the effect Jacob can have on me.

We're both competitive, and he knows that all he needs to do is make something into a game and I'm all in. But I can't be led down that path tonight.

"I can keep a leash on you well enough, but I've never been able to tame Jacob," he replies, a gleam in his eye that hints at something more than he's saying.

Jacob seems to go out of his way to wind Miles up, and sometimes, Miles' determination to not be rattled annoys Jake even more than when they argue. Though, when they fight, it gets heated quickly, and I've had to break them up on more than one occasion.

"I don't pay you enough to tame Jake. Though I do need to come up with a plan to get him to stop fucking around," I grumble, admitting to my friend that I'm no closer to finalising a plan than I was before.

We spend the next hour hashing out some ideas for how I might be able to get Jake to grow up. Admittedly, Miles' suggestion of kidnapping him until he detoxes might not be the worst plan we've come up with—which says a lot about the rest of our shit ideas.

I'm on my second Jack Daniels and Coke—and my last—when I notice Miles' face slip into a grimace, muttering a curse under his breath. I turn in my chair and follow the direction of his gaze, trying to find what it is that has him looking so uncomfortable.

He's looking at the entrance to the club, where Jacob has just walked in with his usual cheeky smile and assured swagger. But I know that's not what caught

Miles' eye. He's looking at the girl who is standing a couple of paces behind Jacob.

Dressed in the shortest, tightest black dress that shows off her shapely arse and tits, and the most sultry red lips, is Chloe Santoro. My dick twitches at the sight of her, and it only takes me a few seconds to realise why Miles is so on edge.

Chloe already looks drunk, swaying on her ridiculous high heels, and she's catching the attention of every man in the room.

My anger rises at the same time my cock does. Miles knows as well as I do, I'm going to end up getting into a fight tonight.

Whenever Chloe lets loose, I always end up having to stop her from doing something stupid.

She can hate me for it all she wants, but she'll thank me tomorrow when she doesn't have to make the walk of shame from some twat's house, while her father lectures her about responsibility.

I tell myself—and Miles—that the only reason I look out for her is because of the peace treaty, and the fact that Jacob is my best friend. He's too off his face to look out for her, so I do it for him.

Regardless of how many times I repeat that to myself, and to anyone who asks, it always sounds like a lie.

No matter how much I want to hate her, or how off-limits she is, there's something about Chloe that pulls me to her. It's a part of me I push down as far as I can, choosing to opt for the easy, obvious explanation instead.

Why is it we always crave something when we know it's forbidden?

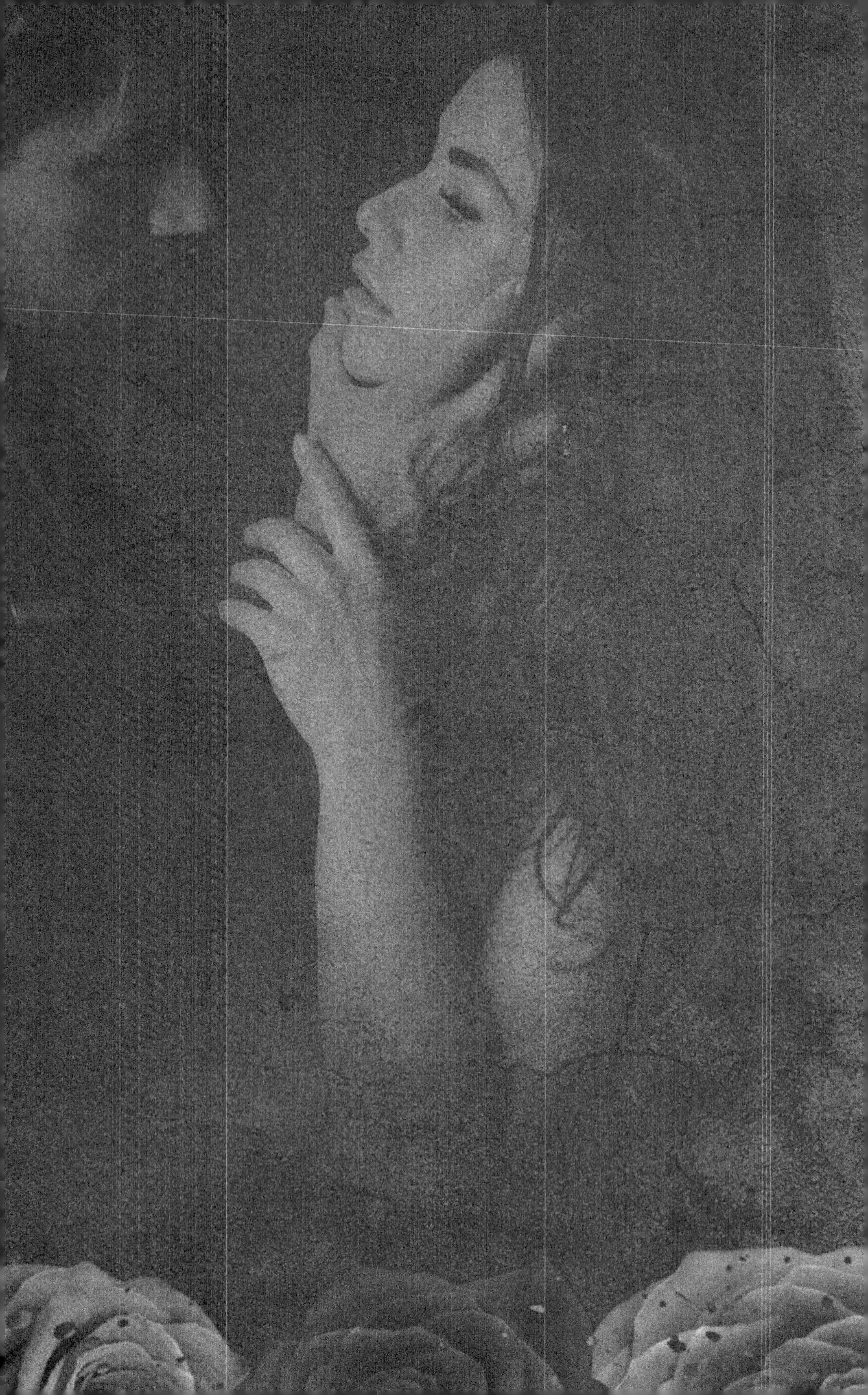

Chapter Three
Chloe

I climb the couple of steps into Caged, tilting slightly on my too-high heels. They would probably be fine if it weren't for the few shots of vodka I did before leaving the house.

There's a pleasant buzz flooding through my system, warming me up to the point I barely notice the chilly bite in the air outside of the club.

Once we're inside, and the pounding of the bass hits me, along with the warmth of all the bodies swaying together in the packed nightclub, I can finally breathe.

The alcohol and the noise have done their job, quieting the incessant voices inside my head to the point I can ignore them entirely. I'm able to be present in the here and now, instead of getting lost in the darkness of the past.

I feel a hand press against my back and freeze, whipping my head around to see who is touching me. My brother, Jacob, is giving me his usual smile, but his piercing brown eyes are looking at me with a little more scrutiny now.

He leans in slightly, bending until his lips are near my ear, and I try my best not to look as stiff as I feel. "You okay?"

I may trust my brother more than most, but I don't like people in my personal space, unless it's my choice. "I'm fine. Let's get a drink," I say through my fake smile, gesturing towards the bar.

He looks at me for another moment, and I hate the way it makes me feel—exposed. I attempt to brush it off, widening my smile to the point my cheeks hurt, as I approach the bar.

I breathe a sigh of relief when I feel his hand drop from my back. I can still feel his looming presence beside me, following me, and I try to focus on the buzz from before.

It doesn't take long for us to reach the bar, and it's even less time before the server abandons who he was about to serve, ignoring their complaints, and heads straight over to us.

With a polite smile, and a respectful head nod, he addresses Jacob. "Mr Santoro, it's good to see you again. What can I get you?"

Jacob smiles at the man's polite respect, but I see him bristle slightly at the use of his surname. It reminds him too much of our dad, and that's the last thing Jake would ever want.

"I'll have a beer, please," he says, before turning to me. "What about you, Clo?"

The server turns his attention to me. "Pink gin and tonic, please."

Without another word, the man moves to the bar behind him to start making our drinks. I take a moment to look around the club, though it's hard to pick out small details as the room is full.

I have a love-hate relationship with this club. *A bit like with its owner*, I think. Then I have to scold myself for thinking of that arsehole at all.

Although Marcus has been Jake's best friend for as long as I can remember, we've never been friends. I have had a crush on him forever, but it's very much one-sided. In fact, I actively try not to find him attractive, by focusing on his fucking miserable personality—but it never works. No matter how much of an arsehole he is, I can't seem to stop myself.

So when I tell myself I'm looking around the club to see who else is here, or maybe to check out the people dancing in the cages, I know I'm just trying to bullshit my own brain.

Of course, I'm looking for him. I just don't know if I'm pleased or not when I don't see him.

The server grabs my attention, letting me know my drink is ready. As I turn to pick it up, I notice there are two shot glasses, filled with what looks to be vodka, next to our drinks.

I turn to my brother, my eyebrow raised in question. "I figured we could do some shots," he replies with a shrug of his shoulders.

He grabs one of the shot glasses and raises it in the air, as though he's going to make a toast. He looks pointedly at the one that's meant for me, waiting until I pick it up. Once I have, his mischievous grin grows.

"What are we toasting?" I ask.

"I mean, we can always toast your engagement," he states sarcastically.

I glower at him until he looks away from the heat in my stare. "I'm not sure which I want to toast more... Our arsehole dad who's selling me off to the highest bidder, or the disgusting prick who bought me."

A shiver ripples down my spine as I think about the meeting yesterday, when I was officially proposed to by Scott Caprillo. Though calling it a proposal seems insincere, as it's not like I was allowed to turn him down.

I had to hold my hand out and let him slide the massive gaudy diamond onto my ring finger, before he placed a kiss on my lips, despite the fact I'd barely spoken to him prior to that meeting.

It took every ounce of strength not to scream, cry, or vomit all over his ridiculously shiny shoes. No matter how much my family warned me this day would come, there was a small part of me that hoped it never would.

I thought my family loved me too much to hurt me like this, to take my choices away.

I should have known what I want doesn't matter. People have been taking things from me my whole life, I just hoped the people who are supposed to love me unconditionally would be different.

Jacob is, and always has been, the exception to this. Despite us arguing like all brothers and sisters do, we are good friends. We've been looking out for each other since we were kids.

With only a year between us, we grew up close, and being brought up in the mafia lifestyle meant there were very few people we could trust except each other.

Jake hates the responsibilities that have been thrust upon him, he never wanted to be the leader of our family. He still doesn't want to be part of this life, and if he could get away from it, he would. So I know he despises the idea of me being used in another one of our dad's power plays just as much as I do.

"Let's toast to the arseholes we hate and love to dream about killing," Jake says, dragging a laugh from my lips as he clinks his shot glass against mine.

We both pour the liquid down our throats, and I'm basking in the delicious burn, when a deep rumbling voice echoes into my ear from behind me, sending a shiver down my spine.

"You wouldn't be toasting about me, would you?"

I don't need to turn around to know Marcus Morelli is standing behind me, and I curse the way my body tingles for a completely different reason at his proximity. His closeness doesn't make me freeze up the way other people do, and it takes every bit of willpower not to think about why that might be.

Jacob chuckles, reaching out to shake hands with his friend. I look up at Marcus, hating how small he makes me feel, even with these ridiculously high heels on. He's not even looking at me, and that sets my teeth on edge more.

"Well, you are an arsehole, but I can't say I've got any plans to kill you," Jake responds.

"Speak for yourself," I mutter under my breath.

Apparently, I wasn't as quiet as I'd hoped when Marcus lazily flicks his gaze over to meet mine. He looks at me with those piercing blue eyes, like I'm nothing more than an annoyance to him, and my temper rages beneath the surface.

"I'd like to see you try."

There's a dangerous edge to his voice that should wind me up, but the deep breathy tone only makes me feel hotter. Blush spreads across my cheeks, and I really hope it's hot enough in here for me to be able to pass it off as being overheated.

"You wouldn't see me coming." It's a much quicker comeback than I was expecting, and I'm quietly pleased with myself...or I am until he opens his mouth with a retort.

He leans in close, his breath fluttering across my ear so that only I can hear. "I'd definitely watch if you were coming."

My heart races, feeling like it's going to beat out of my chest. A shiver ripples down my spine, and I hate how my stomach turns like I'm a teenage girl with a crush.

My mouth flops open and closed like a fish, while my brain whirls, trying to think of something to say to that.

Is he flirting with me?

Before I can come up with a response, he steps in front of me, giving me his back, in a dismissive gesture that stuns me. I'm startled, but mostly I'm angry that he can say something like that to me, and then block me out of the conversation like I'm not even here. To say this man gives me fucking whiplash is an understatement.

He's talking to my brother like I'm not behind him, and I have to lean around him to try and be part of the conversation. Marcus steps in when Jake calls over the server to order more shots.

"I told you, I'm not getting pissed tonight. And you promised me you'd take it easy too," Marcus says in that annoying authoritative voice he uses, sounding more than a little judgemental.

Jake's eyes narrow at him, and I can see he's just as annoyed by Marcus' meddling as I am.

"I said I wouldn't do drugs, and I'm not. I never said anything about drinking."

"Your eyes are like fucking pinpricks, Jake. Don't lie to me," he seethes, but my brother just rolls his eyes at Marcus' judgemental tone.

"I didn't take anything in your club, like I promised. You never said anything about me taking them before I left hope. Loophole!" he cheers, and I can't help but smile when I see Marcus gritting his teeth.

I might not like my brother doing drugs, and I happen to agree with Marcus that he needs to drastically cut back on his partying, but I'm not going to pass up the opportunity to enjoy Marcus being wound up. The tick in his jaw and the fierce look in his eyes betrays just how annoyed he is.

"Since you're already high as a fucking kite, you definitely don't need any more alcohol," he snaps, grabbing the two shots of vodka that the bartender had just placed in front of Jake.

Reaching around his ridiculously bulky frame, I grab hold of the shot glasses. Jake's gaze flicks over to me, and Marcus has to turn around so that he can glare at me. I take advantage of this movement by throwing back both shots, one after the other, before slamming the empty glasses onto the bartop.

"Thanks, I needed those," I state with a very smug smile. Before either of them can scold me like a child, I turn away and head towards the dance floor.

I hear their shouts from behind me, but I can't work out which one is saying what. Honestly, I don't care either. I've had more than enough of people telling me what to do recently. Tonight was supposed to be about me coming out, having a bit of fun, and forgetting all about the life that's being forced on me in just six weeks.

When you have a giant ticking clock hovering over your head, counting down until your life will change forever, it makes you so much more aware of the time you have left. It makes me want to make my own decisions while I still can.

All my life, people have been making decisions for me, telling me what to do, and simply taking it if I refuse. This is all my life will be once I'm a mafia wife. I'll be a trophy wife, forced to obey the rules of my husband, whilst being viewed as a second-class citizen in my own life.

I have six weeks until my life changes forever, and even though I'm no different than I was yesterday when the engagement was forced on me, I want to be different. I want to make the most of the next six weeks, by making all the decisions I can, while I can. It's a false sense of freedom, and it's only temporary, but it's the best I have.

So, I'm going to drink way too many shots...because I can. I'm going to stand in the middle of the dance floor, dancing like nobody's watching...because I want to.

Then I'm going to pick a guy and let him take me home, making sure I'm the one to take all the pleasure I want, not him...because that's what I need.

I need to be the one making the decisions, choosing what I'm willing to do and when I say no.

It may only be temporary, but I'm going to make the most of it while I can.

With this mindset firm, I stand in the middle of the dance floor, surrounded by lots of hot, sweaty bodies who are all losing themselves in the music, and I let go of everything that makes me behave the way people expect.

I turn off the voices in my head, and I let the music infuse through my veins. The bass thrums in time with my beating heart, like they're one in the same. I sway my hips and throw my hands in the air, getting lost in the music.

I'm aware of the bodies around me, but I'm so deep in my own bubble, I couldn't even pick out faces or features. It doesn't matter who they are...I'm dancing for me.

When I feel a firm pair of hands grab onto my hips, the heat of a body crowding my back, I freeze for just a moment. Alarm bells ring in my head at the proximity, and the fact someone is touching me without my permission. I try to take some calming breaths, to push away the not-so irrational fear that is threatening to ruin my buzz.

I turn my head slightly to find a young blonde guy standing behind me, swaying his hips in time with the music as he holds on to mine. Although he has hold of me, and is standing closer than I'd like, he's not pulling me into him the way some guys do.

I take a moment to look him over, his seemingly nice smile being the thing that prompts me to give him a chance. He's a couple of inches taller than me —*nowhere near as tall as Marcus,* I think to myself, before pushing all comparisons to him from my mind.

He looks to be about my age, with floppy dirty-blonde hair that curls slightly on the ends, and green eyes that are a little dull looking. His white shirt is tight around his biceps, showing he has some large muscles on his biceps, but he's bigger across his arms and chest than anywhere else.

He looks like he lifts weights, but focuses more on his upper body, which gives him an asymmetrical look. His top half is bigger than his bottom, and I'm not sure how I feel about it.

Objectively, he's not bad looking. He's got a cute face and a nice smile, and when he moves his hips, it's clear he's got rhythm. I'm also a little impressed he's dancing at all, as not a lot of men like to dance, unless they think it'll get a woman into bed—which could be why this guy is doing it, but there's something in the way he moves that suggests he might enjoy it.

"I'm Sam." He opts to shout at me rather than leaning in, so that I can hear him clearer. I'm pleased he's not leaning more into my personal space.

"Chloe," I reply, before pointedly looking down at where his hands are on my hips.

His eyes follow the direction of mine, but he doesn't let go. Instead, his lips twist into a bigger smile. "I was watching you dance and couldn't help myself. I was wondering if you'd dance with me."

I already am, given you put your hands on my hips without my permission, I shout in my head.

Luckily, the connection between my mouth and brain is severely delayed thanks to the alcohol, and I decide not to say that aloud, since I'm trying to have fun, and be in control of my own decisions. Maybe I want to dance with him.

"I think we can have one dance," I reply, giving him my best flirty smile, hoping like hell it doesn't look as awkward as it feels.

I'm fucking awful at flirting.

His smile widens as his eyes darken hungrily. His grip on my hips tightens and he pulls me against him, my back pressed into his chest. I do my best to ignore the sinking feeling in my stomach that I always get when someone gets a little too close.

I allow the alcohol and the loud thrumming bass to flow through me, loosening my tight limbs as I try to block out everything around me.

I've always loved to dance. There's something completely freeing about closing off your mind, feeling the music consume you, as you move your body without thought. My hips sway in a way I normally don't have the confidence to move them, and my whole body is looser.

As Sam's hands glide from my hips down to my thighs and across my lower abdomen, I squeeze my eyes closed and bite the inside of my cheek to stop the intrusive thoughts from returning.

I call on the deepest parts of my imagination, trying to imagine that the hands on me belong to someone else. The first image that flashes into my head isn't one I want to think about, but he's been the subject of my dreams for as long as I can remember.

No matter how much of an arsehole he is to me, and how often I'm reminded that I'm not supposed to like him, or want him, I can't help myself. There's just something about Marcus that has always drawn me to him, even when I try not to.

I'm not completely delusional. I know the attraction is totally one-sided. I'd even go as far as to say that he hates me.

At the very least, he sees me as nothing more than his best friend's annoying little sister, who he's forced to look out for, even though that's the last thing he wants to do.

He's just too fucking gorgeous for his own good.

Thinking about Marcus seems to work, and the antsy feeling I was getting with Sam's hands on me starts to dissipate slightly, reducing my tension just a tad.

Sam must take this change as encouragement as presses his hard length against my arse. He rolls his hips, thrusting against me in a way that's totally inappropriate for where we are. I try desperately not to care.

Moving one of his hands from my hips, he glides it up my body, over my ribs, before reaching my breasts. Clearly not caring that we're in the middle of a very public dance floor, he takes my breast in his hand and starts to squeeze.

I wince slightly at the firm grip. It reminds me of a clown honking a horn, and I have to bite my lip again to stop the laugh that threatens to break free.

Clearly, Sam isn't very experienced, as he continues to squeeze my boob like it's his very own stress ball, not at all interested in the nipple, which he doesn't seem to realise is the part that gives me pleasure.

Luckily, once he's had a grope of both tits, he lifts his hand onto my head. He grabs my long dark hair in one hand and flicks it over my left shoulder, so it's all falling down the front, leaving my right shoulder bare. This was obviously his intention, as he wastes no time pressing his lips against my neck.

I freeze when his mouth makes contact with my flesh, and my racing heart combined with the bass creates a static buzzing noise in my ears. Nausea ripples through me, and I try to pull in a much needed breath.

Remember where you are!

I keep repeating the instructions over and over in my head, trying to prevent the nightmares from invading my waking mind.

Sam is none the wiser that I've stopped dancing, or that I'm frozen to the spot. He continues peppering kisses along my neck as he grinds his cock against my arse, his fingers digging into my hip, tight enough to bruise.

I try not to focus on the bite of his grip, or him rutting against me, but it's no use. All I can feel is his mouth on my throat. The way he kisses, licks, and sucks on my neck, like he's trying to leave his mark on me for all to see. I want to push him away, but I'm too frozen to move.

As he bites down on my neck, harder than I was expecting, I cry out in pain. My noise is drowned out by the sounds of the nightclub, and given all the people on the dance floor, I may as well be invisible.

"You're so fucking gorgeous. You're gonna look so good with my cock down your throat," he whispers into my ear in between bites.

His breath hits me, and the smell of beer, smoke, and something almost rancid makes my stomach roll. Nausea hits me in extreme waves, and I'm starting to panic that I might vomit in the middle of this dance floor.

Normally, I concentrate on my breathing until the sickness passes, but I can't do that this time. If I get another whiff of his revolting scent, I won't be able to hold back.

His words, combined with the sleazy way he kisses me, makes me feel dirty, and the ants under my skin are back. I want to itch at them, scratching away until I can't feel them anymore.

I gave up on trying to get my skin clean a long time ago, and have since just settled for keeping the ants at bay—something I'm failing at right now.

A drop of moisture hits my cheek, and I didn't even realise a tear had escaped, until I felt it tracking down my face. I squeeze my eyes shut tighter, hoping that will prevent any more from falling.

Do something, Chloe. Don't just fucking stand there like a coward—again. Fucking fight!

My brain yells at me, trying to give me the courage I need to move, but it's pointless. I'm too frozen with fear, lost to the nightmares of the past and the potential horrors of my future.

I try to close my mind off completely, to give in to the inevitable, when everything changes.

The hands and lips that were dominating me are gone, and without the support of Sam's body holding me in place, I collapse to the ground. Before I can make contact with the sticky floor, strong arms grab hold of me. Once I've found my feet, they release me.

I quickly open my eyes, blinking under the brightness of the strobe lights. My vision focuses just in time for me to see a fist make contact with Sam's face. Blood bursts from his nose and he hits the floor like he weighs nothing.

I lift my gaze to see Marcus standing over him, his hands balled into fists, his body practically vibrating with rage. His face is contorted into a snarl, anger dripping from him in droves.

His bodyguard, Miles, is pulling him back, whispering something into his ear that seems to help him calm down. He takes a few deep breaths, his fingers twitching as he tries to loosen his fists.

Sam is unconscious on the floor, but before he has a chance to wake up, the club security guards pick him up in a less than gentle way.

The crowd seems frozen, watching the events unfold. It's at that moment that Marcus realises we have many eyes on us, and he seems to compose himself. Drawing his shoulders back, he runs a hand down his body, straightening out creases that are not there.

All the anger and rage I saw a moment ago is now gone, and the mask of indifference he seems to wear constantly is back in place. He looks perfectly composed, and that's how he wants to appear. To almost everyone, he's pulling it off, but under the gaze of someone who has been watching him for a very long time, I can see the cracks in his perfect facade.

Once Miles is sure Marcus is back in control, he releases his hold on him. Miles says something to him that I can't hear, and their gaze flicks over to me. Marcus' eyes darken, anger flashing in them, but unlike with Sam, I'm not scared.

He stalks towards me, closing the small distance between us before he grabs the top of my arm. His grip on me is tight enough it will probably add to the other bruises I'll have on my skin after tonight.

I wait for my body to freeze, for my heart to race, for fear to overtake me the way it always does when a man touches me like this, but it doesn't come. His grip feels warm, and my skin tingles in a way I never expected.

Before I can register that thought too much, Marcus begins walking away, dragging me with him. His gaze is still locked on mine as he leads me through the crowd of people, not even bothering to look where he's going. People move for him, giving him the respect he's earned in his own club.

People may not know the real business Marcus and Jacob are in, but they know enough to have a healthy fear of the pair. Marcus has earned it just by the dangerous vibe he exudes.

I should be terrified that he's turning all his anger on me. I should be running a mile given the dangerous glint in his eyes. Yet I don't—I can't. There's something about this man that's almost magnetic, and I'm drawn to him—danger and all.

I can tell before we even reach our destination that I'm in so much fucking trouble, yet my body is humming with more excitement than I've had in a long time.

I've always loved pushing Marcus' buttons, winding him up, and I think I'm about to get the perfect opportunity to do just that. No matter what punishment it may earn me.

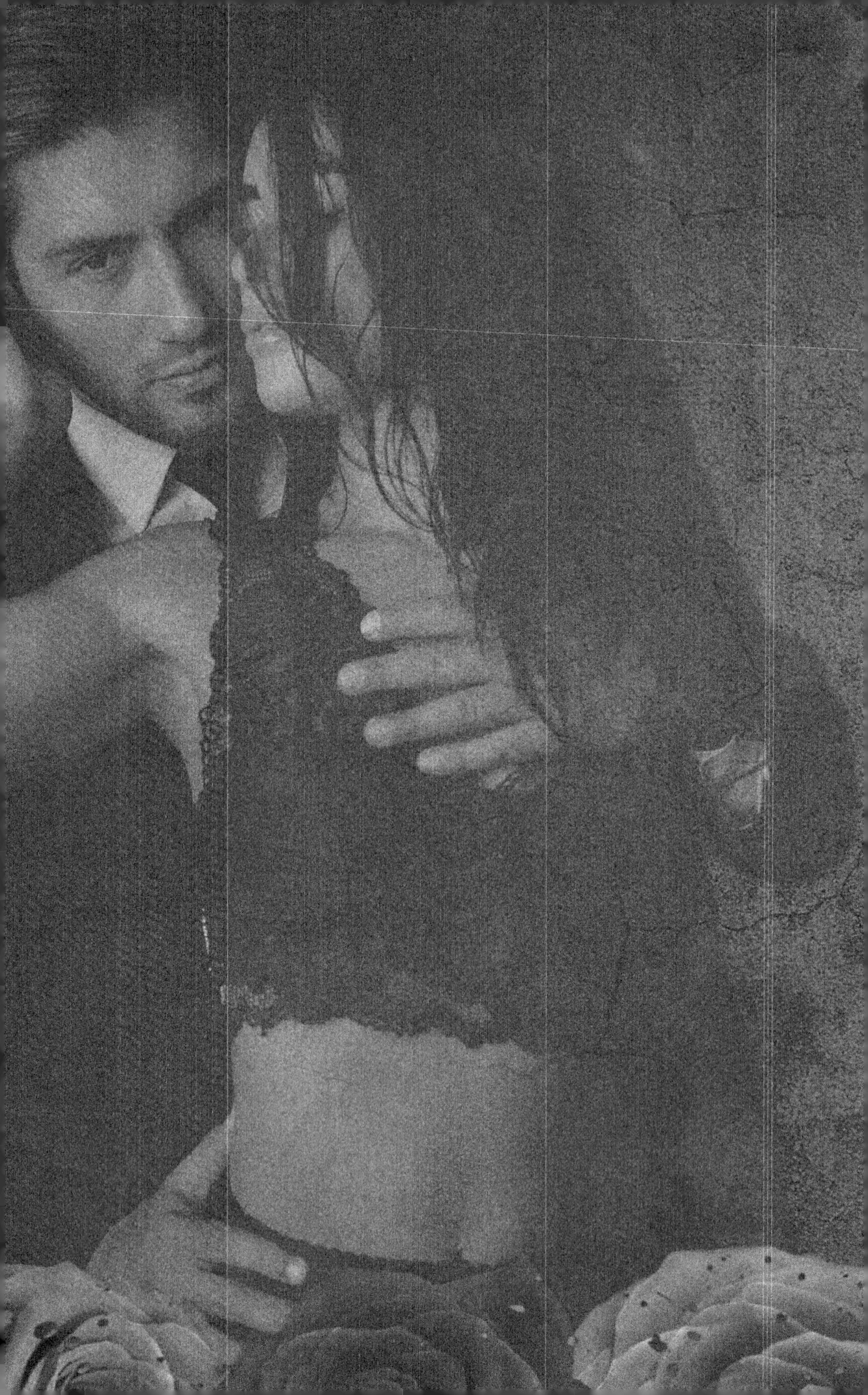

Chapter Four
Marcus

My barely controlled anger is thrumming through my veins, my body practically vibrating as I storm through the club. Even people who don't know who I am know to get the fuck out of my way.

The crowded dance floor parts like the Red Sea as I march through, pulling Chloe behind me.

She shouts at me, but the loud music and the sound of my own heart pounding in my ears, blocks her out. I know my grip on her arm is tight enough to bruise, but I don't fucking care.

Before I pulled her away, my club security was taking care of that arsehole, making sure he knows he's never welcome in this club again. I'm sure they will be issuing him with a strong warning about the consequences if he talks about what happened tonight as well.

He's about to learn very quickly that he messed with the wrong person, and given the fact I own half of this town, it'd be really fucking easy to kick him out. I try reminding myself that option is a bit extreme, but when I'm battling my anger, it's better than killing him.

Just as I reach the back door, that leads to the alley, where we receive our deliveries, Miles steps in front of me. My face contorts into a scowl as I make sure to hold Chloe back, so she can't hear whatever lecture he's about to give me.

"What the hell are you doing, Marcus? I thought our job was to stop the Santoro siblings from going off the rails? Unless your plan was to do something so fucking reckless that it eclipsed anything they do, then in which case, you've succeeded," he growls, his hand on my chest, a warning to take a second to think through my actions.

The only problem is, I'm not thinking clearly. Far fucking from it. "I can't keep an eye on them both. So get your arse back inside and find Jacob. Keep him out of trouble whilst I deal with Chloe," I state firmly, letting him know there's no room for negotiating.

Miles narrows his gaze at me, and those piercing blue eyes of his stare at me like he's trying to read into what I'm not saying. I almost want to squirm under the intensity. He's always known me too fucking well.

"Maybe I should take Chloe home and you should concentrate on Jacob?" he asks.

I shake my head, my glare narrowing until it's his turn to squirm. "No. Just do as you're fucking told, for once, and get out of my way."

My ice cold tone leaves no room for argument, and with an exaggerated huff, he moves away from the door.

Just as I'm about to step around him, he reaches out once more and places his hand on my arm. This time when I look at him, there's a softness to his face that's almost as annoying as his penetrating stare. This is his concerned face, and just for a moment, it makes me regret whatever's about to happen.

"Don't do anything stupid that you can't take back."

Before I can say anything more, he gives me a small head nod and walks away. The brief pause has given me time to catch my breath, and I'm no longer being driven by the rage flooding through my veins.

Now that I can't hear my own heart pounding in my ears, and I'm calming down, I'm thinking clearer. Miles' words of warning echo through my head and logic makes me question what the hell I'm doing.

Or it does until the annoying fucking woman behind me brings it all flooding back.

Chloe's hand hits the side of my arm just a second before her loud, screeching voice seems to vibrate through me, given how close she is to my ear.

"What the fuck are you doing? Let go of me, you arsehole."

I have no idea how long she's been shouting obscenities at me, but it's not until she hits me and is yelling in my ear that I hear them.

Suddenly, all the rage and irritation comes flooding back, pushing my calm away, like the sea bashing over a sandcastle, as ice floods my veins.

My grip on her arm tightens further, but I care even less now. With my other hand, I press the employee code into the security panel, waiting for it to flash green, before I push the door open, pulling Chloe out with me.

The alley at the back of the club is completely empty, and there are only two ways to get in. One is by car, under a security barrier that's manned by staff at all times, and the other is through the door we just used. Since there are no deliveries expected tonight, it's no great surprise that it's empty.

I pull Chloe until we reach a dead end. With tall buildings on either side, and a large brick wall behind us, there's very little light at this end of the alley, just a faint flicker of the security light above the door and the moonlight above us.

As soon as we reach the wall, I quickly spin Chloe around and press her back against it—harder than I initially intended, but my anger is running the show once more. I take a step forward, crowding her with my body, as I tower over her.

She gasps when my chest makes contact with hers, and I watch as she tries to take a step back before realising there's nowhere to go.

Her piercing silver eyes are wide as she stares at me with a mixture of fear, confusion, and what I'm pretty sure is attraction.

She's not attracted to you, dickhead. She's scared of you, I tell myself.

She has every reason to hate me, to fear me. It's how I've been trying to make her feel about me for years.

From when she was eight-years-old, and told me she had a crush on me, so I pushed her over... I've spent all my time and energy making her see that I'm not the good guy.

She deserves a nice bloke who can give her the world, not someone like me. Particularly since her father would have cut my cock off, and that definitely would have broken the fragile peace treaty.

Making her hate me has been my plan for years, and I thought it was working. But recently, as she's been going more off the rails, it's been getting harder to stand by and do nothing. I can tell there's something going on with her, and I want to know what it is.

I'm very aware I shouldn't care, and that it's not my responsibility to try and fix Chloe. In fact, I should be putting all of my effort into sorting out Jacob's issues, but watching her let that fuckwit put his hands all over her was the final straw.

Jake has been rebelling since our final year of high school, worsening after we were handed the key to the kingdom, and it was always going to happen.

Whereas, Chloe's path to self-destruction is something I didn't see coming, and that bothers me much more than it should.

Her tiny voice pulls me out of my own head as her breath flutters over my face. "What are you doing?"

There's none of the bravado she'd had before in the club when she was yelling at me. Now her voice is small and timid, not something I've ever associated with Chloe. She's always been feisty, not afraid to go toe-to-toe with me.

As she stands here beneath me, her body trembling, her eyes wide and fearful, my heart thuds. *What the fuck am I doing?*

Then the image of that guy's hands all over her flashes onto the back of my eyelids, and the anger floods back.

"The better question is: what the fuck were you doing?"

Upon hearing the accusing edge in my tone, her gaze narrows and the timid girl from before fades away, bringing back the one who loves to argue with me.

"Well, I was dancing before some dickhead jumped the guy I was with," she snarls, leaning even closer, so I can see her nostrils flare.

"That wasn't dancing, Chloe. You were a step away from letting him fuck you on the dance floor," I grind out through gritted teeth, as I ball my free hand into a fist, to stop myself from touching her. My other hand remains flat against the wall above her head, helping me to cage her in.

Chloe manages to get her hands up into the miniscule gap between us, and once her palms are on my chest, she tries to push me away, letting out a small scream of annoyance when she's not able to move me.

"Are you calling me a slut? Don't you dare fucking try and slut shame me, Marcus. I've seen you and Jacob do much worse with girls on that very dance floor," she shouts as she punches her fist into my arm.

Using my free hand, I grab hold of both her wrists, lifting them until I can use the hand over her head to grip them both. With her hands restrained above her head, her chest arches in a way that makes her tits look fucking amazing, and it takes all my effort not to stare at them.

I keep my gaze locked on hers, but when her pupils dilate, making her sparkling silver eyes almost black, my cock twitches, hardening even quicker than before.

"I didn't call you a slut, and even if I did, that wouldn't be a bad thing." My voice is deeper and more gravelly than normal, as the anger thrumming through my veins is replaced by something much more potent.

Remember all of the reasons you're supposed to stay away from this girl! No matter how much I shout it in my head, all the reasons I've been focused on for the last few years empty from my brain. My dick is running the show now, and it's going to get me in so much trouble.

Her brow furrows and she looks at me confused. "What does that even mean?"

She pulls her lower lip in between her teeth, biting down on the bright red shade that makes me imagine smearing it in some very dirty places. I shake my head, trying to concentrate, but she's so fucking distracting.

"You say the word *slut* like it's a bad thing, and I don't think it is. If the girl chooses the right person to be a slut with, it can be an incredibly powerful experience," I reply, loving the way her eyes widen with each word.

"Powerful?" she repeats, the pitch raising at the end to make it sound like a question.

"Absolutely. I think if a woman trusts me enough to become a slut for me, that's a massive honour. She's willing to give up a little bit of her control, and that's a big thing, but at the end of the day, she's still the one with all the power."

She shakes her head like she disagrees. "How can a woman giving up her control make her powerful?" she asks incredulously.

The corner of my lip tilts up into a smirk, and I'm actually shocked this woman doesn't know how fucking gorgeous she is and the power that gives her.

"You hand over just a little bit of control, but in return, you get so much more. A good slut has the power to make even the most controlled man lose his senses. A little moan, a sensual kiss, the right touch, you can have even the most important man dropping to his knees to worship you. That's the power of being a good slut."

She takes a moment to mull over my words before the corner of her lip tips up into a mischievous smirk. Before I can say anything, she rolls her hips against me, rubbing herself on my hard cock, as if to prove my own point.

A groan I wish I desperately could hold back rips from my throat, and her eyes widen almost comically as her smile grows. I'm losing control of this situation very quickly, and I had a point to make when I dragged her out here.

My grip on her tightens as I pull back slightly, trying to give my dick a bit of space, as I really don't want to blow a load in my pants, like a teenager who just discovered porn.

Once I've made it clear she's not to move, I gently trail my hand up her body, my fingers ghosting over her ribs. Her breath hitches and her eyes flare dark again.

As soon as I reach the top of her ribs, I lightly brush my fingers over the swell of her breast, before trailing them across her chest to her neck. I spread my fingers out, until they're encasing her throat, and she's forced to tilt her head back a little to accommodate me.

I grip just hard enough to let her know I'm the one in control, but it's not enough to hurt or take her breath away—not yet, anyway. I lean forward until my lips are almost against her ear, and I can't help the cocky smirk that grows when she shudders beneath my touch.

"But you can only be a good slut with the right guy," I whisper against her ear. "That fuckwit in there...he was not the right man."

I press down on her throat, letting her feel how angry I was that she let that jizzbag touch her, when it was painfully obvious she didn't want him to.

All the confidence she had before seems to leave her, and when she speaks, it's barely above a stuttered whisper. "H-how do you know h-he wasn't the right guy?"

It takes all of my control not to roll my eyes. There's no way that arsehole would know what to do with a girl like Chloe, and I'd bet good money on him having a small cock.

I use my grip on her neck to lift her chin slightly as I lean back, making sure she has no choice but to make eye contact with me. When she tries to close her eyes to avoid me, I squeeze her throat. They pop back open, and at first she looks startled, until anger flares in her molten gaze.

"When you were with him, you looked like his touch repulsed you. I bet you were drier than a fucking desert. When you become a slut for the right guy, your pussy will be dripping wet," I growl, my mouth practically salivating at the thought of finding out if she's wet for me.

She shakes her head, disagreeing with me. "It takes more than some dancing and a bit of harmless touching to get some girls wet."

A harsh laugh rips out of me. "That's what women tell themselves to excuse the dickless idiots they're with."

Her brow furrows and she glares at me, but still she doesn't fight to get away from me.

"Bullshit. It takes a lot for some women." Although she tries to sound fierce, she's a lot less sure now than before.

"That's bollocks. You've just never been with the right guy," I say, leaning in closer until my breath hits her ear. "And I can prove it."

I slowly drag my tongue over her earlobe before pressing my lips lightly against the spot on her neck just below her ear. It's barely the ghost of a kiss, but her breath hitches, and I can feel her heart racing beneath my fingers around her throat.

I keep my lips just hovering over the same spot, leaving her in suspense over if I'm going to kiss her again or not, as I let go of her arms.

"Do not move your hands from above your head or I will punish you," I state firmly, and she does as she's told, not moving even a little.

With my free hand, I move it down to the hem of her dress that's sitting high up on her creamy thighs. I tickle my fingertips over her skin, feeling her shiver beneath my touch.

I snake my hand underneath, bunching it up as I lift my hand further. She's barely breathing, frozen beneath me as she waits on bated breath for my next move.

As I reach the lacey fabric of her knickers, I run my finger over the outside of the fabric, swiping through her slit, and as soon as I feel her wetness seeping through, it takes all my control not to fall apart.

My cock twitches in my boxers, straining to be free, to the point it's almost fucking painful. I want to wrap my fingers around my length, as squeezing always helps to relieve some of the throbbing tension, but I don't have a free hand, and there's nothing in this fucking world that's going to make me take my hand away from Chloe's cunt.

"I thought you said you don't get wet that easily, Chloe?" I ask, my voice low and dripping with sex.

She tries to shake her head, but given my grip on her throat and my lips against her neck, she doesn't manage it. "I-I don't."

My smirk grows as I hook my finger into her knickers, pulling them to the side. She gasps lightly as the cool air hits her exposed pussy, and I press my lips against her neck, sucking on her flesh until I leave a mark.

I then swipe my finger through her warm slit, groaning as I feel how hot and wet she is. Her moan flutters over my face, and as I look down at her, I take in the blush of her cheeks, the way her mouth has fallen open slightly as she clamps her eyes shut, completely lost in the moment.

As I pull my finger away, her eyes open and she watches me raise my hand until it's between our heads. We can both see her glistening juices dripping off my finger. Her cheeks flush bright red, and she pulls her lower lip between her teeth, clearly embarrassed that I proved her wrong.

"You look like you're dripping wet to me," I point out, before I lean forward and pull my finger into my mouth, sucking her taste off my skin.

My eyes roll at her sweet, salty taste, and I want to scream at myself for such a fucking reckless move. I should have known that as soon as I have one taste of her, it will never be enough. I want to consume her.

Our gazes are locked together, and her eyes widen as she watches me swallow the taste of her from my finger. Her mouth opens and then closes, like she wants to snark back at me, but for once, she's lost for words.

I decide to capitalise on the moment, and I move my fingers back between her legs. This time when I slide through her slit, I seek out her clit. As soon as I find her hard nub, I circle my fingers around it, spreading her juices as I do.

Chloe's head falls back as a moan escapes from her lips, and she rocks her hips to try and press my hand against her greedy cunt even more.

She looks so fucking dirty, her legs spread wide for me, rocking her hips against me with her dress up around her waist, her head thrown back against the grungy alley wall.

She's a rich mafia princess, who always looks so perfectly put together, and I love watching her turn into a dirty slut just for me. I meant what I said to her before, there's nothing negative about a woman being a slut for the right man.

I may be the one in control of her pleasure right now, but she's the one with all the power. She says stop and I'll walk away without hesitation. She's the one getting all the pleasure, while my cock is straining painfully, trying to get free.

As I rub my fingers over her sensitive nub, her back arches off the wall as she tries to move my hand to where she needs me the most. I press on her throat, just enough to make her neck ache, and to grab her attention.

Her eyes fly open in shock. "Stay still, slut," I growl.

"I-I'm not..."

Before she can finish her sentence, which no doubt was to tell me she's not a slut, I cut her off by pressing one of my fingers into her wet hole. Her loud groan echoes through the alleyway, and my dick throbs.

Her hot, wet cunt clamps down on my finger, and even with just one inside her, she feels tight. I can only imagine how amazing she'd feel gripping my cock as I press into her.

As I work my finger faster, her cries of pleasure get louder, and she forgets all about my instruction that she's not supposed to be moving.

She rocks against me, meeting my movements with one of her own as she chases her release.

I can feel her walls tightening as her pussy gets even wetter than I thought possible. She feels so fucking fantastic. Way better than my shitty imagination has been able to conjure up over the years.

"Oh, fuck... Marcus."

As soon as my name tumbles from her lips, it's like someone douses me in a bucket of cold fucking water. Suddenly, I remember who she is, and all the major fucking reasons I've stayed away from her over the years. I've been deliberately treating her like shit so that this very scenario doesn't happen.

She's my best friend's sister, the daughter of our rival mafia family...and if that's not enough, she's fucking engaged to someone else. Another powerful family that would have no qualms about going to war with us over me taking something that belongs to them. Yet, all of that seems to have fallen from my brain.

Recently, I've watched her go off the rails piece by piece. I've been so caught up with Jacob that I've managed to ignore Chloe's rebellious behaviour. But seeing her throw herself at a guy, letting him touch her, when she very clearly didn't want him to, it was the final straw. She has to have more self-respect than that.

As I said to her, I'm all for her being a slut, as long as it's with the right guy and it's what she actually wants. If his touch repulses her, she should have enough self worth to kick him to the curb.

The way she moans my name brings all this flooding back, and I'm so fucking confused. I love the sound of my name on her lips, and I want nothing more than to hear her scream it at the top of her lungs as I give her the orgasm I know she craves. But, I don't think that will achieve what I need.

I brought her out here to teach her something, and I can't let my own desire get in the way of that. Besides, if I want to avoid starting a war, I need her to go back to hating me...which means there's only one possible way this can go.

She rocks her hips against me with a desperate desire to reach the finish line she's so close to. Her walls flutter around my finger as I flick my thumb over her clit, dragging a deep guttural moan from her lips.

As I feel her start to tighten around me, I quickly pull my finger from her pussy, taking a step back, so my body is no longer crowding hers. She slumps forward as she cries out in frustration, and it's only my grip on her throat that's keeping her from falling to the ground.

Her silver eyes are wide open, and while she stares at me, a mixture of emotions flick across her face—confusion, desperation, need, anger, and then hurt. It's the look right at the end, when she's jumped straight to the wrong conclusion, that is like an arrow to my heart.

She drops her hands from above her head and begins to pull her dress down, covering herself as her cheeks flush red. Humiliation rushes through her, and she tries to drop her gaze to the ground, but she can't because of my grip.

Wrapping her tiny hand around my wrist, she tries to pull me off her, but I'm too strong. "Let go of me," she grinds out, trying to sound strong, but I hear the way her voice cracks at the end, breaking my heart.

She thinks I did all this to mess with her, and that I didn't really want her. The lack of self-confidence drips from her pores, and I want to find whoever caused her to feel this way and rip their flesh from their bones. No girl this gorgeous should ever feel this low about herself.

I step towards her, closing the gap again, loving the way she gasps at my movement, her body betraying the way she wants to behave.

"I didn't stop because I don't want you. I stopped because only good little sluts get to come, and you were not a good little slut tonight. You let that dickhead touch you, when you didn't want him to. You were willing to let him do things to you that you know you didn't want. You need to learn to put your needs first, to control—"

Before I can finish what I'm about to say, Chloe cuts me off. Her voice is full of anger, and my heart breaks as a tear drops from the corner of her eye.

"That's bullshit. I have no control. You say that I'm the one in control, that I have all the power, yet you're the one who can leave me here like this."

I reach up and swipe her tear away, brushing my thumb along her cheek in a far to tender way.

"This is different because I'm trying to teach you. I'm trying to show you that you do have all the power, even if you don't realise it," I explain, not entirely sure how else to show her.

She lets out a harsh humourless laugh. "If that were the case, I'd be in bliss after an amazing orgasm right now. Instead, I'm frustrated, feeling dirty, and so fucking humiliated."

"And you don't think this hurts me?" I snap, as I grab hold of her hand and pull it down between our bodies. I press her small palm against the front of my trousers, forcing her to feel how fucking painfully hard I am right now.

Her eyes widen almost comically, but instead of pulling her hand away like I expect, she shocks me by gripping my length, squeezing in the most fucking ball-tingling way. A low groan rips from my throat and I pull her hand away, watching as her lips tip up into a smirk.

"See...I told you, a good slut has all the power."

"But I'm not a good slut, otherwise you'd have let me come?" It sounds like a statement, but the way she phrases it at the end is definitely a question.

"Correct."

"If I promise to be a good slut for you, will you make me come?" she asks, looking up at me with those fucking hypnotic eyes.

No! No, Marcus, remember all the reasons from before. You stopped for a reason.

"We both know you can never be *my* slut. You belong to someone else, remember?" I point out, hating the way her eyes darken with anger at the reminder.

"Another fucking choice that was taken away from me, forced on me," she grinds out, and I get the feeling she's talking about so much more than just her arranged marriage.

"What other choices have been taken from you?" I ask, hoping I've caught her in a moment of weakness and that she'll answer.

Instead, she pushes at my chest, and this time I let her move me back a step.

She takes in a couple of deep breaths, like she's bordering on panicking, and tears are glistening in her eyes again.

"I've never made a single choice my entire fucking life," she snaps.

"And you'd do things differently, if you were the one in control of making the decisions?" I ask.

She nods, but there's a sadness to her. "There's no point even thinking about it."

"What if I say I can help you?"

Her eyes narrow in suspicion, and even I'm not entirely sure where the hell I'm going with this.

"Help me, how?"

"I'm not sure yet, but if I could give you some time, so you can make different choices in your life, what would you say?"

She lets out another humourless laugh. "I'd say you're talking out of your arse. We both know my life is set on a path that can't be altered."

"I might not be able to alter it, but what if I could delay it? Buy you a little time? A short period where you're allowed to do whatever you want, be who you want. It'll only be a taste of freedom, but it's better than nothing," I explain.

Though I've got no fucking idea how I'll make it happen, if she agrees to it, I'll move Heaven and fucking Hell to give her what she wants.

"I'd ask what you want in return?"

Her suspicious gaze locks on mine, and the corner of my lip lifts further, widening my smirk. She knows me too well—of course, there's something I want from her. Well, actually, there's a lot I want from her, but she doesn't need to know that.

"If I do this for you, I want your help getting Jacob back on the straight and narrow. He's falling off the rails harder than you are, but I need him to get his shit together. If not, your father is going to hand over the reins to that dickhead you're marrying, and I can't allow that to happen," I explain, killing two birds with one stone.

"Jake doesn't want to rule. Getting him to get his head on straight won't be easy," she replies timidly.

"But if we work at it together, we stand a good chance."

She nods like she agrees, but she doesn't say anything. The silence sits between us, and I can almost see the gears turning in that pretty little head of hers.

"So if I help you get Jacob to take responsibility, you'll buy me some time away from this arranged marriage?" she asks finally.

I give her a nod, before clarifying, "I can't guarantee how I'll do it yet, as I don't exactly have a plan, but I'll buy you some time before you have to get married. I'll get you out of your father's house, so you can live a little."

She bites on her lower lip again, like there's something more she wants to say, but she's trying to pluck up the courage. I want to tell her to just spit it out, but I don't. I give her the time she needs, until finally she lets out a little sigh.

"What if I ask you to show me how to be a slut? How to take back all the control?"

My breath hitches and I'm sure my heart fucking stops for a moment. I never, even in my wildest fucking dreams, imagined Chloe would say those words to me. Of course, I want to show her how to be my good little slut, but if I do that, there's no going back. It'll put everything at risk.

"Let me think about it," I reply, not able to turn her down like I should.

Given the smile that spreads across her face, she seems pleased with my answer—she shouldn't be.

"Be careful when you make a deal with the devil, Mio. You might not like what happens."

Her eyes widen, and my cocky smirk grows as I drop my hands. I start walking backwards, not wanting to tear my eyes away from her. She's leaning against the wall, face flushed, panting like she can't catch her breath, with her skirt up around her waist.

She looks like the perfect slut, and it fucking pains me to walk away from her, knowing how wet and desperate she is.

Just before I turn around, I make sure to give her one more thing to think about. "When you rub your pretty little pussy tonight, make sure it's me you're thinking about when you come. It will always be me you think about from now on, even when you're married and he's fucking you with that tiny dick of his. I'm going to ruin you. Make sure you think about that when you fuck your pussy with your fingers later."

Her mouth drops open, but I see the way her body trembles at hearing my dirty words. I turn around, not able to look at her anymore without wanting to walk back over and fuck her against the wall.

My cock is throbbing painfully, and even using my hand tonight won't be enough. I bring my fingers to my lips, trying to drag the last little taste of her off my skin, knowing it will have to be enough for now.

She may have been the one making a deal with the devil, but I'm the one who'll end up in Hell. Chloe Santoro will be my downfall, and I'm not even sure I care.

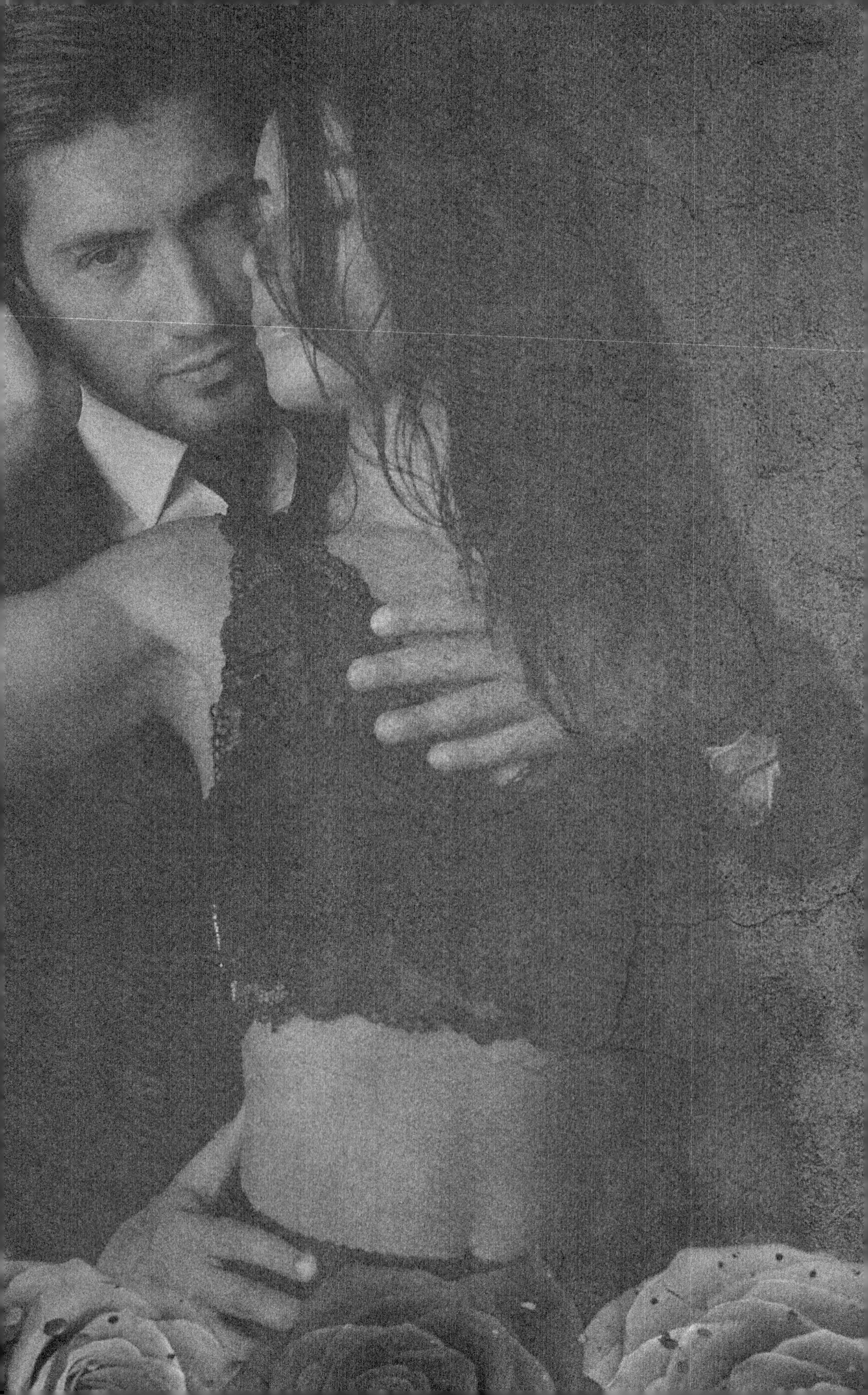

Chapter Five
Marcus

"Wakey, wakey." A loud voice pulls me out of sleep, and when I open my eyes, my vision is instantly flooded with brightness, as I find the curtains have been pulled wide open.

One wall of my bedroom has floor-to-ceiling windows, and they open onto a wrap-around balcony that has a gorgeous view over the city from high up in my penthouse apartment. Normally, I love the view, but right now, all it's doing is making the pounding in my head worse.

I slam my eyes closed with a groan as I lift my hands to cover my ears. Unfortunately, I can still hear Miles' annoying voice. "Wake up, Marcus."

"Fuck off," I growl, not interested in what he has to say.

Sadly, my best friend is a massive arsehole, and doesn't listen to a word I have to say. He rips the duvet off my body, and I groan as the cool air hits me, disturbing my cosy slumber.

"Sorry, but I can't. You need to get up. We have a meeting in an hour, and you need a bucket of coffee and a shower before I get in a car with you," he replies, pulling my hands away from my face, before placing something into my palm.

I squint one eye open enough to see the painkillers he's handed me, and I breathe a sigh of relief when I see he's holding out a glass of water.

With a grumble that's far less polite than he deserves, I take the pills, drinking several more gulps of water afterwards. The cool liquid is refreshing to my dry throat.

"What happened to not letting me drink?" I ask, sounding more gravelly than usual.

"I'm your bodyguard, Marcus, not your mother. Besides, you left and asked me to keep an eye on that fuckwit, Jacob. He's a full-time job on his own," Miles grumbles, as he takes a seat in the chair next to the window.

"That he is," I agree, wincing as I sit up and my head spins.

"What the hell happened to you last night? You went outside with Chloe, and I didn't see you again for nearly half an hour. Then next time I see you, you're downing shots like you're back in college."

Flashes of the night before flicker in my mind, and although my head is hazy, thanks to the hangover, I remember every part of the evening—even the bits I might want to forget.

"Urgh," I groan again, wondering how the hell I managed to get myself into this mess.

Miles chuckles from his seat, and I throw him a glare that would cut a lesser man down, but he just rolls his eyes at me.

"You've been keeping away from her for years. Now you find out she's fucking engaged to some prick, and you think this is the right time to do something about how you feel."

I narrow my gaze at him, balling my hands into fists. "I don't have fucking feelings for her. I've been telling you to stop saying that shit for years. Even if I found her attractive, she couldn't be any more off-limits if she tried, especially now she's engaged."

"So what were you doing in the alley with her? When you came back inside, it didn't look like you'd just been talking. She had a very distinct 'just fucked' vibe about her," he replies smugly, and I have to resist the urge to pick up my gun.

"Don't talk about her like that," I grind out, the anger fizzling under the surface makes me snap much easier than I normally would. "We were just talking. Jacob didn't see us, did he?"

Suddenly, the logical part of my brain takes over and I'm worried. There are a lot of reasons why I've been pushing Chloe away for years, pretending not to see the way she looks at me.

The biggest reason is the peace treaty between our families. Although it's in place now, we are—and will always be—rivals, and it won't take much for the peace to shatter, bringing back the war our fathers have tried to hold at bay for almost thirty years.

"No, he didn't see you. He was too busy trying to convince anyone with tits to sleep with him. Well, that and drinking your bar dry. Man, can that guy down a shot!" he grumbles with a humourless laugh.

We both know how reckless Jacob can be, and I'm sure the assignment I gave my friend was not an easy one.

"Thank you for keeping an eye on him for me."

Miles' glare narrows and he pulls back his shoulders slightly, looking more professional than a moment ago. "Don't ever ask me to do that again. You are the person I'm supposed to be protecting. When I'm on duty, I'm not your friend. Last night, I let you tell me what to do, as though you were speaking to a friend. As a result, I didn't have eyes on you for over half an hour, and barely kept track of you for the rest of the night.

"I know we have the best security staff at Caged, but anything could have happened to you. I wouldn't have been there to do my job because you asked me to be somewhere else. If anything happened, it would have been completely my fault. I may have followed your orders yesterday, but I shouldn't have. It was unprofessional of me, and I'm asking you not to put me in that position again."

No matter how much I glare at my friend, he doesn't back down. He holds his head high, his back ramrod straight, and I know he's serious. I pushed him too far this time, and a sinking feeling sits in my gut.

I drag my hand over my face before running my fingers through my hair in frustration. "I'm sorry. It won't happen again," I grumble uncomfortably.

Miles nods his head once, and then relaxes back into the chair. He knows how much I fucking hate apologising, and like the fucking great friend that he is, he doesn't drag it out for me.

"Good. Are you gonna tell me what happened with Chloe?" He wags his eyebrows dramatically, like I'm keeping good gossip from him.

I groan, resisting the urge to throw myself back into the comfort of my bed. Instead, I get up and head towards the en-suite to get ready for the meeting I'd almost forgotten about.

"Would you believe me if I said nothing?"

Miles lets out a laugh that sounds suspiciously more like a snort. "Fuck, no."

"Will you drop it if I tell you?"

He pauses for a second, contemplating his options. "Okay."

"I made a deal with her. I will help her delay her wedding for a few weeks, in exchange for her help with getting Jacob back on the wagon," I explain, shouting through the door of the bathroom, so he can still hear me while I'm getting ready.

"You're telling me that you had the girl you've had a crush on for as long as I can remember in a dark alleyway, while she was looking hot as Hell, and all you did is talk? I call bullshit," he yells through the door, and I roll my eyes as I finish brushing my teeth.

"I have not had a crush on her—"

Before I can even get the lie out of my mouth, Miles cuts me off. "BULLSHIT!"

"Fine, we fooled around a bit, but it can't happen again." I don't know if I say that more for his benefit or mine.

I can hear Miles chuckle from the next room. "There's no way you can keep away from her. She's been drawing you in slowly like a moth to a flame for years. I'm actually impressed you've not cracked before now."

"Look, you asked and I told you. We're working together to help Jacob. That's all."

"And the fact you offered to help her delay her wedding played no part at all? How the fuck are you going to pull that one off, by the way?"

I wince, wondering the same fucking thing. "I don't know, but if I can do it, I will."

"Of course, you will. You don't want her to marry him," he says slowly, like I'm not keeping up with the conversation.

"She doesn't want to marry him," I grind out.

"That's not how it works in this world, and you know it. She's a mafia princess... She was always going to have an arranged marriage. I'm surprised it's only just been arranged. Most of these things are sorted at birth," he replies, and I hate the way my stomach flips as he reminds me of the world Chloe has been forced into.

Whilst me and Jacob have always known we'd be leaders, and our paths have been set since birth, that doesn't mean our families have an easier time.

I'm an only child, so the pressure on me is immense. Whereas, Jacob has Chloe, and whilst she will never be a leader, the expectations on women in our world are, to an extent, even greater.

Their role is to ensure the longevity of the family. They're raised knowing they'll marry into a family of their fathers' choosing. It'll be a marriage of convenience, not love. It will strengthen their family's position.

Then, once they're married, they'll be expected to produce an heir straight away. They have a level of responsibility that rivals that of the heir, and I couldn't be more glad I don't have a sister to protect from all this bullshit.

"Jacob will want to protect her from it too," I state, knowing my argument is getting weaker by the second.

We all know I'm not trying to help Chloe because I see her as being like a sister to me. There's nothing familial about my feelings towards her.

"Look, we can argue about you denying your feelings another time. We can also brainstorm ideas for how you're going to help Chloe delay her impending nuptials in the car. But for the love of God, please get in the shower and then get out here quickly.

"We have to leave soon or we'll be late. If you're late to one more meeting, your father says he's going to chop one of my bollocks off, and I'm keen on them both. They like being a pair. Now, get a fucking move on," he shouts, and I can't help but laugh.

My father has been issuing threats to Miles for years in an effort to have him keep me in line. He never wanted me to hire a friend as my Head of Security. He claimed it was dangerous, but nobody will put their life on the line for me more than Miles.

We both know Father wanted to hire someone who would spy on me for him, which Miles absolutely won't do. He respects my father and his position of authority, but he's loyal to me.

I shout a few obscenities his way before climbing in the shower. I have to turn it to cold as soon as thoughts of Chloe from last night take over. I only got a small taste of her, and I already know it will never be enough. I want all of her, and all of the reasons I have for keeping away from her are growing more inconsequential with each stroke of my dick.

***

After the day I've had, I want nothing more than to cancel our monthly poker night and stay home, but tonight is more important than ever.

I put myself on a big clock when I agreed to help Chloe delay her wedding, or at the very least get her some freedom before the big day. She's supposed to get married in six weeks, which means I have to put my plan into action today.

Miles and I spent the whole day, when we weren't in boring fucking meetings, hashing out ideas, but none of them seemed to come together until right at the end. I have a plan... well, it's more of a fucking wing and a prayer at this point, but it's all we've got.

After taking some pills to get rid of the headache that's been plaguing me all day, I change out of my suit and pull on my comfy grey sweatpants. Although I hate wearing the suit, my father is right when he says people view me differently when they see me in that compared to my jeans and leather jacket.

I'm quite young for a mafia leader. Most fathers keep hold of their title for as long as they can, only passing over the reins when they absolutely have to. But not in Blackthorn. When the peace treaty was drawn up, it was decided that no ruler shall remain in power beyond their heir's thirtieth birthday.

The idea is that the longer you're in power, the less you'll want to give it up. Also, bringing in new, fresh blood means more up-to-date ideas, and our relatives felt that was the key to ensuring our treaty remains successful.

Although our fathers don't have to hand the position over to us yet, they made the decision to do it in stages. We took on the title of rulers when we turned twenty-five, but our fathers remained in an advisory capacity. Whilst we don't have to answer to them, it would be massively disrespectful not to.

They have five years to mould us into the leaders they want us to be, before they're forced to retire officially. With that being only two years away now, that is why Jacob's father is making plans to replace him if he doesn't get his act together.

After three years in the role, Jacob should be showing the type of leader he wants to be, the same way I am, yet he continues to rebel. Caleb will only tolerate it for so long.

Part of the process of learning the ropes involves building trust and respect with the people who work for me. They may have pledged their allegiance to my family, specifically my father, but that doesn't automatically transfer over to me. I have to earn their respect, and that's what I've been doing.

I've been meeting with each and every business representative. Everyone from upper level managers to lower level pushers. I want to know every single person who works for me, and I need for them to get a feel for the type of leader I am. It's the only way to foster trust between us.

That doesn't mean the meetings aren't tedious as hell. Though today's first meeting was a little more interesting, as I think we've identified a possible rat within our organisation. The fun part will be when we find the rat and I get to show him exactly who he's messed with.

Sadly, that was today's only bit of fun. Combine boring meetings with an awful fucking hangover, and a raging boner that won't go away—since I can't stop thinking about the feel of Chloe's warm cunt clamping down on my fingers—makes for a shitty fucking day.

Even worse luck, poker night is being held at Jacob's flat tonight, which means I have to go out. Granted, he only lives in the building across the street, but still. I pull a black hoodie on and grumble all the way over.

I don't bother taking any security with me. Miles has the night off, and Jacob has more than enough security to cover us both. When I host, I put on a full security team, so it's only fair my team gets the night off when we're at Jake's.

Having said that, I know someone will be on standby watching the security footage, ready to breach in seconds should anything happen. At the end of the day, Jacob's staff are employed to protect him and his family, so I would never be their priority.

After the obligatory pat-down to make sure I've not brought any weapons with me, except the one gun we're each allowed, one of Jacob's security team leads me over to the lift, which takes me up to his penthouse.

Jacob lives in the building opposite mine, but other than the fact we both live in the penthouse, that's where the similarities end. While my apartment has a very modern yet homey feel, Jacob's is a full blown bachelor pad.

His walls are painted navy blue, and wherever you look there's technology to make the room appear advanced. Everything is controlled by a home computer system, even the heating under the floorboards and the blackout covers on the windows.

While my place is light and airy, Jacob's feels dark and stuffy. Every time I walk in here, I want to throw the window open to let some fresh air in, and get some natural fucking light into the room.

If it weren't for the cleaning team he employs, I'm sure this place would look worse than a dirty frat house full of teenage boys who don't know how to work a washing machine.

Jacob is sitting at the poker table already, taking a swig from his beer bottle, when I walk into the room. It's cloudy and stuffy, even though Jacob doesn't smoke.

"Fuck, do any of your windows actually open? You do know what fresh air is, don't you?" I grumble, as I walk into the kitchen and grab a beer for myself from the fridge.

Jake tuts loudly. "You know you sound like a fucking old man, right?"

I shrug my shoulders, not bothering to reply to that. To a perpetual man child, my response sounds like something an old man would say, as opposed to simply an adult. I learnt a long time ago to pick my battles with Jake, and this one isn't worth it.

I take a seat opposite him at the table, drinking down a large gulp of my beer. Beer's not my favourite, but it's become part of the tradition—we play poker, eat crisps, and drink beer.

"You look like shit," Jake says with a grin once I place my drink on the table.

He's not lying. I have bags under my eyes from lack of sleep, and I've been running my fingers through my hair so much, I'm sure it's a mess.

"I can't seem to get over a hangover the way I used to do when I was eighteen," I grumble, hating how fucking old that makes me sound.

Jacob chuckles, but he nods like he understands. "That's why I take the 'hair of the dog' approach."

I roll my eyes at him. "Being drunk continuously is not an option for most people."

"I'm not always drunk. Sometimes I'm just high," he states with a wink. I have to remind myself not to punch my friend.

"You're a real life fucking Peter Pan. The boy who never grows up."

I hate how bitter the words sound on my tongue. Although I need Jake to grow the fuck up, I'm also a little jealous that he's avoided the responsibilities that have been thrust upon me.

Actually, his lack of action as the heir to his side of Blackthorn means I have even more work to do. I've been trying to make sure Jake's family is unaware of his failings. If they knew how little he was actually doing, they'd have gotten rid of him a long time ago.

In our world, business comes first, family second. No matter how much Caleb wants to pass power over to Jake, if he thinks he's not capable of running the Santoros, he'll get rid of him in a flash, without a second thought that he's his son.

Love and family are a weakness, and the family business will always be the priority. Which is exactly why I need to get Jake to stop fucking around, or he may lose more than just his position in the family.

Nobody leaves our world. The only way you get out is to retire, at which point you've proved you're trustworthy, or you die. Jacob definitely hasn't proven he can be trusted, and no matter how much Caleb might love him, he would have no choice to take him out if that's what the family requested.

I need to stop things before that happens.

"What can I say, I have no desire to grow up and turn out like my father." His face wrinkles in disgust, and I can see the anger he's trying not to show.

We've both spent our whole lives promising, even when we do become the full-time leaders of our family, we'll never be like our fathers.

Neither of us have had enough to drink yet to tackle that subject, so I quickly change direction. "Well, I'm hoping you're more hungover than I am, as I could do with a win today," I say with a grin as I nod towards the pack of cards that are sitting unopened on the table.

Jake chuckles as he picks them up and starts to shuffle. "I'm nowhere near drunk enough to lose."

"Well, I need to get you onto the harder stuff then." It sounds like I'm joking with him, but I'm not. For once, I need him to hit it hard, if I'm to stand any chance of this shitty plan working.

"Here, you finish shuffling and I'll get the good whiskey." He hands the pack of cards over to me before heading into the kitchen.

"Don't forget the crisps," I shout, knowing I'm going to need nibbles if I keep drinking this beer.

Jake returns, placing a bottle of whiskey and two tumblers onto the table, before handing over a large packet of crisps. I look at him with disgust. "At my house, I, at least, serve the crisps in a fucking bowl," I grumble, ripping the large pack open so I can grab some.

Jake rolls his eyes at me while pouring two very large doubles of whiskey. He hands one to me, but I set it onto the table as I pass the cards back to him. I think I'll stick to beer for now.

As he shuffles one more time, he glances up at me, suddenly looking more serious than I'm used to. "So, down to official business. Do you have anything outstanding to discuss from the last meeting?"

Whilst on the surface this may look like a friendly poker game between friends, it's still a business meeting, and Jake always treats it as such. He may drink too much and not give a shit about the job, but he does, on occasion, try to be a good leader.

It's actually a massive shame, as I think if he really did put the effort in, he'd probably be a better leader than I am. I'm ruthless and firm, whereas Jake actually cares—possibly too much—but it also makes him a great advocate for the people he rules over.

"All mine were sorted, I believe. What about you?" I reply.

"What happened with Barty?" he asks, his expression now much more guarded.

Barty is the leader of one of the gangs that works for me. He's responsible for a large chunk of the drug income we have, but at the last meeting, Jake told me there had been complaints from some of his gangs that Barty was crossing the border.

When our families split Blackthorn in two, a territory line was drafted. The people who operate on the East side of town are ruled by me, and Jacob has the West. Everyone knows that you don't cross the territory line, it's a breach of the peace treaty. Anyone that's found to be doing so has to be dealt with swiftly.

"I spoke to Barty straight away. He said it was a new pusher he'd brought on board who didn't know the territory line well enough, and crossed it without realising. It's been dealt with," I explain, leaving out the part where Barty was punished for allowing such a mistake to occur.

Even if it was the new kid's fault, the book stops with Barty, and he should have made sure his hires are given enough knowledge. I also made it clear I don't allow anyone under the age of eighteen to work in the drugs game.

There's too much risk of them either taking the product themselves, or pushing it to their friends. What they do when they become an adult is up to them, but we don't sell drugs to kids in my town—a rule both me and Jake agree on.

Jake winces slightly as he deals our first hand. "I'm sorry to tell you, the situation has not been solved. I had four complaints over the last week, all saying the same thing. Barty is moving over into the Upper West side, and he's threatened several members of UW40, the gang who currently deal in that area."

"Fuck!" I growl, slamming my fist on the table. "I take it our first hand is for who handles him?"

Jake nods, a sadistic smile turning up the corner of his lip. This is the way our poker night always goes. When there's an issue that we will disagree over how it's handled, we play for it. If I win, I get to deal with Barty however I choose, but if Jake wins, he can sort it, and I have to accept his methods.

I'm not sure who Barty will want to win this hand. Jake looks murderous, and he will be playing for the right to defend his territory. Whereas, I'm playing for my pride.

Barty lied to me, and he directly went against my orders, which, as his leader, I can't allow to stand. I need to make an example of him.

I always play to win, but some hands are more important than others. However, I can see the intense glare in my best friend's eyes, and I'm a little startled that he wants to deal with this.

The round starts, and I flick a glance at my cards, keeping my face neutral as I see the King of Spades and Three of Clubs. I place the cards back down and assess Jake as he looks at his. As always, he gives nothing away.

"Are there any rules you want to lay down regarding the outcome of dealing with Barty?" I ask, as I throw some chips down to say I'm in the game.

Jake is quick to meet my bid, dealing three cards onto the centre of the table. I keep my gaze neutral as my heart races when each card's turned over.

King of Clubs. Ace of Diamonds. Five of Hearts.

A pair isn't a great hand, but it's better than nothing for now, so I place my bet to let him know I'm still in. Jake assesses the cards for a moment, his gaze giving nothing away.

Is he taking his time to look unsure, to bluff that he's got nothing, when he's actually got a good hand?

"Whatever the outcome, I need his gang to know that they can never deal on the Upper West side again," Jake states, before adding, "Do you have any stipulations?"

What he's really asking is if he's allowed to kill Barty if things go that far.

"As far as I'm concerned, Barty broke the rules, then he lied about it to my face, before breaking the rules again. He had his second chance and he blew it.

"I know he's well connected, and I have no idea where his gang will stand at the end of it, but that's something I can handle. If you kill him, that's fine by me, as long as he's aware that the punishment he's receiving comes with my blessing. I don't want his family blaming you and retaliating," I state firmly.

This has always been a concern for us, whenever the other person wins the right to deal with someone on the rival side. But we made it clear in the beginning that any major action will be undertaken with the other's blessing, unless we say otherwise.

Our teams know that if one of us were to ever make a move without the other's consent, that would be a clear breach of the treaty, and we'd go to war. So we make sure that everyone knows that's not happened.

Jake nods in understanding, taking a sip from his whiskey glass. "I'm not sure if we'll kill him. It all depends on what he says in the interview. You can be there, if you'd like?"

I give him a small smile as I nod. "I think that's a good idea...if you win, of course."

Jake chuckles, throwing his chips in to call me. Another card flicks over, and it takes all my strength not to react when I see the Queen of Spades.

There's the potential for a straight on the table, depending on what Jake's initial cards were. But, given there's a mix of all the suits, a flush is unlikely. It'll all depend on the final card.

I throw my chips in, signalling for him to drop the last card, and he's quick to meet my bid. My heart is racing while I wait for him to flip the card over.

Three of Hearts.

I have two pairs—Kings and Threes, which is a pretty decent hand.

Keeping my expression the same, I throw down double my usual bid, and I have to hold back a smile at the way Jake grimaces at the raise. He studies his cards again, like he's hoping to see something that's not there. Though I'm not naive enough to think he might be bluffing.

He doesn't just meet my bet, he raises it again, and now I'm really worried. He's either going hard on the bluff, or he has something. Either way, my hand isn't a bad one, so I meet his bet. This time, he doesn't raise, he calls it instead.

We both turn our cards over at the same time, and my heart sinks. We both have two pairs, but he's got two Aces, whereas my highest are Kings. Jake whoops and laughs as he throws his arms into the air in celebration, as I grumble and swear to myself.

I take a big swig of my whiskey, allowing the burn to distract me from my loss. Jake begins to gloat, the way he always does when he wins, and he finishes the rest of his glass of whiskey before pouring us both another. He then finishes the beer bottle in front of him too.

As he gloats, a big smile on his face, I note the way his pupils are blown so wide they appear black, only a hint of chocolate around the edges. If he keeps winning, it won't be long before he's really pissed, and that's exactly what I want.

I grab the cards from on the table after he's scooped up his winning chips and begin shuffling them for the next round. "What are we playing for next?" I ask him.

We play a few more hands, dealing with small, almost trivial matters, and as per my plan, the more drunk Jake gets, the easier it is for me to take all his chips.

He's only got a very small pile left, barely enough for this final hand, and that's exactly what I had in mind. I kept this final matter for the end, knowing how hard Jake would go in to win.

"Right, I only have one more matter on my agenda, and since you're done, this will be our last hand. I've tried to do this in a friendly way, but I think we've reached the stage where I need to make it official.

"Last week, you fucked another one of my dancers from Caged, despite knowing they're off-limits to you. You didn't call her back the next day, and when she saw you in the club with another girl, she created a scene. In fact, that doesn't even come close to covering it. She punched the girl so hard she broke her nose. Security removed her, but it was still a scene that could have been avoided, had you stuck to the rules.

"So, for this final hand, I propose we play for the girls in the club. If you win, I won't stop you from being with any of them, but if I win, you can't touch anyone who works there without my permission. What do you say?"

A heavy silence fills the air, and his inebriated state means it's easy to see the emotions that flicker across his face. Intrigue, annoyance, anger, and maybe even a little excitement.

He enjoys messing around with the girls when they're off-limits, but he also knows there'll come a point when I enforce the rules much stricter than I currently do. This is his best opportunity to retain a chance with the girls there.

"I'm in."

I have to bite the inside of my cheek to keep from smiling. He's playing straight into my hands... Now I just need the cards to fall in the right way. I'm not going to cheat, but that doesn't mean I can't carefully manipulate the situation.

The game plays out exactly how I hoped. I have a better hand than I was expecting, but I don't let on. In my hand I have the Four of Hearts, and the King of Hearts. On the table there's the Ace of Hearts, Jack of Diamonds, Three of Hearts, and Four of Spades.

Not only do I have two pairs, there's also the possibility of a flush, if the river card is a Heart. But even if that doesn't come, I still have a pretty strong hand.

Since Jake's pretty tipsy now, he's barely hiding that he's got a good hand. He's raising the stakes quickly and aggressively, which, given the small amount of chips he has left, he'd only do if he was sure he had a good chance at winning.

Now it's time for the next part of my plan. I raise the stakes higher than he has in chips, and he glares at me. "You know I don't have enough chips to meet that bet," he grumbles.

I shrug my shoulders, trying my hardest to look smug, enough to wind him up more. "Well, I guess, you'll have to fold then."

I make it sound like this is about me protecting the girls at the club, so he has no idea I have another motive. He glares at me, taking another sip of his whiskey, though I doubt that will help him come up with a solution.

"I'm not folding. I want to raise the bet," he states, his gaze fixed on mine.

"Too bad you don't have any chips," I reply flippantly.

"Well, let me add in something else of value then," he states, just as I expected him to.

"Look, let me be straight with you, Jake. You wanting to play so badly is a red flag for me. Of course, I'm going to use every chip I have to up the bid in an effort to stop you. You'd have to put something massive on the table to meet me."

I keep my voice neutral, hoping he can't hear the way my heart is racing. It's pounding so loudly, I can almost hear the blood whooshing through my ears.

"You know how much I want free access to the girls at the club. What if I promise not to cause drama?" he asks, wiggling his eyebrows at me like he stands a chance at charming me.

I roll my eyes at him, taking a small sip of my whiskey, just to let the tension build. "I expect you not to cause drama in my club anyway, so that's not a bargaining chip. It's gotta have high value. Something you'd normally never give me."

He lets out a huff. "Fine, you name your price and we'll go all in."

"I don't think you want to give me a blank cheque here, Jake. What if I choose something you would really hate to give up?"

He narrows his gaze at me, though I notice he has to blink a few times, no doubt to counteract whatever blurred vision the alcohol is giving him. I think he may have just realised I have a plan, and I wait for him to call me out on it.

The silence stretches on while Jake ponders my question, before finally saying, "Then I'll have to make a choice, but I won't know until you ask."

I give him a tight smile, trying to hold back the grimace. *Here goes nothing,* I think to myself.

"I want Chloe."

His eyes widen before his face darkens, and he balls the hand that's been resting on the table into a fist. "What the fuck?" he yells.

I hold my hands up, trying to pacify him, as I explain further. "It's not what you're thinking. You know how much I fucking hate Scott Caprillo. He's been a dick for years, and this is the perfect opportunity for me to mess with him.

"For my bid, I want to win your sister for sixty days. She will have to live with me and do as I say during that time."

Jake leans forward, looking more confused than he was a moment ago. "So this isn't about Chloe, it's about Scott? It's not some weird way to get me to give you permission to fuck my sister?"

I laugh loudly, caught off-guard by the abruptness of his comment. "No, this is to mess with Scott. I mean, your sister isn't bad looking, so I wouldn't say no to fucking her, but that's not what this is about."

His eyes darken at my mention of fucking her, and I hate how poisonous the lie feels on my tongue. His sister is fucking gorgeous, and I want nothing more than to claim her and make her mine, but that's never going to fucking happen, so this is the best I can come up with.

"But she's supposed to get married in six weeks," Jake adds, almost as an afterthought.

"If I win, she'll have to delay her impending nuptials. Yet another bonus in my plan to piss off Scott."

Jake lets out a long sigh. "Everyone in my family is going to be so fucked off with me, but I'm in."

"What?" The word tumbles out before I can stop it, shock hitting me when I hear him agree to the deal. I thought I'd have to negotiate a lot more to try and convince him.

"Honestly, I hate the idea of Chloe marrying that arsehole. If you win her for two months, it gives me extra time to come up with a plan to get her out of the marriage. She'll be pissed at me for using her as a bet, but she'll be even more of an arse with you for suggesting it," he says with a laugh. "But anyway, none of this will matter if I win."

He sounds confident, and I have to admit, I'm a little nervous. My plan only goes as far as getting him to agree to the bet, after that, I have to let the cards fall where they may. I just really fucking hope I'm holding the winning hand.

"So, to confirm, this is the bet… If you win, you are allowed to date or fuck any of the people employed at Caged, with no restrictions. But you do still have to be mindful that it's my business, and you need to minimise the amount of trouble you cause.

"If I win, I get full access to your sister for sixty days. Chloe will move in with me, and she'll be expected to do whatever I say. Do we have a deal?"

Jake pauses for a minute, taking in the deal one final time. His gaze is locked on mine, and my heart races. I keep mentally reminding myself to fucking breathe.

"Just one more thing to add… Whilst Chloe has to do everything you say, it doesn't include anything sexual," he states firmly.

I shake my head in disbelief. "I don't need to force women into bed with me, Jake. I would never make her do anything like that. But if she chooses to, that's something else all together."

"You are not fucking my sister," he grinds out, slamming his fist on the table.

"I'm not saying I will, but I'm also not saying I won't. You never know what will happen over the sixty days. Besides, wondering what I may or may not do to Chloe will be part of the torture for Scott," I add on, hoping he buys my excuse.

Jake's never going to give me permission to fuck his sister, but I don't want him to say it can never happen either. I'd never betray my friend, but staying away from Chloe for sixty days, while she's living in my house, will be virtually impossible.

"Fine. If full consent is given by her, then that's okay. Though I would prefer it if you didn't go near her," he grumbles.

"You can always back out of the bet," I remind him, his eyes darken as he glares at me.

"You've got a deal. Draw the last card."

Silence fills the room as we both wait for me to flip over the last card. Jake is leaning over the table, peering at the card as I turn it face up.

The river card is the Six of Hearts.

My heart stops, and I let out the breath I didn't know I was holding. Somehow, I manage to keep my expression neutral, crossing my fingers that I have enough to win.

Jake doesn't hide his excitement, he lets out a loud, "Yes!"

He maintains eye contact with me as he slowly turns over the two cards in front of him, my heart racing a million miles a minute as I wait to see if I've won.

He turns over the Jack of Spades and the Jack of Clubs—giving him three of a kind. I can see why he looks so smug. Under most circumstances, it's not a bad hand.

Without breaking the eye contact he started, I turn over the cards in front of me, one at a time. First the Four of Hearts, and then the King of Hearts. I place them alongside the Ace, Three, and Six of Hearts that are already on the table, making a flush. "I win."

Jake's gaze flicks down to the cards, and then back up at me, taking in the way my lip lifts into a smirk. I want to fucking grin and cheer, but I hold back, saving the celebration for later.

The gravity of the situation quickly hits Jake, and his face falls. His eyes widen and he turns pale. "My father is going to kill me. Chloe is going to kill me."

"Don't worry, you don't have to tell them tonight. I'll come to the main house in the morning." I try to keep my voice casual, but there's a hint of excitement that I just can't hide.

"Fuck! Can't we play again? We can bet on something else?" he asks desperately, but I shake my head.

"Nope. This was the final game. All matters have been dealt with, the way it always is. You know the rules, Jake."

"But this is going too far." His voice takes on a high-pitched desperate edge, and I almost feel sorry for him. I do feel a bit of guilt at the way I manipulated him into this, but if my plan works, he'll benefit from it in the end.

"Sorry, Jake. You know the rules. Once the game is over, the deals are final. I can be there when you tell your family though, if that helps."

He nods his head, taking a big gulp and downing the last of his whiskey, like that wasn't partly responsible for the mess he now finds himself in.

"Fine, I'll call a family meeting for lunchtime tomorrow. We can tell them then," Jake says with a huff.

"You should get some sleep and sober up before then. I'm guessing going into the meeting high as a kite or pissed will only make things worse for you," I suggest, giving him some advice that I really hope he takes.

As we both stand and I head towards the door, Jake lets out a humourless laugh. "The only good thing about this is that I'll get to watch Chloe murder you when she finds out you used her in a bet."

My stomach drops as I imagine how angry she'll be. She may have wanted my help, but I'm almost certain this isn't the way she wanted me to do it.

Though, no matter how angry she is with me, I'm going to enjoy reminding her that she belongs to me. It may only be for sixty days right now, but if things go to plan, I'll make her mine forever.

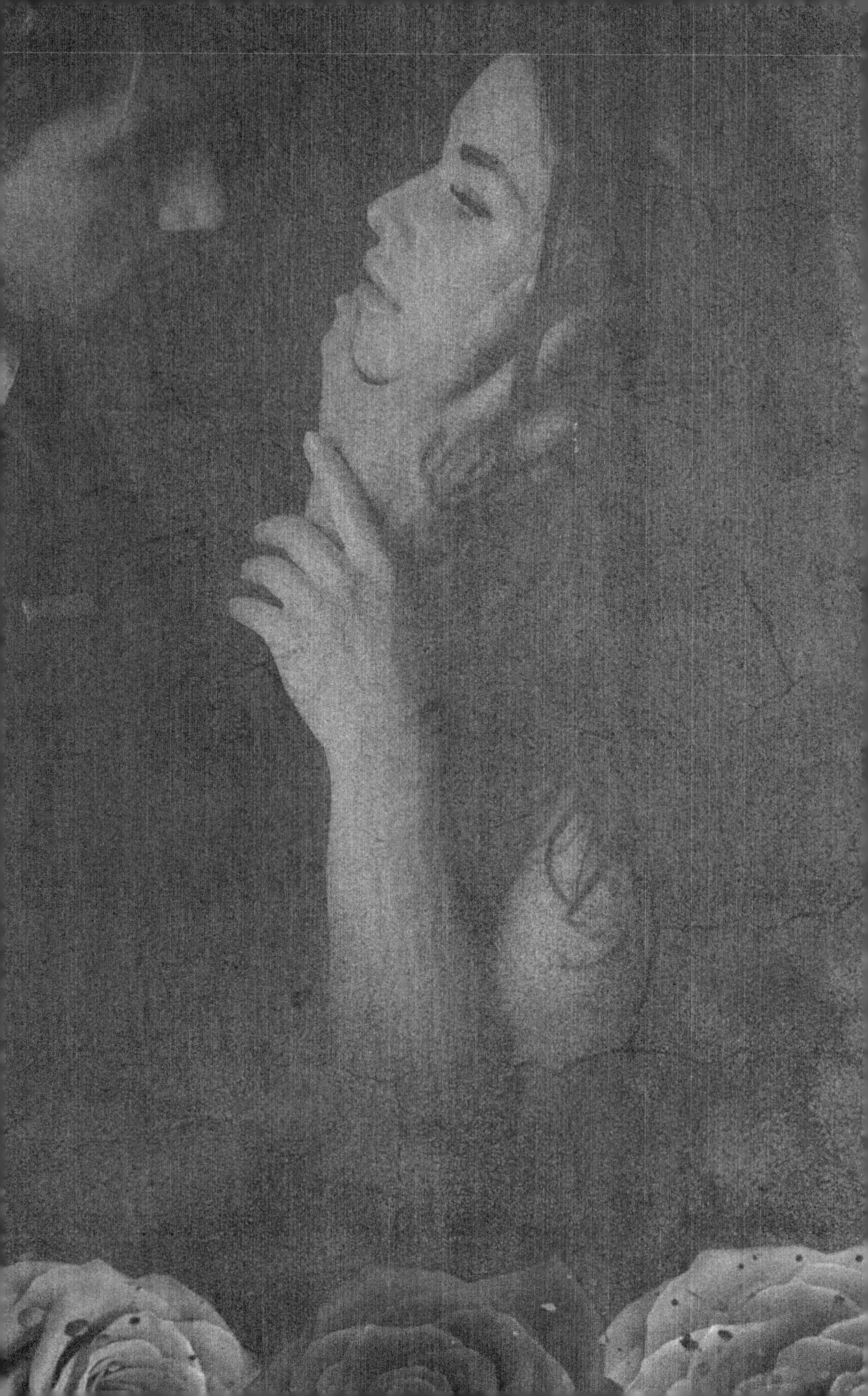

Chapter Six
Chloe

I wake up to a note, summoning me to attend a family meeting at lunchtime. I'm fucking fuming that I'm being summoned like a pet, but that's the story of my life—being given instructions that I blindly follow without question.

The longer I have to stew over the invitation—or demand, as that's what it really is—the more confused I become. I rarely get invited to family meetings. Mostly they just tell me what's expected of me afterwards.

They usually catch me off guard over dinner, letting me know that my future was discussed at a meeting I wasn't invited to, and decisions have been made that I'm just expected to go along with. That's how I found out I was fucking engaged.

Just the word makes me nauseous, nevermind the giant fucking family heirloom engagement ring that's sitting in the top drawer beside my bed. It's not at all my style, but then again, I don't think it was meant to be. The whole point is that you can see the rock from a mile away, and everyone will know who I belong to.

I've only met Scott Caprillo once, and that was the other day when I found out I was marrying him, and he gave me the ring that's worth more than most people earn in a year. Besides that first moment when he slid it onto my finger, I've never worn it since.

I've been engaged for just a couple of days and my life feels like it's spiralling worse than ever. And given the horrors of my past, that's saying something.

I've spent the last two years trying to claw back some semblance of control in my life, and all my hard work has been undone in the blink of an eye. Even though I knew this day would come eventually, I was vastly under-prepared.

So, naturally, I did what any self respecting person would do when faced with a loss of control over their own life...I got paralytically drunk and tried to shag a stranger in the middle of my brother's best friend's club.

What happened with Marcus afterwards will be seared into my brain for all eternity. The way he crowded my body with his, his possessive edge dominating me in a way I never expected to like. His touch took my breath away, and scared me shitless at the same time.

I've had a crush on Marcus Morelli since I was a kid, but I've known it was unrequited since that very first day. I smiled at him and he pushed me over. Ever since, he's made it clear that he only tolerates me because I'm Jake's little sister, and that's all he'll ever see me as.

I've watched him grow up, and the more devastatingly handsome he became, the more his ego grew. He knew he was hot, and that girls were throwing themselves at him every chance they got, and he let them. I've watched him sleep around, leaving a trail of broken hearts in his wake.

Though, to be fair, that was always the girl's own fault. Marcus may be a man whore, but he's always honest with them. He's never wanted a relationship, he only offers no-strings attached.

Yet, no matter how clear he makes this, the girls always think they'll be the one to tame the bad boy. Little do they know, he can't be tamed.

The night before last, in the club, I got a tiny taste of everything I ever wanted with him. I never, in my wildest dreams, thought anything like that would ever happen with Marcus, and when it did, I never wanted it to end. But it did, and I was left aching in the worst way, while wondering if he meant what he said about the deal we made.

What the fuck was I thinking making that deal with him? I have no idea how to get Jacob to stop fucking around.

That's bollocks. I know exactly why I made the deal with Marcus—I will do anything for even just a fraction of his attention. If he really thinks he can delay my marriage, I'll work out how to help him with Jake.

I've been worried about my brother this past year. He's been slowly spiralling since he was placed into the heir position at twenty-five. Though, if we're being honest, he started going off the rails during the last year of high school.

Jake tried to negotiate with Dad, telling him he wasn't ready, but he didn't listen. Marcus was ready to rule, which meant Jacob had to be too.

I hate that I've been so caught up in my own shit this last year that I missed how bad Jacob has become. I had no idea he was doing heavy drugs, or making enemies of the wrong people. In our world, that sort of behaviour is what gets you killed, and I can't have that.

Besides, if Jacob isn't leading the Santoro family, that means our power will pass to Scott when I marry him, and there's no way I want that dickhead to lead.

Desperate to know what the meeting is about, I make sure I'm ready in good time. As I don't normally attend these things, I have no idea who will be in attendance, but there will be an expectation for me to present my best self. Which is why I'm dressed up much fancier than I'd normally be on a Sunday lunchtime.

My black pencil skirt sits just above my knees; long enough to be decent, but short enough to show off my legs, which I accentuate by adding four inch black stilettos.

I pair it with a plain white blouse, leaving the top two buttons undone. The sheerness to the fabric means you can see the outline of my lace bra underneath, and the open buttons show off a hint of cleavage.

I look like a secretary, with a hint of sex appeal. After I've put on a little make-up, mostly to hide the bags under my eyes and the blemishes my mother is quick to point out, I couldn't feel less like myself. I look like the perfect Santoro wife, which I guess is exactly what I am.

Fifteen minutes before the time I'm supposed to meet my family, I head downstairs. The meeting is being held in my father's business wing, which is on the left side of the house.

Unless invited, that wing is off-limits to me. It has a side entrance that Dad's business associates use, so we don't have men with guns traipsing through the house at all hours.

Not that I care. My room is on the top floor, the opposite side of the house to his business wing. I used to share a corridor with Jacob, but he has his own apartment now, though his room is still here if he needs it.

I have my own living space and bathroom, so the only time I'm likely to run into family is in the kitchen, the family dining room, the gym, or the indoor pool. Though, even then it's rare. The house is so fucking massive, we're like ships passing in the night, and I've never complained.

As soon as I reach my Dad's meeting room, I'm thrown to see the door is closed. In our house, everyone knows you don't enter a room where the door is closed without knocking first. Before I even get a chance to knock, one of my dad's security guards walks towards me, clearly having seen me approach on one of the many security cameras littered throughout our house.

"Your father has asked that you wait here until you're called," he states with a clipped, professional tone.

I narrow my gaze at him, trying to work out what the hell is going on. "I was told to attend the meeting at twelve. Has it already started?"

"You are here at the right time," he replies cryptically, his gaze stoic.

I don't know this guard, but that's not a big surprise. My family has a lot of staff members, and it's fucking impossible to know them all, particularly as they rotate around a lot. I may not see this guy again for months.

Some, like my dad's own personal guard, or the ones who guard me regularly, are familiar faces that I remember, but most all blend into one. I hate having guards that follow me, so one of the agreements I made early on with my dad is that I could have a say in who was on my team, and unless it's an emergency, I get the same people.

What can I say? I have trust issues, and knowing that the same guards have been with me for a while helps. Though not a great deal, given I should have had a guard detail with me when my life went to shit, and they weren't there to protect me.

"Could have at least left me a fucking chair to sit on and wait," I grumble, more to myself than to the guard, as I shuffle from one foot to the other. These shoes may look great, and accentuate my legs and arse in a perfect way, but fuck are they uncomfortable.

At this, he looks a little startled, his gaze flicking around uncomfortably, as though he's trying to decide whether he should go and get me a chair, or if it's more important to stay here with me.

In the end, the decision is taken out of our hands when the door to the room flies open and my father sticks his head out into the corridor. He winces when he sees me, and my heart rate begins to accelerate, anxiety creeping in.

"Ah, Chloe, you're right on time," he says.

I resist the urge to reply sarcastically. I know better than to be late, or to sass him when he's in professional mode, and the suit he's wearing indicates this is a formal meeting, which is why I'm now more on edge than I was before.

He opens the door and indicates for me to come in. As soon as I step into the room, my heart stutters. Marcus and Jacob are sitting beside each other, my father's empty seat opposite them.

Jacob is looking down at the table, unable to meet my gaze, which makes me even more agitated. Yet, Marcus' piercing blue eyes are what has my stomach flipping. He stares at me unapologetically, not even bothering to hide the way his gaze travels over my legs.

I'm broken out of my trance when Dad indicates for me to take the seat next to him, opposite Jacob and Marcus. Once we're all seated, the silence hangs heavily in the air, like we're all waiting to see who will cut the tension first.

After a few seconds, Jacob lets out a sigh, and when his gaze meets mine, he looks devastated. My heart is racing so fast, while nausea bubbles away in my stomach.

"I'm so sorry, Clo," Jake says, his big brown eyes pleading with me in a way I don't understand.

I look over to Marcus, who has an unreadable expression on his face, but that signature smirk of his is still there. His eyes are guarded, and that worries me.

"What's going on?" I ask, slightly panicked.

Jacob looks like he's going to respond, but my dad's firm, authoritative tone cuts him off. "As usual, your brother has fucked up, and we're having to clean up his mess."

I turn towards Dad, and I'm surprised to see him looking at Jacob with obvious disdain. He's been struggling lately with Jake's behaviour, and he hates having to cover for him, but he's always been his favourite. I've never seen him look at Jake like this, and I don't like it.

"Don't talk about him like that," I snap at my dad. As all the eyes in the room hit me, I regret my outburst.

The giant grin on Marcus' face almost makes it worth it, until I see the rage my dad is struggling to hold back. "You won't be sticking up for him when he tells you what he did."

This time I turn to Jake, trying to blank out everyone else. Looking straight at my brother, I give him a kind smile. "Tell me, Jake."

He lets out a loud sigh, seeming to deflate at the same time. "I fucked up, Clo. You know how me and Marcus have a poker night every month to work out all the issues we have running Blackthorn?"

I narrow my eyes at him, wondering where he's going with this. "Yes?"

"Well... I was sure I had a winning hand, but Marcus had way more chips than me. If I wanted to match his bet, I had to offer something of great value," he explains, fidgeting nervously in his seat as he picks at the skin on one of his hands.

My brain is working a mile a minute, trying to predict what he's about to say. It's clear he lost the bet, I'm just wondering what high value item he sacrificed. It must be something big for Dad to be involved.

After a few moments of silence, Jake rushes out, "IbetyouandIlost."

The words tumble from his lips, and I struggle to make out what the hell he just said. "What?"

Jake's eyes are wide, glistening with unshed tears, and he looks like he's in pain. He takes a deep breath, almost as though he's trying to pull in the courage he needs to finish his story.

Marcus seems to take pity on Jacob, and fills me in on what I missed. "Jacob made a bet involving you that he lost. As a result, you now belong to me. You will come to live with me for the next sixty days, and you will be expected to do everything I tell you. No exceptions, no loopholes. This was the bet, and now I'm cashing in my prize."

Each word is like a knife to my gut, and I feel as though all my blood is pouring out of me, leaving just a shell. Jacob can't look me in the eye, and my dad looks furious, though I'm not sure who he's mad at most.

"I'm sorry, I don't understand. I'm not a fucking object that can be owned. Jacob can't have used me in a bet, as I don't belong to him," I snap, fixing my stare on Marcus.

The right side of his lip quirks up, like he's challenging me with that fucking cocky smirk. "No, you belong to me." The possessive edge to his voice makes my body tremble, but not in fear like it should.

I push those inappropriate thoughts to one side and focus on the indignation I'm feeling at once again being used like a fucking object.

"I don't belong to anyone." I try to keep my voice firm, hating the way it cracks at the end.

Dad interrupts Marcus before he can say anything more. "Actually, Chloe, you belong to this family. As much as I hate this, Santoros honour their agreements."

My mouth literally pops open in surprise, and as I shake my head at my dad in disgust, I point out the obvious issue he's clearly ignored. "Have you forgotten that I'm supposed to be marrying Scott in six weeks? Surely that's an agreement that we can't get out of either."

At the mention of my engagement, the smirk on Marcus' face disappears and his gaze narrows. His hands, that were resting on the table, are now balled into fists, and he looks seconds away from losing his temper, which is very unlike Marcus. He's usually in complete control, devoid of any real emotion.

My dad lets out a huff beside me. "We will still honour the marriage agreement, we will just ask them to delay it by a couple of weeks. I'm sure we can come up with an adequate excuse."

Now it's my turn to get mad. "Maybe Scott won't want to marry me when he finds out we're delaying the wedding because you're whoring me out for sixty days to our rival family."

Jacob slams his fist down onto the table, startling me. His eyes are wide but fierce. "You are not being whored out. This agreement is not sexual...I made sure of that."

"Oh, well, if you made sure it's not sexual, I don't know what I'm worried about," I reply sarcastically, ignoring Marcus' chuckle.

"Well, I won't say no if you ask nicely."

He ends his cocky comeback with a wink—a fucking wink. We're going to pretend it sent fury rippling through my veins, instead of a completely different feeling. I hate the way he can heat me up from the inside out with just one look, especially when he's not even trying.

This time my dad slams his fist on the table, startling us all. "Don't even fucking think about it, Morelli," Dad growls, leaning towards Marcus in a threatening way.

Despite Dad being the elder, Marcus doesn't answer to him the way we do, and he doesn't cower under the weight of his glare. He maintains eye contact, looking utterly bored by the whole situation.

Fuck, he's going to have to teach me to stand up to my dad like that.

Marcus shrugs his shoulders like he doesn't give a shit, and he's never looked fucking hotter. *God, I hate myself right now.*

"So if this isn't a sex thing, what the hell is it?" I don't aim the question at anyone in particular, and we all seem to wait for someone to answer.

Jacob reaches over and takes my hand in his. "I'm so sorry, Clo."

I want to pull away, but I hate how sad my brother looks. I think he's finally realising the consequences of his actions. It's just too bad I'm the casualty.

"No matter what Mr Morelli's motives are, as you well know, the bets made at their stupid poker nights are binding. As part of the peace treaty between our two families, if we break this agreement, it will be seen as an act of war on our part. I've tried to discuss altering the terms, but Mr Morelli is not amenable. So the bet stands," my dad says through gritted teeth as he glares at Marcus.

"What does this mean for me?" I hate how fucking small my voice sounds.

Dad looks like he's going to answer, but Marcus cuts in. "I'll give you tonight to sort yourself out, and tell your fiancé. I'll be back at nine in the morning to take you to my apartment. Bring what you want, but I'll happily supply anything you need. Your sixty days with me will begin tomorrow."

The smile he gives me is dripping with sin, and I have no fucking clue what to say.

"You're really not going to change your mind, are you?" Jake asks Marcus, sounding so fucking desperate it leaves a pang in my stomach.

Marcus slowly shakes his head, but he doesn't say anything. Jake gets up so quickly his chair slams backwards onto the floor. Without a word, my brother sweeps out of the room in a huff, slamming the door behind him.

I look over at my dad, who has his eyes pinched closed, like we're just annoying children who are interfering in his day, giving him a headache. "Well, I think this meeting is over," he says, pointing at the door.

The look he gives me tells me there's no room for discussion. Once again, decisions have been made on my behalf, and I'm just expected to fucking go along with them. Control has always been a fucking illusion to me.

Without a word, I get up and walk out of the room, very aware that Marcus is following me. I hear him slam the door, but I'm too busy stomping down the corridor, desperate to get away from him.

I trusted him to help me, and instead he goes and fucking does this. What the hell?

My anger is sizzling away under the surface, and I'm desperate to get to my room so I can let it loose. Suddenly, his hand grips my arm, and he spins me until my back hits the wall. Before I know it, we're in the same position as in the alley, his body pressing me up against a wall.

I try to avoid meeting his gaze, not trusting myself. He leans in until his breath is fanning my face, and his voice tickles at my ear. "Aren't you going to thank me?"

I splutter, my eyes widening as my nerve endings prickle with rage. "Thank you? Why the fuck would I thank you?"

He takes a small step back so he can meet my gaze, and he looks genuinely confused by my outburst. "You asked me to buy you time, and that's exactly what I've done. You have around eight weeks away from your fiancé. In that time, I'm sure we can come up with something to make it more permanent."

"You made me your whore. You said you own me," I seethe, genuinely confused how he can't see what's wrong with that.

"I said I own you, not that you're my whore. As I told you the other night, if you choose to be my slut, that's your choice. I'd never force you." His voice is dripping with sincerity, and my brain is spinning.

"I'm confused."

Marcus lets out a small chuckle, and I hate the way my core heats up at the carefree sound. "Honestly, I know I've not gone about this in the best way, but it's all I could think of at short notice. Jacob feels bad, which we can work on. You get out of this house for sixty days, and we've delayed your wedding, which is what you asked for. It might not be the greatest plan, but it's achieved the goals."

He's right, yet I can't help but point out something glaringly obvious that he's failed to mention. "Dad looked so close to breaking the peace treaty over this. And if Scott takes the news the way we think he will, Dad may be forced to take sides."

Marcus' eyes darken, and as he presses his body against mine, I feel his hard length against my stomach. "Your father can make his own decisions. I, personally, can't wait to see the look on Scott's face when he finds out."

I slap him on the chest, which earns me a glare. "You could enjoy this a little less."

His smirk grows as he leans in close again. "I think I'll enjoy this a lot. After all, you wanted someone to teach you what it means to be a slut, to be in control of your own body, and to have power over the man you're a slut for."

My eyes widen and my heart stutters. "What? That was just something we talked about after too much fucking vodka. You said this wasn't about you forcing me into sex."

"I won't force you. It'll be your choice," he states firmly, but his smugness is driving me fucking crazy. I hate how sure of himself he is, when I'm a mess of emotions.

"So if I choose to stay away from you for sixty days, you'd be okay with that?" I challenge.

"Of course," he replies, as he removes a hand that was resting on my hip and glides it up over my ribs, stopping to tuck a strand of hair behind my ear. Then he cups my cheek, rubbing his thumb across my lip in a way that makes my fucking knees weak. "In fact, I'll make you a promise. I won't touch you unless you beg me to."

"Beg you?" I splutter, my brain a fog of emotions, intoxicated by his scent and proximity.

"Yes, you will need to beg me."

I gather as much confidence as I can muster, and hope like hell it's enough to be believable. "I won't beg you."

His smirk grows, and as his thumb traces my lower lip, he leans over until his mouth is almost touching my ear. A shiver ripples down my spine and my core tightens at the feel of his breath on me. "I'm up for the challenge. Game on, Mio."

Before I can even comprehend how much he makes my world spin, Marcus pulls away, and I watch as he saunters down the corridor, like he didn't just leave me in a puddle. I'm so fucking screwed.

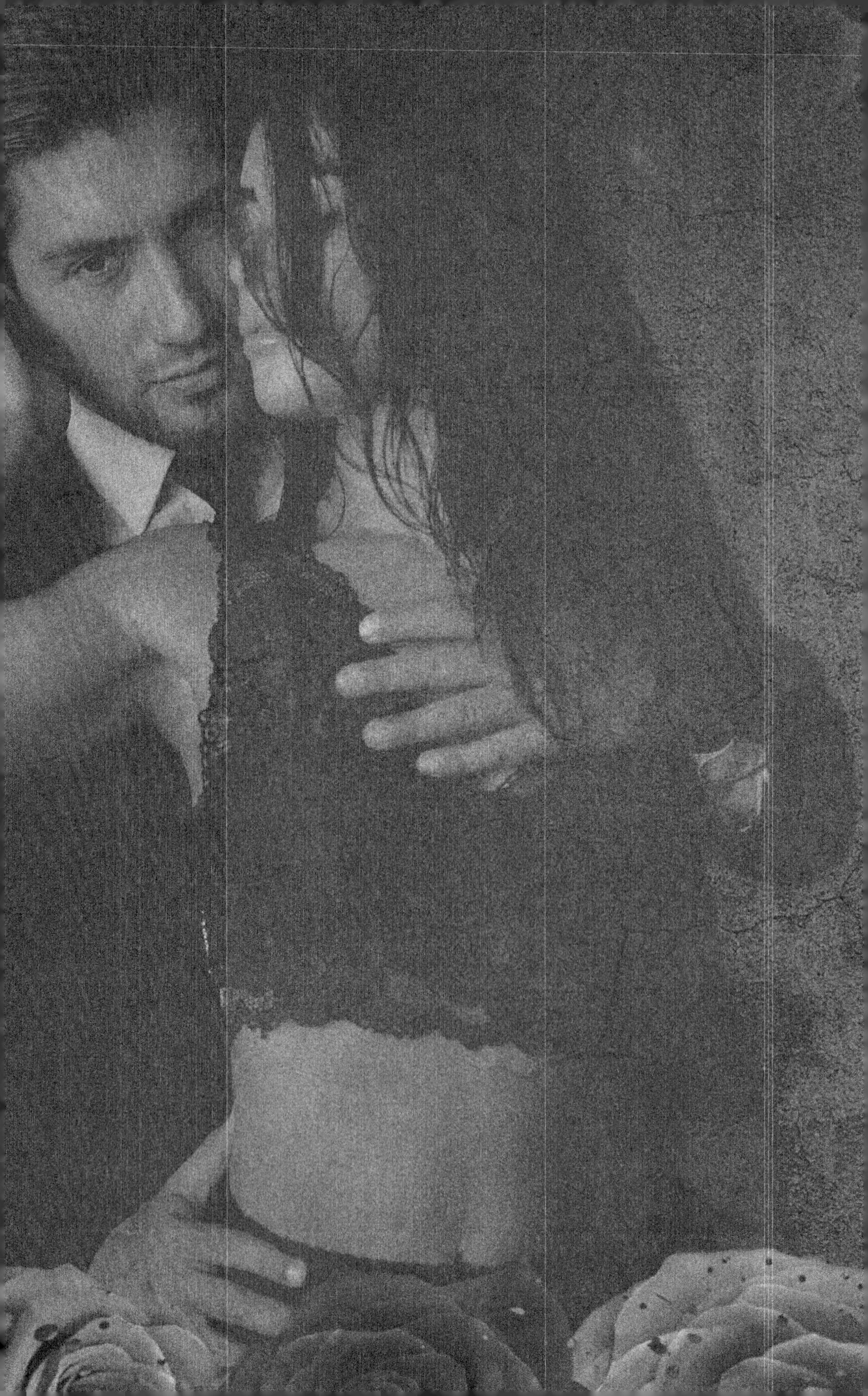

Chapter Seven
Marcus

I expected the evening to fly by, but every time I looked at the clock, it seemed to be ticking even slower than before. I feel almost antsy, waiting for the morning to arrive so that I can collect Chloe.

Miles interrupts my pacing, looking at me with his usual piercing gaze that lets me know he's about to say something I'll probably not approve of. I wait for him to get on with it, but when he doesn't, I find myself snapping at him.

"Just get on and say whatever is on your mind."

He lets out a chuckle, though there's no humour in his eyes. "Do you have any idea what you're doing? I mean, have you even considered what it's going to be like having her living here for the next two months?"

I freeze as his words hit me. Honestly, this isn't the most well thought out plan. It's barely a plan, but it's all I could think of, and so I need to make it work.

"She's an independent woman who can take care of herself. It's not like I've taken custody of a fucking child," I grumble.

Miles rolls his eyes at me. "You've never lived with a woman before. Where's she going to sleep? Have you bought anything that she will need?"

I hold my hand out to stop what I'm sure would turn into a lengthy rant if I didn't. "I have three spare bedrooms, so she can take one of them. And I'm pretty sure she'll bring anything she needs. If she doesn't, I'll buy it for her."

I keep myself from saying that I'd quite like her to share my bed, as I definitely don't want to hear whatever disapproving speech that comment would produce.

"You have no idea what it's like living with another person, especially a girl," he adds, and this time it's me who gives him an eye roll.

"I'm not socially inept, Miles. I can live with another person, I've done it before. Besides, you spend enough time here to almost be considered a roommate," I reply flippantly, and he laughs.

"I'm definitely not your roommate. When I stay here, it's as your bodyguard, or I've passed out drunk in the spare room I call mine. You've never had to deal with any of my bad habits, or any other annoying thing roommates do to each other."

Even though I went to university, I had my own apartment, with Jacob in a matching one next door. I've never had to share with anyone else, and I'm certainly not used to having people in my space all the time. Even my bodyguards don't stay in my home, other than when Miles does occasionally.

I'm an only child, used to getting everything I've ever wanted. Spoiled doesn't even begin to cover it. And I've never had to share. Maybe Miles is right and I'll find this experience much harder than I first thought.

"It's too late now, the deal has been done," I grumble.

"Maybe you should just try and make her feel a little more at home. If this is to be her home for the next two months, she needs to feel like this is her place too, rather than she's just crashing at yours," he adds.

I fix him with a pointed stare as I run my hands through my hair. "How do I do that?"

Miles throws his arms in the air, exacerbated. "You could just ask her?"

"Fine, I'll do that," I grumble, hating that I didn't think of that.

Miles lets out a chuckle as he throws himself onto my sofa, reaching for the remote. "Get some sleep. I have a feeling it's going to be a long few days for you."

I consider throwing expletives at him, but decide against it. "Are you staying in your room?" I ask, and he nods. "I'll save the big room opposite mine for Chloe."

The smile on his face grows. He's reading into what I just said, but I ignore him once again, moving towards my room to try and at least get a bit of sleep before tomorrow.

I hate that as soon as my head hits the pillow, my thoughts are consumed by her, and what it's going to be like having her here—in my space, all the time. I was so caught up in the idea of something finally happening between us, led by my fucking cock, I didn't even consider what I'm getting myself into.

From the moment I woke up, I did everything I could to distract myself from the ever-slow ticking clock. I went to my home gym and ran on the treadmill for a bit, before going down to the pool in the basement of my apartment block to swim a few lengths.

I rushed through my shower, not trusting myself to be alone with my cock for any length of time, without wanking to the thought of her being in my house. So, when the time finally came to go pick up Chloe, I felt like I'd been awake forever, and I'm exhausted.

Since we're going over to the Santoro estate, which is a short drive away, Miles accompanies me and drives. I lose count of how many times I yawn on the journey over, and Miles tries not to laugh.

I fix him with a glare, but that only makes him shake harder. "I have a feeling the next eight weeks will be the death of you."

"You better hope not, given I pay you good money to keep me alive," I retort, much snappier than usual.

"You pay me to protect you from threats, not your own stupidity."

My gaze narrows, as my scowl grows. "I get it, you don't approve."

"I didn't say I don't approve. I'm actually quite excited to see how this will play out," he states, his smirk widening as he focuses on the road.

"Wanker," I grumble, unable to think of a better comeback.

Miles laughs, but doesn't say more. We allow the silence to fill the car as we turn onto the stupidly long gravel drive that leads to the Santoro estate.

Once we've passed security, Miles parks the car off to the side of the house, and we both climb out, approaching the large mansion together. Just as we reach the final step onto the wrap-around porch, the big white door opens and Caleb Santoro is standing there, looking less than impressed.

He looks a little surprised to see me, which is odd given this is the time I said I'd be arriving. Before either of us can say anything, the sound of an approaching car captures our attention. I turn towards the noise, and it only takes me a fraction of a second to recognise the vehicle.

Now I know exactly why Caleb Santoro is answering his own door, instead of having his staff do it. As soon as the black Lexus is parked, the door opens and my father steps out.

Miles leans closer to me, whispering so only I can hear. "Did you know he was coming?"

I shake my head. "I haven't told him about any of this. I didn't know he knew...though I shouldn't be surprised."

"Maximus Morelli knows fucking everything," Miles chuckles, and I agree. My father is a worse gossip than anyone I've ever met. What has me more concerned is whether he's here on my side or Caleb's.

As my father approaches, he looks all business, dressed in the smart black suit he always wears when he's working. I silently praise myself for having the good sense to wear my own suit, as I'd be in for a bollocking if he'd seen me here at the Santoro estate dressed in anything other than a suit.

He walks straight to Caleb, his arm outstretched to shake the hand of his long-term friend and business partner. Although they're not as close as me and Jacob, a peace treaty was built on the foundations of their friendship, and it's stood the test of time—so far.

As soon as he's greeted Caleb, he turns to me. I take a step towards him, my hand out, showing him the respect he deserves as the elder of the family. His grip on my hand is tighter than I'd like, and his stone-faced expression gives nothing away.

Father pulls me in closer, leaning in so only I can hear. "You've got us in a right fucking mess this time, Son. Why the fuck didn't you tell me about any of this?" he growls, and this time when I look in his eyes, I can see the barely restrained anger shining back.

"There's nothing to tell. I have it under control," I reply flippantly, his eyes widening at my tone.

Before he can say anything more, Caleb interrupts us. "Let's go into the living room."

He doesn't wait for us to reply. He turns and walks into the house, expecting us to follow. Shooting another glare my way, my father pulls his shoulders back and follows Caleb. Looking like a chastised schoolboy, I trail behind them, Miles by my side.

When we reach the living room, Jacob and Chloe are already seated on the sofa. Jake looks like he's not slept at all, and the bright red rings around his eyes and pinpoint pupils tells me he's leaning on substances to help him get through this.

Chloe, on the other hand, looks exactly as she did yesterday—perfectly put together, wearing a conservative black dress, not a hair out of place. It's so different from the girl I know, but then again, I look different in the presence of my father too.

"Can I get you a drink, Maximus?" Caleb asks, addressing only my father, like the rest of us aren't even here.

"No, thank you. I think it's best we get this issue sorted out as quickly as we can, so as to not take up any more of each other's precious time," my father replies, like the professional he is.

Before anyone has a chance to respond, a scuffle can be heard from the next room, loud voices carrying through into the living room.

"Mr Santoro asked you to wait in his office," shouts a stern-sounding man.

More noises ring out, and it sounds like someone is fighting in the hallway. We're all staring at where the noise is coming from, and Miles discreetly takes a step closer to me, always on duty.

"I don't give a fuck what he wants. I want to be part of this meeting. Let me in there, NOW!"

Caleb steps towards the door, his face crinkled with anger, recognising who the voice belongs to. Both Chloe and Jacob are up on their feet, wearing matching shocked expressions as they stare at the door.

When the door slams open, I rush to stand in front of Chloe, pushing her behind me, as Jacob moves to my side, blocking her completely from view. Miles jumps in front of me and pulls out his gun from his side holster without a second thought, aiming it at the now open door.

My father has pulled his gun too, aiming at the door, but doesn't have a clear shot as Caleb is in the way.

Time seems to move ridiculously slowly as people draw their weapons, while we watch the door, waiting for the danger to approach. The scuffling gets louder, until finally a man bursts into the room, red-faced and angry.

"What the fuck, Scott?" Caleb yells, as two members of his security team fumble in behind Scott, each with cuts on their faces.

"I told you I wanted to be part of the meeting. I refuse to wait and be excluded," he shouts, puffing his chest out like that will make a difference.

As my brain catches up, I realise who I'm looking at. I don't think I've ever met Scott Caprillo in person, so I'd have no reason to recognise him. But I can't think of any other person named Scott who would be quite as invested in this situation.

I take a minute to look over the man who Chloe will be marrying in just a couple of months. I'm not entirely sure what I was expecting, but he's definitely not it. Perhaps I was hoping for an old bald guy, which Scott definitely isn't.

He looks to be around the same age as me, with a similar athletic build—though I'd like to think I'm a bit more ripped underneath my clothes. His blonde hair has darker roots that suggest he may be ginger underneath the hair dye. He's got a firm jawline and a slightly too wide nose, but otherwise, there's nothing noteworthy about him.

Objectively, he's not a bad looking bloke, yet I can tell by the way his sneer that the guy's a wanker. I also fucking hate the way his gaze is fixed on Chloe, who is standing behind me, trying not to be seen by him.

"I think we need to defuse the tension in the room, before someone gets trigger happy," my father states, grabbing everyone's attention.

At that point, everyone looks around, noting that Miles and my father have their guns drawn, and both me and Jacob have our hands on our weapons, and Caleb's security look to be seconds from pulling theirs too. Given the blood dripping down their faces, they're more likely to shoot Scott than I am—and that's saying something.

"I think that's a good idea. Scott, I need to ask you to calm down, so everyone can put their guns away," Caleb states calmly, though his tone with Scott is cold and firm, letting him know it's an instruction not a suggestion.

"I just wanted to be part of the fucking meeting," Scott snaps, looking like he's seconds away from stomping his foot on the floor, like a child having a tantrum.

My father steps towards him, looking more menacing than I've seen in a while. "Well, now you're part of it. I suggest you simmer down, or I will not hesitate to shoot you."

Scott's brow crinkles, his scowl deepening. He looks like he's going to reply, but Caleb cuts him off. "Why don't we all put our guns away and take a seat? Can I get anyone a drink?"

I shake my head, resisting the urge to laugh at the absurdity of Caleb offering us tea while we have guns pointed at each other. He doesn't wait for any of us to respond, taking a seat in one of the black leather armchairs.

Caleb motions for my father to take the matching chair next to him, which he does, after placing his gun back in his holster. Father looks over at me, his gaze subtly flicking to Scott, before he nods towards the black leather sofa beside me, silently making his wishes known.

With a groan, I let go of my gun and sit on the sofa. Without thinking, I take hold of Chloe's hand and pull her down with me, so she's sitting beside me.

She's so close, I can feel the heat from her thigh against mine, and it takes all my fucking effort not to look at her bare leg.

I keep my hand on hers, while my gaze remains fixed on Scott—the unknown danger in the room. Seconds later, Jacob takes the remaining seat on Chloe's other side, and Miles moves to stand at the back of the sofa, towering over us.

His stance is protective, giving him a good view of the room. I also notice that while he's lowered his gun, he's not put it away. It remains firmly in his grasp, and I don't correct him—neither does my father.

Scott's glare is fixed on where Chloe's hand is linked with mine, his eyes wide and angry. My lip tilts up into a smirk, loving that just me holding her hand is winding him up.

"I will give you five seconds to remove your hand from my fiancée, or I will do it for you, and I can't be held responsible if that happens," Scott growls, and I can't help the laugh that escapes at his pathetic excuse for a threat.

Chloe's eyes widen in panic, and she tries to pull her hand from mine, but I tighten my grip, making it clear I have no intention of letting her go.

"She may be your fiancée, but she's mine for the next sixty days, and there's nothing you can do about it," I reply, much more smugly than necessary. What can I say? I'm enjoying winding this cocksucker up.

Jake groans beside us, shaking his head as Scott practically vibrates with rage. I look over at my father, expecting him to be giving me a death glare too, but I'm shocked to see him trying to hold back a smile. There's even a hint of pride in his eyes.

"Wanna bet? I'll fucking kill you," Scott screams, taking a menacing step forward. He doesn't get far as one of Caleb's security guards grabs his shoulders, holding him in place.

I'm about to cut in with a scathing reply when my father leans forward, his icy cold voice cutting through the room. "I think now would be a good time to remind you who the fuck you're talking to. In case your feeble brain has forgotten, I'm Maximus Morelli, and this is my son and heir, Marcus. We run half of Blackthorn, and even if you're aligned with the Santoros, you know that we still demand the same respect. You'll do well to remember that. I don't take kindly to anyone threatening my son."

The casual way my father leans back in his chair, like he didn't just throw out a thinly-veiled threat, makes me smile. Scott has the good sense to look more than a little terrified as he shrugs out of the guards hold.

Facing my father, he addresses him directly, and I can tell how much it pains him to show any politeness. "I apologise for my rudeness, the heat of the moment got the better of me. I meant no disrespect, but at the same time, I have to stand up for my own honour, and that of my family."

"You feel your honour has been besmirched?" my father asks, and I hear Jacob chuckle beside me at the absurdity of the situation. My father sounds like a posh Lord, greeting his peasant followers. He also looks to be enjoying this much more than I expected.

"Chloe is my betrothed. The marriage contract has been agreed to and signed, so as far as I'm concerned, that is a binding agreement, which she is now trying to refute because of your son," Scott replies quickly, disgust dripping from every word as he glowers at Chloe.

I want to poke his fucking eyes out for looking at her at all, let alone with such disgust. What makes it worse is the way she shrinks in on herself under the weight of his gaze. I need to teach her to never cower to anyone. To hold her head up high, like the beautiful, powerful woman she is.

"I'm aware of the contract you have with the Santoros, but that's nothing to do with me or my son. As far as we're concerned, Marcus won the bet, fair and square, and now he's claiming his prize. Any issues you have should be directed to Caleb," my father adds, pointing at his rival and friend, who looks less than pleased by this.

Caleb lets out a sigh, looking tired. "We still intend on honouring the marriage contract, as I explained to you, we just need to delay it by a couple of weeks. Nothing else has changed."

Scott cheeks redden as he shouts, "Everything has changed. You expect me to marry someone that I know is whoring around? I will not marry a fucking slut."

"Enough!" I snap, fixing him with my deadliest gaze. "Do not talk about her like that."

Caleb points his finger at Scott threateningly. "Do not talk about my daughter like that, or you will face consequences. There is no sexual element to the deal with Marcus, and even if there was, the marriage contract very clearly states that Chloe is not pure—that's something you agreed to."

Chloe shrinks down beside me as her family talks about her sex life like she's not in the room. My blood boils, and the urge to fight for her ripples through my veins like fire.

"I didn't agree to this," Scott snaps, pointing to me and Chloe. "He's touching what's mine, and I have a right to stand up for myself."

Caleb looks like he's about to say something, but my father cuts him off. "This is getting boring. The bet will be honoured. Chloe will live with Marcus for the next sixty days, and then she'll be free to marry you, if she wishes. There is no room for discussion with this."

"We have upheld the peace treaty for a long time, but if you threaten my son again, I will not hesitate to break it. I will wipe out you, and the entire Caprillo family, consequences be damned.

"Now that I've made the Morelli position clear, why don't we hash out the details of this arrangement, so we can all get on with our day." Whilst my father does his best to sound nothing but calm and professional, I can hear the anger in his words, and Scott will do well to take the threat seriously.

I don't think I've ever heard my father threaten to break the peace treaty, and while I don't think he'd ever do it, the threat seems to be enough to get everyone in the room to calm down and think a little more logically.

Caleb clears his throat, clearly uncomfortable. "I think that's a great idea. I'd like to start by requesting that Chloe comes home every Sunday for lunch, so we can catch up with her and make sure everything is okay."

Father nods his head slowly. "I think that's fair—"

Before he can finish, I cut in. "I'll agree to it, but only if I can attend too. While Chloe is in my care, it's my responsibility to ensure her safety."

"She'll be fine at home with us," Jake snaps, glaring at me.

Caleb cuts in with a nod. "We can agree to that. I'm glad to hear you plan on ensuring she's safe with you."

"Of course, he will," my father states firmly, a little disgruntled by the suggestion. "Anything else?"

Caleb and Jake look at each other, but neither says anything. My blood boils when neither of them even bother asking Chloe if there's anything she'd like to add into the agreement. But it annoys me more that she just sits there in silence, blending into the furniture.

Unfortunately, my anger isn't helped when Scott opens his stupid fucking mouth again. "I will need time with Chloe to plan our wedding."

"Fuck, no," I snap, shaking my head.

"Wait a—" Scott leans forward to begin what I'm sure is about to be a tirade, when Caleb cuts him off.

"Marcus, please show a little reason. The wedding will take place mere days after your agreement ends, so it only makes sense that they have time together to plan," Caleb argues.

I shake my head, but my father speaks before I can. "We can agree to one hour per week, but only for the last four weeks. The first four she will be getting settled into a routine with us.

"She'll be allowed contact with her wedding planner at all times, so I'm sure that will ensure things go off without a hitch. I imagine you don't want to be all that involved in planning the wedding, anyway," he adds, fixing Scott with a glare that dares him to challenge him.

Scott is either really bad at reading people or a fucking idiot—I'm not sure which. "I actually plan on being very involved in my wedding. Four hours will not be enough."

"You'll have to make it work," my father snaps, turning his gaze to Caleb, looking for his support.

"I think that's very kind," Caleb adds, in an effort to keep things cordial.

I can't stop my smirk when Scott's face crumples. "Fine, but I guarantee you

I will cancel the wedding contract if I find out she's been fucking him." He points at me for good measure, like there was ever any doubt about who he might have been referring to.

This time when Caleb speaks, all the politeness has gone, and his calming tone has been replaced by anger. "You will not cancel the fucking marriage contract, unless you want to start a war with my family. You agreed to the marriage knowing Chloe isn't pure, and even if she sleeps with a hundred people in the next sixty days, that doesn't change anything about the contract. You will take her."

The way he talks about his daughter makes me so fucking angry. I feel like my whole body is vibrating with rage. For the first time since I walked into the room, Chloe's quiet voice rings out from beside me.

"Please stop talking about me like I'm not even here. Scott, you are talking about me like I'm something you own, just because you have a contract that says I'll belong to you. But Marcus has one too. If you're allowed to do whatever you want with me while I'm yours, then surely you can understand Marcus wanting the same rights while I belong to him."

Her voice is so fucking shy and timid, and not once does she lift her gaze from looking at her hands. If I thought I was angry before, it's nothing compared to how I feel hearing Chloe talk about herself like she's an object that we're passing around.

Given the fact her family hasn't objected, something tells me this is the way she's been made to feel her whole life.

It makes me want to set fire to the whole fucking room, laughing with her as we watch it burn. She's definitely not an object to be owned, and the sooner she learns that, the faster she can take back the power these arseholes have stolen from her.

Scott stutters over his words, clearly not sure what to say. "That's not... I mean, it's not... This is different."

"How?" I ask, fixing him with an arrogant glare.

Scott looks to be contemplating a response when Jake speaks. "Look, Marcus has agreed that this deal isn't sexual. She's not there for sex, and he'd never force her into it."

I mean, that's true, but I won't say no when she begs me...and she will.

For the first time since we entered the room, Chloe looks up at me. Her eyes are almost devoid of emotion, but there's something there, like she's screaming at me to get her out of here.

"I think we're going around in circles now. I would never force Chloe into anything. If something happens, it's because she's asked for it. But even if we do have sex, it doesn't change the fact this is a temporary arrangement. She's marrying you, and you'd do well to remember that," I growl at Scott, hating the way the words taste like ash on my tongue.

Chloe's eyes close, and she looks so fucking hurt, it makes my stomach flip. When she opens them again, there's a slight sheen to them, like my words brought tears to her eyes, and it's like a punch to the gut.

Does she not realise I'm just saying whatever it takes to get this fuckwit to back down so I can get her out of here?

Scott walks over to Chloe and kneels down in front of her, completely ignoring me and Jake. He places his hand on her knee, and when Chloe flinches, I want to plough my hand into his face.

"I'll allow you to go with Marcus, but you better remember exactly what he just said. When this is over, it's me you'll be spending the rest of your life with. I decide how comfortable your future will be. Remember that," he states far too calmly, while squeezing her thigh so hard, her skin turns white.

I'm about to punch him when Miles lays his hand on my shoulder, warning me not to do anything rash. He's right, of course. With this, I can bide my time. I'll select the best time, and when he least expects it, I'll strike. There's no way I'm letting him get away with a threat like that.

Besides, if he's dead and buried in an unmarked grave, I won't have to worry about what will happen in sixty days when I refuse to let Chloe leave. I suspect, given how protective I'm feeling towards her, once I have her in my world, I won't ever let her go.

When I get her home, I have sixty days to show her who she really is. It's not just about showing her how much of a slut she can be for me—although that part will be fun. I need to build her confidence, give her back the power people have taken from her, until she sees the same person that I do.

As soon as we get home, it's game on!

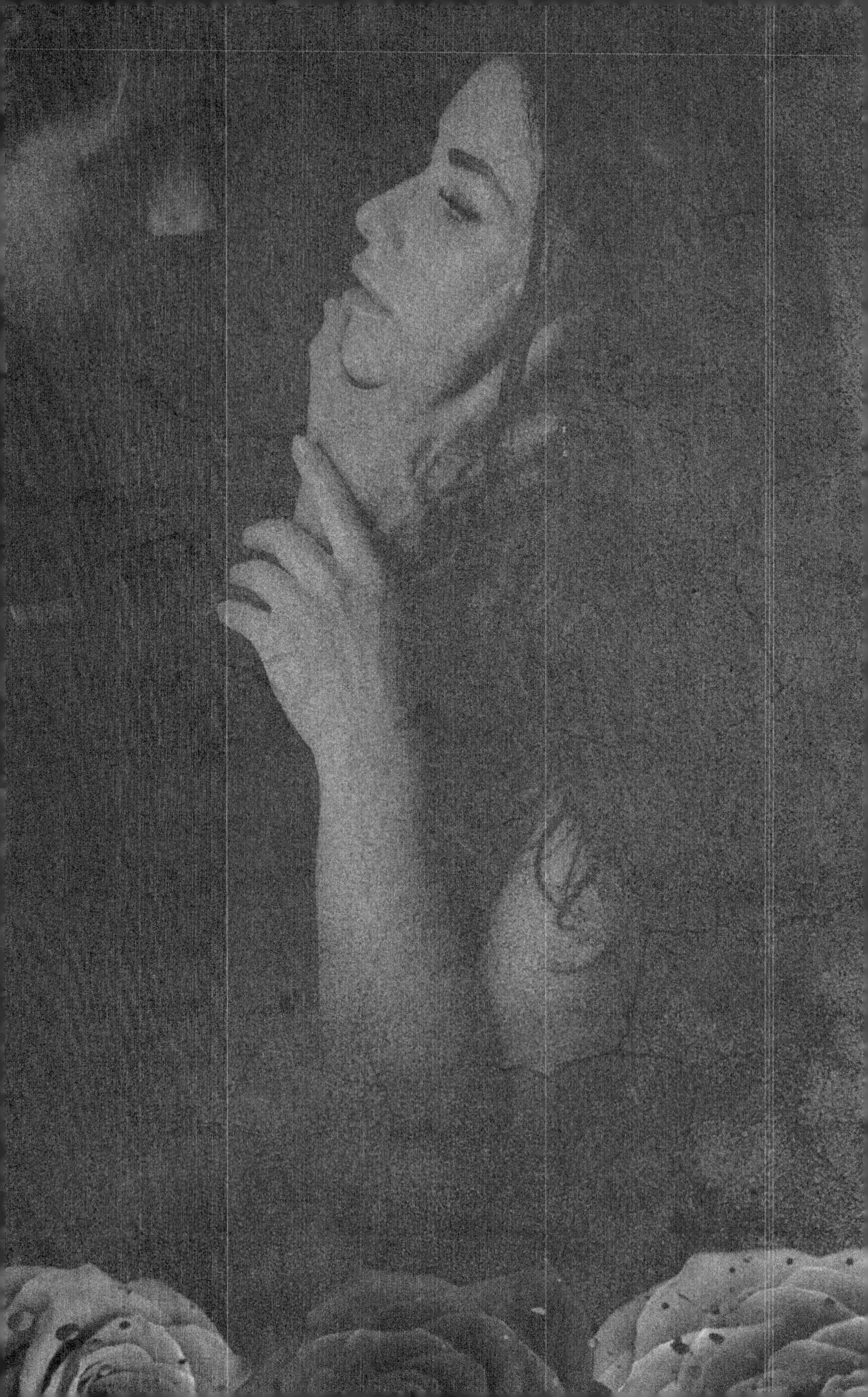

Chapter Eight
Chloe

The journey to Marcus' penthouse seemed to be over in a flash. We sat in deafening silence, neither wanting to be the first to speak. Instead, I shuffled around on his ridiculously comfy leather seats and stared out at the passing scenery.

All manner of thoughts were rushing through my head. While I'm fucking annoyed as hell that yet another decision has been taken away from me, and I'm being treated like an object being passed around, I can't say I'm entirely upset by the situation.

After all, this is exactly what Marcus promised he'd do. I may not like his methods, but I'm out of my parent's house for a while, and my wedding has been delayed, which was all I wanted.

It just fucking irritates me that Marcus, of all people, was able to get me out of the mess I was in. I'm also not entirely sure what to expect from this little arrangement.

According to Jake, Marcus owns me for the next sixty days. I have to do whatever he tells me, no questions asked—that alone makes me grind my teeth in frustration. I may have been raised to follow orders, but it doesn't mean I fucking like it.

Also, I hate how much my stomach sank when Jake clarified that nothing sexual would happen between us. I mean, don't get me wrong, I wasn't exactly thrilled that my brother was whoring me out after losing a bet, but I can't deny my mind went to a very dirty place—one I quite like the thought of.

Ever since that night at Caged, to say Marcus and his dirty words have been on my mind would be a fucking understatement. His words have been echoing through my head so often that I could probably recite them. I don't even want to think about how many pairs of knickers I've ruined thinking about him, dreaming about him.

It wasn't just the sexual chemistry that pulled me in. Yes, him calling me a slut did stupid things to me, but the promises he made meant more. He said he could give me back the control I've been longing for—something I stopped hoping for a long time ago.

Initially, I was convinced it sounded stupid, like something a guy would say to get a girl into bed. *'Be my slut, do as I say, and you'll feel like the one with all the power'*.

Then I remember how I felt in the alleyway. When Marcus looked like he was struggling to control himself, that made me feel powerful. He's the most put-together, controlled man I know, yet he was struggling to do the right thing because of me.

In truth, I want nothing more than to claim back the control that was taken from me a while ago, but I also want him. No matter how much I tell myself I don't, there's something about Marcus Morelli that draws me in. He's forbidden and dangerous, that one guy you know you're not supposed to like, so of course you do.

Even when he's pushing me away, being the perfect arsehole I'm supposed to hate, I still like him.

He doesn't treat me like I'm fragile. He doesn't baby me the way my family always has. He's not afraid of telling me things I don't want to hear, because he knows it won't break me—I've survived much worse.

So why did it hurt so much when he said nothing sexual would happen between us?

As soon as he said I'd have to beg him, I saw red. The slutty side of me was on her knees, begging already, but the girl fighting to claw back some semblance of control held firm.

I told him I'd never beg him, and the responding look was pure sin. I saw the challenge, and I didn't know what the hell to think.

The confusing swirl of words and emotions have been on repeat in my brain, and I've reached the point where I have no idea what to expect while I'm with him.

Honestly, it's driving me crazy, which is why I've decided to confront him as soon as we arrive at his penthouse. I just hope I can hold my nerve.

Although Marcus and Jake have been friends nearly my whole life, it occurs to me, when we pull up to the tall high-rise building, that I've never been to Marcus' penthouse, despite it being across the road from Jake's.

I've been to Morelli Manor, the large stately home his father lives in, where Marcus grew up, but I've never been here.

We pull into the underground parking garage, and after being let in by security, Marcus pulls into a spot at the very end of the row, nearest the lift. As soon as I climb out, I'm overwhelmed by the amount of ridiculously expensive cars. I don't have to be a petrolhead to know that there's a lot of super cars here.

He catches me staring, and looks like he's about to say something, but instead, he turns and starts walking towards the lift.

I stand near the boot of his car, and when he realises I'm not following, he looks over his shoulder at me in confusion. "What? Do you not like lifts?"

I roll my eyes and point to the boot of his car. "All my bags are still in the boot, remember?"

He shakes his head with the look of confusion growing to the point you'd think I had a third boob. "Someone will come and collect them. They'll be in your room before I finish giving you the tour," he states, sounding more posh than usual.

"I didn't know you have staff for that sort of thing," I state bluntly.

Obviously, his family has money, as does mine. In fact, Morelli Manor is even bigger than our house, with way more rooms and land. His father has staff that work at the Manor, but other than the security staff Marcus always has with him, I didn't know he had his own staff at the penthouse.

Marcus just shrugs his shoulders like it's not a big deal. "I don't really. I have security staff that are responsible for keeping me and this place safe, and they usually help out with things like this. They won't go through your bags, but they will scan them to make sure it's safe before taking them to your room.

"I also have a woman who helps take care of the place. She does all the cleaning and sorting, but that's it."

"I was expecting you to say you have butlers, drivers, and private chefs, like at Morelli Manor," I confess, my cheeks heating as I blurt out my thoughts.

He shakes his head with a small smile. "I moved out to get away from all of that. Anyway, shall we go in?"

He points to the lift, and I realise that the whole time we've been talking,

I've just been standing by his car like a crazy person. I rush over to him, knowing my cheeks are going to be even fucking redder than they were before.

The lift arrives within seconds, and as the door opens, he places his hand on my lower back to guide me inside. "After you," he says, his voice a deep grumble.

Fuck, my stomach flips and my skin tingles where his hand is against me. It's barely even a touch, yet my nerve endings feel like they're on fire.

He guides me into the lift, and I turn to face the door once we're both inside. He drops his hand, so he can press the button for the penthouse, and it seems to take fucking ages for the doors to close. I choose to ignore the way my body seems to ache over the loss of his touch.

With each nanosecond that passes, it's like the air starts to sizzle around us. He's standing so close, I can feel the warmth from his body.

Thanks to the romance books I read, I'm now analysing our proximity in the confined lift, sexy thoughts flashing into my head like a dirty movie.

I want him to push me up against the lift wall, to slide his leg in between mine until I'm grinding on his thigh. I want him to wrap his hand around my neck while his other arm cages me in, completely dominating me. I want to feel the press of his soft lips against mine as he swallows my moans with his kiss.

The loud ping of the lift announcing we've reached our destination pulls me out of my fantasy, and I have to blink a few times to clear my mind.

Am I sweating? I feel like I'm sweating in places I didn't know I could sweat.

The biggest problem with the fantasy is that I already know, if anything were to ever happen between me and Marcus, my imagination wouldn't even come close.

That one incident in the alleyway taught me that. His actions and domineering presence caught me off-guard in a way I never expected.

Now I know that my imagination is woefully lacking—and given how wet my knickers currently are, that's saying something—I'm a little worried about anything happening in real life. I have an awful feeling that Marcus Morelli has the power to break me, and I'm not sure I want to stop him.

As the doors open, Marcus walks out first, motioning for me to follow. As soon as I walk into the hallway, I'm stunned. I don't know what I expected, but this is not it.

The long corridor has several doors on either side. Despite it having no windows, the space is so light and bright, with crisp white walls and beautiful black picture frames. The black wooden doors contrast so well with the sleek white walls, making the place look elegant in an unexpected way.

"This is where you can hang your coat and leave your shoes," Marcus says, pulling open the door on the immediate right of the entrance to reveal a small utility room.

There's a row of coat hooks along one wall, with shoe storage along the floor. There's also a splattering of umbrellas, bags, and other random items, that all seem to have their own place.

Marcus removes his shoes, and it seems so weird to see him in just socks. He takes off his jacket and hangs it on the door, loosening his tie as he does. Without giving it much thought, I take off my uncomfortable heels and place them beside his, as I slip off my coat.

Before I can reach up and place it on a hook, Marcus takes it and does it for me. It's so domesticated that it completely throws me, and I'm once again lost for words. Luckily, I don't need them, as Marcus leads us out of the utility room and continues the tour.

The apartment has three guest bedrooms—though one seems to have been claimed by Miles, his Head of Security—a small office, two bathrooms, and a master suite that has a small sitting room, a large bedroom, and a fucking gorgeous en-suite.

The claw tub alone grabbed my attention, until I saw the multi-jet rainfall shower big enough to fit several people inside. Hell, it's even got a bench seat in there, so you can sit and enjoy the water streaming over you.

Damn, I wish this was my bathroom instead of Marcus'.

Don't get me wrong, the bathroom that he tells me will be all mine is gorgeous. It has a large jacuzzi tub that I could spend hours in, and a waterfall shower similar to his, but there's just something missing.

Every room he shows me is more beautiful than the last. Decorated in bright whites, black, and grey, it looks like it's been done professionally. Everything is sleek and clean, but there's also a nice homely feel to it.

Even though I wasn't expecting a bachelor pad—that's just not Marcus' style—I didn't in my wildest dreams think he'd live somewhere as beautiful as this.

Though, as I wander around, I note the lack of a personal touch. There are no photos on the walls, no memories dotted about. The house looks immaculate, but it doesn't tell me anything about Marcus.

As he leads me to the final guest bedroom, he looks a little hesitant for the first time during the whole tour, like he's unsure what I'll say. With his hand on the door handle, he turns to face me.

"Honestly, I wasn't sure what you'd want your room to look like, and given I didn't really have much of a plan, I'm sort of winging it. But after talking to Miles, I know it's important for you to have a safe space while you're here. I want this place to feel like home while you're here.

"I've left it how it was, for now, but I figured we could decorate it any way you'd like. If there's any particular furniture you'd like, let me know and I can get it for you. Basically, it's your space, and you can do what you want with it. Of course, I'll pay, and help with decorating, so you don't have to do it all yourself."

The words rush out of him in a way I've never heard before. He's almost babbling, saying whatever comes into his head, and I hate how fucking adorable it is.

Without thinking, I reach out and place my hand on his arm. His gaze flicks to me, his eyes darken in a way that makes my thighs clench.

"Thank you," I whisper, hoping it's enough to convey what I'm feeling, while stopping his adorable rambling.

We both stand frozen, just staring at each other as the air around us seems to crackle. As always, Marcus regains his composure much quicker than me, and he pushes the door to my new room open, breaking the weird bubble we just found ourselves in.

I take in the room, and I'm shocked by how much I like it just the way it is. Compared to the other rooms, this one feels the most homely.

It has pale blue walls, deep mahogany furniture, and the biggest bed I've ever seen, with a deep midnight blue duvet covering it. Seeing the cute little throw cushions in various shades of blue scattered over the top makes me want to dive onto the bed.

"It's beautiful," I say as I cast my eyes around the room again, catching more cute little details, like the fluffy rug on the floor.

"Like I said, you can change anything," Marcus replies gruffly, like he thinks I might not mean it.

"I don't want to. I really do love it."

This time when his piercing gaze fixes on mine, that signature smirk of his turns into an actual smile. "I'm glad you like it. Nobody's ever stayed in here before."

"Why do you have so many rooms if you don't have guests?" I blurt out.

He shrugs his shoulders. "Miles has claimed one of the rooms, and then the other I showed you is the one I tend to use for when people stay over, as it's the furthest away from my room.

"With this one being right beside mine, I've always left it empty, but I meant what I said, I want you to have a space that's all yours. Having a room no one has ever stayed in before seemed to fit that bill."

Without thinking, I reach out and grab his hand, squeezing as I smile up at him. "Thank you, that means a lot."

He looks down at where our hands are connected, not even blinking. I should pull away, but the warmth from his touch is too much. My whole fucking hand is tingling, and I can't bring myself to drop it. I'm a little surprised that he hasn't.

In true Chloe fashion, my brain decides to ruin the moment with a bit of verbal diarrhoea when I say the first thing that comes into my head, consequences be damned. "Did you mean it when you said you wouldn't touch me while I'm here?"

His eyes flick between mine and our hands, his brow furrowing as my words ring loudly in the air. Clearly misunderstanding my question, he lets go of my hand quickly, almost like it burnt him.

"Sorry, I did say I wouldn't touch you," he mumbles, taking a small step back, as if trying to clear his head. But that's the last thing I want.

Finding a confidence I didn't know I had, I take a step towards him, crowding his space.

"Actually, you initially said you wanted to teach me to be a slut, to help give me back the control I crave, but then you said you wouldn't touch me. Forgive me for being a little confused."

The last part comes out much snarkier than I'm expecting, and Marcus tries not to smile when he hears it. This time, he takes a step towards me, closing the already small gap, so he's very much in my personal space.

In fact, he's so close I can feel the warmth of his breath fluttering over my lips, and my mouth suddenly feels very dry. Even running my tongue over my lower lip doesn't seem to help.

I hear an almost unperceivable gasp, and my eyes flick up to Marcus, who's watching my tongue trace its path. He looks almost hypnotised, but then his face scrunches up like he's in pain.

"I meant it all. I can give you everything that you're looking for. I can teach you and torment you, without ever touching you. If you want me to touch you, you'll have to beg first, and I'll only do it when I want to," he explains, his gravelly voice rasping beside my ear, sending a shiver down my spine.

"I don't understand."

Talk about stating the fucking obvious. I can't think clearly when he's this close, and all the blood has evacuated my brain for other areas.

"Sit!" he snaps, pointing at the bed.

There's a small part of me that wants to tell him I'm not a fucking dog and I don't take demands, but all good sense appears to have left my brain, and I'm seated on the edge of the bed before I know it. My legs move of their own accord, propelled by my vagina.

"You want to be in control? You want to feel powerful?" He phrases them like questions, so I simply nod, my mouth far too dry to find actual words right now. "Do you believe you can achieve that by giving up control?"

My brain spins as I try to make sense of his question. "How can I gain control by giving it up? That doesn't make sense."

He chuckles as he takes a step back, pulling off his tie at the same time. My eyes are wide as fucking saucers as I watch every movement, my heart racing in anticipation.

"When it comes to sex, I have to be the one in control. I call the shots, I make demands, and I expect the person I'm with to follow them without hesitation. I prefer to be dominant, and I like the girl I'm with to submit. But that doesn't mean I'm the one with all the power. Something like that requires trust," he explains, throwing his tie on the floor.

I take in a shuddered breath, my skin suddenly feeling really fucking overheated.

It doesn't come as a great surprise to me that a man like Marcus enjoys being in control—he practically oozes that Alpha persona. What surprises me is how much I like the idea of submitting to him.

After everything I've been through, I swore I'd never let another man take anything from me, including control, yet there's something about this that appeals to me.

"If you're dominating her, surely you're the one with the power. She has to do as you say." My voice sounds so quiet and unsure, because I am. I need him to help me make sense of what he's talking about.

He lets out a deep chuckle, that smirk of his growing. "No, she doesn't have to do as I say, she *chooses* to. There's a big difference.

"If you give over control to me, that's something you've chosen to do. I haven't taken it from you, and you can still claim it back. You set boundaries, and are able to say when things become too much.

"I might be the one calling the shots in the moment, but you're the one creating the rules to play by, and any guy who has ever made you believe different is a fucking arsehole," he growls, his eyes flaring with anger at the mention of my past.

For a moment my heart stops, and I wonder if he knows my secret, but that would be impossible. I've never told anyone, so there's no way. He's just hitting closer to the mark than I'd like.

"I'm still confused," I admit, hating how foggy my brain feels when he's looking at me with those gorgeous blue eyes, like he can see into my soul, and it scares the shit out of me.

"Why don't I show you how much control you really have?"

Before I can respond, he reaches down and slides the zipper to his trousers open. My heart stutters and my breathing turns into panting as all the air is sucked from the room.

He's still standing a fair distance away, and he hasn't moved closer, so my mind is working a million miles a minute to figure out what the hell he's doing.

As soon as the zipper is down, he pulls his white shirt out of the waistband of his trousers, and I ignore the way my breathing hitches when I catch sight of the patch of skin just above, and the trail of hair leading into his boxers.

His trouser button is still fastened, and I have to mentally scream at myself to stop looking at the bulge that's threatening to break through where his zip was.

"Most women think it's easy for men to get a hard-on. That our dick perks up at the first sight of a pretty girl in a tight dress, and when we were horny fucking teenagers, that's true. But the older we get, the more selective we are. It takes more to turn us on, and at my age, I've learnt exactly what I like.

"You could bring a random girl in here, with big tits and a bare cunt, have her get naked and shake her arse, and there's a good chance I wouldn't even get a semi. I'm much more particular about what I like," he says gruffly, as he begins to unfasten the top button of his shirt.

Wrong fucking button.

I hate the way I'm screaming in my head, wishing he was opening the button on his trousers instead, but I can't deny I'm fucking hypnotised by him. Not just his deeply seductive, slow, purposeful movements, but also the words.

I have no idea where he's going with this, but someone could set off a bomb in the next room and I still wouldn't move.

With each button he opens, he keeps his gaze locked on me, and I can hear my heart pounding in my ears. I open my mouth to say something, anything, but I can't seem to find the words.

He watches my mouth twist as I try to form words like a human, and when I give up, that fucking self-satisfied smirk of his grows.

Just as he begins exposing the hard lines of his abs, his words cut through my haze. "I know exactly what I like, and believe it or not, it's incredibly hard to find."

That catches me unaware, and before I know it, I'm blurting out, "Why?"

He lets out a little sigh, that I see more than hear as my eyes are glued to his fucking god-like chest, watching as he pops the last of his buttons and his shirt falls open. My mouth gapes, and I worry that I'm drooling.

"In the past, I may have been willing to try with someone, but now I'm not.

People who watch too many Disney movies would say I've kissed all the frogs, and now I'm waiting for the real thing," he says with a shrug of his shoulders.

A very undignified snort breaks free, and I slap my hand over my mouth in a delayed attempt to cover up the awful noise. But the mere idea of Marcus referring to himself as a Disney princess is one of the funniest things I've heard in a long time.

As soon as he hears my laugh, his eyes darken and he takes a step towards me. I feel like prey trapped in the path of a predator, and I'm too frozen to move. "What's so funny, Mio?"

There's that word again. I need to ask what it means, but I'll stick to answering his question—for now. "You are no Disney princess."

His smirk grows wider and he seems almost dangerous as he takes off his open shirt, throwing it onto the floor. My eyes are fucking wide as saucers, and I'm not sure I'm even blinking. My gaze is focused on the hard ridges of his pale, beautiful chest.

"I never said I was... I know I'm the villain in every story, but my point still stands."

When he says the word villain, his tone is almost a growl, as though that will make me more afraid of him.

"So, how do you know if you've found the real thing?" I ask, trying to get us back on track...whatever the hell track we're on.

For the first time, he breaks our eye contact, and he drops his gaze down to his trousers. I watch with rapt attention as he slides his hands over the waistband, until he reaches the closed button. When he finally pops it, my heart skips a beat.

As he begins sliding them over his hips, he lifts his gaze to meet mine once again, and his eyes are almost dark, hooded with the same lust I'm sure he sees reflected back. I pull my lower lip in between my teeth, biting to distract from the way my body is practically vibrating with nervous energy.

Teenage me daydreamed about this moment practically every fucking day and night, from the moment I first realised I had a crush on my brother's best friend.

No matter how much I told myself I shouldn't, that he's an arsehole, that he doesn't feel the same...none of it mattered. You can't help what your brain thinks about when left to its own devices, and mine has been thinking of Marcus for years.

I've imagined every scenario you could possibly think of. I've pictured every inch of his body in my head. I've dreamt of every possible thing that he could say to me...or so I thought. Because nothing in the world prepared me for this.

My imagination was woefully fucking inadequate at dreaming up Marcus, as this real life version is so much better.

His trousers drop to the floor and he steps out of them, kicking them to the side with his foot. Marcus stands before me in just his tight black boxers, and it's impossible to miss the bulge that's straining against them.

I must have been staring for much longer than is acceptable, as Marcus lets out a short laugh, pulling my attention back to that cocky smirk of his. "This is how I know," he states confidently, taking his hand and gripping his hard length over his boxers.

As his hand wraps around his shaft, Marcus lets out a low groan, and I gasp loudly, my core clenching at how fucking hot this is. His eyes are fixed on me, but I can't meet his gaze for long, my attention is pulled away when I see his hand move.

Marcus slowly palms his cock through his boxers, sliding his hand over his length, and I watch transfixed as it grows. As his cock becomes erect, his motions become more obvious. He slides his finger over the head of his cock, before moving back to the base, squeezing when he circles his hand around it.

"You did this," he states loudly, and it's enough to pull me out of the bubble I was in, stuck staring as he strokes his hardening length.

"What?" I mumble, completely fucking flustered by the whole situation.

My eyes meet his, and they're so dark, my breathing stutters as I pull in a desperate gasp. The corner of his lip tilts, revealing the cutest fucking dimple, and I hate how he can be so fucking sexy and adorable, all at the same time.

"Do you have any idea how fucking gorgeous you are?" he growls.

I shake my head slightly, my heart racing at the intensity of his words. Nobody has ever made me feel so much with one sentence. The fact he's attracted to me is baffling, but telling me I'm the one to make his body react this way is something else. I'm lost for words.

Well, if I thought I was lost for words before, it's nothing compared to when his hand disappears under the waistband of his tight black boxers. His large hand palms his cock, the black fabric preventing me from seeing anything except the outline of his movements.

"Each time I think of those fucking delectable curves of yours...or the way your skirt clings to your arse...or how your tits are pushed up to show off the most perfect cleavage...my cock gets impossibly harder. As I think of your sexy body, all the blood rushes to the head, making it pulse almost painfully."

His words are deep and breathy, with an almost gravelly tone that makes me squeeze my thighs together. Though I suspect it's far too late...my knickers are beyond ruined.

"Do you know how many times I've stroked my dick whilst thinking of you?

Wondering what you look like without clothes, if your body is even fucking hotter underneath the tight dresses you wear. I think about how tight you are, and how fucking wet your little cunt gets when you think about me. Do you think about me?" he adds, looking almost shy at the vulnerability behind his question.

I feel like my mind has a few seconds delay on it. I'm still processing Marcus Morelli's confession that he strokes his cock while thinking about me, so my brain barely registers the question.

When it does, I don't know what to say. He's being honest with me, but to tell him the truth now requires a level of trust I'm not sure I have yet.

Unfortunately, Marcus has a secret weapon, and he uses it to make me lose the last bit of good sense I had. He pulls the waistband of his boxers down just a fraction, showing me the purple engorged head he just mentioned, and at the sight of the pre-cum dripping from his tip, my brain becomes fuzzy.

"Yes." It's barely above a whisper, but when that smirk turns into a genuine smile, I know he heard me.

"Good girl," he replies, and an honest to God shiver ripples down my spine. *Why did that sound so unbelievably sexy coming from him?*

Using his thumb, he swipes a bead of pre-cum off the tip and spreads it over the head, before his hand disappears behind the fabric once more.

"I'm a man who has to be in control at all times, yet you have power over me that I never gave you. It doesn't take much from you and my dick is standing to attention, throbbing like I'm a teenager with no bloody control. Can you imagine how much of a fucking mess I'd be if you were actually trying to turn me on?" he says with a chuckle.

"I-I... I didn't even know you liked me. I-I thought you...hated me," I stutter, shaking my head rapidly, like that might change how bloody mind boggling this entire scenario is.

Marcus lets out a dark chuckle, but there's no humour there.

"I definitely never hated you. I hated how you made me feel. You were off-limits, and I wasn't allowed to find you attractive. I told myself repeatedly that you were nothing special.

"Still, you looked at me with those big fucking silver eyes, like you could see past all my bullshit, and that scared me. So I treated you like shit. I pushed you away and made you think I hated you, in the hope that you'd stop looking at me like you are right now." His voice gets deeper and more urgent, and as the final word leaves his lips, he's almost growling at me.

My mouth flops open, and once again I have no idea what to say. I thought I'd done a better job of hiding my schoolgirl crush, but it's a bit too late now.

"I-I...I didn't..."

My words trail off, and I'm honestly not sure what I was about to say. Luckily, Marcus doesn't need me to reply.

"You never stopped looking at me, and I have no idea if that's a good thing or not. There's a million bloody reasons why this is a bad idea, and I don't give a shit about any of them. But I do stand by what I said before, I refuse to touch you until you trust me."

Before I can even think about what I'm saying, the words tumble from my lips. "I do trust you."

A sad smile crosses his face, like he doesn't believe me, and I want to fight him, but his next sentence catches me off-guard.

"Then tell me why you need to take back control. I saw the change in you that began nearly a year ago. I was too consumed watching your brother fall apart, I missed the exact moment it happened to you, but when I started seeing the signs...I knew something big had occurred."

My heart is racing, there's a loud buzzing in my ears, and I'm suddenly feeling really fucking dizzy. It's like the walls are closing in around me, and my breathing starts coming in short and sharp until I'm panting, desperately trying to pull in air, yet never getting enough.

Even though Marcus says he knows, I'm certain he doesn't, otherwise he wouldn't have asked. But the fact he knows something happened, that scares me. Though not half as much as him wanting to know. Marcus isn't the type of person who lets things like this go.

"I-I...It's... I mean, it's nothing," I stutter, as sweat runs down my back.

Marcus shakes his head, but he doesn't look disappointed in my answer. It's almost like that's what he expected me to say. "Okay."

The way he says that one word sets me on edge. "I mean it," I snap.

"Okay," he repeats, which just winds me up even more.

"Stop saying that!"

The small almost sad smile morphs into that cocky smirk of his again, and his moodswing catches me off-guard. "We both know something happened. You can deny it all you want, but until you trust me enough to tell me about it, there will be no touching."

I swear my vagina would have groaned with despair if it could. I want nothing more than to have those big, strong hands of his on my body, but talking about my past is out of the question.

I've spent over a year trying to push it from my mind, and although I've been wildly fucking unsuccessful, I've managed to keep it a secret, and I don't plan on breaking the promise I made to myself.

I don't know where the hell it comes from, but I try to turn the tables on him, to play him at his own game.

"That means I can't touch you either, though. You will have to walk around with blue balls if you stick to this."

He shakes his head, a wicked smile on his lips. His hand moving pulls my attention down to his cock, as he pulls his length out of his boxers. I have to hold back a fucking gasp at the size of him.

I blink rapidly a few times, wondering if I'm seeing things, but I'm not. He's really that fucking big.

He wraps his hand around the base of his shaft, and he's so wide, he almost struggles to get his fingers to meet. As he begins dragging his hand up and down his hard length, my body tingles and I'm frozen, staring at his movements.

"As much as I'd love for this to be your hand, I'm a patient man. I can wait, and I'll continue using my imagination. I'll picture what those pretty red lips of yours would look like stretched wide as I slide my cock into your mouth, imagining what your throat feels like swallowing around me. I bet you'd be able to take me deep, with a bit of practice."

Fuck, now I really am going to have to throw my knickers away. I don't think I've ever been wetter than I am right now. I have to clench my thighs together to try and alleviate a bit of the pressure that's building in my core.

Yet, Marcus seems intent on pushing me even further into madness. "I bet if I were to slip my fingers into your knickers right now, I'd find you dripping wet. I can see you shimmying your hips, trying to clench your thighs together to ease some of that throbbing ache. Do you want to touch yourself right now?"

Hell fucking yes, I do, I shout in my head, but in reality, I stay silent. I've never touched myself in front of someone else before, and my self-conscious part holds me back.

"I bet if you were to slide one of your fingers in now, your pussy would be so wet and tight, wouldn't it?" he asks, as he continues to run his hand up and down his shaft. I watch with rapt attention as his movements get quicker and more uncoordinated. "I can only imagine how tight your cunt would be if I were to push my cock in deep."

A shuddered moan leaves my lips as my imagination goes haywire. That's exactly what I fucking want, and he's driving me crazy.

I nod, hoping that will be enough to let him know what I want, but I'm not that stupid. He won't back down on his earlier request, and I can't...

"I'm squeezing my hand tighter, and I still don't think it's anywhere close to how you'd feel. My cock is throbbing at the thought of sinking into you, watching as your cunt swallows all of me, stretching you more than any man has before."

Oh, my God, his dirty words are nearly enough to make me orgasm right now, without him even touching me. That's how much he's setting my body on fire, and it's like the most delicious form of torture, as he's showing me what I could have, knowing this will never be enough.

"I'm so fucking close," he growls, squeezing his cock as beads of pre-cum leak from the angry-looking tip. "This is all you, Mio. You have the power to make me fall apart."

He looks at me with wide eyes, like I'm a fucking Queen, and my heart races. I've never felt as powerful or as sexy as when Marcus looks at me the way he is now.

"Do you want me to come for you?" he asks, giving me power over him.

"Yes."

As soon as the word leaves my lips, Marcus lets out a roar as he explodes over his hand. He throws his head back, slams his eyes closed, and groans loudly as he slowly works the last bits of cum from his shaft. Most of it sprays into his hand, but some hits his stomach or the floor.

My eyes never leave his dick, watching with each spurt as he rides out the orgasm I gave to him without even touching him. My mind is blown, and my whole body is tingling. I doubt it would take more than a few strokes to my clit before my own orgasm rips through me, and it's taking all my effort not to reach between my legs.

Marcus is panting loudly, and I slowly drag my gaze up his body to find his eyes are now open and latched on me, his expression dark and glazed with lust. "Next time, you'll get on your knees so I can paint you with my cum. Or better yet, you can do it for me with your mouth. You'd like that, wouldn't you, Mio?"

Words have gone and all I can do is nod, which earns me a cocky chuckle that makes me want to snap at him, if only I could remember how to speak.

"All you have to do is tell me what I want to know, then I'll touch you as much as you'd like." His smug expression is enough to bring me around, just a little.

"I can touch myself, thank you." It sounded much more confident in my head.

"I'm sure you can, but now you know that I can drive you wild without ever touching you. I can promise, you'll cave before I do."

Before I can even begin to argue with him, which would be pointless as we both know he's right, he turns his back to me, sliding his sticky cock back into his boxers. Picking up his discarded clothes, he walks out of the room, leaving me frozen to the spot.

It's not until I hear his bedroom door close that I snap out of the trance he left me in. I'm so fucking screwed.

There's something about Marcus that hypnotises me, and he's right when he says I want nothing more than to give my body over to him. But the problem is, although I think I trust him, I'm not sure I'll ever trust anyone enough to divulge my secret.

I have a feeling this is just the beginning. Marcus is going to do whatever it takes to get me to cave, to give myself over to him, but the only way that'll happen is if I give him the one secret I vowed never to share with anyone.

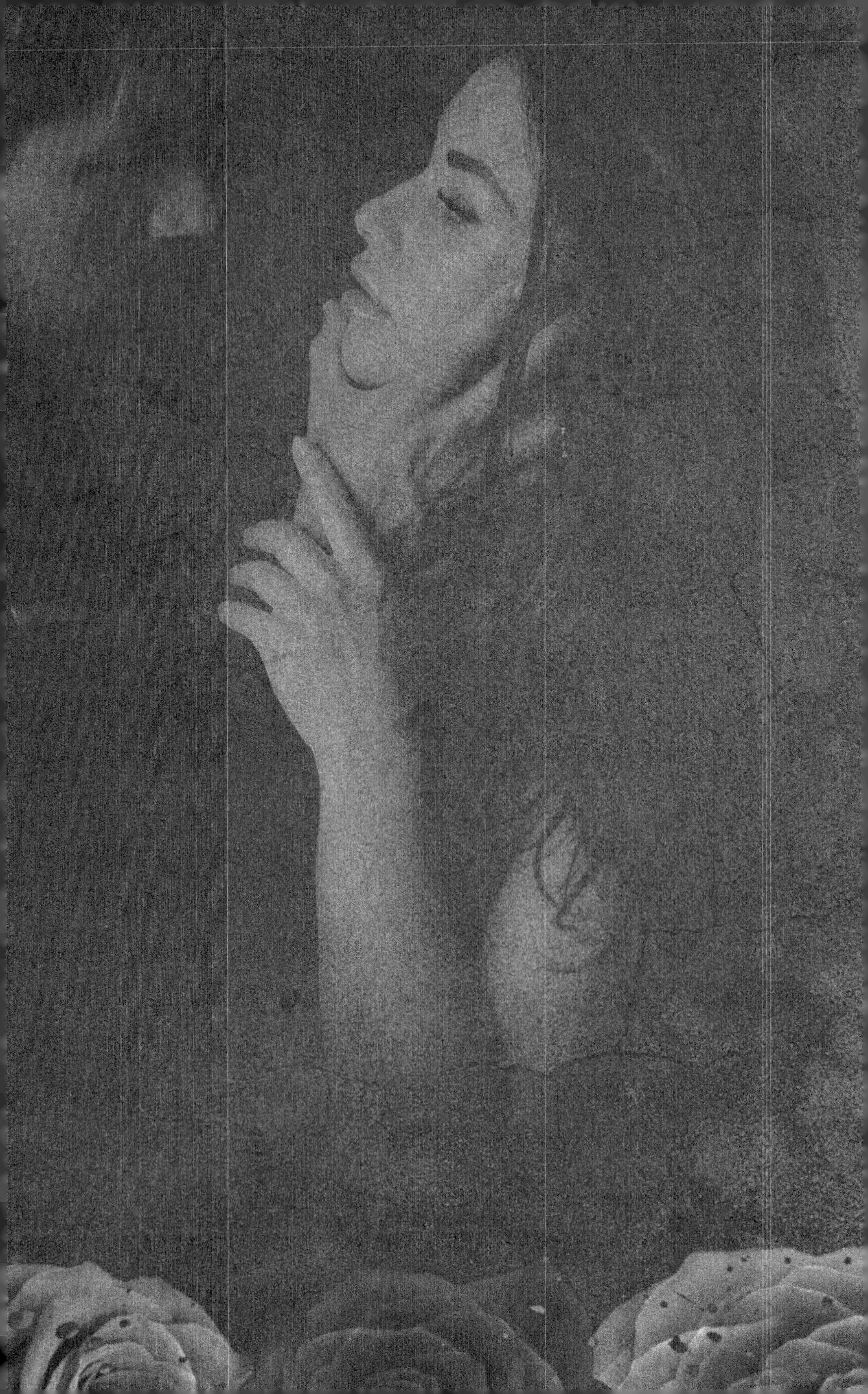

Chapter Nine
Chloe

As expected, I got very little sleep that night, despite the large, bouncy bed being the most comfortable I've ever slept in. I tossed and turned, throwing the sheets off every few minutes in a feeble attempt to cool down my scorching skin.

Watching Marcus stroke his hard cock as he talked about me was one of the most erotic things I've ever seen. His dirty words dripped off his tongue like liquid lava, and my body responded in a way I never expected.

My nerve endings sizzled like they were crackling with nervous energy. I was heating up from the inside out, fire bubbling beneath the surface, desperate to burn free.

Don't even get me started on how wet my knickers were. Watching my very own live sex show had me wetter than I'd been in a long time, but when he opened his mouth, I was dripping for him.

My thighs are probably red raw from how hard I ground them together, squirming to try and alleviate just a little bit of the maddening ache.

It didn't take long after Marcus left for me to slide my fingers between my folds, and it took even less time for me to bite down on my lip, desperately trying to swallow the cries of pleasure that threatened to break free as I fell apart. I don't think I've ever come so quickly or easily. I barely touched myself.

The problem was...even after having a toe-curling orgasm, my body was still on fire. My core ached and my pussy throbbed, like it was missing something, and I knew exactly what that was.

I was so close to walking out of my room, straight into Marcus', and begging him to fuck me.

If he wasn't demanding to know my secret, I would've begged him in a heartbeat. He wants me to trust him, and I think I do, but telling him my darkest, most shameful secret has nothing to do with trust. Some things are better kept in the dark, and this is one of them.

All those fucking amazing things he said about me, the way he made me feel like a beautiful, powerful Queen, it will all be diminished to nothing if he were to find out about the skeletons in my closet.

As much as it pains me, and no matter how much my pussy aches for him, he won't change my mind.

Instead, I'll have to spend the rest of my time here tossing and turning, rubbing my clit until it's sore and sensitive, imagining it's him. It's nowhere near as good as the real thing, but it's all I have right now.

I'm going to hold out the tiniest bit of hope that Marcus caves first, and that he's so overcome with the need to touch me, he forgets all about his stupid request.

So, as I laid there in the early hours of the morning, in a sleep-deprived haze, I came up with a plan.

I need him to break his own rules and touch me, without me having to tell him my secret.

All I need to do is entice him enough that he can't help himself. I need to make myself appear as sexy and as unavailable as I can, and hopefully that will drive him wild, the way he does to me.

With a plan in place, I finally manage to get a couple of hours of sleep, and it's just after half past seven when I find myself wide awake again. I still feel oddly uncomfortable in my own skin.

It's like I'm at war with myself... Part of my brain is focused on all the negative self-hatred that's been consuming me for well over a year now, whereas there's a nagging pit in my stomach that keeps replaying all the fucking amazing things that Marcus said about me, remembering all the ways he made me feel beautiful and special.

He's not the sort of guy to just say things, so I have no doubt he meant every word. But believing them is something else altogether.

I get the feeling Marcus isn't one to let the subject go until he's sure every word has sunk deep into my marrow, until it's so intrinsically a part of me that I have no choice but to believe them. I don't know if that's a relief or absolutely terrifying.

I've hidden behind my shame and self-loathing for so long, I can barely remember who I was before. But maybe I don't need to remember who I used to be, and after all this time, I can focus on finding out who I am now.

With the thoughts running through my brain so much that I feel weighed down, and my flesh still tingling and unsatisfied, I pull myself out of bed with a groan. Sleep is long gone, so I may as well find some coffee.

After using the en-suite, I pull on some sweatpants, as I don't think I can walk around Marcus' flat in just the baggy T-shirt I usually sleep in. I pull my hair into a messy bun on the top of my head, hoping that a bit of fresh air blowing around my neck will help cool me down.

Remembering Marcus' tour the night before—focusing on his tour of the apartment rather than what happened afterwards—I head in the direction of the kitchen. I'm shocked to see the light is already on, and there's someone sitting on a bar stool at the island in the middle of the room, but it's not Marcus.

I freeze in the doorway, and the man drags his eyes from his phone to look at me, his smile growing as he sees me.

"Morning. Do you want some coffee?" he asks, pointing over to the coffee machine on the counter.

I quickly recognise Miles. He's been part of Marcus' security for as long as I can remember, and his friend for longer than that. We all went to the same school, but I was never close to him, and over the past few years, I've only ever seen him by Marcus' side.

He's usually perfectly put together in a suit with his dark hair slicked back, which is totally different to how he looks now.

When he stands, his black sweatpants are baggy and hang dangerously low on his hips. The tight white T-shirt clings to his chest, and is almost see-through enough for me to see the hard ridges of his clearly defined abs.

His dark hair, that is usually gelled back, hangs loose around his face, and is long enough to curl slightly at the ends. A few errant strands fall in front of his eyes, and he flicks them away without much thought.

He's also wearing dark-rimmed reading glasses that I've never seen on him before, and I have to admit, they give off a very sexy geek vibe that is totally at odds with his usual look, but a lot more appealing.

When he gives me a small smile, a dimple appears on one cheek, softening his whole face. He looks so much younger than he normally does, his face rounder and more boyish than when he's in professional mode, looking stern.

I smile back, but I'm still thrown at him being here instead of Marcus. "Erm, hi. Yes, please," I stutter, grateful he's offering to make the coffee, as the machine looks complicated.

As he walks over and begins operating the machine, he talks to me over his shoulder. "I know you know who I am, and that we went to school together, but I'm going to formally introduce myself. I'm Miles, Marcus' Head of Security, and his best friend."

He turns to me, his cheeky smile growing as he hands me a steaming hot mug of coffee. It looks to be made just the way I like it, which is weird as I don't remember telling him that I take milk. I look up at him in confusion.

"Er, thanks. I'm Chloe." I feel like an idiot stating the obvious, but Miles doesn't seem to care. I can't help but ask, "How did you know how I take my coffee?"

He lets out a soft chuckle. "I'm observant," is his only reply, which is far too cryptic for me. "Did you sleep okay?" he asks, distracting me before I can get him to elaborate.

"Not too bad. The bed is lovely," I admit, taking a sip of the coffee that is exactly how I like it.

"You can sit down, if you'd like," Miles says, pointing to the bar stools on the opposite side of the island.

With a grateful nod, I move around to the stool, placing my coffee on the island before I jump up—it's harder than I expected since I'm short. Miles chuckles as he watches my effort, and when I shoot him a glare, he covers his face with his hand.

I'm about to say something when a deep voice from the corridor interrupts us both. "Morning." Marcus' sounds deep and gravelly, thanks to sleep, and it makes my core clench.

How the fuck does this guy have the ability to make me squirm with just one word?

Both me and Miles say good morning back, and without another word, Miles jumps off his stool and moves over to the coffee machine. He also grabs a loaf of bread from the bread-bin and takes it over to the toaster.

I'm watching what Miles' doing, so I feel Marcus take the stool beside me before I see him out of the corner of my eye.

His body gives off a warmth that heats up my side, and when his arm swipes across mine, goosebumps erupt across the flesh, right the way down to my fingers.

"Would you like some toast too, Chloe?" Miles shouts, his back to me as he places some bread in the toaster.

"Yes, please." Fuck, I hate how squeaky I sound, but I can't help being affected by Marcus' proximity.

I concentrate on my breathing, trying to get my racing heart to slow down, but he blows any chance of that happening when he leans closer to me. His breath tickles my cheek, and it's almost like I can feel the ghost of his lips touching the bottom of my ear.

I freeze, scared to move in case he actually plans to put his lips on my skin. I try to ignore the shivers that ripple down my spine as each breath he takes feathers over my cheek. My grip on the coffee mug tightens, it's a miracle the damn thing hasn't cracked.

"If you keep staring at him like that, I'm going to be forced to kill my best friend, and I'd really hate to do that," he growls, his words barely above a whisper, so that only I can hear.

I turn to face him, my eyes comically wide, as I can't quite believe what the hell he just said. "What?!"

The corner of his lip tips up into that signature smirk that both infuriates me and turns me on. "I much prefer your eyes on me."

I shake my head. I'm so fucking confused, I don't know what the hell to say. "I-I wasn't... Not like..."

Before I can tell him I wasn't looking at Miles, and even if I were, it wasn't in the way he thinks, he cuts me off. "It doesn't matter how you were looking at him. I want to be the only guy you look at."

I roll my eyes. "Possessive much?" I snark, and that fucking smirk of his grows.

"I'm very fucking possessive, Mio. While you're here with me, you are mine. Remember that," he growls.

There's that fucking word again. I'm going to ask him about it, but the rest of his words soon force all other thoughts from my head.

"I thought I was here as a deal to help you with Jake? The bet was just a cover so you could meet your end of the bargain."

He lets out a dark, humourless chuckle. "If that's what you want to tell yourself, that's fine. We both know you're here because you want to be mine. I'm willing to wait until you're ready to admit that. But, in the meantime, I won't accept you looking at other men."

My mouth flops open, and I have no idea what the hell to say to that. Luckily, Miles interrupts us by placing down a plate filled with buttered toast, glaring at his best friend as he does.

"Stop being an arsehole. We were only talking. I was being polite and making her feel welcome."

Both men stare at each other, neither one wanting to break away first. For a few seconds, it looks almost like they're having a silent conversation with each other. One born out of years of friendship and understanding one another.

Miles is the first to look away, and I'm not surprised—Marcus is a stubborn fucker, who no doubt hates to lose.

"Help yourself to some toast, Chloe," Miles says to me, before turning back to his friend. "I'm going to get ready. We need to leave for the meeting in half an hour."

Miles doesn't wait for Marcus to respond. He grabs a slice of toast and walks off in the direction of his room. Although Marcus said it was his on the tour last night, he didn't say he lived here.

"Does Miles live here?" I ask.

"Some of the time. He has his own flat, but he spends a lot of his time here. He's the only member of my security that I allow in the apartment, the rest guard me from in the hall or outside of the building.

"If the threat level is high, Miles will generally stay with me. Often he stays because he can't be arsed to go home, or because he wants company. We've been friends forever, and he's worked for me for so long, we just go with the flow. He's welcome here anytime. Is that a problem?"

I contemplate that for a moment, and I can't help but wonder what Marcus would do if I said it was. "No, he's always seemed like a nice guy," I admit.

Although Marcus scowls, he nods his head in agreement. "He's the best."

Silence stretches between us as we both eat our toast and drink our coffee. I'm acutely aware of every movement he makes, and each time his arm catches mine, or his knee brushes against my leg. I've never been so conscious of another person before.

After a while, the silence becomes deafening, and the building tension grows to the point I have to talk. "So, you have a meeting today? Erm... What do you need me to do?"

We've never really spoken about what I'm supposed to do while I'm here. In fact, we haven't really talked at all. There wasn't exactly a job description for what 'belonging to him' entails.

Marcus' brow furrows and the confusion on his face is evident. "What do you mean?"

I let out an annoyed huff. "Well, when you brought me here, you didn't exactly give me instructions of what you want me to do while I'm here. I know I'm supposed to help you get Jacob on the straight and narrow—which I still think is a bloody impossible task—but other than that, I have no idea what I'm supposed to do for you while I'm here. What does belonging to you entail?"

Marcus lets out a chuckle, and I shake my head at the emotional whiplash I get around this guy. "You're not one of my employees, Chloe. The whole reason you wanted to get away from your family and the arranged marriage was so that you could figure out who you are... That includes finding out what it is you're passionate about. What did you do at home during the day?"

My cheeks begin to heat, and I'm sure they're turning bright pink. "Honestly, I did whatever my parents told me to do. I attended social functions, with the intention of getting our family name out there, particularly charity events.

"Mother drags me shopping a lot, and then I do very stereotypical things like spa days, manicures, beauty treatments, trips to the hairdresser...things like that."

"Why do I get the impression you hate all of those things?"

I let out a humourless laugh. "Because I do hate them. Don't get me wrong, it's nice to have a massage or a manicure every so often, as a relaxing treat, but that's not what this was. Even going to the gym wasn't about me enjoying myself, it was always about the end result. Everything I was forced into had the end goal in mind—the creation of the perfect society wife."

"So you don't have any hobbies or things you like to do for fun?" he asks, sounding exasperated.

I shake my head. "Nope. Everything has been to make me better wife material. I took piano lessons so I was more cultured. I speak Latin, which I'll never fucking use, but it gives me an edge over women who can't speak it.

"I took etiquette lessons to learn how to be the perfect woman, and still attend once a week to make sure my habits don't slip.

"Together with my mother, we run two charities, but with the exception of planning the fundraising galas and balls, I have no idea what our charities do. There's not a single thing in my calendar that I chose for myself."

I don't know whether Marcus looks more shocked or angry, he's always so reserved with his emotions. I only catch glimpses of them, and they're gone so quickly, it's nearly impossible to get a read on him.

"Well, you can use your time here to do exactly what you want to do. If you want to go to the gym or swim, we have the facilities here, but you can go on your own terms, not because someone is telling you that you have to.

"Other than that, I suggest you think about what you actually enjoy doing. You've spent your whole life with other people's voices filling your head, telling you what to do. When all the other voices are silenced, you can finally listen to what yours is trying to tell you. Find what it is you're passionate about, and grab the opportunity with both hands."

"Okay," I reply, not really sure what else to say.

"Just do me one favour," he asks, and I look up at him, giving him my full attention. "Stay in the flat, just for today. I haven't had a chance to sort out security for you, or to even discuss that with you. We can talk when I get back, but just for today, please, stay inside."

It might be the first time he's ever said the word *please*, and so I agree, even though I want to argue with him about the security issue. I agreed to move here to be free, not to have a whole new set of staff follow me around. But we won't have time for that argument right now, so I bite my tongue…for now.

"Thanks," he says with a small smile, clearly being able to see how much I want to fight him on this. "Just spend the day getting to know the real Chloe. Forget about all the shit your parents have forced you to do, or the person they've made you become. While you're here with me, you can be whoever you want to be. You just have to take the time to search for her."

I let Marcus' words sit with me for a bit, hating how right he is. I haven't heard my own voice in a very long time. I've just been going through the motions, doing as I'm told, almost on autopilot. That's why my life has started to feel like a monotonous drone, as I'm not doing anything for me.

Now I can change that… As thrilling as the idea is, it's also terrifying. I'm not even sure who I am without the person I pretend to be for my family, so tapping into that is bloody scary.

Marcus and Miles leave for their meeting, and I sit at the stool in the kitchen for a long time, just looking around at everything. I marvel at all the modern utensils and equipment that Marcus has, which seems totally out of character for him.

I don't know why, I just don't see Marcus standing here in his modern, fully kitted out kitchen, doing something as menial as cooking.

Yet, it's an image that I can't get out of my head.

Marcus dressed in his low slung grey sweatpants, cooking me breakfast with that cocky smirk that shows me he's aware I'm not just drooling over the delicious cooking smells.

Fuelled by the bizarre image, I find myself wandering around the kitchen, pulling cupboards open and looking at all the different things inside. I'm half way along when I find a stand mixer that looks almost brand new, and for the first time in a long time, I hear the voice Marcus told me to listen to.

A memory from so long ago hits me, and a lump in my throat forms because I'd almost forgotten this.

When I was about eight-years-old, whenever I'd visit my Momma—my dad's mum—we would bake together. No matter how many members of staff she had to help her, when it came to the kitchen, that was all Momma.

She would bake her own bread early in the morning, usually before everyone else had woken up, so from the moment we opened our eyes, that smell of freshly baked bread filled the house.

She would cut me a still-warm slice and add some butter, telling me all about how much better things taste when you make it yourself.

Although she was a great cook, and could make just about anything she tried her hand at, baking was her passion. She would bake cakes, desserts, pies, anything she fancied that day, and they would always turn out better than the pictures in the recipe books.

Every time I stayed at her house, she would fetch a little step so I was tall enough to stand next to the counter with her, and I'd help with whatever cake she was making that day. I'd watch in amazement as we mixed the ingredients together until they formed the smooth, creamy batter.

She'd laugh whenever she caught me sticking my finger in the bowl, so I could taste the batter without her knowing. And even though she'd tell me off, once the cake was in the oven, she'd always give me a spoon, so I could eat whatever mix was left in the bowl.

I'd stare at the oven, watching with amazement as the thing we created together started to harden and grow, until it finally took the shape of a cake. Not many little girls would sit there for almost an hour watching cakes rise in the oven, but I was mesmerised.

The thing I loved most was watching her transform the almost boring-looking cake into a masterpiece. How had I forgotten that my Momma used to enjoy decorating cakes?

Every birthday, we would always have the most beautifully decorated cake, like it came from an expensive bakery, when really, Momma had just stayed up for hours making sure it was perfect.

She only made cakes for family and friends, for fun, and I used to love watching her mould the fondant into little designs.

I still remember her teaching me how to make roses, and I'd help her when she had lots to make for a flower cake she was doing for one of her friends.

I don't recall ever being as happy as I was in the kitchen with her, and my heart breaks that until this moment, I'd forgotten all about it.

Momma died when I was nine-years-old, and I felt like a piece of me died with her. She was the first person I had really lost, and I'd never really known grief before, but even at a young age, I knew the pain I felt wasn't one that'd ever go away. It may diminish until things are easier and memories are more distant, but it never goes away.

Nobody else in the family liked to bake or cook. Mum definitely didn't. She hates doing anything that might be considered manual labour, or beneath her. I don't think we even own any baking equipment in our house.

We have a private chef who cooks all our meals for us, and I can't remember the last time I was in our kitchen.

As thoughts of my Momma fill me, I look around Marcus' pantry, smiling when I find exactly what I was looking for. I promised not to go outside, and I'd hate to break it so early on, but I would have done if he didn't have everything that I needed.

Using the memory to guide me, I start baking a vanilla cake. I have no idea how I still remember the ingredients and the quantities off by heart, but I do. I get lost in the moment, and for the first time in forever, I follow my heart.

By the time Marcus comes home, he finds me right where he left me, in his kitchen, only the sight before him is very different. There are used pots and pans littering every surface, and I'm pretty sure I look like I'm in the middle of the war zone. I have flour all over me from where the bag exploded in a plume as I tried to open it.

But the smile on my face isn't one that will be dimming any time soon. "I baked," I state the obvious.

His lip tilts up, as does his eyebrow. "I can see that."

I point to the baked goods on the island between us. "I baked some bread, and used the excess dough to make a couple of little bread rolls. Then I made a Victoria sponge cake with cream and jam... I had to use pre-made jam as we didn't have the ingredients for me to make my own, but I can grab them another time, as it's much better when you make your own.

"I then made these shortbread biscuits, and both the chocolate chip and white chocolate cookies. I'm quite pleased with how soft the cookies are. You can have one now, if you want, they're probably still warm.

"Oh, I also made an apple crumble, but that's got about another ten minutes left in the oven. It'll be really nice with the custard I made," I add, pointing over to the pan that's sat on the stovetop with a lid covering it.

"So, you bake?" he asks, a hint of amusement in his voice.

I nod my head enthusiastically. "When we've had the security talk, I'm going to look at hopefully taking some classes. I'd like to learn how to make celebration cakes."

The smile on his face grows, and it's not even a fraction of the one on my face. "It looks like you've found something you enjoy."

"I used to bake with my Momma. I'd just forgotten all about it until you told me to forget all the shit with my family. I was looking around the kitchen, and when I found the mixer, it all came flooding back.

"She used to love making big celebration cakes for us, and she was great at it. She was teaching me everything she knew when she died. Nobody else in the family bakes, and I wasn't allowed to take lessons as my mother said baking wasn't a skill men valued in a high-society wife. I was told I'd have a chef and wouldn't need to know how to do something as menial as cooking."

"I think your mum is very wrong on this one. Everyone knows the way to a man's heart is through his stomach, and I happen to love apple crumble," he says with a wink, and my heart races.

"Well, you're in for a treat then as I'm going to cook us a meal tonight too. It's the least I can do to thank you," I tell him, leaving no room for him to shoot me down.

I want to cook for him, and the idea of sitting down for a meal with him, almost like a date, sends a shiver of anticipation down my spine.

"You don't have to thank me. I have very selfish reasons for helping you, and we both know that. Don't forget, I'm the bad guy in this story. But I'm not going to say no to a home cooked meal." His voice is deep and gravelly, and as he stares at me, his bright blue eyes darkening, I can see the dangerous side that he's desperate for me not to forget.

The problem is, the more time I spend with him, the more I don't care about that side of him. I like him, and the way my body responds to him scares the shit out of me. I have a feeling Marcus Morelli has the power to break me, and I just might let him.

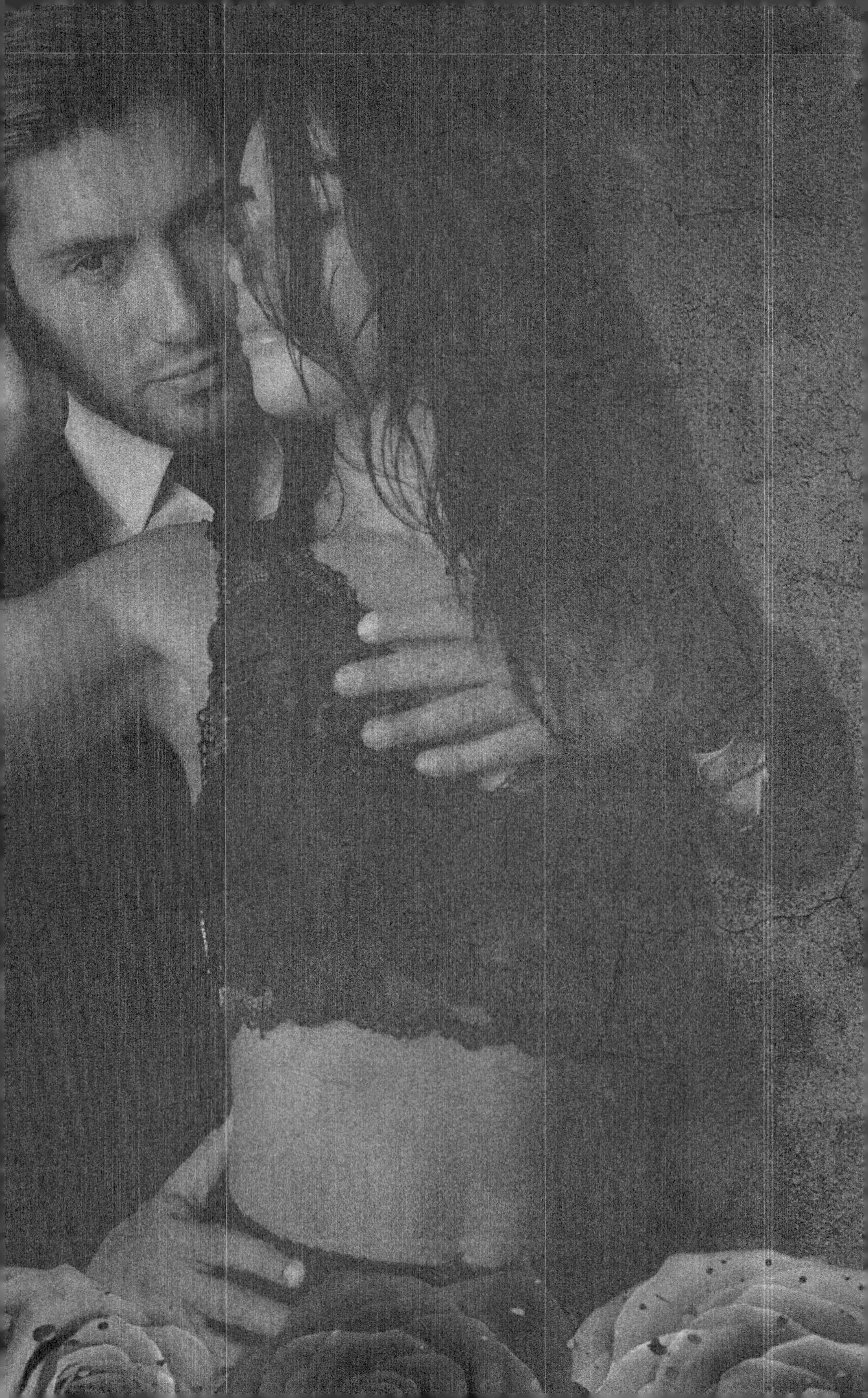

Chapter Ten
Marcus

Watching Chloe traipse around my kitchen like she's lived here her whole life is both a massive turn on and a headache all rolled into one.

This was supposed to be simple—bring her here, use her for the sex I've been thinking about since she developed tits, have her help me get Jake back in line, and then send her back to that tool Scott like it never happened.

I was a stupid dick for thinking that I could fuck her out of my system. I've not even really touched her yet and I can't fucking get enough of her. She's going to be my drug of choice, and that scares the shit out of me.

Even though she's here with me now, and her family haven't been able to stop it, that doesn't mean anything has changed between us. She's still fucking forbidden, not to mention engaged to be married.

Besides, I don't do relationships, and that's exactly what Chloe deserves. She doesn't need another fucker who just wants to use her for sex, and right now, that's all I could give her.

Even if I wanted a relationship with her, it could never happen. It would be a direct breach of the peace treaty, and the Santoros would declare war on us, putting Chloe directly in the middle of a battle between me and her family. I'm most definitely not worth that, and she doesn't need that kind of hassle either.

So, I plan to enjoy her fully while she's here, whilst holding on to my real motives. I have to remember what's at stake if my dick decides it wants more from her. We can have sex, but that's it. No future, no feelings, nothing.

Despite knowing all this, repeating it over and over in my head, the image of Chloe cooking in my kitchen in those ridiculous little shorts she wears, with flour on her face, will stay with me for much longer than it should.

I stand in the doorway, just watching her. She has her headphones in, and she's dancing around the kitchen with a bright smile on her face as she cooks. It's the most relaxed I've seen her in a long time, making her pretty face seem younger.

She's not wearing any make-up, but she doesn't need any. Her bright silver eyes sparkle, and the heat from the oven has given her cheeks a rosy glow. Then there's her plump pink lips that look so soft, as she runs her tongue along them, tasting her food.

She's wearing the most ridiculous black cotton shorts that stop just under the swell of her arse, and her milky thighs and legs are on full display. Even if I tried not to look at her arse—and I'm not sure why the fuck I wouldn't—I'd be drawn to her by the way her hips sway to the music only she can hear.

Her curves are enough to make a man's mouth water. Full hips that are enough for me to grab hold of as I pull her into me. And even though she's wearing an oversized baggy T-shirt, it does very little to hide her amazing tits.

As it's so loose on her, it hangs off one shoulder, showing off her bra strap and the start of her rather impressive cleavage. It says a lot about the girl that she can look so fucking gorgeous with just one shoulder on display.

I'm having some very inappropriate thoughts about sinking my teeth into her collarbone, marking her to show everyone that she's mine—even if it is only temporary.

She must catch me standing in the doorway, staring at her, as she stops in the middle of a very sexy hip shimmy, her eyes going wide while she grabs her phone off the counter, no doubt to turn off her music, before pulling the earbuds out.

"Sorry, I didn't hear you come in," she mutters, her already flushed cheeks becoming redder.

"That's because I didn't tell you I was here. I thought I'd take in the show for a bit first," I reply, my lips tilting into that smirk I know she loves when the flush over her cheeks spreads down across her chest.

I wonder how far down it will travel, I think to myself, feeling my cock twitch again, having already started to harden at the sight of her gorgeous curves and swaying hips.

"Oh," she squeaks, her gaze quickly flicking down to the pan on the stove as she picks up a spoon and starts to stir. "I dance when I cook."

"I can see that." I try to hold back the smile that's threatening to overtake me, loving how embarrassed she's getting.

"Dinner is almost ready. Where would you like to eat?" she asks, clearly trying to change the conversation.

I nod my head towards the small dining table in the corner of the room. "I'll set the table. What would you like to drink?"

I move towards the drawer where we keep the placemats and then the one with the cutlery, as silence fills the air while Chloe ponders my question.

"Erm, do you have wine?"

She sounds unsure, like she's worried I might say she can't have wine with her meal. There's clearly more to her behaviour that I'm missing, but now's not the time to unpick everything.

"Of course. Do you prefer red or white?" I ask.

She tilts her head to the side, pondering my question. "Well, I've made chicken alfredo pasta with garlic bread and a side salad, so whatever you think would go best, I guess?"

The final words lift in tone, making it into a question, and I realise she's somehow managed to avoid answering what she likes, and has made it into what I want instead.

"You didn't answer the question. What type of wine is *your* favourite?" I ask, stressing that this is about her.

Her face scrunches up, like she's wincing. "Well, I like either. I will drink whatever you decide to open."

I shake my head as I stalk over to her, purposefully keeping my strides slow so she can see me coming. She's frozen to her spot in the kitchen, and I'm thankful she's already taken the pasta off the stove and placed it onto our plates, as it would be burning right about now.

Her eyes are fixed on my slow deliberate movements, stopping only when I'm right in front of her. I'm so close, I hear the small intake of breath when I stop in front of her, my fierce gaze fixed on hers.

"This is not a difficult question, Mio. I don't give a shit about what you think the right answer is, or whatever the hell you were saying about trying to please me... All I want to know is what your favourite wine is," I growl, loving the way she trembles as my breath flutters across her face.

If I take one tiny step forward, she'd be able to feel how hard I am for her, and I'd be able to touch her lips with mine, to see if they're as soft as they look. But I keep myself frozen to the spot, waiting for her to answer.

"Sorry," she mutters, her gaze dropping down to the floor, so she doesn't have to make eye contact with me. "I'm so used to just doing whatever I'm told, or what other people want. I can't remember the last time someone asked me what I like."

Her voice is so small, and that murderous rage begins to flare to life under the surface, making me want to go back to her family home, so I can punish every last person who made her feel less than she is.

"Do you even like wine?" I ask through gritted teeth.

She quickly nods, though she still doesn't lift her head to meet my gaze. So I place my fingers under her chin and lift until she has no choice but to make eye contact with me.

"I do. I actually prefer rosé, but I drink any," she mumbles, her eyes flicking around slightly before she finally holds my gaze, pulling her shoulders back just a touch, like she has found a little of her confidence.

I can't help but smile at her honesty. "I like rosé too. I have a nice bottle that I think you'll like. Sit and I'll grab it," I say, pointing to the table before I head to the corner of the kitchen, where I keep a wine rack.

I scan the rows of wine, landing on the bottle I was thinking about. On my way to the table, I grab two wine glasses and the corkscrew before taking my seat opposite Chloe.

She's already placed the food and has taken her own seat, though she appears to be waiting for me before she starts to eat.

The smells in the kitchen are amazing, and they've become even better once all the food is together on the table. My mouth is almost watering, and not just from the gorgeous girl with dark hair and stupidly short shorts.

"This smells delicious," I tell her with a smile as I uncork the wine.

After doing the bullshit test that you see posh twats like my father do, despite having no clue what the hell I'm looking for, I deem the wine to be fine and hand a glass of the rosé over to Chloe. She doesn't even bother with the theatrics, and just takes a small sip instead.

A low moan breaks from her lips over the rim of the glass, and it hits me straight in the dick. "You're right, this is so good."

"I like hearing you say that I'm right," I joke, and Chloe rolls her eyes at me, picking up her fork to begin eating her pasta.

I have to drop my gaze. I can't focus on my own food when I'm watching her cheeks hollow as she sucks a string of pasta into her mouth, or the way her tongue licks the sauce off her lip. My dick throbs painfully, and I have to discreetly use my hand to adjust myself, so I can make it through this meal without blowing my load in my boxers.

"Is now a good time to have the security talk you mentioned this morning?" Chloe asks after taking another sip of her wine.

I wince, hoping I could delay things a little longer before having this particular argument. Jake used to tell me stories about how much she hated her security, and the rebellious phase she went through where she'd lose them at every available opportunity.

"We can..." I start, sounding just as hesitant as I feel. "What are you used to?"

"Back home, we had the main security staff that guarded the house in general, though we were free to move around the house without having anyone follow us. Naturally, my father has significantly more security than the rest of us.

"Whenever I'd go out, I had a couple of guards who were specifically assigned to me, and they'd be with me whenever I left the house. They'd have to stay with me at all times," she explains, sounding annoyed.

"I think that's pretty standard for most people in our line of work," I reply with a shrug of my shoulders.

"You don't have guards in your house," she snaps.

"That's because I own the whole building. I have guards covering every possible entrance, and you need a fingerprint to get in the garage and the lift, so there's no way anyone who shouldn't be in the building is getting in. Plus, I have CCTV that's constantly monitored, and plenty of security that can be in my flat in seconds, if I need them," I reply, watching as her eyes grow wider.

"You own the whole building?" she asks incredulously.

I chuckle at her look of bewilderment. "Yes, I do." I pause as she shakes her head in disbelief, though I've no idea how she didn't know this already. "So you're used to having guards with you when you go out?"

She nods, though I catch the way her nose wrinkles like she's just smelled something bad. "As they're still assigned to me, I can just call them whenever I need to leave."

I shake my head rapidly. "No, absolutely not. You'll have to use my guards."

Her fork is almost in her mouth and she pauses, looking at me in confusion. "What? Why?"

"While you're here with me, you're under my protection, which means you have to use my staff."

"But I know my guards, they've been protecting me for years," she replies, her food now long forgotten as she stares at me with those fierce silver eyes.

"Look, those guards are loyal to your father, and I can't trust them," I reply calmly, feeling the tension in the room growing, just the way I thought it would.

She shakes her head, disbelieving. "My father would never let anything happen to me. He needs me, remember?"

I grit my teeth, hating her casual mention of her engagement responsibilities. "We have pissed a lot of people off by doing this, and that puts a target on both our backs. I don't trust anyone, even your father. Everyone in my world is opportunistic, and if the right scenario presents itself, your safety may not be someone else's primary concern, but it always will be for me."

At first, I think her features are starting to soften at the mention of me wanting to keep her safe, but then her gaze hardens once more. "What about who I trust? I don't know your staff. How am I supposed to just trust them?"

"That's fair," I reply, taking a sip of my wine. "I've spoken to Miles, and he has a guard who used to be assigned to his sister, but she doesn't need security right now, and he thinks it'd be a perfect fit for you."

If the phrase "if looks could kill" was right, I'd be six fucking feet under right now. Her silver eyes are almost molten as she glares at me.

"How do you know that he'd be the perfect fit for me? I have strict rules for who I'll let guard me, and you've not even bothered to fucking ask what they are."

Her tone both angers and thrills me. Chloe is usually so meek and quiet, obeying every instruction thrown her way by her family, yet I've always known there was a feisty girl with a backbone in there. Seeing her use that fire on me is exciting, but fuck does it make me want to punish her for using that tone with me.

"What are your fucking rules?" I snap, my hand curling so tightly around my wine glass, I'm surprised it's not smashed.

"I refuse to be guarded by a man." Although she holds her head high as she says it, I don't miss the way her voice breaks at the end, and my anger quickly dissipates, only to be replaced by confusion.

I've known Chloe since I was a kid, and although I've made sure to push her away, making it clear I'm Jake's friend and not hers, I thought I knew her. When you grow up with someone, particularly someone who caught your attention from the first time you met, it's hard not to notice every little thing about them.

How the fuck did I not know she won't be guarded by a man? And more importantly, why does she feel the need to have that rule?

I think about her recent wild behaviour, and her desperate need to claw back some control in her life, and I can't help but wonder if those things are linked. I really hope I'm putting two and two together and making five, because the alternative is fucking soul destroying.

A million things flash through my mind as I think about what to say, struggling to find the right words. It's not hard...I just have to tell her that it's a female guard. But that requires logical thinking, which I clearly don't have right now.

"Who hurt you, Chloe?" I say through gritted teeth.

Her brows fly to her hairline as her eyes widen, her mouth pressed into a tight line. Her whole body becomes rigid, and when she tries to talk, no words come out, but I can hear her loud and clear.

"I-I...I mean... It's not... No one," she mumbles, struggling to form a coherent sentence.

I want to lean over, to place my hand on hers in a reassuring way, but her body language is screaming at how tense she is. Besides, if I touch her, I'm sure she'll be able to feel the barely contained rage that's making my hands shake.

"Did. Someone. Hurt. You?" I repeat, punctuating each word in a way that lets her know I'm not dropping this.

She takes a shuddered breath and her eyes become glassy with unshed tears. Although she shakes her head, saying no, it's weak, and we both know she's lying.

"Can we just leave it?" she says, her voice barely above a whisper.

"Is this why you're trying to take back control? Why you were drinking too much and sleeping around? Is it all linked?" The questions tumble off my lips just as quickly as they enter my brain.

That deer-in-headlights look gets worse with each question, and I know I should be filtering them, rather than just saying the first things that come into my head, but I can't. I'm barely holding in the rage as it is.

I'm one second away from flipping the table, grabbing my gun and shooting every guy she's been in contact with over the last eighteen months, just to be sure I've got the one who hurt her.

Is that a bit overkill? Yes, but I don't give a shit. I've never been possessive or protective over a girl before, but this doesn't even feel like a choice to me. It's like there's a dragon inside me that's blasting his way to the surface, determined to protect and claim revenge on what's his. Dragons hoard treasure, and some part of me sees Chloe as mine—my treasure.

She slowly shakes her head, her silver eyes glistening with tears she's no doubt forcing not to fall, and I hate how fucking small and broken she looks. "I don't want to talk about it."

Everything in me is screaming that I need to force her to tell me, that I have to know who it is, so I can wipe the shit-stain from the Earth for good, but I know that she'll never forgive me if I force her to talk about this before she's ready. I want her to trust me enough to tell me on her own.

So despite my raging dragon that I'm struggling to control, I let out a huff and try to uncurl my fists.

"Fine," I say through gritted teeth, before forcing myself to soften just a little. "I want you to be able to talk to me about anything, so I'm willing to wait until you trust me."

I see the ghost of a smile tip the corner of her lip up, before it quickly turns into a frown, her face looking blanker than I've ever seen it. As the words drip from her lips, I've never heard her sound colder. "I don't trust anyone."

My anger flares once more, but I concentrate on keeping my breathing steady so that she doesn't notice. "It sounds like you have reasons for that. But, I promise, I'll prove to you, over time, that you can trust me."

She looks at me in disbelief, but there's a small amount of hope shining in her eyes too. This beautiful girl hasn't had anyone on her side for the longest time, and I'm determined to change that.

Chloe looks like she's struggling to find the words to respond, so I quickly try to change the subject. "And in response to your earlier assumption, the security guard Miles has assigned you is a female. She's actually one of the best we have."

Her eyes narrow, like she's not sure she believes me. "If she's the best, why isn't she guarding you?"

The corner of my lip tips into my signature smirk. "Because I have Miles. Besides, his sister is the most important person in the world to him, and her life was put in danger simply because he works for me. We knew we had to keep her safe, and that meant assigning her the best, which is Kim."

She leans forward, her eyes boring into me like she's trying to see deep into my soul. She's trying to work me out, and I fucking hate it. I'm a closed book for a reason. "Why isn't she with her now?"

I let out a huff, grimacing as I'm reminding of how fucking much I hate this part of the story.

"She's safe now. When the threat level became too high, we had no choice but to move her into Morelli Manor, as the security there is safer than anywhere else."

"Why do I feel like you're leaving out parts of the story?"

I let out a humourless laugh. "Because I am. I'm not exactly thrilled about it, and neither is Miles, but when Courtney, his sister, moved into Morelli Manor, she grew close to my father."

"Grew close?" she repeats annoyingly.

"Too close," I reply cryptically, and just a few seconds later her eyes widen comically as she gets what I was hinting at.

"How old is Courtney?" Her voice has taken on a ridiculously high pitch, and

I don't blame her. There's a reason we've been trying to keep the scandal hidden.

"She's nineteen."

Chloe's laughter fills the air, and I hate how fucking young she looks as she takes pleasure in my misery. "So your dad, who is at least in his fifties, is sleeping with a nineteen-year-old, who he was supposed to be looking after for his son?"

"Yes," I grind out, which only makes her laugh more.

"It's like the plot of a dirty romance novel," she jokes. Then, as if she just realised something, her eyes begin to sparkle as she leans closer to me. "If Maximus marries her, your step-mum will be younger than you."

I close my eyes to try and block out the mental imagery her suggestion brings up, and I ball my hands into fists as I grind my teeth together.

"That's not going to happen," I say, as I take a much needed gulp of my wine.

"Why? Is it just sex for them?"

Before the word sex has even left her mouth, I'm half spitting out my wine, and half choking on it. I quickly bring my other hand up to my mouth to catch the spraying wine, as I carefully put the glass down on the table.

My coughing becomes desperate as I try to clear the liquid out of my lungs, to replace it with some much needed air.

Chloe quickly stands and rushes over to me, slapping me hard on the back. My eyes widen as I look at her, wondering what the fuck she's doing. As the burning in my throat dies down, and I'm able to pull in a few sharp gasps of air, she continues to hit me.

"Stop. Hitting. Me."

"Oh, my God. Are you okay?" she asks, gently running her thumb under my eyes to brush away the tears that had escaped while I was choking.

"Are you trying to fucking kill me?" I rasp, my throat burning as I try to speak.

Her brow furrows as she pouts, a very cute mixture of concern and frustration marring her beautiful face. "How am I trying to kill you?"

"First, you bring up my father's sex life, which we will never speak about again, and then you beat the shit out of my back so hard I'm bound to have bruises," I growl as she stands there, glaring at me.

"When someone is choking, you're supposed to slap their back to help," she replies incredulously, her hand on her popped hip making her look very serious.

"That's only when there's something that needs to be dislodged, not because wine went down the wrong fucking way," I snap, sounding much harsher than I intended.

"You could just say *thank you*."

"For what? How would you like it if I started smacking you?" I ask.

If I hadn't been so focused on her, I may have missed the very subtle changes that occur at the mention of me smacking her. Her eyes widen just slightly, becoming darker at the same time. Her breath hitches before becoming shallower, like she's struggling to catch her breath. Then there's the way she very slowly rubs her thighs together, like she's trying to alleviate an ache between them, and I can't help but smile.

She looks like she's trying to think of something to say, but I beat her to it. "Well, it seems you might like the idea of being spanked."

The deer-in-headlights look is back, but the way she squirms isn't just from feeling uncomfortable. She's getting turned on, and my dick twitches at the thought, as does my palm.

"I-I... I mean, I..." She fumbles over her words, not making any sense.

As the grin on my face widens, I stand abruptly, causing her to take a stumbling step back, her eyes wide. She manages to find her balance and freezes in front of me, though it looks like it's taking every ounce of strength she has not to back away from me.

It takes only a couple of small steps before I'm standing so close that she has to tilt her head back slightly to look up at me. Her pupils are blown, and the blush on her cheeks confirms she's turned on, but her eyes flick around like she's nervous too.

I'm reminded once again that someone hurt her enough that she now has to look for danger in the most innocent of gestures, and my murderous dragon flares his ugly head once more.

I have to remind myself that the way I stalked across the room towards her, trapping her with my piercing gaze, can hardly be classed as innocent.

"Have you ever been spanked before?" I ask, my voice deep and raspy.

She shakes her head. "No."

"But you'd like to try it." I phrase it as a statement rather than a question, as her body has already answered on her behalf.

Still, she nods her head, the flush on her cheeks reddening further as she drops her gaze to the floor. I reach up and place my finger underneath her chin, tipping her head back until she has no choice but to look at me.

"I would like nothing more than to turn your sexy arse red, marking you with my handprint," I growl, loving the way her breath hitches at my words. "But that would require me touching you, and I can't do that yet."

"I-I... What if I-I said you could?" she mumbles, pulling her lower lip between her teeth.

"You can beg me all you want, but I can't do it until I know you trust me," I state.

"I do... I think I do trust you." The words rush out, though she sounds a little uncertain.

"I'll know you trust me when you tell me who hurt you." I don't want to ruin this moment between us, but I really do have her best interests at heart when I say this.

I don't just want to know who he is and what he did so that I can rip him to pieces—though I will very much fucking enjoy doing that. I need to know what trauma she's endured, so I can make sure nothing I do is a trigger for her. I want to help her use sex to heal, not to make things worse.

She may think she trusts me, and she probably trusts me enough for us to have meaningless sex, but I'm not some random stranger she's picked up in a club that she'll never see again. I'm not going to fuck her and walk away, leaving her unsatisfied.

If we do this, I want to make it very fucking pleasurable for her, and to do that, I need to know what her limits are—which she's not ready to discuss yet.

"I may never be able to tell you that. But I still want you to show me how I can take back control. You promised you'd show me," she pouts, her eyes fixed on mine in a challenge.

I pause for a moment, wondering if there's a way I can do this and still remain firm. I let out a huff as an idea comes to me like a flashing lightbulb moment.

"I can teach you control... I can even punish you... All without actually touching you. But I promise, by the end, you'll be craving my touch so much that you'll want to beg me, but the rules haven't changed.

"I won't cave because you've begged me, and I won't give in, no matter how much I might fucking want to. The only way I'll touch you is if you've told me everything.

"This isn't me sexually blackmailing you into telling me your secrets, it's for your own safety. I want you to tell me, but I also want it to be your choice. Do you understand?"

She lets out a harsh laugh, looking at me in disbelief. "You think that you're going to be able to drive me so crazy, I'll want to tell you all my secrets, just so you'll fuck me?"

I casually shrug my shoulders as I give her a nod. "Yes, and I won't have you accusing me of blackmailing you."

"You do realise that no guy has ever properly given me an orgasm. The fact you think you can make me lose my head, without even touching me, says a lot about you. I knew you were cocky and egotistical, but this is next level." She laughs, and I roll my eyes.

"Call me whatever you like, but you'll see for yourself soon enough. I just want to make sure, for the record, that you know my intention is not to force you to tell me anything," I repeat, wanting to make sure she's very clear on this.

Although she doesn't appear to be taking what I have to say seriously, she nods her head. "Fine, I agree that if I do, by some miracle, decide to tell you all of my secrets, it will be because I want you to know them, not because I want you so badly I feel like I have to spill my guts."

Even though her tone becomes more sarcastic as the statement goes on, I'll take it. She may not believe it's possible right now, but I plan to show her just how truthful I am. I'm going to make her fall to her knees, begging for me to finally touch her.

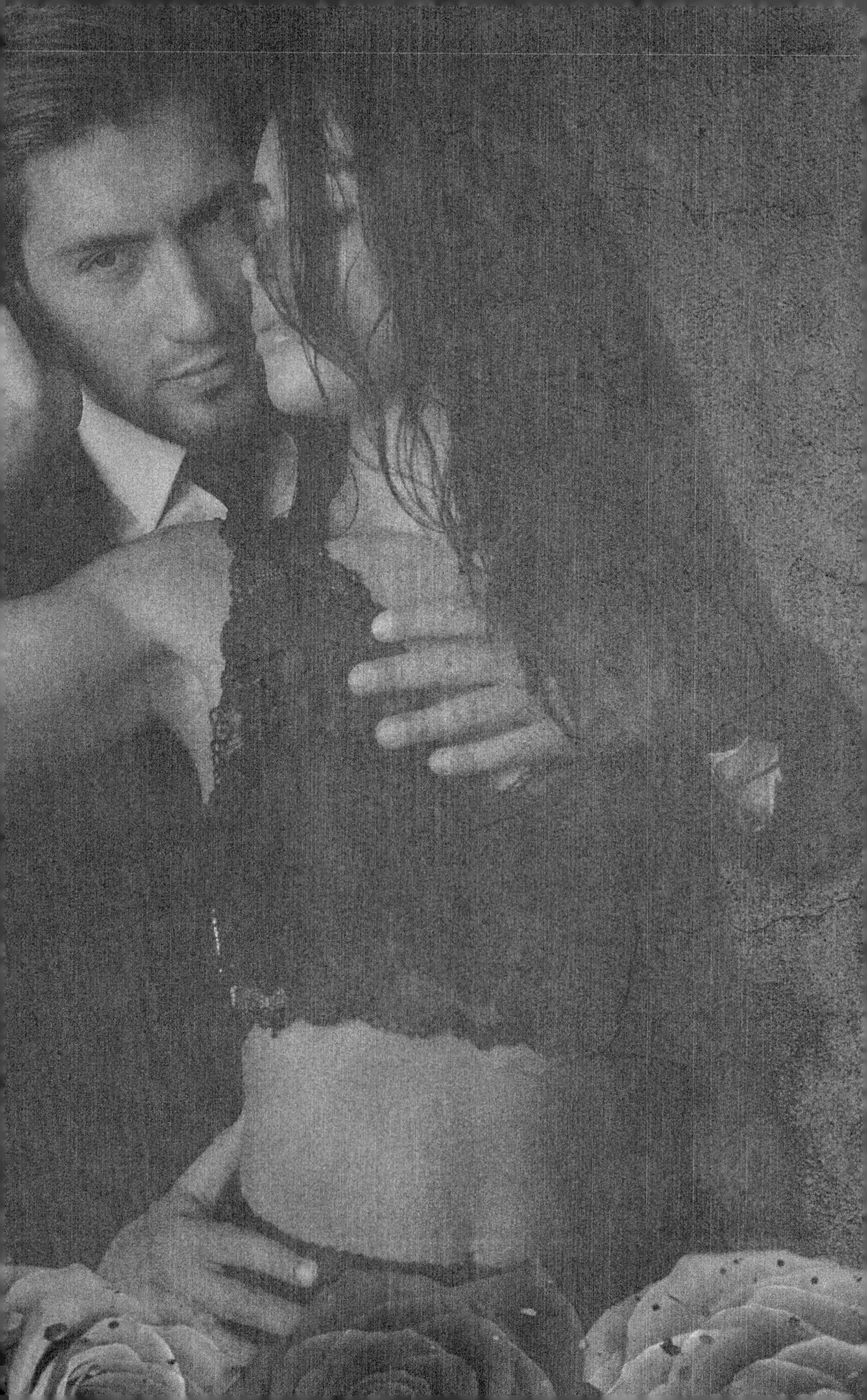

Chapter Eleven
Marcus

Silence swirls around us, both waiting to see which of us is going to break the tension first. I'm enjoying the way Chloe is trying not to squirm far too much, and I'm heavily regretting my decision not to touch her. There's nothing I want more.

Why the fuck am I trying to be the good guy when we both know I'm very fucking bad for her?

I take a step away from her, hating the way my body seems to drop in temperature just from not having her warmth near me, but I need the space to keep my head clear.

Turning quickly on my heel, I abandon the dinner dishes and our unfinished wine glasses, and walk into the living room. I drop down into the big arm chair opposite the sofa, taking a deep breath as I do.

I want to turn back, to make sure she's following me, but I don't want her to feel like I'm forcing her into anything. This has to be one hundred percent her choice, so I prick my ears up, listening for any movement. When I hear the soft pads of her feet following behind me, I have to fight back my smile.

Once she joins me in the living room, she stands in between my chair and the sofa, her eyes flicking nervously around the room as she tries to decide where to sit. After a second, with a huff, she drops onto the sofa opposite me. Her eyes fall to the floor, but mine remain fixed on her, watching the way she shuffles around, trying to get comfortable.

I clear my throat to grab her attention, and once her gaze is locked on me, I lean forward slightly, opening my legs wider to appear more laid back. "So, tell me, after the other night, did you think about me?"

Her eyes widen again, and the side of my lip twitches as my smirk grows. As her cheeks redden further, she looks like she's not sure what to say.

I love the way she squirms, feeling uncomfortable with my blunt approach, and so I push things further.

"You remember, when I took my big, hard cock out and wanked myself while you watched. You were hypnotised watching me pump my hard shaft, not taking your eyes off me as I blew my load at just the thought of your sexy body. You do remember that, don't you?" I ask sarcastically, my voice deepening with each dirty word.

Her throat bobs as she swallows air, her head tilting just the slightest, like she's ashamed to admit she remembers. "Yes," she whispers, barely audible, but it rings loud in my head.

"What I want to know is what you did after I left. Did you think about me? Did you picture my dick as you put your fingers on your dripping pussy?"

"I-I... I didn't—" Before she can finish whatever lie was about to tumble from her lips, I cut her off.

"How wet was your pretty pink pussy after watching me? Were you dripping into your knickers? Don't lie to me, Mio," I state firmly, loving the way her nostrils flare and her eyes darken as lust takes over.

As she shuffles on the seat, she tries to be discreet about it, making it look like she's simply trying to get comfortable, but I don't miss the way she grinds her thighs together, like she's trying to alleviate an ache that I'm desperate to help her with.

Her eyes drop to the floor so she doesn't have to look at me, but she finds her voice after a short pause. "I was so wet."

My dick twitches at the desperation in her voice, and I ache as my hard length presses against the confines of my trousers, trying to break free.

"Did you touch yourself? Was your wet cunt aching so much that you just had to use your fingers to take away the pressure?"

I watch as her breathing increases, until she looks like she's panting, unable to take full breaths. I bet her heart is beating so fast and loud that she can hear it thudding in her ears.

She slowly nods her head, and the blush on her cheeks has started to spread down over her chest, redness slipping underneath her T-shirt. I can't help but wonder if the swell of her tits are bright red too.

"Use your words, Mio," I state firmly.

"What does that word mean?" she mumbles, her gaze firmly locked on mine now as she searches for the answer. I can't help but chuckle.

Although both me and my father have lived in Blackthorn our whole lives, our family are originally of Italian descent. My great-great grandfather moved over from Italy a very long time ago, and the Morelli's have lived in England ever since.

Though we still have some distant relatives that none of us see that still live in Italy, we rarely go back there. My father's mother is the only one who wanted to feel some kind of bond with her ancestors, and she chose to learn Italian. The rest of our family barely knows anything other than the odd curse word.

Growing up, I used to love watching my grandma move around the kitchen as she cooked, talking to herself in Italian. Despite only having been to Italy a few times, she still cooked like other Italian women, with recipes that were handed down through the generations.

My grandma was by far my favourite person, so when she offered to teach me Italian, of course, I said yes. She also taught me a bit of cooking at the same time.

I still remember her squeezing my cheeks when I turned thirteen, telling me that any woman would find me irresistible if I could cook her a nice meal and compliment her in the beautiful language.

The idea that I could win over a girl, and spend a bit of extra time with my grandma, was more than enough of an excuse for me to learn Italian. She wasn't remotely surprised that I picked it up easily, boasting to everyone who would listen that I was a natural.

I still remember my father scoffing at me, saying I was wasting my time, that I should spend my time learning something useful rather than a language I'd rarely speak. Naturally, that made me spend even more time perfecting the language, until I could both write and speak it fluently.

Although I hate to admit it, my father was right that I barely use the language I spent so long learning. We rarely deal with anyone who doesn't speak English, and even when we communicate with our contacts in Italy, my father insists they speak English so he can understand.

In fact, since my grandma passed away almost a decade ago now, I've barely spoken the beautiful language. Choosing only to drop the odd word when I don't want the other person to know what I'm saying—usually as a way of insulting them whilst they're none the wiser.

With Chloe, calling her Mio is my own little inside joke, and I'm not ready to let her in on it yet. I've been using it randomly since we were teenagers and she's never looked it up, so I think she's waiting for me to tell her what it means, which is fine by me.

Ignoring her question, I try to get the subject back on track.

"I asked you a question. Answer me," I growl, leaving no room for arguments.

She's torn between fighting me, demanding I tell her what the nickname means, and obeying me. There's a submissive buried deep inside Chloe, and I'm desperate to bring her out to play.

"What was the question?" she rushes out, looking confused and a little flustered.

I have the bite the inside of my cheek to stop my smile from ruining the stern expression I'm trying to maintain. "I asked if you used your fingers to help with the ache in your wet pussy after watching me wank."

The nod of her head is so slight, had I not been paying attention, I may have missed it. Then she remembers my instructions and finds her voice, though it's low and croaky. "Yes."

My smirk grows as my dick throbs painfully at the images I'm conjuring in my head. "Did you just rub your clit until you fell apart? Or did you plunge your fingers into your tight cunt, wishing it was my hard cock instead?"

With each dirty word, she chews more on her bottom lip, her chest rising and falling rapidly. The way she rubs her thighs together is becoming more noticeable, and I can tell she's just as worked up as I am.

I want nothing more than to slide my zipper down, take out my hard cock, and stroke it until I blow all over myself, but I can't do that this time. This has to be all about Chloe.

"Both," she squeaks, and I can't help the low groan that slips free at the thought.

Her eyes widen as soon as she hears it, and she looks shocked that her words could elicit such a response from me. I'm surprised she hasn't notice the large tent in my trousers yet, and I'm reminded once again that this girl has no idea how fucking perfect she is.

"Take off your shorts," I say.

"What?" she blurts out, her hands moving instinctively to press against the small fabric that's doing a piss poor job of covering her legs.

"I said...take off your shorts," I repeat, deliberately slowing my words down as I enunciate them more clearly.

She shakes her head, looking a little panicked. "I'm not wearing anything underneath," she whispers, and my smile grows, showing my teeth in a way that probably makes me look like a predator.

"Good."

I wait, and Chloe looks to be warring with herself, torn over what the right thing to do is. I see the moment she makes her decision, as her face that had been crinkled while deep in thought suddenly relaxed. Her gaze drops to the floor, and she takes a big deep breath before she reaches up to grab the waistband of her shorts.

Without hesitation, most likely as she's worried any pause may cause her to lose her nerve, she lifts her arse just enough to wiggle the shorts down her legs. Once they fall to her ankles, she uses her foot to flick them to one side.

Her creamy thighs are now fully on display for me, and saliva floods my mouth as I think about how soft her flesh would be against my lips.

"Open your legs, Mio," I demand, loving the way her eyes flick up to meet mine, the blush on her cheeks worsening.

With a confidence I wasn't expecting, she widens her legs, not stopping until I can see her pussy. She doesn't have any hair there at all, and I have to bite my lip to stop myself from moaning. My cock is pressing so hard against my boxers, it's almost painful now.

"Lift your feet onto the sofa and spread your knees as wide as you can."

She follows my instructions, her gaze still locked on mine, and I drag myself away from her molten silver eyes to look at her body. Her pretty pink pussy has a slight glisten to it that lets me know she's wet, and my hand itches to touch her.

"Take your T-shirt off." My voice is deep and husky now, dripping with lust.

"You have all your clothes on." I hear the challenge in her words, but her voice is barely above a whisper.

I wonder if she is pushing me, or if this is just her asking for what she wants. It's a really hard decision for me, as I want to reward her for finding her voice and asking for what she wants, but if I remove even one item of clothing, keeping my restraint will be a challenge.

"I do," I reply, loving the way her glare narrows on me in challenge. "This isn't about me, it's about you. Now, take off your top, Mio."

She shakes her head as she rolls her eyes, but at the same time, she reaches down to the hem of her shirt and begins lifting it. I'm sure she's going at a fucking glacial pace to drive me mad, revealing a fucking centimetre of skin every few seconds.

It seems to take hours from her revealing her pierced belly button before I catch a glimpse of the underside of her bra.

I'm not sure if she's doing it on purpose to wind me up, but it's working.

Each sliver of creamy soft skin that's exposed seems to push me further into madness.

I never lose control. I'm always the one in charge of every interaction, never once letting my urges get the better of me. Yet with Chloe, I'm tempted to throw the rule book out the window as I fall to her feet, giving her whatever she wants.

Man the fuck up, Marcus, I remind myself. I'm supposed to be doing this to help Chloe, and I need to stop letting my cock distract me from the plan.

As she throws her T-shirt in the same direction as her discarded shorts, I suck in a breath at the sight of her sitting on my sofa, legs spread wide open, wearing just a lacy black bra. I don't think even my wildest imagination could create something so fucking sexy.

"Bra off," I snap, not trusting myself to say anything more.

With her gaze fixed on me, her confidence growing as she watches me fall apart just looking at her, she reaches back to unclip her bra. Once it's open, she wraps her arms around her chest, so the fabric can't fall away. She pauses like that for a moment.

Chloe squeezes her eyes shut, and I watch as she slowly takes some big deep breaths. I don't miss the way her hands that are holding her bra in place tremble.

"Are you okay?" I ask, worried I may have pushed her too far, too fast.

Silence fills the room as she doesn't respond. Then, when she seems to have gotten full control over her breathing, she reaches for the bra strap on her left shoulder. Her hand still has a slight tremble, but nothing like before.

She lowers the strap, pulling her arm out, and repeats the motion with the other arm. The only thing holding her bra in place is the arm across her chest. It's pressed so tightly against her that her tits are squashed, looking like they're trying to burst out of the bra cups.

Even though her response is a little shaky, her eyes are fixed on mine and she doesn't look away. "I'm okay."

She then drops her arm, catching the bra with her other hand. The fabric falls away from her body, exposing her fucking amazing tits, and she throws the bra in the direction of all her clothes.

I want nothing more than to look at her tits, but I know it's taking a lot for her to maintain eye contact with me right now, and I want her to know how much it means to me that she trusts me with this.

She's putting herself in an incredibly vulnerable position, being naked and exposed while I'm clothed and assessing her. I couldn't be fucking prouder, and I let her see that as a genuine smile replaces my usual smirk.

The moment she sees how real my smile is, and that it's all for her, she relaxes completely, her face lighting up and making her look even more beautiful than she did before. If only she knew, this is the smile I reserve just for her.

I don't think I've ever seen a girl look this fucking gorgeous before, and it's taking every ounce of self-restraint not to walk over to her and devour her the way I have so many times in my dreams.

I can't do that yet, I have to make this about her, but that doesn't stop me from looking. Once I know she's okay with what's happening, I allow my gaze to drop from her face.

Moving slowly, so I can take in as much of her as possible, I drag my gaze over every inch of her fucking incredible body. Even though her eyes are fixed firmly on me, showing the confidence she's trying to portray, the rest of her face gives her away.

The red glow of her cheeks is a dead giveaway that she's a little embarrassed, but as the flush travels down her neck and across her chest, it gives her a glow.

Her lower lip is pulled between her teeth, plump from where she's been nibbling at it as a nervous gesture. It's made her lips appear pinker and fuller, and I can't stop imagining what they'd look like wrapped around my cock.

I quickly move my stare from her lips, as I'm really not trying to give myself a hospital-inducing case of blue balls. I follow the direction of her flushed skin, down her neck and across the subtle curve of her collarbone.

Her round, perky tits are just the right size, and I know if I were to cup one in my hand, it would be slightly more than a handful, which is fucking perfect for me.

As I drag my gaze over her peaked nipples, I can't help but wonder if it's the coldness of the room that's hardened them, or is she as turned on as me?

Moving my gaze away from her tits is a struggle. I feel like a teenage boy who just found a nude magazine and is looking at his first ever pair. These may not be my first, but they are pretty fucking perfect.

Get a grip, Marcus, I think to myself, before the rude version of me responds with, *I would very much love to get a grip of those.* Great, now I'm having conversations with myself. I think all the blood has left my brain and is firmly in my boxers right now.

With much more effort than I'd like, I continue my lazy perusal of Chloe's body. Her skin looks so soft, and she has curves in all the right places. Although she's sat down, I can see the soft curve of her stomach and her hips, which only makes me want to see her arse even more.

The twinkling of her belly button bar catches my attention, and I want nothing more than to fall to my knees in front of her and kiss every inch of her skin. I want to touch her, to know if she's as soft as she looks. The need to hold her curves, to grip her hard enough to leave my mark on her, so she'll know exactly who she belongs to.

I never get possessive over women. In fact, I rarely ever see a woman again after one night. I never lead them on, they always know where I stand, and that I'm not looking for any more than one night.

Yet, as I stare at this beautiful woman, with curves in all the right places, I can't help but think that one night wouldn't be enough. It wouldn't give me enough time to devour every piece of her, to learn her body in a way that nobody else ever has.

I suspect that one taste of her will have me hooked like a drug, and I'd willingly fall into addiction for her.

As I finally drag my gaze over her pink pussy, taking in her glistening folds, she starts to squirm under the intensity. It looks like it's taking all her effort not to close her legs, or to use her hands to cover herself up.

In fact, her hands are balled into tight fists, clutching at the sofa cushions on either side of her so tightly that her knuckles have turned white.

"You are so fucking beautiful," I growl, breaking the deafening silence that seems to be combining with the growing chemistry, creating a tense atmosphere.

Hearing the deep, raspy growl in my voice, she lets out a gasp. As I was assessing her, she must have taken the time to do the same, as her gaze is now locked on the tent in my trousers. I can't help my smirk as I take in her awe-like expression.

"Is your pussy wet right now?" I ask, tilting my head in that direction so she's forced to look down at herself.

She gives me a small nod, but I fix her with a hard stare, reminding her of the rules—she must use her voice. "Yes." It's small and shy, but I smile when she does as she's told.

"Use your finger and tell me how wet."

She flicks her gaze between me, her hand—that's still curled in a fist around the sofa cushion—and her very exposed cunt. She looks so uncertain, and I watch as her chest rises and falls slowly while she no doubt tries to claw back some of her anxiety.

When she finally lets go of the sofa cushion, I involuntarily lean forward, like I need to be as close to her as I can.

She reaches down with one hand, resting her arm on the inside of her thigh, and uses her fingers to part her lips. With her other hand, she swipes her finger through her slit.

A low groan echoes around the room, and I'm not entirely sure which one of us it came from. This is fucking torture, yet I can't look away.

She drags her finger slowly from the bottom of her slit to the top, and as she reaches her swollen clit, she gently presses against it, making her gasp. Her eyes screw shut as she loses herself in the moment, gently circling her hard bud.

I'm so fucking hypnotised watching her, but I'm supposed to be using this to teach her about control, and once I've mentally chastised myself for what I'm about to do, I get things back on track.

"Stop!" I snap.

Her eyes fly open, her fingers stilling on her clit as she looks at me, very confused.

"What? Why?" she rushes out, her brow furrowing.

"Did I tell you that you could play with your clit?" I keep my voice stern, my cold stare fixed on her so she can see I'm not happy.

She shakes her head. "No."

"What instruction did I give you?"

She opens her mouth a couple of times, her nose crinkling as she tries to remember, before she finally says, "You asked how wet I am."

"Did you answer me?"

"No," she replies softly, dropping her eyes down to the sofa, looking like a child being told off.

"Eyes of me, Mio. Answer me, now." Before I've even get the full instruction out, her molten silver eyes flick back up to meet mine, and I love that they're darkened with lust.

"I'm very wet," she mutters, her voice giving away just how shy she's feeling right now.

"Are you as wet as you were the other night, when you were playing with your dripping cunt, thinking of me?"

Her breath hitches, and it doesn't take a genius to tell she likes dirty talk. I'd also hazard a guess that she has either a praise kink or a degradation kink—maybe a combination of the two. I look forward to finding out.

She takes in a breath before the words rush out. "I'm not as wet as I was that night, but I'm getting there."

My smirk grows as the redness in her cheeks that had been starting to fade worsens once more.

"Show me."

Her eyes widen almost comically as her brows fly so high they're almost in her hairline. "What?"

I hold back a laugh at how high-pitched her tone is.

"Drag your finger through your slit, then lift it up and show me just how dripping wet you are." I make sure to say each word slowly, dragging out the instruction so that the excitement builds for us both.

I can see the war in her eyes. She's torn between not wanting to do something that she thinks is embarrassing, that she's clearly never done before, and needing to do exactly as I tell her.

She needs to remember this is a teaching experience, as well as a whole fucking lot of fun, so in my stern voice, I remind her that disobeying me isn't the smart option.

"You've already earned yourself one punishment for touching yourself without my permission, you don't want to earn a second for not doing as you're told."

"Punishment?" she splutters, looking both horrified and a little intrigued.

"If you want me to teach you control, that means giving yourself over fully. I own you. If I tell you to do something, I expect you to do it straight away. I'll never ask you to do more than you're capable of, but I will push you," I tell her.

"I'm still not entirely sure how me giving you all the control, submitting to you, helps me to feel in control," she mutters, rolling her eyes like a petulant teenager who is one step away from a pouting tantrum. My palm is twitching already.

"You'll just have to trust me," I say, turning her own words back on her. She thinks she trusts me, and now is the time for her to prove it.

I'm sure there are certain things that she trusts me with. She knows I'll keep her safe, and that I'll make sure she has a good time, but in my opinion, that's just superficial trust. I want her to put her life, her heart, her soul in my hands, knowing I'll protect them as though they were my own. Only when she feels that will she tell me her secrets.

There's a nagging voice in my head that keeps telling me I don't need that level of trust to make her submissive, the superficial version would work perfectly for the sex stuff. It's how I've done things with other girls in the past. As long as they trust me with their bodies, that's all I need.

So why do I want more from Chloe?

I've known for years that nothing can ever happen between us. She's the very fucking definition of forbidden, and I risk starting a war, igniting the old rivalry with her family if I break the rules for her.

No matter how fucking amazing the sex might be, it's not worth causing unrest in Blackthorn, and me potentially losing my best friend.

Sex is all I can ever offer her. I'm not capable of more, so why am I asking her to give me all of her?

I push those heavy thoughts from my mind, not wanting to acknowledge or deal with the conflicting emotions. Instead, I do what I do best and concentrate on my throbbing cock, and the beautiful naked woman in front of me.

Her soft, low voice drags me back to the moment. "What punishment?"

"We can discuss that at a later date, but for right now, you just need to remember that every time you disobey me, or do something I'm not satisfied with, you are adding to it. Do you understand?"

She nods her head, and it only takes a second of me glaring at her for her words to tumble out as she remembers the rule. "Yes, I understand."

"Are you going to do as you're told?" I ask, my brow rising in challenge.

With a small sigh, she says, "Yes." At the same time, she moves her hand back to her pussy and screws her eyes shut.

Repeating what she did before, she slowly drags her finger through her slit, starting at the bottom, pulling it all the way up to her clit. Learning from last time, she rubs her finger over it gently, but she doesn't give it any more attention, though it's clear by the way her eyes screw tighter that she really wants to.

She then brings her finger up and holds it in front of her, though her eyes are still firmly clamped shut.

"Open your eyes," I snap, and she does.

Our gazes both fix on the finger she's holding up in front of her face. There's no denying the glistening wetness that is soaking it, and I have to bite the inside of my cheek to stop myself from moaning.

"So fucking wet, Mio," I growl, and I'm sure she's watching my bright blue eyes darken with pure lust.

I want nothing more than to move over to her, take her finger in my mouth, and devour every last drop of her. I have to grip the chair arms to keep myself still.

"Now I want you to show me how you played with yourself last night. I want to watch as you touch your dripping cunt, wishing it was me." My voice is so deep and raspy, I barely recognise myself.

Her eyes snap up to meet mine, and I can tell she's nervous, but she must see something in my gaze as she doesn't hesitate to move her hand. Her dripping wet finger is on her clit straight away, but she takes her time, spreading the juices over her sensitive nub, her breath hitching as she does.

With each stroke, she gets lost in herself, and though her eyes appear to be fixed on me, she's totally immersed in the experience. I don't think she'd have any idea if I left the room.

Ha, there's no fucking way. Someone could drop a nuclear bomb and I still wouldn't move from this spot.

I watch with rapt attention as her fingers explore her pussy. She starts slowly, using her fingers to spread her juices around, getting her clit and her lips nice and wet. Each time she tentatively circles her clit, a shiver ripples through her, and her head lulls back just a little.

Once she's made sure her fingers and her pussy are dripping wet, that's when she starts to lose herself. She alternates between rubbing her fingers over her clit, pulling a moan from her lips, before moving back to gently tracing circles around it, making her tremble.

I'm leaning so far forward now, I'm about a minute or two away from falling head first out of my chair. I'm so fucking enthralled by her movements.

The way her chest rises and falls in short gasps as her breathing speeds up. The way the red on her chest glows brighter as she gets hotter. The way her head falls back and her eyes roll when she hits a particularly good spot, unable to stop the groan from filling the room.

"Does that feel good, Mio? Is your pussy getting wet and tingly each time you press your clit?"

She makes a noise that sounds like confirmation, mixed in with a loud groan as her fingers press hard on her clit. I'm sure I heard the word *yes* in there somewhere, and watching her lose control like this makes me smile.

Before I know what I'm doing, I'm out of the chair. I use the last of my self-restraint to stand when really all I want to do is crawl on my hands and knees across the room, settling in between her legs. Somehow, I manage to retain a little of my dignity, and I walk over to her instead.

Chloe has no idea I've even moved. She's so lost in her own head, her eyes scrunched shut, so she hasn't seen or heard me approach. It's not until I speak, and she hears how close I am that her eyes fly open in surprise. "Does that feel good?"

Her eyes lock with mine and she nods her head rapidly.

"Yes." It sounds more like a breathy moan than a word.

"Do you like having me watch you while you play with your wet pussy?"

"Fuck, yes," she moans, as she presses her fingers harder against her clit.

I bet if I were to slide a finger into her tight hole right now, I'd feel her walls starting to tighten around me. She looks like she's getting closer to the edge, but I'm not ready for this to be over yet.

"Do you like being a dirty little slut? Do you like teasing me as you rub your clit like a naughty whore?"

Her breath hitches and her eyes widen as she hears the dirty words, and I smile as I expose her love of degradation. I had a feeling, and I couldn't be more fucking pleased that I was right.

"I'm... I'm not a-a slut," she mumbles, in between gasping for air.

I lower myself so that I'm sitting on the sofa beside her, so close my knee is touching her bare thigh, and she doesn't take her eyes off me the whole time. I lean in close, so my lips are right beside her ear, my breath fanning across her cheek.

"That is exactly what you are, Mio. You are *my* slut. You are my dirty little whore, and that is something you should be so fucking proud of.

"You can be a high-society lady out in the real world, but when you're here with me, you are my slut. You live to bring me pleasure, and in return, I will show you how good your body can really feel.

"Being a dirty slut isn't a bad thing, as long as it's just for me," I tell her, feeling the way her body shivers with my words.

She gasps, her eyes rolling, and I can tell she's nearing her orgasm. My words had just as much effect on her as her fingers rubbing at her clit. But she still has more to learn, and I'm not ready for this to be over.

As a soft moan drips from her lips, I reach down and place my fingers over hers, stopping her movement. She's wet and warm, and it takes every bit of strength and self control that I've amassed over the years to not let her orgasm.

I want nothing more than to see what this beauty looks like when she falls apart, but this is a teaching moment too.

A loud groan of frustration rips from her throat as she turns to glare at me, rocking her hips as she tries to gain the little bit of friction she needs.

"Marcus, what the fuck?!" she yells, trying to pull her fingers away from the firm hold I have over them.

"Did you ask to come?" I ask slowly, calmly, the complete opposite of the way Chloe is feeling.

"What?" She shakes her head, a bead of sweat dripping from her forehead as she continues to glower at me.

"You heard what I said. If you're my slut, that means I have full control over you. I say when you come, and until I give you permission, you will not come," I state firmly, watching as her eyes widen and she continues to shake her head, disbelieving.

"I-I can't... I can't stop myself," she mutters, her eyes finally dropping to look at the floor instead of shooting daggers my way.

I can't help the cocky smirk. "That's because you've never tried. You want to be in control of your body... Well, this is where you start. No matter how much you might want to come, you have to do whatever it takes to hold back."

"How?"

This time when her shy eyes meet mine, my stomach flips in a way it's never done before. This fucking girl is my weakness, and I'm already breaking all of my rules for her.

"Do you want me to show you?"

She freezes for a moment, her eyes assessing me, before she finally says, "You are going to touch me?"

I hate the hope that is tinged with every word. She's really making it difficult to stick to my stubborn fucking rules.

I shake my head, my heart racing at the way her face falls, so I quickly explain. "I meant what I said, I won't touch you until you trust me enough, but that doesn't mean I can't help you a little, if you want me to?"

I pointedly look down at where my fingers are already resting over hers. I know, *technically*, I am touching her, but it's not in the way either of us wants, so I'm going to maintain that I'm sticking to my rules—mostly.

"Yes, please." Her voice is so low and shy, and it's like she has a direct fucking line to my cock, that twitches and aches painfully against my boxers.

"What's the rule?" I ask her, as I slowly move her fingers until they're hovering just above her clit, her breath hitching in anticipation.

I freeze there, waiting for her to reply. "I have to get permission before I come."

"Good girl," I say with a smirk, loving the way her body shivers beneath me from the praise. "What happens if I don't give you permission?"

The deer-in-headlights look is back, and she pulls her bottom lip in between her teeth as the intensity of the situation triggers her anxiety again. I wait, giving her time to find the words.

After a short silence, she takes a breath and finds her voice. "I have to do whatever I can to stop myself."

"Good, and what happens if you can't stop? What happens if you come without my permission?" I ask.

This time she looks genuinely confused, and shrugs her shoulders as she admits, "I don't know."

"If you come without my permission, that makes you a very bad girl, and it will add to your punishment in a big way. The only way for me to be sure you'll follow the rules is if you're punished for not following them. Does that sound fair?"

Her mouth flops open. "Punished, how?"

My devilish smirk grows at her expression. Although she looks apprehensive, and a little scared, there's also excitement and intrigue glistening in her silver eyes.

Although I don't think she wants to be punished, there's probably a part of her that wants to know what the punishment would be, and if she'd enjoy it.

"Well, that all depends on how much you break the rules. I think for now we should concentrate on you being a good girl, so you can receive your reward, shall we?"

At the mention of a reward, she nods her head rapidly, and I can't help but chuckle. I then use the control I have over her hand to move her fingers where I want them, following the path I'd take if there were no barrier between us.

I drag her fingers through her slit, groaning low against her ear as I feel how hot and wet she is against my skin. I make sure her digits are coated in her juices before moving them back to her clit.

I follow the pattern I watched her take before, circling the hard nub before gently rubbing over it. I keep up the rhythm, varying the speed and pressure I use, listening to the way her breathing hitches when I find a spot that's particularly sensitive.

I'm leaning in close, so I can both reach and see what I'm doing, and Chloe seems to have taken advantage of my proximity by leaning against me. As her breathing picks up, and she edges closer, she leans into me more, until I'm the only thing keeping her upright.

I fucking love having her so close. I can feel the warmth of her body seeping into mine, heating me in a way I've never felt before. Each time her chest rises and falls, it's like it's an extension of me. When a shiver ripples through her body, it keeps on going through me too.

"More," she breathes, her head rolling back to rest against my shoulder, her eyes falling shut as pleasure takes over. "Please."

I press my fingers harder against hers, and a deep guttural moan rips from her lips. Even though I'm barely touching anywhere except her fingers, I can tell her walls are tightening, her whole body is tensing as she gets closer to her release.

"That's it, Mio. Does that feel good? Are you pretending it's my fingers that are on your dripping cunt right now?" My deep, raspy voice tickles her ear and she trembles in response.

"Yes, fuck. Please, please. I'm so close. Can I... Can I come?" she mumbles, the words tumbling from her lips as she pulls in a breath.

I don't respond, except to increase the pressure of her fingers on her clit, forcing her to rub faster and harder, until a string of almost unintelligible curse words fall from her lips.

"I'm going to... Please, Marcus... I need... I can't... Can I come? Please?" Her begging grows more frantic as her body begins to tense. Her eyes are screwed shut, her head thrown back against my shoulder still, and I know she's close.

Just as she's about to fall over the edge, I grab hold of her fingers and pull them away from her no doubt aching pussy.

"Nooooo. Marcus, what the fuck?" she shouts, sounding more like a desperate cry with a touch of anger.

"You don't have my permission to come yet, slut," I reply simply.

Her eyes fly open, and once more she's giving me a death stare. She tries to close her legs, to squeeze them together to help with the throbbing I'm certain she can feel, but I've already captured her leg with mine, locking her in place.

She then tries to pull her hand away, but I'm stronger, and she knows her attempt will be futile.

Her eyes are glistening with unshed tears as she looks at me, pleading with me in a way that almost breaks me. "I need to come, Marcus. Please."

"You will come, but only after you've learnt to control your body. You have to push yourself to the edge, and when you finally fall, it'll be like nothing you've ever experienced."

Before she can argue with me, I pull her hand back in between her legs, giving her the touch she's so desperate for.

I repeat the same process as before, but as her clit is already super sensitive, it doesn't take long for her to turn into a panting, begging mess, desperate for release.

"You are so fucking gorgeous when you beg me like this. Does this feel good?"

"Yes," she replies, the word turning into a moan at the end.

"Can you imagine if it were my fingers on your clit? We both know I wouldn't be able to stop there. I'd have to press my fingers deep into your tight pussy, feeling your walls clamp down around me as I fuck you.

"Maybe I'd even attack your clit with my tongue while I'm fucking you with my fingers? Would you like me to lick that pretty pussy of yours?"

I whisper the dirty words into her ear, loving the way she trembles beneath me with her growing orgasm. It builds quickly, and soon she's not even listening to me, she's too busy begging and pleading.

"Please, let me come. I'm being a good girl. I need to come. Please, please, Marcus. Please, may I come? I'll do anything." Her words are coming out so fast, it's difficult to make them all out.

The smirk on my face grows as she begins to lose control, but as soon as I feel that tell-tale pulsing in her pussy, I rip our hands away. Her loud cries of pleasure and pain fill the room, and this time she doesn't stop the tears from streaming down her face.

"I-I can't... Please, Marcus... I can't... I need to come," she begs, her body flopping down against mine as her silver eyes plead with me.

"Does it feel good, Mio?" I ask, kneading my hand into her thigh to stop me from exploring the rest of her body.

I want to run my fingers over her nipples, to find out if she's as sensitive as I think she'll be. I want to plunge my fingers into her cunt, to feel how tight she really is. But I can't do any of those things, so I stick to grabbing hold of her thigh so tight, I'm sure she'll have bruises in the morning.

Good, I want her to wear my marks.

"It feels good, but then it hurts. I'll do anything, please, just let me come. You can use your fingers, your cock. You have my permission to do anything, but please, let me come."

My smile grows and my cock twitches, begging me to do as she asks. No matter how much I really want to bury myself in her right now, to feel her milking my cock with her tight walls, we've come this far, and I have to finish the lesson.

"Oh, love, I know it would feel so much better if I were the one to make you come, but this is about you. You need to have full control over your body, and when you know you have that, you can give it over to me."

She looks like she wants to say something, but I cut her off by moving her fingers back between her legs. I bring her close to orgasm, only to deny her, another four times. By the time I pull our fingers away the final time, she's a blubbering mess. She's begging and pleading with me, but she's fully in control, just where I want her to be.

Once she's calmed down, I move her fingers back to her sensitive clit, and start the process again. It takes mere seconds to get her to the edge, her abused clit now hypersensitive, not needing much encouragement anymore.

As with every other time, Chloe starts to beg me, pleading with me to let her come. The posh girl is gone, and in her place is a foul-mouthed dirty slut who is desperate for release, and she's never looked more fucking gorgeous.

"Please, please, Marcus, can I come?" she begs, her knuckles still white as she holds onto the sofa cushion beside her with a death grip.

"You can come, Mio," I whisper into her ear.

Her eyes fly open, her sparking silver gaze locked on me, assessing me like she's not sure she heard me correctly. "I can come?" she clarifies.

With a smirk, I nod. "Yes, slut. I want you to fall apart on your fingers, imagining that it's me touching you. Think about how fucking amazing your orgasm will be when I finally do touch you. You know I won't hold back, I'll give you everything you didn't know you needed."

"Yes," she screams, as she gives in to the impending orgasm.

"Come for me, Mio," I instruct, and she does as she's told.

Chloe's head falls back against my shoulder again, as her whole body begins to tremble. Her breathy moans turn to cries of pleasure, until she suddenly screams my name.

I hold her, my fingers becoming drenched around hers as her release ripples through her, her body trembling and twitching as she rides the wave. It takes every bit of strength I have not to blow my load in my fucking boxers.

Hearing my name on her lips, like she's worshipping me, is almost enough to tip me over the edge. I haven't come without someone touching my cock in a very long time, and I'm not about to start now, though I'm closer than I'd ever like to admit.

It takes a good few minutes for Chloe's breathing to return to normal, and I choose to ignore that mine's also coming out in rough pants. I was much more affected by watching her come than I expected.

When she's finally breathing normal, her body no longer trembling, Chloe begins to pull her fingers away from her abused pussy, and that's when I remember mine are still encasing hers.

I allow her to move, and I shift my body so I'm no longer trapping her in. Although she closes her legs, she doesn't attempt to cover herself up, and I can't help but smile at that.

After a few seconds, Chloe breaks the silence with a short chuckle. "That was…"

Her words trail off, and I fix my gaze on her, waiting for her to finish, but she doesn't, so I try. "Good? Intense?"

She chuckles again. "Yeah, definitely good, but very intense. I've never done anything like that before."

"Did you feel like you had more control over your body?" I ask, since that was supposed to be the original task.

She thinks about it for a moment, before finally nodding. "Yes. At first, I didn't think I could hold back. I didn't think it was possible to simply stop myself from having an orgasm. I've always kinda thought that once it starts, you don't stop it. I mean, I have them so infrequently, why the hell would I want to stop it?" she jokes, and I can't help but chuckle along with her.

"Did it feel more intense when you finally did come?"

This time she doesn't hesitate to answer, she nods her head rapidly. "So fucking intense. I felt it throughout my entire body."

My smile grows when I see how much she enjoyed herself. "Good. For your first lesson, you did well. You just need to remember, from now on, I own you. I control all of your orgasms.

"If you're lonely and horny at one in the morning, you better get your arse into my room and beg for me to let you come, because you are not allowed to without my permission ever again."

"What? That's not… I can't do that!" she blusters, her cheeks flushing bright red again.

"You can, and you will. I meant what I said before, I own you now. Every orgasm belongs to me. If you come without my permission, I will punish you."

She pauses for a moment, deliberating my words. She crosses her arms defiantly, and I try to ignore the way it pushes her tits up in the most fucking magnificent way.

With a mischievous glint in her eye, she looks at me in challenge. "How would you know if I came without your permission?"

My devilish smirk grows, and her eyes widen as she takes in my predatory gaze. "You are my slut, I will know."

"I-I dont... You won't—" Before she can even fumble a full sentence together, I cut her off.

"You're my dirty slut, but you're also a good girl. I have a feeling it won't take long for you to beg me. You will go to bed tonight dreaming it was my fingers that got you off instead of your own.

"Soon my fingers won't be enough, and you'll start to fantasise about my cock. It won't be long until you're spilling all your secrets, begging me to make you my dirty whore in all the ways you crave."

Her mouth flops open, and she looks like she's about to argue. I'm keen to hear whatever retort she comes up with, but I want to leave her thinking of my dirty words.

I lean over until my lips are almost touching her ear, my breath tickling her cheek. "Goodnight, Mio. I'm going to have some very nice dreams about your sweet pussy. Sleep well."

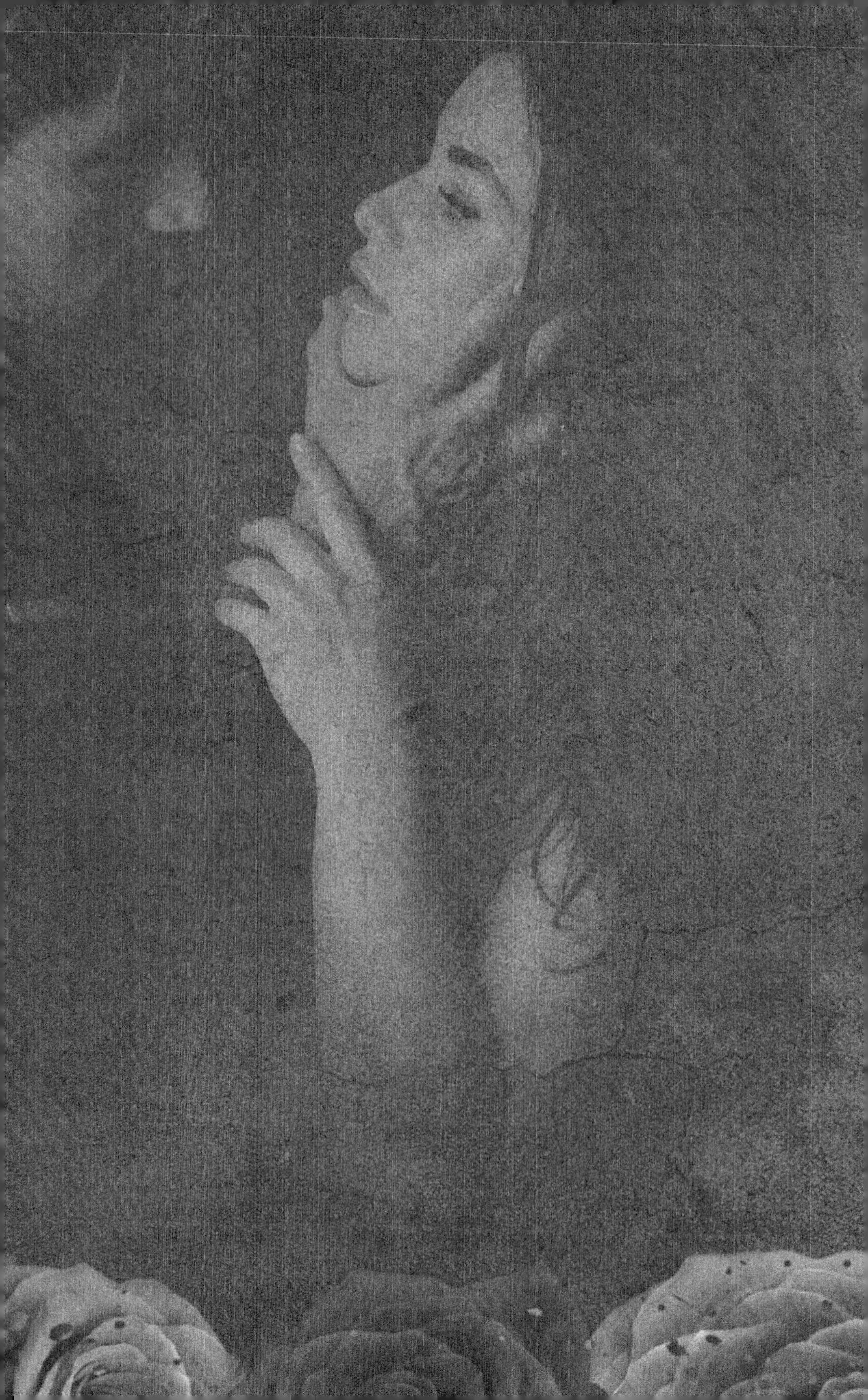

Chapter Twelve
Chloe

After Marcus gave me the most mind-blowing orgasm, without ever really touching me, I wasn't sure how things would be between us. Naturally, I spent the whole night tossing and turning, wanting nothing more than to reach down, to alleviate the throbbing ache between my thighs, but all I could think about were his instructions.

Logically, I knew there was no way he'd know if I decided to touch myself—at least, I don't think he would—yet something still held me back. The experience with him was so much more than just having the most intense orgasm of my entire life.

For the first time in a very long time, I actually felt in control of myself. I've always felt betrayed by my body, hating the way it shows how I feel, even when I don't want it to.

I know all teenagers probably dealt with that at some point, particularly teenage boys getting a hard-on at the most inconvenient of times. But for me, it's not about the way my cheeks flush when I'm trying to pretend I'm not thinking about Marcus. Those slight giveaways, I could handle.

My issue is with the way my body reacts even when my mind is telling it to behave another way. The way my nipples peak as though I'm interested, even though I'm completely terrified. Or the way my pussy gets wet when my clit receives any attention, even if my brain is screaming that I'm not actually enjoying it.

I've always hated that lack of control, knowing I might come, even when I really fucking don't want to.

What Marcus gave me back was so much more than just control. He showed me that my body is mine, and if I don't want something to happen, no matter how hard or painful it may be, I can stop it.

I wanted nothing more than to give in to him after the first time he brought me to the edge. I wanted to lose myself in his touch. I wanted to experience the pleasure he was capable of giving me, but he never lost sight of what he was trying to teach me, and I'm so grateful for that.

Even when I was begging and pleading with him, offering him anything and everything he might want, he never relented. He showed me that even though he was the one who controlled my pleasure, and ultimately gave me permission to find my release, I was the one with the real control.

I could have orgasmed after the first time he edged me, but by the time he told me I could come, I was so in control that I could have held off had I wanted to—though I very much fucking didn't want to.

Since he first proposed the idea of me submitting to him, to learn how to control my own body, I thought it was all bullshit. How can you give up control to gain control? But he was right, and although I now wake up each morning very fucking sexually frustrated, I'm also a hell of a lot more empowered than ever before.

I don't know what I expected to happen after that night, how I thought things might have changed between us, but I definitely wasn't expecting for nothing to be different.

Every morning, I'd get up and drag my arse into the kitchen for my morning coffee, only to find Marcus already there, my drink waiting for me. We exchange the same pleasantries… Did you sleep well? What are your plans for the day? It's nice weather today, isn't it…

Not that I'm complaining, as I like talking to Marcus while we move around the kitchen, both getting ready for the day ahead. At times, we'd venture into slightly more personal questions, getting to know a little about each other as we ate.

But it was like we'd both circle the elephant in the room, not once discussing what happened between us.

We would then just go about our day. Marcus would leave for whatever meeting or job he has that day, and I'd smile and wave him off, before trying to decide what to do with myself.

I met my new security guard, Kim, and it took me a couple of days to get to know her, but I quickly learnt why Miles thought she'd be the best fit for me.

She's such a quiet, unassuming person, but that never stops her from voicing her opinion if I want to do something she thinks is unsafe.

There were a lot of butting heads at first, but we quickly got to know each other, and now I actually don't mind her being around all the time.

She's easy to talk to, and despite my father drilling it into me from an early age that our staff are not our friends, I'm starting to consider Kim as one.

Once we created boundaries, and she explained to me what she needs to do to keep me safe, we started to work together. I told her all about my desire to learn more about baking, and she did some research to find a class that I could attend.

She needed to make sure the building was secure, and that the instructors passed all her security checks, but once she gave her approval, I signed up without hesitation.

The class was only for a couple of hours each day, but they're the most free I've ever felt. For the first time in my life, I'm doing what I want to do, and I'm loving every minute of it.

As soon as I'd get home from the class, I'd jump straight into the kitchen, practising the techniques I learnt that day, whilst making dinner for that evening.

Although Marcus has never asked me to do this, it kinda feels like the only way I can contribute. He's at work all day, the least I can do is make him a nice meal for when he gets home.

The first couple of days he came home to find the meal ready and waiting for him, I could tell he was surprised. He looked at me with that intense gaze of his, assessing me to see if there was something he was missing, if I had an ulterior motive.

Every time he looked at me suspiciously, I'd roll my eyes and remind him that it's just food. I'm not poisoning him, and I'm certainly not doing it so I can get something out of him. It's nothing more than a way to thank him.

It took a couple of days, but he stopped looking at me suspiciously, and started actually looking forward to whatever I was cooking that day.

He came home late on Saturday, looking like he hasn't slept in weeks, and I wasn't really sure what to do. Although we've settled into this comfortable existence where we talk about inconsequential things and eat meals together,

I'm not sure we are friends. Yet, at this moment, I think a friend is exactly what he needs.

Marcus brings over a bottle of wine as I place the food I've made on the table. We don't normally have wine, so it must have been a long day for him.

When he left this morning, I could see the bags under his eyes, and the paleness to his skin that had been getting progressively worse over the last couple of days, but even compared to this morning, he looks exhausted.

"How was your day?" he asks as he sits down, taking a slightly larger than normal gulp of his wine straight after.

"It was good, thank you. We learnt how to make different sugar flowers today, and I had a lot of fun practising. My first few didn't even resemble flowers, but by the end of the class, I think I got the hang of it," I reply, unable to keep the smile off my face as I think about how much fun I had in class.

I'm almost at the point where I could attempt to make my first real celebration cake, but there are still a few more techniques I want to learn before I try.

"I'm glad you're enjoying yourself." The small smile he throws my way is so genuine, and I have to avoid thinking about how much that tiny gesture makes my heart race.

"What about you? How was your day? You look like you've had a particularly rough one," I say, hoping I'm not pushing things too far between us.

Marcus is very particular, and doesn't really like to talk about his work. He will give me a rough overview of if he's had a good day or not, but that's about the extent of it.

I learnt after the first day that there's no point asking, as he'll just ignore me, so I have no idea what prompted me to push him today.

He lets out a sigh before taking another sip of wine. "It's been a fucking long day," he replies with a groan, running his fingers through his hair as soon as he's placed his wine glass down.

His long dark locks stick up at all angles, making him look completely ruffled in the best way, and I have to bite my lower lip to keep from staring at him.

It's so unfair that even in his most exhausted state he manages to look fucking gorgeous, I think to myself.

"What happened?" I ask, taking a bite of my potatoes.

Marcus looks at me for a moment, but there's no malice in his eyes. He seems to be warring with himself, and so I keep quiet while he works through whatever is going on in his head.

After a short time, he lets out a huff followed by a sigh. "Things have been a little...rough lately between your family and mine. Jacob isn't really speaking to me, and your arsehole fiancé, Scott, is making things difficult at every turn.

"I found out today that Scott is gathering his resources. He's doing it discreetly, and he's not left any sort of usable trail, but it's not hard to see what he's doing. When he marries you, he plans to have Jacob ousted so that he can take over—"

Before he even had the chance to finish the rest of his story, I cut him off, blurting out the first thing that came to my head. "That would mean starting a war with you."

Marcus slowly nods his head, his lips pressed together in a tight line. "Exactly. I think he plans to become the leader of your family, and with the Santoro resources, combined with his family supporters, he'd stand a very good chance in a war against me."

I shake my head in disbelief. "That will never happen. There's no way my dad will hand over the reins to anyone except Jacob. He's his heir," I point out the obvious.

Marcus' eyes scrunch up as he grimaces. "Sadly, Jacob has been going further and further off the rails recently. He's making lots of mistakes, and even though I've been trying to cover for him, word is slowly reaching people.

"He's making your family look weak, and that's something your dad will not tolerate. Jacob isn't exactly hiding the fact he doesn't want this job, and the people aligned with your family are starting to notice.

"If they start to question his ability to lead, it will make it very fucking easy for Scott to stage the rebellion I can see coming from a mile away."

As soon as he's finished speaking, his whole body seems to sag, like the weight he's been carrying around with him has been lifted.

He appears almost lighter, and I can't help the small smile that spreads across my lips at the thought that opening up to me has helped to relieve some of his burden.

Now I just need to think how I can actually help him...and my wayward brother.

"We need to come up with a plan to fix this. Blackthorn will go to shit if Scott gains power. I know the most obvious solution would be for me not to marry him, as he can't gain any of our power if he doesn't marry into the family, but it's not as simple as that. We also need to make not only Dad, but all the people who work for us, see that Jake is a good leader," I explain, my brain ticking away as I try to think of a plan.

Marcus chuckles, the hint of a smirk on his face. "Before we do that, we actually have to make Jacob into a good leader. Even if he weren't getting drunk or high every day, and was taking the job seriously, the fact he hates it means he doesn't really make an effort.

"It's clear to anyone paying even the slightest bit of attention that he doesn't want the job, and until he looks like he wants to rule, nobody will take him seriously," Marcus says with a shrug of his shoulders.

"How the fuck do we do that? I mean, making other people think he's a good leader isn't too hard, as it's all about creating the right image, but getting Jacob to actually want to do the job, and to do it well...that's something else entirely," I snap, sounding a little harsher than I intended.

"There used to be a time when both me and Jacob looked forward to taking over from our fathers. We hated living in their shadows, and wanted the opportunity to prove the sort of leaders we could be. I have no idea when that changed for him.

"I keep trying to think back, to see if there was a catalyst, but I just don't know. I feel like such a shit friend for not seeing it," he admits, his cheeks flushing just a little as he shows me a vulnerable side to him that I never expected to see.

"You're not a shit friend, Marcus. I lived with him, and I have no idea when he changed either, or what caused it." The words feel like ash on my tongue, and I hate admitting that I missed it too. He's my brother and I love him... I should have seen the change in him before he became this wild.

"You were going through your own shit," Marcus says, then he shocks us both by reaching out and placing his hand over mine.

It's almost like he does it without thinking, and as soon as our skin touches, we both look down at where his big palm is encasing my smaller one.

The skin on the back of my hand is tingling, and I wonder if he can feel it too. He's looking at his hand like he's not sure how the hell it got there, and I can see the war in his eyes as he considers pulling away.

I don't want to lose the warm contact, so I take the decision away from him by turning my hand over and lacing our fingers together.

His eyes are glued on the way our hands fit together, and his breathing appears to speed up slightly. I'm so used to him trying to maintain eye contact with me, I'm a little thrown when his gaze remains locked on our hands.

"I should have noticed you too." His voice is low, barely above a whisper, but my heart stutters under the intensity of his words.

I squeeze his hand, and this is all it takes for Marcus to lift his big blue eyes up to meet mine, making my stomach flip. "It's not your job to look after us."

His eyes narrow as he shakes his head. "Jacob is my best friend, and you... I should have noticed. I knew you were both spiralling, but I can't pinpoint exactly when it happened. Did something happen to you both?"

His question catches me off-guard. I don't like thinking back to that time, but I try to remember if Jacob started acting out before or after me.

"No, or at least, I don't think so. I have no idea what happened to Jake, but he had already started to drink more and do drugs before...my incident."

I don't really know how to explain what happened to me without actually telling him, and although labelling it as an 'incident' fucking diminishes what I went through, it's all I can think of on the spot.

Marcus' nose crinkles while his other hand tightens into a fist, and I can tell he's angry on my behalf. I can't help the way my lips tip up into a smile, as for the first time in a long time, I feel like I actually might have someone who is on my side, someone who will fight for me.

He looks like he's struggling to find the right words, so I decide to help him out. "We need to find out what Jacob's trigger was. Until we know why he's behaving the way he is, we can't help him. Telling him to do better, to be better, won't work. We have to get to the root of the problem."

Marcus lets out a humourless laugh. "You make that sound so fucking easy."

I shake my head in disbelief. "He's your best friend. Surely you can talk to him about it?"

This time when Marcus laughs, it's a full belly laugh. He throws his head back, and the sound echoes around us. He looks younger than I've ever seen him, his face and eyes bright with humour, and butterflies flutter in my stomach like I'm a teenager all over again.

"We may be best friends, but we aren't girls. We don't talk about our feelings, Chloe," he chuckles, rolling his eyes at me like I should know that.

I mean, I don't really have any friends, but I always thought that if I did, the whole point of the friendship would be that the other person is there for you, as a shoulder to cry on, a listening ear when you need them the most. I know guy friendships aren't exactly the same as girls, but I always assumed they had some version of this.

"But you talk to each other? Couldn't you find some other way to bring it up?" I ask him, watching his head tilt as he considers my suggestion.

"I mean, I could, but I'm not really sure how," he admits.

I give him a reassuring smile as I squeeze his hand. "I can help. I will think about how you can approach it, and then we can give it a try."

Marcus looks at our conjoined hands again, before lifting his gaze to meet mine. His eyes darken and a mischievous look spreads across his face. "We're having our first check-in dinner with your family tomorrow, so we can make a start then."

I narrow my gaze at him, wondering what it is he's not saying. "Why do I get the impression you're deliberately not saying something?"

He chuckles before leaning over the table until he's so close I can feel his breath against my cheek. "Because that's exactly what I'm doing. You didn't think I forgot about your punishment, did you?"

My eyes widen as my brows shoot to my hairline. "What?"

His lip tilts into that fucking devilishly sexy smirk of his, and his lips flutter beside my ear. "Get plenty of sleep tonight, Mio. You'll need all your energy for your punishment tomorrow."

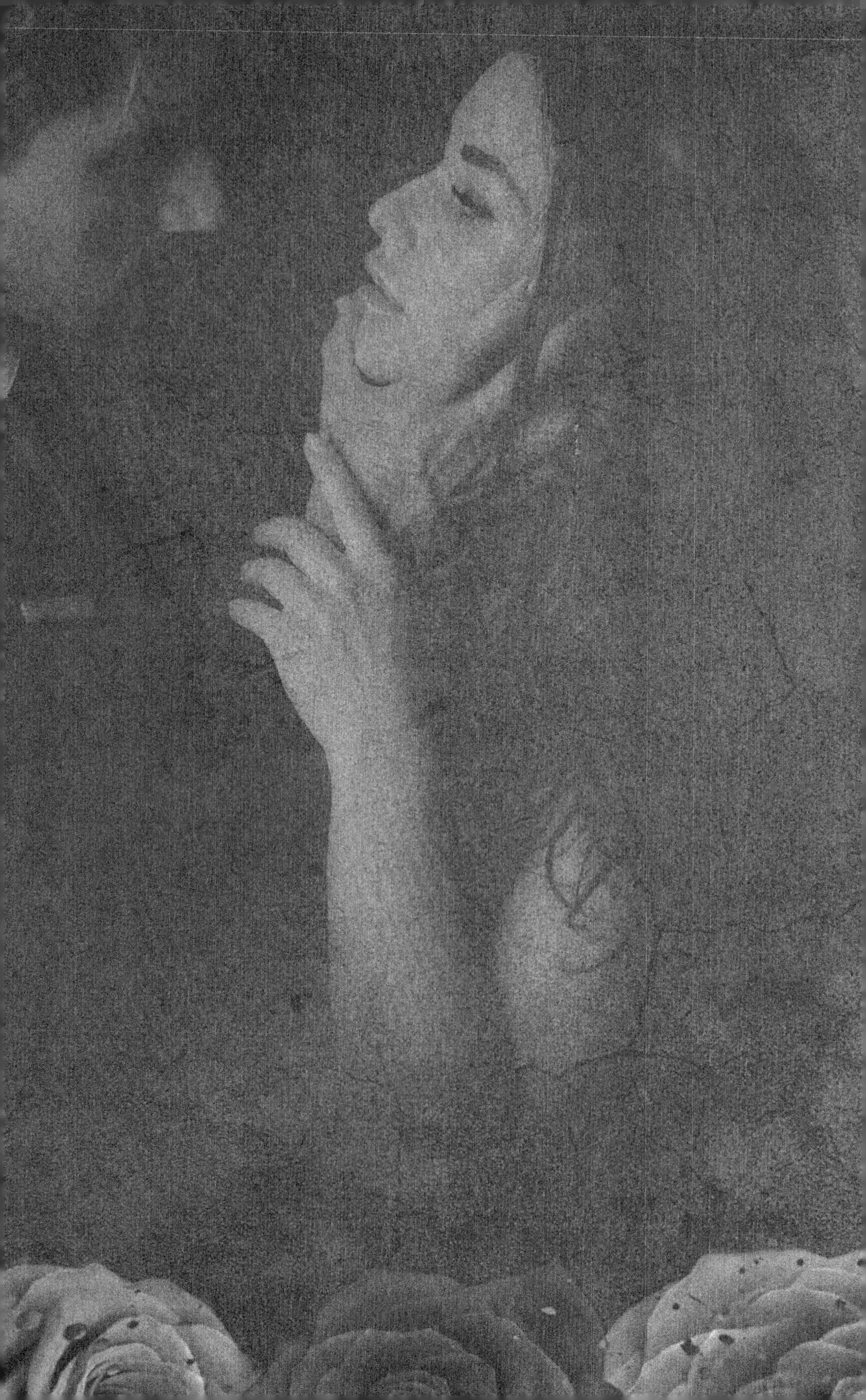

Chapter Thirteen
Chloe

"**G**et plenty of sleep tonight, Mio. You'll need all your energy for your punishment tomorrow."

Those damn words were on repeat in my head the whole fucking night. Every time I closed my eyes, just to get a little bit of sleep, I was consumed with thoughts of what that might mean.

I may not be the most sexually experienced person in the world, and my past sexual history has all been distinctly vanilla, but that doesn't mean I don't read the odd spicy book, or watch porn.

But the problem with doing either of those things is that it doesn't exactly help me narrow down what the word 'punishment' means to Marcus.

According to some people on the internet, it may be a much worse version of the edging he taught me the other day, with a bit of spanking thrown in—which I can honestly admit I'm intrigued about.

However, that does seem to be a somewhat mild form of punishment, and there are a million different forms on the punishment scale. I saw one video where the woman was completely tied up, dangling from the ceiling wearing nothing but rope.

Her tits were roped together, she had a ball gag in her mouth, and her hands were tied behind her back. Her hair had been tied back, but not in a normal way.

The tie seemed to be connected to something, and as I followed it, my eyes nearly popped out of my head when I saw it connected to the hook in her arse. So, every time she moved her head, it jostled the hook that was deep in her arsehole.

While the guy was swinging her around, flogging and whipping different parts of her, he'd be teasing her pussy. I have to admit, when he started hitting her clit with a riding crop, I was cringing and rubbing my thighs together in sympathy, while she cried and shook with what looked to be an earth-shattering orgasm.

I quickly realised that watching porn was only going to terrorise me. And that's how I found myself struggling to sleep, wondering how to tell Marcus that I don't like the idea of having a hook in my arsehole, or being suspended from the ceiling while he tortures my clit.

It may do it for some women, and I'm not above experimenting, but there are just some things I'm already certain I won't enjoy.

Aren't people in BDSM relationships supposed to have contracts or something? I think to myself, before chuckling as I remind myself that the only experience I have of BDSM relationships is through books and the internet, which can be vastly inaccurate.

The problem with staying up all night, looking at porn while panicking, is that eventually my mind drifts away from worrying, and that's when I started thinking about all the things I might enjoy trying with him.

I should have known watching porn was a bad idea. Now I'm horny as fuck, and I daren't touch myself. I'm already being punished, I don't want to make it worse.

So, naturally, when I wake up in the morning, having only got a couple of hours of interrupted sleep, I'm tired, cranky, and unbelievably fucking horny.

I have a couple of hours before we're scheduled to leave for my parents' house, and I should probably get a little more sleep, but now that I'm awake, the nerves are back.

I'm a little surprised when I stomp into the kitchen to get my morning coffee to find that Marcus isn't there, though my usual mug is next to the coffee machine waiting for me. Next to it is a note explaining he went for a run and will be back soon.

While I'm waiting for the coffee to brew, I pop some bread into the toaster.

My parents will have had the chef go all out with a big Sunday lunch, so I don't eat much.

Once I have my coffee and toast, I take a seat on one of the stools at the island and begin reading a cake decorating book I bought the other day. It has some interesting techniques I want to try for creating more realistic sugarpaste flowers.

I'm so lost in reading the instructions, I don't hear the door to the apartment click open. It's not until one of the stools opposite me scrapes on the floor that I flick my gaze up to see what made the noise.

My mouth drops open at the sight of a very sweaty, topless Marcus who has his head thrown back as he gulps from his water bottle. I watch the way his Adam's apple bobs as he swallows, and I find myself swallowing hard too. His hair is wet with sweat, making it look darker, but it still flops around in the most unbelievably sexy way.

I watch as sweat droplets make their way down his face, along the curve of his throat, down to his very naked chest. I'm sure my eyes look like something out of a fucking cartoon as they pop out of my head at the sight of the drops trailing over his ripped abs.

Don't even get me started on his Adonis-like V that disappears below his running shorts. The guy is literally a god walking amongst us mere humans here on Earth, and given the way his lips curve into that fucking smirk of his when he catches me staring, he knows exactly the effect he has on women—me specifically.

"See something you like?" he drawls, winking at me when I finally drag my gaze up to his face.

What I bloody hate the most is that whilst his body is a work of art that I'd happily stare at for all eternity, it pales in comparison to his face.

Those bright blue eyes sparkle in a way that makes you get lost in them. His long eyelashes are the type that women pay good money to replicate, and make his eyes look hooded and sexy.

Then there's that smirk of his that I'm sure he only pulls out because it makes him look smug and arrogant, and he knows it melts women's knickers. But for me, his smirk is nothing compared to when he shows me a genuine smile.

His cheeks plump up until the cutest dimple appears, and it not only makes him look his age, as opposed to the older image he tries to portray, it also makes him seem so much more relaxed. Maybe that's why he doesn't use it all that much.

I blink rapidly a few times, trying to pull my dirty mind out of the gutter—

and the very sexy images it is currently producing—to bring me back into the room.

What did he just ask me?

Marcus clears his throat again, although it sounds an awful lot like he's coughing to hide a laugh, and that helps to sober me up. I glare at him as he lifts his brow in a challenge.

"What?" I snap eventually when I can't remember what the hell he just said.

I was aware of his mouth moving, but I was so lost staring at him that I didn't pay enough attention to what he was actually saying.

"I said...do you like what you see?" There's an arrogant edge to his voice that makes me prickle.

Of course, I like what I see. A fucking blind person could see I'm attracted to him, but that doesn't mean I'm going to admit it. Particularly, when he's looking at me with that cocky, knowing stare.

"Sorry, I was reading my book and got lost in my own head for a moment," I say, pointing to the book in front of me that I had very obviously stopped reading in favour of ogling him. But it's the best cover up I could come up with on the spot.

Marcus chuckles, rolling his eyes as he moves towards the coffee machine, pulling out his usual mug.

"Of course, you were. You definitely hadn't forgotten all about whatever you were reading so that you could stare at me instead," he jokes, sarcasm dripping from every word.

I grind my teeth at his smugness. "Wow, you certainly think a lot of yourself. I'm surprised you managed to get in the kitchen with that big head of yours."

I'll admit, it's not my best comeback, but it's all I've got. I blame his body still being on display, it's clearly messing up my brain.

Marcus stops just behind me, making me jump, as I hadn't realised he was so close. He leans over, his chest crowding my back as he places his head beside mine. His stubble rubs along my cheek as he edges closer to my ear.

As his breath fans over my face, a shiver ripples down my spine, and my breath catches. He's so close, the heat from his almost naked body warms me up, my core burning from his closeness.

At first he just hovers over me, his breath fluttering against my skin, and I wait for whatever he's about to do.

My eyes drift closed as I take in his deep, woodsy smell with a hint of mint, and I question how the hell he still smells amazing even though he's dripping in sweat.

He drags a breath in and I freeze when his lips gently brush against my ear, my heart racing so fast I can barely keep up. "My head is getting bigger the longer I look at you in those sexy sleep shorts. Wanna feel?"

His voice is deep and husky, and as he asks his question, he presses his body against my side until I feel the unmistakable outline of his hard length pushing against my hip. I have to bite my lip to stop the all-consuming groan I can feel building from escaping.

Would I sound completely desperate if I said hell yes?

Get it together, Chloe, I mentally chastise myself. *He already knows you like him, don't make it any easier on the arsehole.*

After mentally berating myself, I take a deep breath to help steady my nerves before opening my eyes again. I turn my head just slightly, so his lips are almost against mine. The urge to taste him grows, but I push it away, needing to stay strong, just for another moment or two.

His eyes are locked on mine, and I can see he's just as affected by this as I am, and that brings me even more joy for what I'm about to do.

With as much confidence as I can muster, praying that my voice doesn't break and betray me, I reply, "Sorry, I'm busy. You'll have to feel yourself."

While Marcus stands there blinking, clearly not sure he heard me correctly, I place my hand on his naked chest—fucking hell, he's rock hard—and push him away from me.

As soon as there's enough of a gap, I jump down from my stool and practically run from the kitchen. Just as I reach my room, I hear Marcus let out a string of curse words and I chuckle to myself.

I'm not sure if I just made the situation worse, particularly if he plans on going forward with the punishment he's been teasing me with, but it feels quite good to have taken back a little bit of the power, even if it won't last.

I spend the next couple of hours trying to relax, before getting ready for dinner with my family. Since I'm going back home, all the expectations that are usually placed on me will be back, and I have to keep that in mind as my mother will be extra observant, I'm sure.

Which is why I spend far too long making sure my make-up is just perfect, and the outfit I've chosen is one she'd approve of, instead of being my own preference. I stare at myself in the mirror, ignoring how deflated I look, but giving a nod of approval.

I make my way into the living room to wait for Marcus, only to find he's already there. I expected to see him in the suit he normally wears around my family, so imagine my surprise to see he's wearing black faded jeans that hug his arse and thighs in just the right way.

The tight black T-shirt clings to his body, but the leather jacket he's wearing over the top is what makes me drool. Well, that and the biker boots.

He looks like danger and sin personified, and my stomach flips the more I look at him. His all dark attire compliments his floppy black hair, but it makes his bright blue eyes and plump pink lips stand out even more.

Fuck, he's far too gorgeous for his own good.

While I'm unabashedly checking him out, he appears to be doing the same to me. Only, while I'm openly drooling over him, he looks to be a little confused. There's no heat in his eyes, and it makes me squirm in a completely different way.

I want to break the weird tension, but I have no idea what to say. There's no way to ask him if he likes what he sees without coming across as needy. Besides, it's clear he doesn't like what he sees, and that makes my heart sink.

"What are you wearing?" he asks. There's no malice or disgust in his voice, just curiosity.

I look down, taking in the knee length black skirt that I've paired with matching black Mary Jane's, nude-coloured tights underneath to give my pale legs a bit more colour, and the off-white blouse that has a soft floral pattern decorating it.

Everything is crisp and well pressed, fitting to my body in a way that shows off my figure without emphasising my curves—just the way I've always been told to dress when in the company of others.

"It's one of the outfits my mother selected for me to wear when I meet with Scott. It's supposed to show I'm feminine without clinging to me in a way that makes it obvious I'm too curvy," I state, practically repeating my mother's words back to him.

Marcus' eyes darken, and an angry expression crosses his face as he begins stalking over to me. I stand still like a deer-in-headlights, and I really do feel like I'm being trapped by a predator.

I take a step back until I hit the wall behind me, giving me nowhere to go, and Marcus just keeps coming.

He stops mere inches from me, his body crowding mine, making me feel so fucking small, but I'm not even remotely scared. My heart is beating so loud, it's a miracle he can't hear it, but it's not through fear.

"I'm only going to say this once, Chloe, so I want you to listen very fucking carefully. You are perfect. Don't listen to a word your mother says. She's just jealous that her daughter has such a fucking killer body and she doesn't.

"Your curves are one of the best things about you, and when I finally am allowed to touch you, I plan to mark every one, holding on to them as I claim you as mine. Do I make myself clear?" he growls, and I can't keep the shit-eating grin from lighting up my face.

Did he really just say I'm perfect? Every girl wants to hear that, but for Marcus Morelli to be the one who says it, to little old me, I genuinely feel like I might faint from shock.

"Thank you," I whisper, not really sure what else to say to him. There really are no words to adequately show this man just how grateful I am for what he just did.

"Don't mention it. Now, what's with the make-up?" he asks, and I can't help my brow furrowing in confusion.

"What do you mean?"

Before I've even got the sentence out, he grabs hold of my hand and pulls me into the main apartment corridor, stopping in front of the large floor-length mirror that's hanging on the wall in between two doors.

He places both hands on my shoulders and turns me until I'm standing in front of the mirror, and he's behind me, his head towering over mine as we both stare at our reflections.

I take a moment to look, wondering what he means. My make-up looks flawless, and that confuses me further. The way he voiced the question made me think I had mascara smudges everywhere, or lipstick on my teeth, but there's nothing I can see.

"What's wrong with my make-up?"

He takes a moment, and it almost looks like he's trying to find the right words, which makes me even more nervous. Marcus isn't exactly known for his tact. He's blunt and honest, so I'm not sure why he's holding back.

"The last few days here, you've barely worn any make-up," he starts, and I nod in agreement. I'm about to explain but he cuts me off and continues.

"Whenever I've seen you out and about, or at the club, your make-up always looks so different to how you're wearing it now. I'm not really sure how to explain it, as make-up definitely isn't my thing, but with the exception of your dark eyes and red lips, you barely look like you're wearing anything.

"Whereas, right now, it's clear you have a lot of make-up on, but they're all quite neutral colours. It's almost like you're trying to make your face look natural but with a filter on."

I listen to everything he's saying, and he's not wrong. My mother always says that women should look like they're not wearing any make-up, opting for nudes and tan colours that give off a perfect, airbrushed finish, which is the look I opted for today, knowing I'd be judged by her.

When I choose my own make-up, Marcus is right, I tend to go for a really dark smokey eye, usually with a metallic glittery finish to make my silver eyes pop. I add a little blush and highlighter so that my cheeks stand out, and a bright red lipstick to show off my plump lips, and that's about it.

I rarely wear a full face of make-up, preferring to go without, since I have to wear it constantly when I'm with my mother, or people from high society.

My gaze flicks over and meets Marcus' in our reflection, and I try to find the words to explain to him. "This is how I'm expected to look, but it's not what I would choose."

It's a very simplistic version, but it's the truth.

When Marcus looks back at me, he gives me a knowing smile, and his eyes are kind. He nods his head, like he understands. Then again, the suit he usually wears is probably part of the uniform he's expected to present to the world, so maybe he does get it.

He looks at his watch for a second, then turns to face me. "Right, you have ten minutes. Get changed into something you want to wear, but make sure it's still a skirt, and do your make-up however the hell you'd choose.

"Don't wear what your parents would expect, just dress for yourself. It's what I decided to do." He gestures to his more laid back attire, and I can't help but smile.

"It suits you." Understatement of the fucking century.

"Thanks. Now, get a move on," he states, turning me around and pushing me in the direction of my bedroom.

My mind is whirling, my thoughts spinning a million miles a minute as I second guess myself. I want to dress my own way, to look the way I prefer, but years of being trained by my parents is hard to overcome, particularly in ten bloody minutes.

So, I decided to do as Marcus suggested. I don't think, I just feel. I wipe all the make-up off and start again, opting for my usual smokey eye with a silver glitter to accentuate my eyes.

I use a slightly heavier black liner than normal, thinking that if I'm going to rebel, I might as well go all the way, adding just a touch of mascara to complete the look.

I then use a darker shade of red to the one I wear in the club, as I want my lips to look plump without standing out too much. Once I've added a bit of blush and highlighter to emphasise my cheeks, I take a look in the mirror. The reflection I see shining back, smile and all, is the most familiar version of me I've seen in a while.

With only a few minutes left, I rush over to my closet. I didn't bring much clothes with me, and so that's making my decision harder. A lot of my casual stuff I rule out straight away—my mother would have a heart attack if I showed up for Sunday lunch in my black leggings or ripped jeans.

All of the skirts I have are Mother approved, which means they don't qualify, but Marcus was adamant about me wearing one.

That's when a dress on the end hanger catches my eyes. It's a small white sundress with little yellow flowers on it, which sounds perfectly innocent, but the dress is far from sweet.

The thin spaghetti straps connect to a low sweetheart neckline that shows off a generous display of cleavage. The top of the dress itself has boning in it similar to that of a corset, with wire underneath the cups, which pushes my boobs up enough that I don't need to wear a bra.

The boning stops at my waist, and the white fabric flares out from there, stopping mid-thigh. It's long enough to cover everything, but shorter than my parents would approve of, and that makes me smile.

The white fabric is pale enough that it's almost see-through, without actually showing off too much. Well, I have to opt for no bra and a pair of very small lace knickers with thin sides, so the fabric isn't too visible, but it adds to the look, making me feel very sexy.

I opt for a pair of black ballet flats, as I don't particularly enjoy wearing heels, and this is supposed to be an exercise in me picking what I like.

I take a moment to look at myself in the mirror, and I can't help but smile. I'm also very glad I remembered to shave my legs yesterday, as there's a lot of my creamy white skin on display right now. But I can't deny that the way the dress clings to my curves makes me look shapely and...dare I say it, a little sexy.

I just know my mother isn't going to approve, but I don't care.

I walk out of the room, a genuine smile on my face as I hold my head up high. This time when Marcus catches a glimpse of me, I get the reaction I was hoping for all along.

At first his eyes widen comically as he takes all of me in, but then his gaze darkens with lust. I watch as his tongue darts out and sweeps along his lower lip, like he's trying to taste me. Then, when I expect his lip to quirk up into that cocky smirk of his, he surprises me by giving me a genuine smile.

"Now you look like you," he states, his voice gravelly and rough in a way that makes my stomach flip. "You look so fucking sexy, Mio."

My lip tips up into a small smile, and I can feel my cheeks starting to heat up. "Thank you."

"I'm really going to enjoy punishing you now," he growls as he slowly begins walking towards me.

"Now?" I squeak, wondering what the hell he has planned. We are cutting it fine as it is, and there's nothing my parents hate more than tardiness.

The devilish smirk on his face grows as he gets closer to me. I know better than to back away, even though everything in me is telling me to. He stops when he's right in front of me, towering over me once again.

He reaches into his pocket and pulls out a light pink oval-shaped item that has a string attached to one side of it. He holds the piece of string, letting it hang between us, right in front of my face.

"Do you know what this is?" he asks, and I shake my head.

He waits, glaring at me, and that's when I remember how insistent he is that I use my words instead of head gestures. "No, what is it?" I ask, intrigued.

His eyes sparkle with mischief as he leans in closer, his breath fanning across my cheek. "This, Mio, is a love egg. It's connected to a remote control on my phone. Here."

He takes hold of my wrist, turning it so he can place the love egg in my hand, and I curl my fingers around it, shocked at how soft it is. He then takes his phone out of his pocket, and after a couple of taps of his fingers, the egg in my hand begins to vibrate.

My eyebrows shoot into my hairline when it finally hits me exactly what this is. I've heard about them before, but I've never seen them in real life, which is why I didn't recognise it. The name never triggered a recollection either, but now I'm very aware what it is, and what it does.

It's at this exact moment that it suddenly hits me... This is my punishment.

"You don't expect me to use this, do you?" I blurt out, looking like he's lost his ever-loving mind.

Marcus chuckles, but his face remains very serious. "I absolutely do expect you to use it. This is your punishment, which means it's not optional. You are going to put the egg in now, and you will keep it in until we return home after lunch."

He's barely finished his sentence and I'm shaking my head frantically, repeating the word 'no' over and over again.

"You've lost your fucking mind. I can't go to Sunday lunch with my family with a fucking sex toy in my knickers," I blurt out, and Marcus full belly laughs at my outrage.

He then leans over until his lips are almost touching my ear. "It doesn't sit in your knickers, Mio. The egg belongs in that tight little pussy of yours."

Once again, my cheeks are so inflamed you could probably fry an egg on them, if it weren't for the way I'm rapidly shaking my head to protest.

"No. Absolutely fucking not. How the hell am I supposed to walk with this in? Even when it's not turned on, it'll feel too full. I can't do it."

Marcus takes a step back, and thankfully, with a press of a button on his phone, he turns off the vibration. His eyes glare at me as he fixes me with a stern expression.

"This isn't up for debate, love. This is a punishment. If you don't want to make things even worse, I suggest you put the damn egg in right now, so we can be on our way."

"Worse? How the hell can it get any worse?" I splutter.

This time when his lip tilts up, his smirk is pure evil. "You forget, I have control of the egg. If I need to make this punishment more severe, I can always turn the vibration onto its strongest setting at the worst possible moment. Say when you're hugging your dad goodbye, or getting a lecture from your mother on how you're dressed?"

I blame the stress of the whole fucking situation, as it never even occurred to me that he might activate the bloody vibration whenever he chooses.

"You can't be serious? You plan on using that thing on me whenever you choose? No fucking way," I snap, putting my hand on my hip for emphasis. I'm about one freak out away from stomping my foot for good measure.

Marcus lets out a dark, humourless laugh as he takes a step towards me, his stern glare fixed on me. "This isn't up for discussion, Mio. Either you put the egg in, or I will. But remember, the longer you delay it, the worse I will make things for you."

There's a dark threatening edge to his voice that tells me he's not messing around.

"I-I don't... I mean, how..." My words trail off as I struggle to admit that I've got no fucking idea what I'm doing.

Clearly, I'm giving in, as I don't want to make this punishment any worse than it needs to be—or already will be—but I don't know the first thing about inserting a love egg.

I have a small bullet vibrator, but I've only ever used it on my clit, I've never put it inside. Then again, if it were a normal vibrator, I don't think I'd have any problems, but the egg isn't exactly a standard shape, and it's making me nervous.

Marcus reaches out and takes the egg from my hand, before slowly moving it up to his mouth. I then watch with my mouth open—most likely with drool dripping down—as he sticks out his tongue and swirls it around the egg.

In a motion that's far too fucking sexual, he proceeds to get the egg as wet as he can, even going as far as sucking the tip of the egg into his mouth, while sticking out his tongue to swirl around the edges. It's so erotic, and I can feel my core heating with each swipe of his tongue.

Once the egg is coated, he holds it by the string, that sexy smirk of his back again. "Here you go."

Fuck, those three little words, combined with everything else, has probably ruined my knickers to the point I will need to throw them away, or maybe just burn them.

I don't know what the hell possesses me to utter the next words that come out of my mouth, but once they're out in the world, there's no turning back.

"Can you do it for me?"

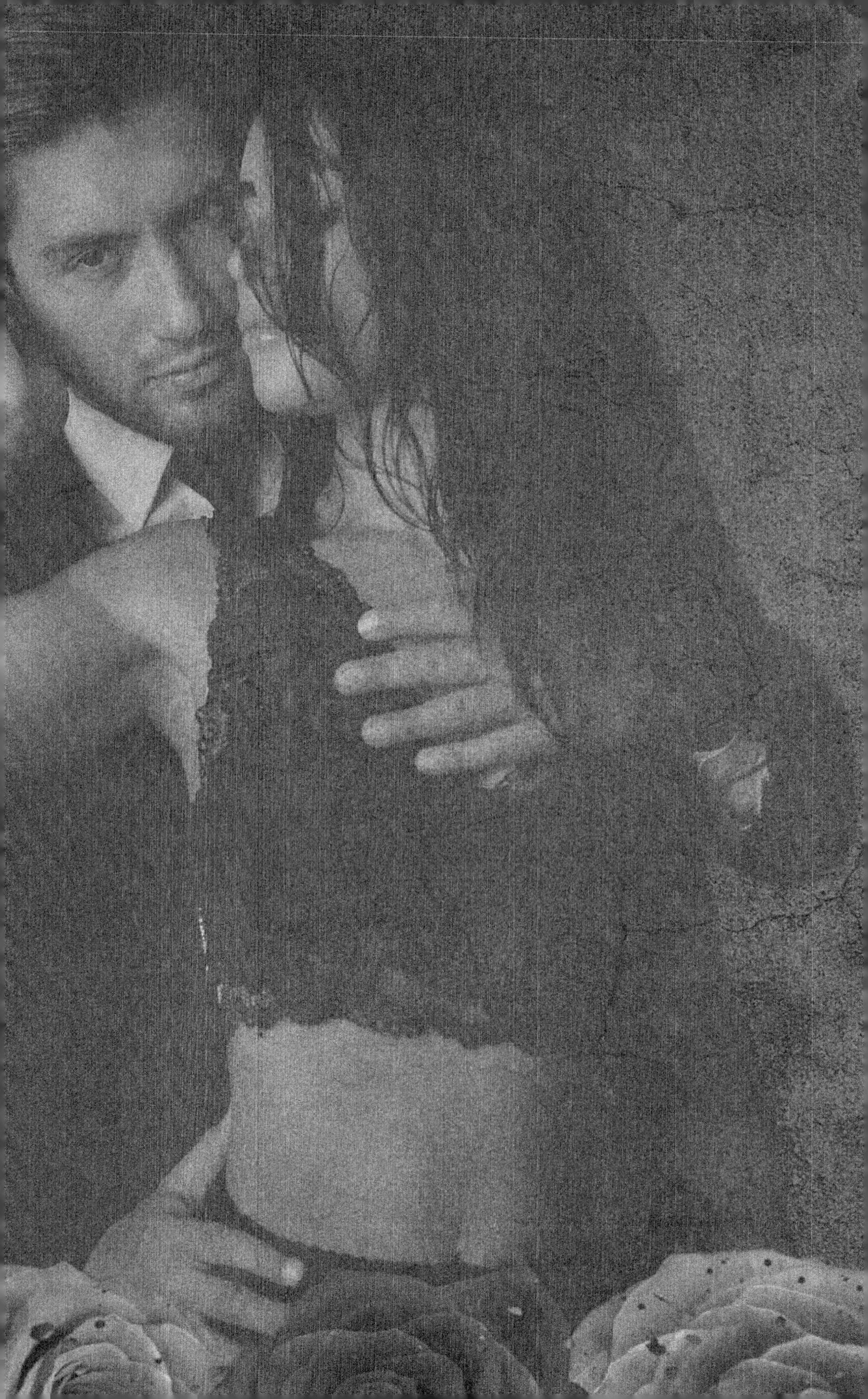

Chapter Fourteen
Marcus

"Can you do it for me?"

Those few innocent words nearly brought me to my fucking knees. This is supposed to be Chloe's punishment, so why does it feel like I'm the one who's being tortured?

After she changed out of that ridiculous outfit she was wearing, and took off the excessive amount of make-up, she emerged from her room looking exactly like the woman I've gotten to know over the last week. But also the girl I've been trying not to see from afar for years.

I don't think I've ever gone this long without fucking a girl, but why the hell would I go looking for something meaningless and random when I have the most gorgeous woman waiting in my house?

Granted, I can't touch her yet, and the blue balls it's giving me is starting to become a fucking nightmare, but I know we're getting closer.

I'm showing her that she can trust me, whilst also helping her take back control of her body. At this point, I'm starting to think that whatever her secret is, it can't be worse than the horrors I'm imagining inside my head. So much so,

I'm already plotting the brutal deaths of everyone involved. I know someone has broken Chloe, and I intend on making them pay.

But first, I'm going to help her gather all her broken pieces, so she can create an even stronger version of the woman she was before.

I take a deep breath as I keep my gaze locked on her sparking silver eyes, startled when I see no hesitation reflected back. I swallow hard, hoping when I speak that my voice doesn't betray just how close I am to breaking all my rules.

"Take your knickers off and bend over the back of the sofa," I instruct, my voice thankfully holding firm.

Even though she looks a little nervous, she barely hesitates for a second before she reaches up under her little white dress and begins removing her knickers. As the hem of her dress lifts, I catch sight of more of her creamy thighs, and my cock twitches painfully.

Even though I wanked in the shower before getting dressed in preparation for today, my dick clearly can't remember, growing harder with each bit of flesh she exposes. I bite the inside of my cheek to hold back my moan as she slides white lace down her legs.

Once she steps out of them, she holds the knickers in her hand, clearly unsure what to do. Without thinking, I reach over and take them from her, stuffing them into my jeans pocket. Her eyes widen comically as her gaze flicks rapidly between my face and the pocket now housing her underwear.

"What are you doing?" she blurts out, making me chuckle.

"I'll give you these back when you need them. Now, bend over."

She looks like she's about to argue with me, until she catches sight of my stern expression, reminding her that I will add to her punishment if she continues to disobey me.

Her eyes narrow at me in a scowl, but that's the extent of her rebellion as she slowly moves towards the back of the sofa.

I can't help but smile, when she's not looking, at how fucking adorable she is when she's trying not to sulk. I like her rebellious streak, but I fucking love when she obeys me.

Once she reaches the sofa, she begins to lean over it, her chest moving towards the cushions as her back curves, forcing her arse to stick out. Her dress has risen up, and I can see the roundness of her arse cheeks peeking out underneath the hem.

My cock throbs painfully, and I have to grip myself through my jeans, readjusting slightly to dull the ache that only seems to be growing the longer I look at her sexy body, bent in the perfect way, presented to me.

Then she turns her head until she's looking over her shoulder at me, a shy but mischievous smile on her face as she asks, "Is this how you want me?"

Fuck, yes! I've seen her in this position so many different times in my dreams, but my imagination has vastly let me down on this one—the real thing is so much better.

I walk towards her slowly, wanting to drag this moment out for as long as I can, mentally saving this image for later.

I want to remember every minuscule detail, every curve, so that when I wrap my hand around my dick later, this will be the exact image I see. I want it to be perfect.

The closer I get, the more my fingers start to twitch with the overwhelming urge to touch her, and that's when I remember that I can't. It's going to be hard enough putting the damn egg in without doing more, but I doubt I'll be able to stop if I touch her the way I want to.

"Reach back with your hands, pull your dress up above your waist, and then spread your arse cheeks wide," I say, my voice raspy with lust.

Her eyes sparkle as the flush on her cheeks spreads down over her neck, creating a trail that I want to follow with my lips. Even though she's slow with her movement, almost hesitant, she follows my instructions without complaint.

As soon as her dress is bunched around her waist, exposing her bare cunt for me, a groan rumbles from my throat, and I don't even try to hide it.

Chloe looks shocked that the noise came from me, but as soon as she sees my hand cupping my denim-covered hard cock, her eyes sparkle and her smile widens.

With both hands, she reaches back and parts her arse cheeks, showing me her glistening pink pussy, and I'm so fucking gone. I moan loudly, taking a step closer to her.

"So fucking gorgeous, Mio," I growl. "You have no idea how much I want to touch you right now."

I watch her throat bob as she gulps, looking a little nervous, before her shy voice asks, "So why don't you?"

I can feel my resolve snapping as this fucking gorgeous girl makes me forget all my own rules. Seeing her wet and waiting for me, it's like my own personal brand of kryptonite. She's my weakness, and at this moment, I don't even fucking care.

I take a step forward, fully intending to take her for myself, when a buzzing in my jeans pocket pulls me out of the moment. I scowl, wondering who the hell I'm going to have to kill for interrupting me.

I hold a finger up to Chloe, indicating I need for her to give me a moment, as I pull the phone from my pocket. I let out a string of curse words when I see it's a text from Miles.

> **MILES**
> We have to leave in five minutes. You're already late. Whatever you're doing, stop. I will come up and drag both your arses down if you're not in the car in five minutes. And before you threaten me, these are the orders you gave me. It's my job to make sure you both get to lunch, no matter how much neither of you want to go.

Another string of expletives leave my mouth as I consider, for just a moment, if I could manage without Miles if I kill him. When I've determined he's too valuable to me, so I can't murder him, I vow to come up with a way to give him a case of blue balls to rival my own.

Miles rarely dates, or fucks around, so it will be hard, but when the time comes, I vow to cock block him just as badly as he's just done to me.

There's a very small part of my brain saying this is probably a good thing. I was about to go too far, throwing all of my rules out of the window, but more importantly, I forgot that I'm supposed to be doing this to help Chloe, not just because my dick is so painfully hard it might genuinely fall off soon.

"Everything okay?" Chloe asks, her gaze scanning my face, assessing me. I smile when I see she's still in the same position, exposed and wet for me.

"Yeah, everything is fine. It was just Miles, threatening to come and get us if we don't go down to the car soon," I explain.

Chloe looks torn between standing up and going to the car, and staying where she is to follow my rules. Thankfully, her submissive side wins out and she stays still.

"I better put this in quickly so we can go."

I bring the egg to my mouth once more to make sure it's still wet enough. Her hands are holding her open wide enough for me to see her entrance, but I kneel down to get a better look.

Once I'm on my knees, I'm so close that I'd only have to lean forward the slightest bit and my tongue would be on her clit. I'd know what she tastes like, but we both know when that happens, a taste will not be enough.

Gently, I use the tip of the egg and slide it through her slit, capturing as much of her juices as I can to help. Her gasp as she feels the egg touching her most sensitive place is like music to my fucking ears, and is part of the reason I press a little firmer when I reach her clit.

Chloe lets out a long, deep groan and I almost come in my boxers. The urge to tease her more is overwhelming, but the last thing I want is for the arsehole I call my best friend to storm in here and find Chloe bent over the sofa.

So, I slowly slide the egg back down, stopping at her hole. I press forward slightly, hearing Chloe's sharp intake of breath as I begin pushing the egg into place.

As the largest part of the egg stretches her, Chloe hisses, and I grip her arse cheek, kneading her flesh to distract her. "Take a deep breath, Mio. Almost there."

"Okay," she whispers, her voice shaky and gravelly, but she does as I instruct and pulls in a deep breath.

As she breathes in, I gently press the rest of the egg in, watching with fucking amazement as her tight cunt swallows it, closing until only the string is left slightly visible.

"Ohhh," Chloe moans as the egg gets deeper into her pussy, filling her.

I reach up and capture both of her wrists in my hands, pulling them away, so she can stop holding herself apart. I almost groan in pain when I can no longer see her wet slit spread open for me, but the image is seared into my brain for all eternity, and that will have to do for now.

I give her arse cheeks a squeeze, simply because I'm not ready to stop touching her yet, then I push up from my knees to stand over her. I take a moment to appreciate the view from this angle, wondering what it would look like watching my cock plunge into her while she's bent like this.

Focus, arsehole. You have to leave now, I remind myself.

After giving her arse one last stroke with the palm of my hand, loving the way she trembles beneath my touch, I lightly trace my hand up over her hip, until I reach the hem of her dress. Begrudgingly, I cover her exposed flesh.

"Stand up," I instruct, helping to straighten her dress as she does.

Chloe stands in front of me with a strange look on her face, and I can't quite decipher what it means.

"Are you okay?" I ask.

She nods her head, though her brow is furrowed like she's not completely sure. She shifts around from one foot to the other, and her mouth falls open into an O. "It feels so strange...and full."

Fuck, I can just imagine how tight she is.

"You should try walking a bit," I suggest, since discussing how tight her cunt is didn't seem like the right thing to say.

She nods at me, her hand still in mine as she takes a few tentative steps. After the first couple, her scrunched up face starts to relax, when she realises whatever she's feeling isn't as bad or as strange as she maybe was expecting. But after a few more, her eyes widen and her brows shoot up as a little moan slips free.

"Fuck," she groans.

My cocky smirk grows as I can only imagine what she's feeling. "What?" I ask innocently, which earns me a glare.

"At first I just felt sort of full, but when I walk around, there's an almost enjoyable pressure when the egg hits my more sensitive spots. I can feel the pleasure building each time it happens. It's not enough to make me come, I don't think, but it feels good," she explains.

I give her a mischievous grin. "Don't forget, this is supposed to be a punishment. It's not about making you come, Mio."

"What? So you're just going to drive me crazy, push me to the edge, but never let me come?" she asks, looking a mixture of confused and angry.

"I might let you come, but that all depends on if you're a good girl for me. You have to take your punishment first. Now, we better go before Miles comes storming in to get us," I say, heading towards the door, pulling her behind me.

Chloe squeezes my hand to get my attention, and I turn to look at her. "I need my knickers, Marcus."

I shake my head. "You'll get them back when I decide." She opens her mouth to argue, but I cut her off. "Don't argue with me or you won't get them back at all."

She looks stunned. Her eyes narrow at me, and the glare she throws at me is sharp enough to wound me, if I weren't enjoying myself so much.

She pulls her hand out of mine, the only act of rebellion she can think of, and folds her arms across her chest, her bottom lip sticking out in a pout.

Thankfully, she doesn't argue and follows behind me as we make our way to the car. Miles is standing beside it with a face like a slapped arse, throwing a glare at me that rivals the one Chloe is giving me too. I roll my eyes at them both.

"You're late," Miles says through gritted teeth.

I point over at Chloe. "Sorry, someone needed a little help getting ready."

Her eyes widen for a second before she's back to shooting daggers at me when she hears me blame her for our tardiness. Miles doesn't seem to believe me anyway, tutting at me as he opens the car door for Chloe.

"You look lovely, Chloe," he says, as he helps her climb in.

For just a second, a moment of irrational jealousy that I've never experienced before threatens to overwhelm me, and I genuinely consider stabbing my friend.

Then the logical side of my brain reminds me he's just being nice, trying to put her at ease, and I climb into the car with a groan, wondering where the hell that possessive side of me came from.

"Thanks," Chloe mutters as she slides into the back seat, pulling at the hem of her dress as she does, clearly not wanting to show off any more flesh, or risk flashing too much.

Once both me and Chloe are seated in the back, Miles climbs into the front and turns on the engine. He looks at me through the rearview mirror, and we have a silent conversation that we've perfected over years of friendship.

I motion for him to put up the privacy window and he rolls his eyes at me, the threat in his gaze more than evident, but he does it nonetheless.

Chloe watches as a window begins to rise in the middle of the car, partitioning off the front seats from the back. It's a very handy tool if I need to have important meetings or calls that I don't want to be overheard, or in this case, if I want to do something I don't want someone else to see.

Although we can still see Miles, he can't see us because of the one-way privacy glass. It's also soundproof, so no matter how much noise we make, until we activate the intercom, Miles won't be able to hear anything.

Once the window is up, Chloe looks over at me, no doubt wondering what the hell is going on, but when she finds me on my phone, she seems to relax just a tad. She doesn't interrupt me, assuming that I'm working—I'm not. Instead, I'm messing with the settings on my phone, waiting for the perfect time to play.

Chloe turns away from me to look out of the window, relaxing back in her seat. She shifts about for a second, her brow furrowed until she finds a position that she's most comfortable in. When she's relaxed, that's when I activate the egg.

I start on a low setting, but even that's quite powerful when you're not expecting it.

"Oh shit," Chloe groans, her body tensing as she sits up straight, her eyes widening as she turns to look at me.

My lip tilts into a smirk as I watch the flush on her cheeks redden, her eyes darkening with lust. Her body becomes rigid, since she's not used to the sensations, but as her mouth falls open on a moan, she begins to shuffle around.

"Something the matter?" I ask, sounding just as cocky as I intended.

She turns and scowls at me, but before she can come back with what I'm sure is a witty retort, I turn the level on the egg up a notch.

A moan rips from her as she arches her back from the chair, sticking her tits out in the most fucking gorgeous way. She moves her hands out to her sides, looking for something to grab hold of, but settles for clenching them into fists when she can't find anything.

Her eyes are dark and hooded, her cheeks flushed with small droplets of sweat appearing on her brow as she pulls her bottom lip in between her teeth, no doubt trying to fight back the noises she's desperate to make.

Loving the way her body is reacting, I turn the egg up to the middle level, and she's not able to stop the moan from escaping this time.

Her eyes lock on mine, and I'm not sure what she's trying to say, but they're pleading with me for something. The silver in them is barely visible, looking almost black as her pupils are blown so wide with lust.

I watch as Chloe begins to rotate her hips whilst clenching her thighs together. She almost looks like she's humping the seat, her pelvis rocking as she tries to chase the pleasure the egg is giving her.

"Oh fuck," she mutters. "So good. It feels...so, so fucking good."

I chuckle as her words become more unintelligible, my eyes drawn to the hypnotic way she's rolling her hips. She then lifts one of her hands and begins to massage her breast, rubbing her thumb over her nipple until the stiff peak is showing through her white sundress.

I'm mesmerised as she controls her body, embracing the feeling the egg is giving her, whilst helping to get herself off. I imagine what she'd look like sitting on my cock rolling her hips in this way, rubbing her nipples as I grab hold of her, pulling her down onto me hard.

"Fuck, I'm so close," she moans, her eyes screwing shut as she loses herself in the sensations.

The corner of my lip tilts as I watch, one hand gripping my cock tight enough to help ease the growing ache as it presses against my jeans. It's almost fucking painful, and the urge to pull it out and stroke myself as I watch her grows.

"Shit, I'm going to come," she whispers, followed by a long drawn out moan that echoes around the car.

Her hips rotate quicker, her fingers squeezing her nipple just a little harder as she chases her pleasure. Her face is scrunched up, but her mouth has fallen open as she throws her head back against the seat of the car.

Just when it looks like she's about to come, I quickly turn off the egg.

"Motherfucker," she shouts loudly, her eyes flying open as she turns to glare at me. "What the fuck?"

She then moves her hand over her thighs, trying to slide it between her legs, but I grab hold of her wrist.

"Don't even think about it, Mio. Have you forgotten the rules already?" I snap, trying to keep my stern expression.

She looks a little startled, before saying, "Sorry."

I have to bite the inside of my cheek to stop myself from smiling. "What's the rule?"

Chloe deliberately looks down at her legs, pulling her dress down from where it's risen up as she does. "I'm not allowed to come without permission."

I nod my head. "And were you about to come without asking me first? From where I'm sitting, it looks like my dirty little whore was so lost in her own pleasure, she forgot all about making me happy."

"I forgot to ask," she admits, sneaking a quick glance at me out of the corner of her eye. I keep a stern look on my face, though it's getting harder to do.

"This is supposed to be a punishment. Do you think bad little sluts like you should be allowed to come during a punishment?" I ask, loving the way she shivers when I degrade her.

She shakes her head. "No."

I pause for a moment, watching as she continues to shuffle in her seat, desperate for just a little relief, and then a wicked idea enters my head. "That's right. How badly do you want to come right now, slut?"

"So badly. Please, can I?" she asks, fluttering her lashes at me.

I do a long dramatic pause, as though I'm thinking, when really the thought is already there, but now I have time to actually consider the outcome, I'm starting to worry. Still, I say it anyway.

"If you are really that desperate to come, then you can…" Her eyes light up and she begins to smile, until I continue with the catch. "But only if you open the partition and let Miles see and hear everything."

The deer-in-headlights look is back, and she shakes her head rapidly, narrowing her gaze at me until it becomes a glare. My heart stutters when I hear her say, "Not a fucking chance."

That's the outcome I was hoping for, but for just a moment, I wondered if she was desperate enough to do it. I'm normally not territorial or possessive, and it's a test I've put a couple of women through.

Miles doesn't really care, and is used to my antics. But the thought of him seeing Chloe in that way makes my skin prickle, and I start to feel nauseous.

It would appear I'm more protective and possessive over her than I first thought. Normally, that thought would consume my brain for a long time, as I try to work out what the hell it means, but I don't have time for that, so I try to push it away, knowing it will no doubt rear its ugly head when I least expect it.

"Well, it would appear you're not all that desperate to come then," I state, my voice sounding almost sing-song.

Her scowl deepens. "I will never be desperate enough to have an orgasm in front of people."

She sounds so sure of herself, I can't help but chuckle. "We'll see."

"What the hell is that supposed to mean?" she snaps, her hand on her hip as she glares at me defiantly.

"Mio, you've only had an introductory lesson in edging so far. Just wait until

I've been edging you repeatedly for days, refusing to let you come after bringing you to the edge multiple times an hour, every hour, for days.

"After a while, you lose all sense of propriety and standards, embracing the dirty whore you are just for me, and you won't give a shit where you come or who is watching, just as long as you get the release your cunt desperately craves."

With each word, her breathing starts to increase until she's almost hyperventilating. I can almost hear her heart beating out of her chest as she picks at the skin around her fingers.

Her eyes travel from confused to annoyed, to intrigued, to out right turned on, and it's clear that even though the thought is a little daunting for her, if not horrifying when she first heard it, there's also an element of intrigue, and that's the part I was hoping to see.

"I-I...I don't... I'm not..." She struggles to produce a proper sentence, and I have to bite my inner cheek to stop myself from smiling or chuckling at how flustered she's getting, the redness on her cheeks spreading down her neck now.

"It's fine. I won't make you do anything you're not comfortable with. I think we should probably have a proper conversation about all of this when we get home tonight," I explain, and she lets out a sigh of relief.

Although I lean more towards being Dominant during sex, I'm not immersed in the BDSM lifestyle. I don't do scenes or contracts, and I don't have to dominate each time we fuck. But that doesn't mean I'm not aware of some of the elements that come with the lifestyle.

I wouldn't ever do an official contract, but I always make sure that whoever I'm with is aware of the situation before we get into anything. Chloe is the only person I've ever broken this rule for.

Normally, I make sure the woman is aware that this is most likely a one-time thing, and that I will never want a relationship.

I usually make sure we agree on the adequate form of contraception—insisting on using a condom, but I prefer if she's on the pill too—and I make sure neither of us have any sexually transmitted diseases, for obvious reasons.

I also find out exactly what they're into, and more importantly, what it is they are not willing to try. There might be things they've never tried before, but are open to experimenting, and if those things align with what I like, then I'll happily give them a go.

This has always been important for me, as I never want to go too far with a woman. I may not give a shit about seeing them again, or even remember her name, but that doesn't mean I want to traumatise her in any way. I want her to walk away from the experience just as satisfied as I am.

So why the fuck have I clearly forgotten all of these rules with Chloe?

I may be refusing to touch her, but I'm barely keeping to that rule, and some of the stuff we've done so far are things I wouldn't dream of entertaining before going over the rules.

Then I remember that she has trauma in her past that I don't know anything about yet, and I want to stab myself for being so fucking stupid. Knowing this, I should be extra hesitant with her, abiding to the rules more closely, not forgetting them.

It's pure fucking luck that I've not triggered her yet, and I can't have that happen. If she's not going to trust me enough to tell me what happened to her, we definitely need to establish boundaries.

Well, we can do that tonight, as I want to see where this punishment leads first. Fuck, I really am being led around by my dick, even when my brain is screaming at me to think logically.

"I get the feeling that conversation is going to be really bloody awkward," she says with a laugh. "But it's probably necessary. As long as you know there might be things I don't answer."

I nod my head in understanding. "The conversation isn't just another tactic to get you to share your secrets. I know you'll tell me when you're ready. This is about making sure we're on the same page, and that I'm not pushing you too far out of your comfort limits."

Before I've even finished my sentence, she bursts into laughter, throwing her head back with a bright smile on her face.

"Marcus, I'm about to have Sunday lunch with my family wearing no knickers, with a vibrating love egg in my vagina, whilst trying to hold back any noises that give away how fucking amazing it feels… I think we passed my limits a little while ago."

The sound of her laugh is almost hypnotic and my stomach flips, though I'd never admit that for fear of sounding like a lovesick teenage girl. I shake my head, my smile growing as I see how much brighter she looks when she's truly happy.

"Trust me, we're not anywhere near your limits yet. I'll admit this is to push you, but if it were a limit of yours, you'd never be doing it. You'd have refused, and I'd have let you, but you didn't. You can hide it all you want, but there's a dirty slut hidden inside, and I intend on bringing her out, just for me."

Before either of us gets the chance to say more, the car comes to a stop and the engine is turned off. Miles waits a few seconds, like he always does before beginning to bring down the partition window.

Before it's open, I reach over and pull Chloe's skirt down, making sure Miles doesn't see more than he should.

"We're here," Miles shouts as he climbs out of the car to open Chloe's door.

I watch as she shuffles to the edge of the seat, biting her lower lip as she tries not to make any noise, even though I'm sure the love egg is making her incredibly hot, given how close to the edge she was not too long ago.

I open my door and climb out, just as Chloe reaches my side with Miles trailing behind. Without thinking, I hold my hand out for hers. She looks down, her brow furrowing at what I'm sure is an unexpected gesture.

I'll be honest, I'm not entirely sure why I did it, it just felt right. After just a couple of seconds of hesitation, she reaches out and grabs my arm, looping hers through mine, in a much less personal way than holding hands.

I hate the way my stomach drops, and I push it away, plastering a blank mask on my face, so she doesn't see how affected I am. As we begin walking towards the front door, she leans in closer so that only I can hear.

"I want nothing more than to hold your hand, Marcus, even if I was a little shocked you offered. But, do you see that red car over there?" she asks, pointing to the obnoxiously bright flashy sports car that's parked a couple of spots down from ours.

"Yes."

"That is Scott's car. I had no idea he would be here, but walking in with you will be bad enough, I don't even want to imagine how much he'd kick off if we were holding hands," she explains, grimacing when she says the name of her fiancé.

"Shit," I mutter, wondering why the hell he's here.

I want to tell her that I don't give a shit about Scott, or what anyone else thinks. They know she belongs to me for the next few weeks, and that entails whatever I say it does. But that will be opening a can of worms I'm not prepared to deal with right now.

The door in front of us opens, silencing us both. Caleb Santoro is waiting on the other side, his face twisted into a scowl as he drags his gaze over the both of us, no doubt taking in our relaxed attire compared to the sharp suit he's wearing.

As we reach the entrance, he plasters a fake smile on his face, and holds his arms open wide. "Chloe, darling, it's so lovely to have you home again."

Chloe freezes beside me, clearly not used to her father being so openly affectionate with her, letting me know this is all an act—what I've yet to figure out is why.

With a quick glance at me, she gives her father a tight smile before dropping my arm to allow him to embrace her. Even from here I can tell it's an uncomfortable, forced gesture. "Hi, Dad. Nice to see you again."

As soon as he drops his arms, Chloe takes a step back to my side, and Caleb turns to me, his smile now a lot more forced. "Marcus, we're so glad you could make it."

The smirk that I'm wearing is definitely not fake. I have a feeling I'm going to enjoy this lunch more than I should. Particularly if Scott is here too. "I wouldn't have missed it for the world."

Caleb looks startled by my jovial tone, but remembers the manners a rich guy like him is supposed to have, and ever the gracious host, he opens the door wide and gestures for us to come in.

I step through, but before Miles can follow, Caleb holds out his arm. "I don't think it's necessary for you to have your security here, given this is supposed to be a family meal."

Miles looks like he's about to argue, but I cut him off. "Then consider him here as a family friend."

"That's not—"

Caleb starts to protest, but to my amazement, Chloe interrupts him. "I invited him, Dad. He's here as a friend, not security."

Both myself and Miles turn to Chloe, no doubt wearing matching shocked expressions, but it's nothing compared to the murderous glare Caleb is throwing at his daughter. He's obviously just as surprised as we are to see Chloe talking back for the first time. I can't help but think I'm rubbing off on her already.

I'd really fucking love to be rubbing off on her, I think, my mind taking a very dirty mind, until Caleb interrupts my inappropriate train of thought.

"Fine," he grinds out. "Follow me."

Without even looking at us, he walks away, leading us through the maze of hallways, towards their formal sitting room. Chloe wraps her arm around mine again, pulling me closer to her with a smile. She looks over her shoulder at Miles and motions for him to follow us.

"Thanks," he mutters so only we can hear.

I'm not sure what we would have done, but I know my friend well enough to know that he would never have let me step foot in this house without at least one member of security.

While we have a peace treaty in place with the Santoros right now, it doesn't change the fact we are rival families, and the agreement will always be fragile, particularly if they find out I'm defiling their only daughter after I promised I wouldn't touch her.

"No problem. Just try not to kill anyone. Either of you," she says to us both, but her fierce glare is fixed on me.

I roll my eyes. "I make no promises."

"He'll be on his best behaviour," Miles states, discreetly punching me on the arm in a warning.

Before I can retaliate, we reach the formal sitting room. I take a moment to scan the room, force of habit given the world I live in. I'm always doing a risk assessment, looking for threats, as well as identifying all the exit routes, or anything that might be suspicious.

I know Miles is doing the same, probably to a much higher standard than me, but my father raised me to be constantly vigilant, as there are plenty of people out there who want me dead.

Chloe's mother, Fiona, is sitting on the edge of the sofa, one foot hooked behind her other ankle, her back completely straight—the picture of high class etiquette.

She's wearing a matching skirt suit in a pale pink colour, a white blouse underneath, with matching pink heels. I'm sure, given how posh the outfit looks, it's designer, and I'd hazard a bet that the jewellery she's wearing would buy some people a house.

For her age, she's not a bad looking woman, but it's clear she's had a lot of work done to keep up with the younger society women. There was a big scandal almost a decade ago when Mrs Santoro came home from a break with new tits.

Eighteen-year-old me was very impressed, as they were a hell of a lot bigger than what she had before, and she wasn't afraid of showing them off.

Now, a decade later, they look out of place on her. It's not known how many other surgeries she's had, but if I had to guess, I'd say she's definitely had a face lift, liposuction, a bum lift, as well as lots of rounds of Botox and lip fillers.

I'm not sure there's anything natural about her at all, which is ironic as she's desperate to come off as a natural beauty. It's why she insists on Chloe wearing a shovel full of make-up, with the purpose of making her look like she's not wearing any.

What she doesn't realise is that her daughter is a natural fucking beauty, and she looks amazing without any make-up.

Caleb takes a seat on the sofa beside Fiona, picking up his amber drink from the coffee table in front of him. He doesn't bother to make any introductions, just gulps down his drink, ignoring the tension in the room.

On the wingback chair beside their sofa, Jacob is lounged back, looking worse than the last time I saw him. I catch Chloe out of the corner of my eye, wincing when she sees her brother.

He's got dark bags under his eyes, and his skin looks pale and clammy. His head is tilted, resting on the back of the sofa, like he doesn't have the energy to even hold his head up.

Jacob is usually immaculately dressed, as he's had the same lessons drilled into us as I have since we were little. Though today, he looks like he's wearing the same crumpled clothes from last night, and given he appears to hardly have had any sleep, that's not a great surprise.

I then catch sight of Scott on the opposite sofa, a little shocked to see his father beside him. He's got grey hair and a beard, but other than that, he's a match for Scott.

Since the Caprillos are aligned with the Santoros, my family don't have much dealings with them, though I know my father has met with Ewan Caprillo on occasion.

As I stare at his slightly familiar face, I wonder if I've met him before too. There are so many people in our line of work, and I struggle to remember all the people that are loyal to me, let alone those loyal to the Santoros.

I'm a little startled that out of everyone in the room, Ewan is the one to speak first.

"How lovely to see you again, Chloe, dear," he says in an extremely fake, cheery voice as he stands from his place on the sofa, and reaches out a hand for her.

Chloe freezes beside me, her gaze flicking between all the people in the room. She lets go of my arm, releasing a small sigh as she does, before stepping forward to shake his hand.

"It's nice to see you too, Mr Caprillo. I wasn't expecting you, so it's good of you to join us."

"Well, after hearing the news that the wedding was being delayed, I thought it was best to come in person to make sure everything is alright," he states, his voice taking on an edge that I don't appreciate.

His gaze flicks over to me, and it's clear I'm not his favourite person. Naturally, that makes my cocky smirk grow.

"Everything is good, thanks for asking. I know you've mostly had dealings with my father, but as a formal introduction, I'm Marcus Morelli," I state, sounding just as much of an arsehole as I intended to.

"I know who you are," he snarls, looking down his nose at me.

"Clearly, you don't. If you did, you'd know the right amount of respect to show me," I reply, my voice taking on a dangerous edge.

Chloe places her hand on my arm, no doubt as a warning, and Miles takes a step closer to me, always having my back. The older man wrinkles his nose, looking murderous, and that makes me smile even more.

Scott clearly has a higher sense of self-preservation, as he quickly stands. "Marcus, let me formally introduce you. This is my father, Ewan Caprillo."

Though he's addressing me, he's giving his father a pointed stare, motioning with his head for the man to offer me his hand.

When he begrudgingly does, I almost want to refuse, but Chloe squeezes my arm, looking up at me with those bright silver eyes of hers, and I relent. I shake his hand, making sure to squeeze a little tighter than is necessary.

As I'm doing that, I watch Scott turn to Chloe, dragging his leery gaze over her body for just a fraction too long. "Chloe, baby, I've missed you."

His tone is sickly sweet, and Chloe freezes when she hears the term of endearment, her grip on my arm now so tight it will probably leave bruises. I drop Ewan's hand and turn to scowl at Scott.

How the fuck can he miss her? He's only met her a couple of bloody times!

"I-I, erm—" Chloe mumbles for something to say, only to be interrupted by her mother, who has at some point moved to stand on her other side.

"I'm sure Chloe has missed you a great deal too, haven't you?" There's a hard edge to the last part as Fiona shoots daggers at Chloe.

"Yes," Chloe replies through gritted teeth, forcing her lips into a tight smile.

Thankfully, one of the household staff that works for the Santoros walks in then, breaking up the increasingly thick tension in the room.

I don't recognise the young man, but Caleb goes through staff like nothing I've ever seen. I'm guessing he's awful to work for.

The young man sounds incredibly nervous as he speaks. "Can I get any of our new arrivals a drink?"

Chloe lets out a sigh of relief, grateful for the interruption. "Yes, please. I'll take a glass of rosé."

Fiona scoffs. "We're having roast beef for lunch, Chloe. You'd be better with a red Bordeaux," she states, before turning to the young man. "Bring her a small glass of that instead."

Chloe seems to deflate before my eyes, giving her mother a tight smile and a polite nod. Anger sizzles beneath the surface of my skin, making me twitchy. "Actually, I'd prefer a glass of rosé too. I'm happy to share a bottle with Chloe."

The young man seems a little startled, and all eyes flick over to me. Chloe appears both relieved and a touch concerned that I have the balls to stand up to her mother.

Fiona and Caleb are both glaring at me, as are the Caprillos. Jacob is so out of it, I'm not even sure he's aware of what's happening right now.

Silence fills the air, the tension becoming thick as we all wait, seeing who will be the first to break. The young man, whose eyes have become wide and scared the longer we've all stood there, is the one who speaks first.

"I'll grab you those drinks right away," he squeaks, practically running out of the room.

"We should probably move into the dining room. Dinner will be served shortly," Fiona says haughtily, trying to sound like the gracious host, but struggling to keep the venom out of her tone as she looks at me.

It's actually sort of strange, as me and my father have always been treated with the utmost respect whenever we've visited the Santoros home in the past.

For a moment I wonder if this bet, claiming Chloe as mine, even just for a few weeks, is really worth all this. I mean, the relationship our families have been building for years is on rocky footing for the first time in decades, and it's all my fault.

I know I should feel bad, and I should be prioritising the peace treaty we have with the Santoros over anything else, but I can't. There's something about Chloe, and now that I've had a sample, I don't know how the hell I've managed to push her away over the last few years.

Her family filters into the dining room, Scott and his father walking with them, whilst me and Chloe hang back for a second. Miles has stayed by my side, just as I expected he would, and I look over to the chair, only to find Jake's eyes closed.

Chloe leans closer to me, shaking her head, a look of despair on her face. "He looks so much worse than last week," she says, her voice breaking at the end.

I move over and kneel down in front of Jacob, placing my hand on his shoulder to rustle him awake. He doesn't even murmur, so I use both hands to jostle him more forcefully.

His eyes spring open as he jolts up, his head flicking around as he scans the room, a startled expression on his face. "What the fuck? What's going on?"

Chloe kneels down beside me, and I smirk when I hear her hiss, no doubt from the love egg rubbing her in just the right way as she moves. She places her hand on her brother's arm and gives him a comforting smile.

"Hey, bro. You fell asleep. I'm here for Sunday lunch."

His eyes flick between his sister and me, like it's taking a few minutes for his brain to catch up, but once it does, his gaze narrows on me, though he talks to his sister.

"Are you okay, Clo? Is he looking after you? You can tell me if he's done anything he shouldn't have done."

I ball my hands into fists at the assumption that I'd ever hurt Chloe. It irks me that someone who is supposed to be my best friend, who has known me for most of my life, would even suspect me of being capable of something like that.

Chloe looks over at me, and the bright smile she gives me is enough to calm my growing anger.

"Marcus is taking really good care of me. I'm actually having a great time. In fact, I was going to ask you to come over some day next week, so we can catch up properly. You know, without prying eyes and ears."

She nods her head towards the dining room, reminding us that any conversation we have here could potentially be overheard.

Jacob looks over at me, no doubt waiting for me to confirm Chloe's story. "It's true. I'm taking care of her, but I know you won't believe me, so you can come over and see with your own eyes."

"Fine."

Chloe's eyes light up. "That's great. How about Tuesday evening? We can all have dinner?" She looks so hopeful, there's no way I'd turn her down.

"I'm available," I confirm.

Jake looks between us, no doubt seeing the way Chloe is smiling at me, that shy blush on her cheeks that she gets when she's thinking naughty things while looking at me, and he lets out a reluctant sigh.

"Fine, I'll be there."

Before either of us can say anything more, Caleb's booming voice echoes through from the other room. "Children, join us in the dining room, now. It's rude to keep our important guests waiting."

I see the way both Chloe and Jacob bristle at being called children, and I let it slide that I'm probably their most important guest. I stand, reaching out for Chloe to take my hand, so I can help her up.

She takes it, and once we're standing, instead of letting go, she laces our fingers together as we head towards the corridor that leads to the dining room.

Jacob eyes our joined hands and lets out a frustrated huff as he climbs to his feet. Before he's even made it fully upright, he begins to wobble, swaying from one foot to the other.

He tries to take a step before he's ready and he loses his footing, stumbling forward as he sways.

It's clear he's going to fall, but both me and Chloe are too far away to do anything about it. Just as I'm expecting him to hit the floor, he doesn't.

Miles, with his super-fast reactions, has sprung into action, and grabs hold of Jacob before he face-plants the floor.

Miles' arms are wrapped around Jacob as he pulls him back up, helping him to find his feet, even though he's clearly still wobbly. As soon as Jake's feet are firmly on the floor, and he's no longer bobbing around, he looks up at Miles.

Miles is a few inches taller than Jake, and is looking down at him with concern, and something else I don't quite recognise. There's a moment where they're just looking at each other, as if neither can believe Miles got there in time to help Jake, and the tension between them grows.

Then, out of nowhere, Jake's face scrunches into a scowl and he brings his arms up in between them, placing his palms on Miles' chest. He pauses just for a few seconds before pushing him away. Miles is so shocked by the action, he stumbles back, eyes wide and confused.

"Get the fuck off me. Who the hell do you think you are? Don't ever fucking touch me again," Jacob yells, pushing Miles again in an act of aggression.

I move to step in, but Miles shoots me a stern glare with a slight shake of his head. This isn't just about the fact he can look after himself—which I know he can—this is also about who Jacob is, and the peace treaty we have to maintain.

Not to mention, both Jake and Miles are my friends, and if I get involved now, it'll look like I'm choosing sides.

Although I've been friends with them both for years, Miles and Jacob aren't friends themselves anymore. I've no fucking clue when it happened or why, but I think we were around seventeen-years-old when they just stopped seeing each other as friends, and they basically pretended one another no longer existed.

I've asked them a million times if something happened, and they stringently deny it, stating that they both realised they're from very different worlds, and didn't get on without me there as a buffer.

I didn't believe them, but after a year of trying to force them to get along again, I gave up.

They seemed quite content just being cordial with each other when needed, whilst otherwise pretending the other person doesn't exist. This is the first time there's ever been any open hostility between them, and it catches me off-guard.

I know Jacob's high, and that's not helping, but the way he's looking at Miles, and speaking to him with such venom, makes it very fucking clear these two had a falling out.

Great, another fucking problem I'm going to have to solve.

Miles takes a step towards Jacob, looking angry and confused. He grabs hold of Jake's shirt, scrunching it into his fist as he pulls Jacob towards him.

"Push me again, Pretty Boy, and I'll make you regret it."

There's a venom in Miles' voice that I've not heard in a long time, and Jacob is right to look scared. His eyes are wide open, but his nostrils flare as he scowls at Miles.

He brings one of his hands up to grab Miles' wrist where he's holding onto his shirt, but uses the other to try and push him again.

This time, Miles isn't caught off-guard, and he doesn't move. Jacob isn't small, and before he started going off the rails with drink and drugs, he used to work out regularly, and he still has some of that bulk and strength, but he's let himself go too much to be any sort of match against Miles.

Although Miles isn't big and bulky like you'd expect a security guard to be, he's on top of his fitness, and he's a lot stronger than he looks. He lifts weights and does a lot of cardio, so despite his lean appearance, it's all muscle, which is why Miles doesn't falter even a step when pushed by Jake.

"How dare you fucking threaten me? This is my house. Don't you know who I am? Get the hell out of here, now!" he yells, looking almost manic as he snarls at Miles.

Miles rolls his eyes and laughs. "Do you have any idea how much you sound like a pampered fucking prince, Pretty Boy? Next you'll be telling your daddy on me, while throwing your gold rattle out of your pram."

Well, that doesn't help to calm Jacob down at all. In fact, I rush forward quicker now when I see him pull his fist back, getting ready to strike.

Luckily, Miles' has seen it and grabs hold of his hand before he's able to make a move, and I get there just in time to grab Jacob and pull him away from Miles, who looks to be enjoying the situation far more than he should.

"Jacob!" Chloe shouts, grabbing his attention. "What the hell are you doing? Miles stopped you from falling, and that's how you repay him?"

Jacob drops his gaze to the floor, looking thoroughly chastised by his sister. For a moment, it seems like he's going to say something, but loud footsteps pull our attention to the corridor.

"What the fuck is going on in here?" Caleb shouts, taking in the scene before him.

I've got my arms wrapped around Jacob, clearly restraining him, while Chloe looks frazzled by the whole situation. Miles is standing off to the side, looking far more amused than is appropriate right now, and I can just imagine the conclusions Caleb is jumping to right now.

Chloe, who is thinking quicker than the rest of us, jumps in. "Sorry, Dad. Jacob wasn't feeling too good, and when he stood up, it looked like he was about to faint. We were all just checking on him, making sure he's well enough before we came through."

Caleb takes one look at his son, and it doesn't take long for him to believe the story.

"You do look like shit, Son. Drink a glass of water, pull yourself together, and for fucks's sake, no more alcohol for you. We'll talk about this tomorrow. The rest of you, get your arses into the dining room before my wife has an aneurism."

Caleb turns on his heel and storms off. I loosen my hold on Jacob as I ask, "You good?"

"Yes," he mutters, though I'm not entirely sure he believes himself.

"Right, then let's get this damn lunch over and done with," I say, walking over to Chloe's side.

She takes my hand in hers without thinking, and I look over my shoulder at Miles and Jacob, who haven't moved.

"This isn't over," I tell them threateningly. "I want to know what the fuck happened here, and I won't be fobbed off."

I leave no room for discussion, pulling Chloe with me as I lead her into the dining room. Footsteps follow behind us, but their quiet whispers are too low for me to hear what they're saying. At least they aren't arguing.

Chloe leans in, tugging on my arm so I tilt down a little, just enough that she can whisper in my ear. "I'll be glad when this fucking meal is over. I have a feeling it's only just beginning."

A mischievous smirk spreads across my lips as I look down at her. With my other hand, I reach into my jeans pocket and pull out my phone. Chloe's brow furrows in confusion, and I turn to her at the same moment I press a button on my phone.

The love egg she'd almost forgotten about begins to vibrate as I turn it onto the lowest setting, her mouth falling open as she looks at me in panic. "You're right, this is only the beginning. You didn't forget about your punishment, did you, Mio?"

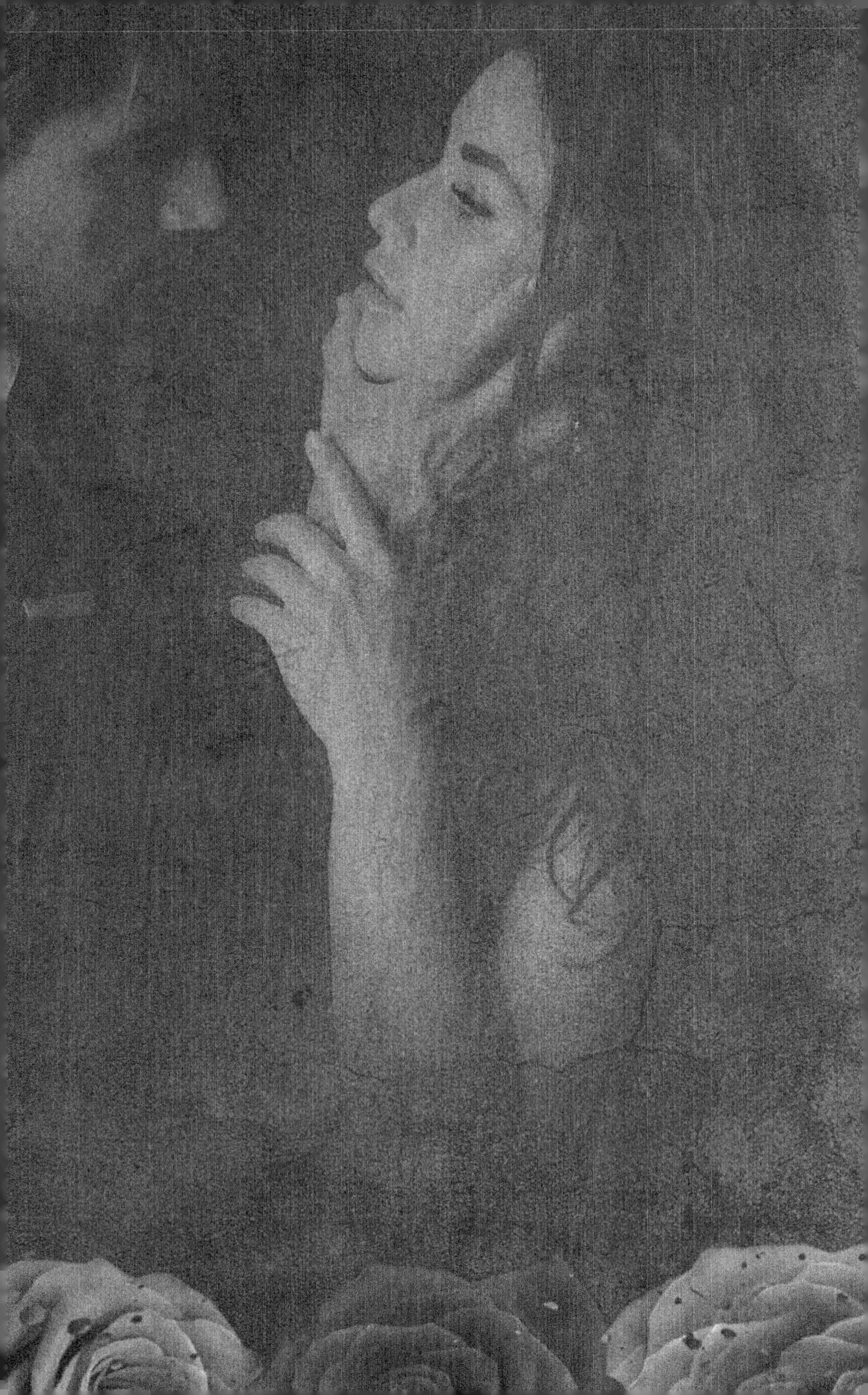

Chapter Fifteen
Chloe

J ust when I thought this fucking meal couldn't get any worse, Marcus activates the bloody love egg. I mean, it's not like I'd forgotten it was there. It's more I'd gotten used to the full feeling.

Although everything is extra sensitive—especially after Marcus took me to the edge in the car before leaving me hanging—the egg is giving off more of a pleasant fullness than anything else.

Whenever I walk, it rubs in the most delicious way, but the sensations aren't enough to do anything more than get me even hotter than I already am.

That is until he starts the vibrations. I know it's only on the lightest setting, but after being so close to an orgasm earlier, the sensation is making my legs go weak.

I look over at Marcus, my eyes pleading with him, but that cocky smirk of his just grows, and I don't know whether I want to slap him or kiss him. He's too fucking sexy for his own good.

My brain is an absolute mess. I was already a nervous wreck about coming home, not knowing what to expect. Then Marcus encouraged me to change, to step away from the rules my parents forced on me when I was living with them, and although I can't deny it felt totally freeing, that doesn't mean I'm not anxious as hell.

As soon as we arrived, Dad looked like he was ready to tear the peace treaty up and go to war with Marcus right here, and it was made even worse by some arsehole inviting Scott and his father. Talk about a stupid fucking decision, which had everyone on edge.

Then my mother took one look at how I was dressed, and her face morphed into disgust. She looked at me the way you'd look at your shoe after you realise you've stepped in dog shit. Still, she tried to control me, making decisions for me about the type of wine I should be choosing.

I'm not going to lie, when Marcus stood up to her on my behalf, had I been wearing any, my knickers would have been ruined without the aid of the egg. I've never really had anyone stand up for me before, and I stopped fighting for myself a long time ago, so to see him do that, it broke down one of the many walls I've built around my cold, fragile heart.

If the start hadn't gone bad enough, then there's the whole mess with Jacob. I knew he was going through a rough time, but I've only been gone a week and he's almost unrecognisable. He's a mess, and his eyes are wide as saucers after taking fuck knows what.

Then he started on Miles and it was like I'd been transported into the fucking Twilight Zone. I didn't know whether to hit him or cry. I hate seeing my big brother so messed up, but I'm fucking furious that he'd take it out on Miles like that.

I got the feeling there was something going on between them that I was missing, and the threat Marcus threw their way tells me he doesn't know either, but he wants to find out just as badly as I do.

My head is already a mess of confusing information, and all the thoughts that accompany the punishment are almost too much. For a moment, I'm so lost in the sensations from the egg, feeling the fullness and the vibrations, that all rational thoughts leave my brain completely—then the panic returns.

Oh, my God, is he going to keep doing this while we're having lunch?

Is he going to turn it up, because if he does, I'm not sure I can cope with that?

How the hell am I supposed to sit still with the vibrations buzzing around, driving me crazy?

Can anyone hear the vibrations?

Fuck, I really need to moan...

My brain is moving a million miles a minute, and I can hear Marcus' evil chuckle beside me as he continues pulling me towards the dining room. He leans in closer until I can feel his breath against my ear, sending a shiver along my spine.

"This is the ultimate test of how much control you have over your body, Mio. You have to control yourself, your facial expressions, and especially your noise. It won't take much for your whole family to see exactly what's going on.

"Whilst I like knowing what a dirty little slut you are, it's just for me, nobody else. That little cum-stain, Scott, will never know the noises you make when you come, so I expect you to hide them. Do you understand?"

As soon as he says Scott's name, he scowls, looking furious at the idea that Scott might one day know exactly what I sound like—though I doubt even when he's my husband that he'll be all that concerned with my pleasure. I'm guessing he's a selfish lover.

"I-I...I don't know if I can," I confess.

The vibrations are making my nerve endings prickle, and my whole body feels like it's an electric current buzzing around, just waiting to explode, and I'm not sure I know how to stop that from happening.

"You have to. If you're a good girl and take your punishment, I'll make sure you're rewarded."

My heart stutters when he calls me his *good girl*, and I blame the brain fog on the next words that slip out of my mouth. "Will you be my reward?"

His eyes darken as that cocky smirk of his morphs into a rare genuine smile. "Do you want me to be?"

I don't even hesitate, I'm nodding my head rapidly before he's even finished asking his question. "Yes!"

He chuckles, and my cheeks flame at how eager I sound. To be fair, this damn love egg is driving me crazy, and I've been desperate to come since the car, so I'm not exactly thinking rationally. But it doesn't change the fact that I want him—I've wanted him for a long time—I'm just now being honest about it.

"And what exactly are you willing to give me?" His voice has taken on a low growl, whispered in my ear for only me to hear.

That's when I realise we're standing in the entrance way to the dining room, and everyone who is already seated is staring at us.

I give Marcus my best flirty smile as I say, "Anything and everything."

He lets out a low groan, his darkened gaze letting me know he's very pleased with that suggestion. "I'll remember that."

With a tap of his phone, the vibration ends and I let out a sigh of relief, though the smirk on Marcus' face lets me know this definitely isn't the end of my punishment.

Is it wrong that I'm kinda pleased by that?

Focus, I mentally tell myself as I look around the table, trying to find the best place to sit. I never thought deciding where to sit would be as tactical.

My dad is at one end of the table, my mother at the other. Ewan is seated on Dad's left side, with Scott beside him. There's an empty chair between Scott and my mother.

On the opposite side of the table, there are three empty seats, and so I pull Marcus towards them.

Before I can get around the table, my mother stands and stops us. I don't miss the way her gaze flicks down to where Marcus' fingers are clasped with mine, or the way her eyes darken and her nose wrinkles.

"Chloe, darling, you take this seat here beside me. That way you can catch up with me, and we can do a bit of wedding planning with Scott," she says cheerfully, gesturing to the empty seat between her and Scott.

Marcus' face darkens, his free hand balling into a fist by his side, and he looks to be seconds away from arguing with my mother.

Before he can, my father's booming voice interrupts us. "Jacob, come and take your seat beside me."

My brother doesn't bother to argue, he just keeps his head down as he walks towards my dad's end of the table. He sways a little, still looking a bit unsteady on his feet.

Miles, for some strange reason, follows behind Jake, looking like he's ready to catch him if he falls again.

I have no idea why Miles is showing Jake even the tiniest bit of kindness after the way he treated him, but it just confirms to me that Miles is one of the good guys.

Once Jacob has taken the empty seat beside my father, Miles takes the seat next to him, opposite Scott. Which leaves just one seat remaining, and Marcus has no choice but to sit between my mother and Miles, opposite me.

I can tell he's not happy about it as he's still not let go of my hand, or made any attempt to move towards the chair.

"I'll be fine," I say to him, giving his hand a reassuring squeeze before I reluctantly let go. My skin feels cold, almost like it's mourning the loss of his warmth.

I lower myself into the chair my mother gestures to, and watch as Marcus walks around the table, pulling out his own seat with a huff.

I have to bite my lip to prevent myself from gasping as the amazing sensations in my pussy become more intense when I'm seated. If it's possible, I feel even fuller.

I ball my hands into fists, trying to focus on keeping my breathing normal as my heart rate begins to speed up.

Once we're all seated, only a few seconds later, several members of staff flood into the room. They all have something in their hands, and I can't keep track of what each of them are doing.

One of them brings wine, filling up everyone's glass with a deep red vintage, though there's another person who brings rosé for me and Marcus.

Another person places freshly baked bread rolls onto the mini plates beside us, while someone else brings out tiny pots of handmade butter.

As they're all moving around with expert precision, not once getting in each other's way, four more servers enter, each carrying two bowls of soup, which they place down in front of all of us at the exact same time.

Once the soup bowls hit our placemats, the man overseeing the whole process, our long-term butler, Bastien, who is standing at the head of the table beside my dad, claps his white-gloved hands to get our attention.

Bastien is an older man, probably in his early sixties, and though he's worked for my family since I was a child, I know very little about him. I was always told not to talk to the help, and would regularly get into trouble whenever I did.

"Your first course is a luxurious homemade mushroom soup, made with freshly foraged ingredients, and served with a soft, fluffy sourdough roll that was handmade this morning, along with lightly salted butter that was hand-churned by our staff," he states proudly, the slightest hint of his French accent still present even though he's lived in England for the majority of his life.

My mother preens beside me, puffing out her chest as she smiles fakely.

"Thank you, Bastien. We pride ourselves in making sure that the staff here make everything from scratch, and that we use all local ingredients. It's important we support local companies," she states, talking to nobody in particular.

When the hell did she start using that super-posh voice? Has she always put on a really snooty, high-pitched voice when we have company and I've just never noticed?

Whenever I'm forced to attend things like this—and that's often given my parents love to entertain guests as it gives them the perfect opportunity to show off—I tend to blank the events out, moving through them on auto-pilot. Still, you'd think I'd have noticed my mother using a fake voice.

"That we do, darling. Now, let's eat," my dad says, giving my mother a large smile.

As we all dig in, I hope like hell we can eat in silence to get this meal over with quicker. I should have known I wouldn't be that damn lucky.

Scott leans closer to me, and as he's a bit taller than me, this gives him the perfect angle to leer at my cleavage from above.

His face is closer to mine than I'd care for it to be, but I keep my eyes on my food, trying to let him know I'm not interested in talking to him.

"So, Chloe, how have you been? I think we should start talking about the wedding, and more importantly, my expectations for when we're married," Scott states in what I'm sure is supposed to be a seductive tone.

I turn to face him, concern spiking through me at the way he's grinning at me. "What do you mean?"

His eyes light up, and it's obvious I just walked right into his plan. "Well, once we're married, there will be certain rules you'll need to follow, and expectations you will have to meet, but as my wife, you'll want nothing more than to please me."

My grip on my soup spoon tightens to the point I'm surprised the silver hasn't bent. My whole body is tense, and I'm sure he can see that reflected in my stern expression, yet Scott doesn't seem to care.

"Like what?" I ask through gritted teeth.

This is one of those moments in life where I know I'm not going to like the answer, yet I can't help asking the question anyway—and as soon as Scott opens his mouth, that's confirmed.

"Well, for starters, I will set ground rules on what you can wear and the image you want to present to other people. Whilst I like you in this dress, you have skin on show that I wouldn't want anyone but me to see," he says, trailing his finger down my bare arm for emphasis, before dropping his hand to my thigh, trailing his fingers down until he touches the exposed flesh there too.

I freeze, squeezing my eyes shut as I bite the inside of my cheek so hard that I taste copper. Small droplets of blood hit my tongue, but I barely register them as all I can feel is his hand on my leg.

When Scott starts to speak again, his voice is even closer, his lips are practically touching my ear. "I will love taking you whenever I want, however I want. In fact, I might make it a rule that you have to be naked every evening, waiting on your knees for me in the bedroom, ready for me to give you some attention, but only if I choose to."

His hand begins to travel higher, under the hem on my skirt, and my stomach rolls. The small amount of bread and soup that I've managed to eat threatens to make a reappearance, and my heart is pounding so fast, if my eyes were open, I'd probably be dizzy.

"I expect my wife to follow my every command. You will attend high society functions if I say you can, and you'll organise charity events that make me look good, but other than that, your only job will be to make me happy.

"You can go out to make yourself look better, so manicures, pedicures, waxing, massages, things like that, but that's all. No friends, no hobbies... Your whole life will revolve around me, your husband. Do you understand?"

My heart is racing as panic seeps into my bones and I can barely catch my breath. I squeeze my eyes shut tighter, hoping this is all a nightmare and I can make it go away.

Then I feel Scott's fingernails digging into my sensitive flesh. He's squeezing so hard, I'm surprised he's not drawn blood. There will definitely be bruises.

"I said, do you understand?" He sounds more angry than he did the first time he asked me, and I know I need to reply, so I don't wind him up more, but I don't think I can make my voice work.

A short sharp buzz from the table distracts me enough to open my eyes. The sound of a text message coming through on my phone is both a welcome relief and a bit confusing, as everyone who normally texts me is sitting in the room with me.

I reach over to pick up the phone and Scott's grip on my leg tightens. "It's rude to use your phone at the dinner table, Chloe," he chastises, sounding like my mother.

I turn to him, trying to find as much confidence as I can muster so that my voice doesn't shake. "Sorry, but it might be important."

I quickly use my fingerprint to open the lock screen on my phone, and for the first time I'm grateful for the privacy film that Marcus insisted on me putting over my screen.

I thought it was just paranoia, but he insisted, and I couldn't be arsed to argue—now I'm glad, as Scott can't read the screen from his place beside me.

If he were really desperate, he could hover behind me and he'd be able to read it with no issues, but it'd be clear to everyone what he's doing, and I'm guessing since Scott is still trying to keep up appearances, he doesn't do this. His grip on my thigh, however, remains firm.

> MARCUS
>
> I'm about thirty seconds away from taking out my hidden gun and shooting that cunt in the head. Is he hurting you? After the soup, excuse yourself to the bathroom and text me.

I look up at Marcus, but his gaze is fixed on his soup, like he's completely unaware of the situation around him. I should have known he'd notice what Scott was doing.

I'm not even a little shocked to learn he's got a hidden gun. Surprisingly, I feel safer knowing that.

Although Marcus appears uninterested to the casual observer, I've gotten to know him well enough over the last week to see he's anything but. He's gripping his spoon so tight, his knuckles have turned white. His other hand is under the table, no doubt edging closer to his weapon the longer this goes on.

While his eyes appear to be fixed on the spoonfuls of soup he keeps bringing to his lips, I catch his gaze flicking over to me constantly before moving over to Scott. His eyes darken and his murderous expression flashes for just a second, making him look more dangerous than normal.

I quickly slide my phone into the small clutch bag I brought with me, that's sitting on the table beside me, knowing that will make it easier for me to take my phone with me if I'm able to pull off this plan.

Once my eyes meet Marcus', I give him what I thought was a discreet nod, but when Scott's nails drag hard across my skin, I'm sure he saw. I hiss before quickly biting my lip to stop any more noise from slipping out.

Scott leans in closer, anger practically radiating off him now. "No wife of mine will be a whore. If you look at him again while I'm in the room, when you become my wife, I will beat your arse with my belt so badly, you won't be able to sit down for a week. Not that I'll care. As long as you can still kneel to swallow my dick, that's all I need."

I look over at Scott and see that he means every single word. His eyes have darkened, and his lips are pressed into a tight line. Instead of looking dangerous, like Marcus does, he just looks like an angry little man who is trying to exert power over me, and whilst I may be scared shitless, there's a very small part of me that's trying to fight back.

I try to channel all the confidence Marcus has been trying to instil in me, and as I lean closer to Scott, I imitate Marcus as best I can. "If you even think about putting your tiny cock anywhere near my mouth, I'll bite it off."

For just a fraction of a second, his eyes widen in shock, and that little part of me that's been silenced for so long does a leap of joy, but then his expression darkens, his nostrils flaring as rage takes over.

"Why you little bitch—"

Just as his grip on my leg becomes too painful, my father puts his spoon down loudly, clinking it against the China as he speaks to the room. "Well, that was lovely. Did everyone enjoy their soup?"

As mutters of approval flood around the table, I take the opportunity that's presented itself. "Yes, Dad, it was really delicious. May I be excused just for a moment, so I can use the restroom?"

I hate the fact I'm a grown woman asking for permission to use the bathroom, but my family has strict rules, and nobody gets up from the table before my dad without his permission.

My mother, sounding like I'm disappointing her once again, chimes in. "Really, Chloe. Disrupting dinner like this isn't appropriate."

It takes every ounce of willpower not to roll my eyes at her, particularly when Scott joins in to support her. "Your mother is right, Chloe. It's rude to leave the table in the middle of dinner. I'm sure you can wait."

The edge to his tone makes it clear he doesn't want me to argue with him. Out of the corner of my eye, I see Marcus getting twitchy, looking like he's about to intervene.

That's when I see Miles reach over to place a hand on his arm, before he leans closer to him, no doubt telling his friend to calm down. I'm grateful for Miles' help, as Marcus would only make this situation worse.

I need to say something, and quickly. Then I remember the one trump card all women can play when they're being controlled by men. "If I could wait, I would. Without going into details that aren't appropriate dinner conversation, I'm simply going to say that I need to be excused due to women's issues."

The room, made up predominantly of men, goes silent for a moment. Those magic words had more of an effect than I was expecting, as Scott quickly removes his hand from my thigh.

I almost laugh at the absurdity that a grown man is worried he might accidentally touch menstrual blood. But, hey…the plan works better than I could've imagined, and I fight to hold back a smile.

My father clears his throat, sounding uncomfortable. "Of course, you may be excused, darling."

I give him a grateful smile as I stand, smoothing down my skirt as I push the chair back so I can get around it, grabbing my bag as I do.

As I'm about to turn around, I give Marcus a cheeky wink that only he can see, loving the way he tries to hide his smile as I walk out of the room.

I practically sprint to the nearest bathroom, locking the door behind me as I pull out my phone. There's a message already waiting for me from Marcus, and I don't hesitate to read it.

MARCUS

Good girl, you followed my instructions well. Now, tell me, was that cum-stain hurting you? What was he doing?

CHLOE

As he leaned in to speak to me, he put his hand on my upper thigh, which is when I started to freak out. When he got annoyed with me, his grip tightened, and his nails dug in a lot. I think it'll bruise, but he hasn't drawn blood.

There's a pause, and I can see Marcus has read my message, but he's not typing anything. I've not heard a gunshot, or any kind of commotion, so I'm assuming he's just trying to pull himself together before replies.

MARCUS
Anything else?

CHLOE
No. Just stuff he said, that's all.

MARCUS
Like what?

CHLOE
Too much bullshit to go into details in a text, but he was letting me know what he'll expect from me when I become his wife. He also said that if I look at you one more time while he's in the room, when I do go to live with him, he'll beat my arse so badly with his belt that I can't sit down for a week.

MARCUS
Motherfucker.

CHLOE
Apparently he doesn't need me to be able to sit, as long as I can kneel and swallow his cock, that's all he wants.

MARCUS
I'm going to kill him.

CHLOE
Don't worry. I told him that if he even thinks about putting his little dick anywhere near my mouth, I'll bite it off.

MARCUS
Good girl!! I'm still going to kill him. But only after I've peeled the flesh from his fingers. I hate that he touched you.

Fuck, that statement alone should scare the shit out of me, but instead, I get a tingle down my spine that confirms just how much Marcus' dangerous side excites me.

And his possessiveness... I'm trying not to read too much into it, but it's almost like he really does see me as his. I'm just not sure if that still comes with a ticking clock attached.

Prized Possession

> CHLOE
> I wouldn't say no to that, but if I'm going to have to marry him, I guess you can't really maim him.

Why the fuck did I just send that?

I don't know if there's some part of me that's trying to poke a very agitated dragon just to see what he does, or if I'm just an idiot.

I wait for a little while, and no text comes. I'm staring at my phone, my grip on it tightening the longer the message remains read but unanswered.

Just as I'm about to give up and put it away, the vibrating egg starts again, startling me to the point I have to bend over and grab the sink cabinet.

Fuck, I think he's put the egg on a much higher setting, and my whole body feels like it's on fire. My core is heating up, getting me wetter as my grip on the counter and my phone tightens.

Then I hear the tell-tale buzz of the phone, letting me know he's finally text me back. I can barely hear it over my heartbeat pulsating through my ears. A soft moan escapes, and I have to bite down on my lip to stop any more noise from getting free.

I try clamping my legs together, but that only makes things more intense. I can't help squirming around, trying to get into a position that helps alleviate some of the ache.

That's how I end up leaning over the counter, my arse in the air, my legs spread wide as I rotate my hips to help the egg move around.

I look like I'm waiting for someone to come along and fuck me from behind, and shit if that idea doesn't really bloody appeal to me right now.

In the distance, I hear another buzz coming from my phone, and I drag myself back into the moment just enough to check my messages, knowing exactly who they'll be from.

> MARCUS
> You are not fucking marrying him. And for reminding me of that, I'm going to start the punishment again…
>
> How does it feel, Mio? You better not forget the rules.

Shit, does he really expect me to be able to text him back while I'm like this. I can barely get my brain to work for long enough to read his messages, let alone send another back. Before I can, another message comes through.

> MARCUS
> You better come back now. People are wondering where you are.

My breath hitches as I realise what he's saying. He wants me to go back into the room while the egg is vibrating like this. I can barely stand upright.

I pull myself together long enough to reply to him.

> **CHLOE**
> Please, it's too strong. I can't walk, let alone come back in the room and have dinner with my family.

> **MARCUS**
> You want me to lower the setting?

> **CHLOE**
> Yes, please.

> **MARCUS**
> If I do that, what do I get?

> **CHLOE**
> Anything. Whatever you want, you can have it.

> **MARCUS**
> That's a dangerous thing to promise a man like me, but I'll accept.

Before I've finished reading his text, the egg drops down to a much more manageable level. The vibration is still intense, but that's because my body is incredibly sensitive already.

It's a small miracle that I didn't come. The egg gets me all hot and bothered, but it isn't enough to push me over that edge.

Once I've caught my breath, I send Marcus a quick text before quickly making my way back to the table.

> **CHLOE**
> Thank you. I will make it up to you. I'll be a good girl, just for you 😊

I get to the table just in time to see Marcus reading my message, and the way his blue eyes darken makes my core tighten. He looks up at me and the fire I see shining back is enough to make me shiver. I really wish dinner was over so that we can go back home.

"Is everything okay, Chloe?"

I'm aware of people talking around me, but my attention is solely on Marcus and the way he's looking at me like he wants to devour me. It's not until my mother places her hand on my arm that the fog lifts.

I blink a couple of times, trying to clear the sex-filled haze that's descended over my brain, as I look over at my mother.

"Jacob asked you a question," she says, looking very annoyed that she's having to talk to me. She even points over at my brother, so I can follow along.

I look across the table, only to find that everyone is staring at me. Miles and Marcus look amused, Jacob seems concerned, while everyone else appears to be annoyed at me.

I fix my gaze on my brother, slightly shocked to see he's participating in the discussion at all.

"Sorry, Jake. What did you say? I missed it."

"I just asked if you're okay?" he replies, his gaze flicking between myself, Marcus, and Scott.

"I'm fine, honestly. Just women's problems that I won't go into," I say, giving him a small smile to try and reassure him.

My dad cuts in, "Great, now we can enjoy the main course."

As soon as he announces that, the room floods with staff once more. The same pantomime continues as they bring food, announcing how fresh and homemade everything is, while my parents boast and preen like damn peacocks.

I'm distantly aware of what's going on, but the gentle vibrating continues to pull my attention away. I try to keep an ear out, in case anyone talks to me, but it's not easy when my whole body feels like it's on fire.

My mother decides this is the perfect time to discuss wedding planning, and the more questions she asks me, the harder it is for me to focus. I can see Marcus getting more agitated, to the point he's cutting his meat with far more aggression than is needed.

"We will have to find a time to go wedding dress shopping. It's already going to be hard enough getting a dress at the last minute, and since you're not small enough to fit in a sample size, that will only make it harder," she says, looking down her nose at me.

Before I can respond, Scott cuts in. "What's the difference between Chloe's size and the sample sizes?"

"Well, wedding dresses do run on the smaller side, but I suspect Chloe would need to drop a dress size to fit in a sample," my mother replies, dragging her gaze over my body in a less than satisfied way.

Scott shrugs his shoulders. "Well, I'm sure Chloe can drop a dress size before the wedding. I'd actually prefer that."

I must have fallen into some kind of bizarre world. My mother and my fiancé are basically calling me fat, telling me I need to drop a dress size before getting married to a man I hate, while the man I do want to be with sits opposite me, glaring at everyone like he wants to kill them, all while a fucking love egg vibrates in my pussy, driving me crazy.

When the fuck did this become my life?!

"You can do that, can't you, Chloe?" My mother directs her question at me, though I'm not really sure she's even looking for me to respond.

Scott clearly doesn't need me to reply, as he does it on my behalf. "Of course, she can. I'll set her up with a personal trainer I know, and they can sort her out with a diet and exercise regime that will make her look amazing."

"Absolutely fucking not," Marcus snaps, hitting his fist on the table, startling us all.

"Marcus, you—" My mother starts to address Marcus, but he simply cuts her off.

"In case you've all forgotten, Chloe will be with me for the next few weeks. Which means it's my decision if she gets a trainer or not. And I will not allow it. She doesn't need to lose any weight, she looks amazing the way she is," Marcus snaps, and I can't keep the smile off my face that he's sticking up for me.

"That's not your fucking decision to make. She's going to be my wife. This thing with you is just temporary, and you'd do well to remember that," Scott snarls, glaring at Marcus while he sits there with that cocky smirk of his.

I expect him to fly off the handle, but I'm surprised to hear Jacob cut in. "Actually, Scott, you're the one who needs to remember your place. You may be aligned with us, but we rule side-by-side with the Morellis. Meaning, Marcus is just as much your superior as I am.

"You may not like that he owns Chloe for the next few weeks, and you have a right to be unhappy about it, but you must never forget the hierarchy. Marcus is a leader, and you will show him the respect he deserves.

"You'll also honour the agreement made between me and him regarding Chloe, whether you like it or not. If he says she doesn't need a trainer and won't be going on a diet, you will honour that, and quite frankly, I agree with him. Do I make myself clear on this?"

Everyone around the table has matching looks of astonishment on their faces. I think that's the most I've heard Jacob say in a long time, and I don't think I've ever seen him so authoritative.

Although Scott looks pissed, he nods his head at Jacob, giving him the respect he demands. Through gritted teeth, and despite him clearly not wanting to, Scott turns to Marcus. "My apologies for stepping over the line."

"See that it doesn't happen again," Marcus deadpans, clearly refusing to accept Scott's poor attempt at an apology.

I have to bite my lip to stop from laughing at the way Scott balls his hands into fists. He's grinding his teeth so loudly, I can almost hear them.

Luckily for us all, Scott doesn't attempt a comeback and remains silent, though he continues to glare at Marcus. What's worse is that Marcus isn't paying him any attention, his gaze is fixed on me.

The rest of the meal passes by extremely slowly, and by the time the dessert plates have been cleared away, I'm ready to burst. Although the mild vibration isn't enough to push me to the edge, having it running constantly has left me in a state.

I'm hot, sweaty, and so fucking desperate to come.

"Well, this has been lovely. We'll have to do it again next week," my dad states, and I have to bite my lip to stop a sarcastic laugh from coming out as a snort. This meal has been far from lovely, and I think everyone at the table will agree.

He makes it sound like next week is a suggestion, but we all know it's not.

Ewan, who has remained reasonably quiet for most of the meal, is the first to respond. "I can't thank you enough for inviting us. It's a pleasure to get to know you all better, especially since it won't be long until we're all one big family."

When he says the last part, his glare is fixed on Marcus, waiting for him to react. I'm not sure if he just doesn't care, or if Miles is doing a good job of keeping him calm, but Marcus doesn't even bat an eyelid, let alone respond.

My mother, on the other hand, takes the opportunity to interfere. "Oh yes, we can't wait. Can we, Chloe? We will start wedding planning very soon, making sure it's an event befitting the occasion."

Her eyes are fixed on me, and I know she's waiting for me to respond. "Oh yes, it will be, erm, great."

I couldn't sound any less enthusiastic if I tried, and both Miles and Jacob snicker across the table, though they quickly stop when my mother glares at them.

Marcus, who doesn't look amused in the slightest, cuts in. "Well, we should get going."

"Won't you stay for an after dinner drink?" my dad asks. "That will give my wife and Chloe some time to discuss the wedding."

As my dad is speaking, a wicked grin spreads across Marcus' face, and that's when I feel the vibration on the egg increasing. I let out a gasp, my eyes wide as everyone around the table turns to look at me.

My cheeks are heating, no doubt turning a bright shade of red as I grab hold of my dress, just for something to squeeze.

I bite the inside of my cheek, trying my hardest to remain still, as everyone continues to stare at me, but it's nearly fucking impossible not to fidget with this damn egg setting me on fire.

"Are you okay?" my dad asks, looking at me with concern.

"Sorry, just a bad cramp," I blurt out, struggling to come up with anything better.

There's silence in the room, and I'm mentally praying to anyone that will listen to start talking. I'm worried they'll be able to hear the egg if it stays too quiet.

"We definitely should get going then," Marcus says.

My mother looks like she's going to object, and we're all shocked once more when Jacob interrupts. "Yeah, if Chloe isn't feeling too well, it's best you take her home. I'll see you guys out."

"Thank you," I say, giving my brother a genuine smile.

As I move to stand, the egg must shift slightly, as all of a sudden, it hits just the right spot and I have to bend over, a low groan slipping out. I look up at Marcus, using my eyes to silently beg him to turn the vibration down before I come in front of my family.

"Oh darling, you clearly aren't very well. You need to go home and rest right away," my dad says, looking extremely worried about me. *If only he knew.*

"Here, let me escort you to the car," Scott says as he grabs hold of my hand.

"That won't be necessary. I've got her," Marcus snaps as he takes my other hand in his.

With a bloke on each side, I feel like I'm in the middle of a fucking tug-a-war, and all I really want to do is have a fucking orgasm, not referee a pissing contest.

Jake walks over to us and shakes his head. "Stay here, Scott. I'll see them out. Marcus, lead the way," he instructs, taking my arms from them both so I can walk with him.

Miles grabs hold of Marcus' arm and practically drags him out of the room, but just before he gets to the door, Miles shouts back over his shoulder, "Thank you so much for having us all over for dinner. It was lovely. We'll see you all again at the same time next week."

How Miles can remain so calm in situations like this impresses me, but then again, it is his job to remain calm under pressure. *Maybe he can teach me how to do it?*

He doesn't wait for anyone to respond, and we all say goodbye as we walk towards the car. Jacob hangs back with me, and I'm grateful he's threaded our arms together, as I'm struggling to walk thanks to the damn egg.

Every so often, it hits the most delicious spot, and my legs go weak.

"Chloe, you have to be honest with me, are you safe with Marcus?" Jacob is looking at me with a deep, penetrating stare, almost like he's trying to see what I'm hiding.

"I promise, I'm safe. Come and visit us at his apartment, and you'll see for yourself," I reply, amazed I'm able to keep my voice steady.

"So you're really just unwell?"

Shit, I hate lying to my brother, but I can't exactly tell him the truth.

"It's just cramps."

"Okay, I'll be over on Tuesday evening."

I give him a smile. "Will you make sure you're sober, please?"

He rolls his eyes at me, but I hold firm. "Fine."

I pull my brother in for a hug, but don't hold it for as long as I usually do. Having someone so close to my body, when all my nerve endings are prickling, and I'm so fucking turned on, is not a good decision. Thankfully, he doesn't seem to notice.

Marcus and Miles are standing beside the car when we join them. I let them know that Jake has agreed to visit us on Tuesday. I'm a little shocked when it's Miles that speaks to him.

"Don't even think about showing up hammered, Pretty Boy. If you are impaired in any way, or I suspect you've taken anything, I will send you away without a moment's hesitation. It's my job to keep them safe."

Jake glares at Miles, looking extremely annoyed, but after a brief stare-down, he nods and sighs. "Fine. I've already promised I'll be sober."

"Good, I just wanted to make it clear."

Miles doesn't wait for a response, he walks around to the drivers side and climbs in. "Your bodyguard is an arsehole," Jake grunts, and Marcus chuckles.

"Well, you seem to bring out the worst in him," Marcus replies. "Thanks for agreeing to come and visit on Tuesday. You won't regret it."

"Make sure I don't," he says, before turning to me. "Take care of yourself."

He pulls me in for another hug, and I have to bite my lip and tense my body. It's over quickly, and once he turns back to the house, I climb into the car, Marcus following behind me.

As soon as the door closes, the car starts. I notice the partition is already up, and I waste no time turning to Marcus.

"Please, do something," I beg.

"What do you mean?" he asks nonchalantly, looking far too smug.

"The egg is driving me crazy. I'm so fucking turned on, but it's not enough. I need more." I sound high-pitched and desperate, but I don't care.

"Pull up your dress and show me."

I do as I'm told, shuffling until my dress is bunched up around my waist. I then slip my shoes off so I can pull my feet up onto the chair, as I spread my legs wide. The cool air hitting my exposed pussy makes me gasp.

Marcus' eyes widen as he watches me expose myself to him completely, having lost all my inhibitions. He groans as he sees I'm dripping wet. "So fucking wet, I can see it from here."

"I need more," I beg again. "Please, will you touch me."

Marcus freezes for a moment, and I can see he's warring with himself. He's clearly torn between sticking to his rules and throwing the rulebook out so he can have me. Maybe I just need to push him a little more.

I reach down with one hand and rub my fingers over my clit, a loud moan falling from my lips as my back arches from the overwhelming sensations. His eyes are fixed on where I'm touching myself, my fingers getting wetter with each swipe.

"It doesn't feel as good if I do it myself," I moan, pleading with my eyes.

"Fuck," he growls, though he still doesn't move. "You're going to be the death of me."

This time, I'm the one with the wicked smile as I maintain eye contact with him. "Surely that's not a bad way to die?"

He chuckles as I press harder on my clit, rocking my hips in a way that moves the vibrating egg against that sweet spot deep inside, making me practically purr.

For the first time, Marcus looks torn...almost like he's in pain, and I've never felt sexier. Even though he's the one controlling the egg, and I need his permission to come, so all my pleasure is essentially in his hands, I'm the one that's able to make him come undone just looking at me.

Seeing how much he affects me is making him lose all control, and that's a heady power I never expected.

"Please, Marcus. I need you," I beg once again, my body getting more and more tense as my pussy drips with desire.

"Fuck, if I do this, you *will* tell me what I want to know. Do you agree?"

The way he's staring at me, his eyes alight with so much fire and passion, makes it clear this isn't really a question. If I want him, this is the price I have to pay.

The thing is, I've been thinking about telling him anyway. Not all the details, just enough to placate him.

Although I don't want my secret to get out, I'm beginning to trust Marcus enough to keep it safe. But the real reason is that I crave him too much, I'll spill all my secrets if it means I can have him.

"Yes, I promise."

As soon as he hears the words, his breath hitches, like he wasn't sure I'd agree. His bright blue eyes darken to the point they're almost black and my heart races when he looks at me like he's a starving man who wants to devour me.

"Pull out the vibrating egg," he instructs, and I do as I'm told.

Once I have a hold on the string, I gently begin to pull the egg out. It's still vibrating, and the feel of it moving makes my core tighten, making me extra sensitive. I close my eyes, just allowing myself to feel the sensations as I focus on keeping my breathing even.

As the egg reaches my hole, I feel it stretching me slowly as I pull it out. When the egg is at its widest part, stretching me in the most delicious way, that's when I feel Marcus' large hand on top of mine.

My eyes spring open, but I no longer find him sitting beside me. Whilst my eyes were closed, Marcus lowered himself onto the car floor, kneeling between my legs. Those dark eyes of his are level with my glistening pussy, and I freeze, unsure what to do.

Marcus moves the hand that's over mine and takes the piece of string from me, so he's in control of the egg. He doesn't pull it out further, and the stretching combined with the intense vibrations are driving me insane.

I try to rock my hips, desperate to relieve even just the slightest bit of the ache that's building, but he places his other hand on my thigh, holding me in place.

"You're so fucking wet, Mio," he growls, licking his lips.

"Please. More." I can't even form proper sentences, I just know that I need him to give me what I crave.

He chuckles, the corner of his lip tipping into that smirk that both infuriates me and turns me on, but before I can comment, he starts rolling the egg. At least, that's what I think he's doing.

The widest part is still stretching me, but he's moving it in a way that's doing it even more.

My moans become uninhibited and I'm panting frantically as only his hold on my hip stops me from rocking into the amazing feeling. Yet, still it's not quite enough, and Marcus seems to know that.

"Tell me what you want, Mio. What does my beautiful little whore need?"

"You," I breathe, dragging the word out like a plea.

"You have me."

I shake my head frantically. "No. I need...more."

"Use your words, love," he snaps, his fingers digging into my thigh is a way that I know will leave bruises. Yet, unlike with Scott, I don't care. I want this man to mark me, to make me his.

"Please, make me come," I beg.

Marcus then quickly pulls the vibrating egg out. I go through a myriad of sensations as he does. The stretching and pleasant burning sensation worsens for a second, and then once the largest part is out, the vibrations become more intense around my clit, pushing me right to the edge of insanity.

Once the egg is all the way out, my core feels both numb and alive at the same time, yet there's this awful empty sensation that I wasn't expecting.

The constant vibrations have left my pussy feeling almost numb, yet it's like everything is prickling with heightened sensitivity, and I know it won't take much for me to come now. I just need Marcus to give me that little bit more.

"How do you want to come, Mio?" he asks, his voice deep and husky.

"However you choose. I meant what I said, I'll take you any way I can get you."

Wow, talk about speaking before thinking. I'm just putting it all out there today, aren't I?!

Though, given the way Marcus' face darkens as his eyes become hooded, it appears I've said the right thing. I watch in awe as he brings the egg to his lips and begins to suck my juices from the sex toy.

As soon as he tastes me, his eyes screw shut and he throws his head back with a groan. "Fuck, I shouldn't have done that. I knew one taste of you would make me lose all fucking control."

As his eyes fly open, he moves so quickly I can barely keep up. He throws the egg onto the seat beside me and grabs hold of my arse with both hands, pulling me a little further down the seat until both of my legs are hooked over his shoulders.

I barely have enough time for my gasp to slip free before he thrusts one of his long fingers into my soaking wet pussy. We both groan at the same time, mine turning into a longer moan when he adds a second finger.

His long digits stretch me in the most amazing way, and it's mere seconds before my already sensitive pussy is building towards release.

"Oh, fuck. I'm so close," I mewl, gasping for breath as he rocks his fingers in and out of me, stretching me with each thrust.

"You're so fucking tight, Mio. Fuck, you would squeeze my cock like a vise." His voice is so deep and gravelly, and I can hear the way he's struggling to hold it together.

"Oh, please... Please, Marcus... Please, can I... Can I come?" I mumble in between desperate gasps for air.

"Do you want to come for me, slut? Do you want to come all over my fingers like a good little whore?" he asks, and I am nodding my head so much, I'm surprised my neck isn't aching.

"Yes, yes... I want to come for you."

Marcus pauses for a second, his fingers deep inside, and I'm sure he can feel my walls fluttering around him as I chase my release. He leans in closer until his lips are right over my clit, and he blows air on my sensitive nub, making me shiver and groan.

"This is supposed to be a punishment. Do you think you've been a good enough little slut for me to reward you?"

"Yes." I can't think clearly enough to say anything more.

"Beg me, slut," he says as he starts to move his fingers again, curling them in just the right way that I see stars.

"Fuck, fuck, fuck, fuck," I scream, unable to say anything more.

To make things worse, that's when Marcus presses his lips onto my flesh, flicking his tongue over my clit before sucking it into his mouth. My back arches as a desperate sound I've never made before is ripped from my throat.

"Please. P-please, Marcus. I need… I have to… Can I-I…come?" I beg, my voice becoming more high-pitched and frantic with every flick of his tongue.

He chuckles against my pussy, the vibration sending a tremble through me as I attempt to writhe around, his arm now wrapped around my leg, so that he can press his hand against my lower stomach, keeping me in place.

His fingers and tongue are like magic, and my whole body is on fire. Every nerve is crackling, and I'm teetering on the edge, mere seconds away from falling. I'm holding back as best I can, but won't be able to for much longer.

"Hold on, love. You can do it," he says in between slow licks through my slit.

"No, no, I can't. I need…I need to come. Please. Please. I'll be your good little slut. I'll do anything you want. I promise, I'll do whatever you want, just, please, let me come."

I'm not even sure what the hell I'm saying anymore. All I know is my begging is becoming more frantic as I struggle to keep control over my body.

I'm barely aware of anything going on around me until I feel the car come to a stop and the engine turns off, which means we're home. Any second now, Miles is going to open the door and this will be over.

Suddenly, the very real possibility that Marcus might leave me in this state hits me, and I begin to panic.

"Please. Please. Can I come? Can I come? I'll be good, just for you. I'll be your slut. I need to come now. Please."

Each word becomes more desperate, and Marcus continues pushing his fingers deep into my pussy like he's not heard a word I said.

I reach over and grab hold of his hair, pulling at the dark strands to the point I'm sure it's hurting him, but he doesn't seem to care. He continues licking and sucking my clit, whilst fingering my pussy with increasing speed.

"Come. Now!" He mumbles the words against my clit, but I hear them loud and clear.

As soon as I hear the instruction, my body follows the command.

Every muscle tenses before my orgasm hits me like a fucking truck. My body twitches and spasms as my walls clamp down on his fingers, getting wetter with each moan that rips from my throat.

I cry out as my release rips through my body. My grip on Marcus' hair tightens as my thighs practically squash his head between them. I'm sure my walls are clamped so tightly around his fingers, he couldn't remove them even if he wanted to.

As I look down, Marcus is staring up at me, his tongue out as he gently flicks it over my clit. His dark eyes are hooded, and he's looking at me like I'm the most beautiful thing he's ever seen. I don't even think he's blinking, not wanting to miss a moment of my orgasm.

When the last ripples of my release finally work their way out of my system, I'm panting as I try to claw back some much needed air, but my body finally begins to relax. Marcus pulls his fingers out of my exhausted pussy, making me wince at how empty I feel when they're gone.

I watch with a smile on my face as he lazily licks them clean, making sure to get every drop of me off them. He then leans down, that cocky smirk on his face as he drags his tongue along the length of my slit, making me shiver.

"Now I've tasted you, there's no going back. You're mine," he growls.

His words both terrify me and make my heart soar. All I've ever wanted is for him to want me, I'm just not sure he means it in the same way I do.

This will only ever be about sex for him, whereas I'm ready to give him all of me, even though I'll get my heart broken in the process.

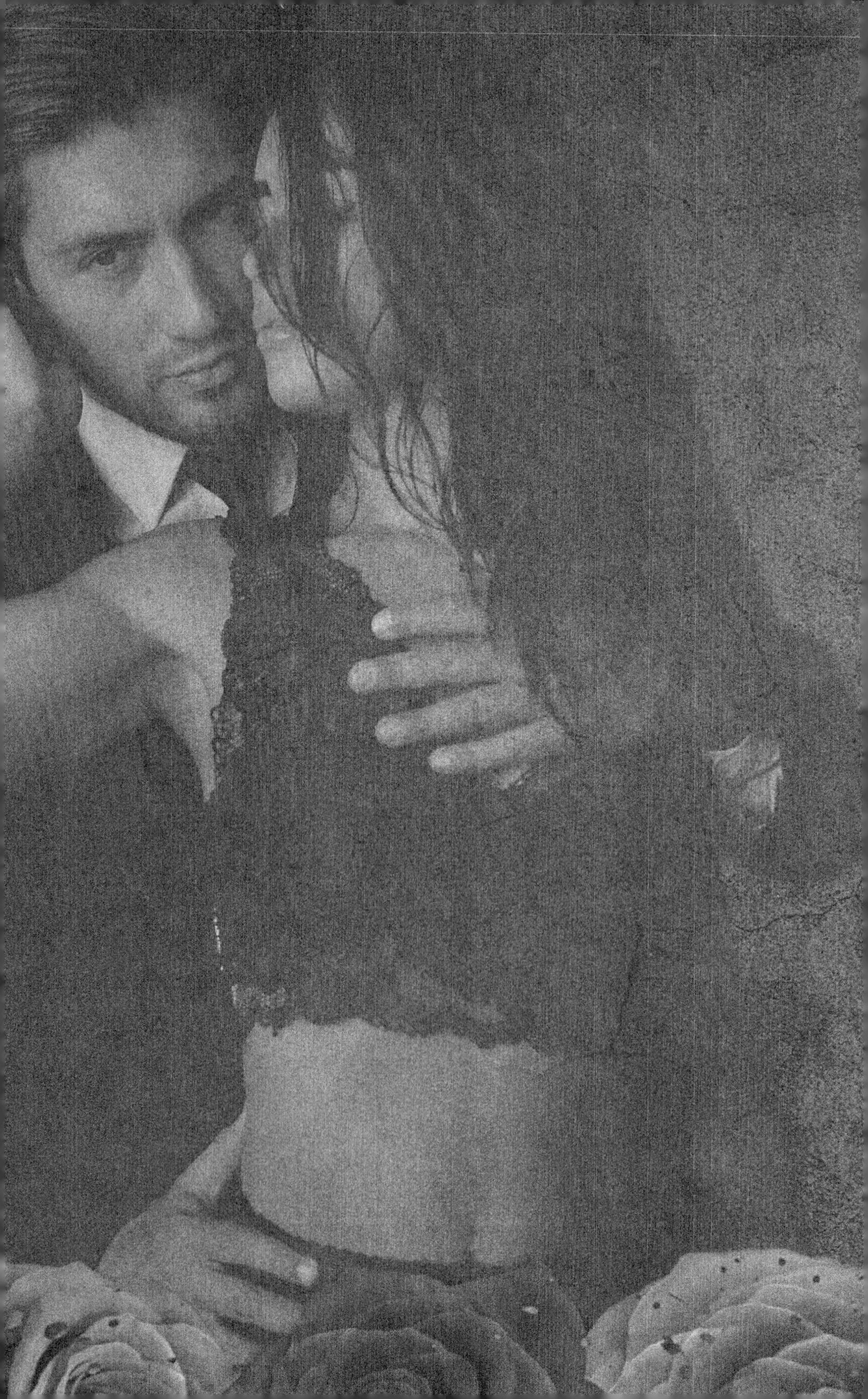

Chapter Sixteen
Marcus

Four. That's the number of times I have wanked to thoughts of Chloe since we left the car yesterday evening. That's rivalling teenage Marcus when he first discovered boobs, and isn't something I've done to this degree for many years.

I mean, since I started having sex, I haven't needed to use my own hand all that much. Yet, here I am.

As I watched her fall apart on my fingers, feeling her tight cunt cling to them as her taste flooded my tongue, the only thing I could think about was how my dick would feel in their place. I wanted to pick her up, carry her into my bedroom, and never let her leave.

Sadly, my brain kicked in and I remembered all the reasons I'm supposed to be showing restraint.

She's starting to learn to control her body, and she's definitely becoming confident enough to ask for what she wants, but it doesn't change the fact she's been through something traumatic, and until I know what it is, going any further with her could be harmful—and I never want to hurt her.

So, begrudgingly, when we got to the apartment yesterday, I made up a lame excuse about having work to do, and I've locked myself in my room ever since.

The look of disappointment on her face made my cock twitch, as it's clear she was expecting for more to happen between us when we got inside. I just need to do this the right way.

I was hoping by this morning, after a wank and some sleep, I'd be able to think with my head instead of my cock, but I'm still just as fucking wound up as I was when I went to bed.

In fact, after a night of dreaming about her moans and the way she tastes, I'm more exhausted and turned on than yesterday.

I couldn't be more grateful for the strong coffee I grab myself when I stomp into the kitchen, or that she's not there to torture me with those ridiculously short pyjama's she sleeps in.

Half way through my second mug, I'm finally starting to feel more human and less like a horny teenager when I hear Chloe's door open. I keep my gaze firmly locked on the contract I'm reading on my phone, though I have no idea what it says as I'm listening intently to each footstep that brings her closer.

"Morning," Chloe mutters, her voice low and shy.

I lift my gaze up to meet hers, only to find her staring down at her feet as she shuffles from one to the other. Just as I thought, she's wearing those stupidly short pyjamas that stop at the top of her thighs. I'm sure if she turns around, I'll be able to see the swell of her arse.

The top isn't much better. The straps are tiny, the neckline dips low enough to show off her generous cleavage, and the material is so thin, I can see the outline of her hard nipples poking through.

The hem of the vest stops just above her belly button piercing, showing off a stretch of pale skin between that and the start of her low-hung shorts.

She's got curves in all the right places, and even though her stomach isn't as perfectly flat as some people prefer, I happen to like my women more natural, and to me, Chloe is perfect.

Since her eyes are downcast, I allow myself a long moment to appreciate her glorious body, though it causes my cock to harden painfully once more.

"Morning," I grumble, sounding much more irritated than I intended as I discreetly readjust myself in my sweatpants. "Coffee?"

Her gaze slowly lifts to meet mine, and although the blush on her cheeks spreads, she gives me a small smile and a nod. "Yes, please."

I stand to grab her a mug, making it just the way I know she prefers, and I turn back to find she's already grabbed her usual seat on the stool across from me.

Once her drink's ready, I slide it over to her. "Thank you," she says as she takes her first sip, the low moan she makes causes my dick to twitch painfully.

This woman is going to be the fucking death of me, I think to myself.

We drink our coffees in silence for a few moments, and although I pick up my phone to make it look like I'm busy, I've read the same line around seven times, and I'm still not quite sure what it says.

I'm too busy casting glances at her over my phone, hoping to catch her stealing looks at me.

After a few minutes, Chloe clears her throat awkwardly, trying to get my attention.

"So... I know this is a little embarrassing, but we're adults... I think we should talk about what happened yesterday," she says, pulling her back straight in an attempt to look more confident than she sounds.

"Okay," I reply, dragging the word out in a way that makes it clear she's the one who needs to do the talking, not me.

She takes a deep breath, the grip on her coffee mug tightening until her knuckles turn white, and she lets out a sigh.

"I, erm, I enjoyed yesterday very much... Well, parts of it... I just, well, I wasn't sure if you just reacted in the heat of the moment, and would regretithismorning."

Although she starts off stumbling over her words, the last part tumbles out in a rush, making it hard for me to catch the end.

"What?"

"I'm worried you regret what happened between us, since you broke your rules," she repeats, her gaze firmly locked on her coffee mug.

I chuckle, which makes her eyes snap up to meet mine. "Yes, you made me lose control, which never happens, but that doesn't mean I regret it."

"You don't?" The way her voice lights up, full of hope, it almost guts me.

"No, I don't. But I still stand by what was said in the heat of the moment. If you want anything more to happen between us, you have to be honest with me. I'm not saying it just because I want to know, although I do, I'm saying it more to protect you.

"People who've experienced trauma can be re-traumatised very easily, and I will not be the person to trigger you," I explain, and her eyes widen slightly.

"So this whole time you've wanted to know so that you wouldn't hurt me? I thought you wanted to know so you could get revenge."

I'm sure she can see the dangerous expression that crosses my face as my smirk turns evil.

"Oh, I do plan on getting revenge, but that's just a benefit. The main reason is to keep you safe."

"Oh," she says, her brow furrowed.

"Did you mean it yesterday when you said you were going to tell me? I was worried you were just saying that to get what you wanted," I admit, watching as she cringes at my words.

Fuck, I never thought she'd lie to me.

She lets out a sigh. "Honestly, I was so desperate for an orgasm yesterday, I would've told you anything you wanted to hear. Then, once we got back home, the more I thought about it, the more fear took over.

"I've kept this secret for a while, and saying it aloud makes it real. I didn't lie to you yesterday, but this morning, I'm not entirely sure I can go through with it."

My stomach rolls and I feel like she's just stabbed me in the gut. I knew she was in the sort of headspace where she'd have said anything, but I really thought she meant it.

Then again, it probably wouldn't have changed anything. I wanted her badly enough to break all my own rules, so that's on me. It's a mistake I won't make again.

"Fine. I get it," I say through gritted teeth.

I swallow the last mouthful of my coffee before going to stand, until I feel Chloe's hand on mine. She's leaning over the island, her eyes misty with an almost distraught expression on her face.

"Please, don't leave," she whispers.

Fuck, I want nothing more than to give in to her, but I can't.

"Sorry, I have some work to do," I mutter, pulling my hand free as I stand from the stool.

I walk towards the exit, but Chloe jumps from her stool and blocks the way. She places her hand on my chest, stopping me from going any further.

"Please, just let me explain."

"There's nothing to explain. You've made it perfectly clear," I snap, sounding harsher than I intended.

Chloe grabs hold of my arm and pulls me towards the living room. "Just come and let me explain."

I don't know why, but I allow her to drag me until we're both sitting on the couch. She's so close, I can feel the warmth from her thigh against mine. I have to block out her fucking fantastic smell, and the way she feels against me, as it almost hurts to think about.

"Fine. What do you want to say?"

She rolls her eyes at my tone. "You're right, I have experienced trauma. I've never talked about it before, and for a long time, I tried to pretend it never happened, but it did, and I've never been the same since.

"Even admitting that to you is hard, but not because I don't trust you—I trust you more than anyone else. It's just...talking about it makes it real, and brings it all back.

"I've spent so long trying to forget, and I'm worried that telling you about it will put me back in a very dark place that I spent a long time clawing my way out of."

Well, fuck, now I feel like a right jackass.

I focus on my breathing, trying to control the anger enough that she only sees the concern I have for her, as I don't want to scare her away.

I tuck the rage away into the back of my mind, saving it for when I need to unleash it on the person most deserving of it.

"I understand that, I do, but when you were in that dark place before, you were all alone. Now you have me to help you," I say, meaning every single word.

She lets out a shuddered breath, and I can see the tears welling in the corner of her eyes, threatening to break free. This time when she speaks, her voice is barely above a whisper, and I have to strain to hear her.

"I'm worried you'll look at me differently when you know."

I shake my head vehemently. "No fucking way. There's nothing you could tell me that will ever change the way I look at you."

Her eyes widen as she fixes her gaze on mine. "You promise?"

"I promise," I reply, taking hold of her shaking hand.

She closes her eyes and pulls in a breath, and I let her have as much time as she needs. The silence sits between us, and I rub my thumb along the back of her hand in slow, reassuring strokes, letting her know that I'm still here, and I'm not going anywhere.

"It was about eighteen months ago. My mother set me up on a date with the son of one of her society friends. His father is aligned with Dad, and he agreed that our date would be a good match.

"I'd never met him before, though I remember Jacob saying that he didn't really like him, so he must know him in some way," she starts, finally opening her eyes to look at me.

I give her a small, reassuring smile, encouraging her to continue, and she does.

"Although there was nothing formal in place yet, Mother made it quite clear that the outcome of the date would be a marriage contract if she got her way—which she always fucking does," she snaps, looking murderous.

"I'd been avoiding any dates that could possibly lead to a marriage offer, as it's the last thing I wanted, but Mother knew what I was doing. She made it clear I couldn't put it off forever.

"Marrying someone of their choosing, strengthening the Santoro name was quite literally my only job, and the clock was ticking."

How I manage to keep the hand holding hers from shaking with rage is a fucking miracle. I have to curl my free hand into a fist just to try and claw back some semblance of control. We're not even at the worst bit of the story, and already I'm angry.

To know her parents were pushing her to marry is one thing, but to make her feel like that's the only reason she's here on Earth is something else.

It's also starting to look like the guy who hurt her was someone her parents set her up with, and if that's the case, the peace treaty is going to be on really shaky grounds, as I'm going to want to murder them all.

I focus on slowing my heart rate down as I keep my breathing steady, making sure my face doesn't display any of what I'm feeling. I keep my eyes locked on Chloe as she continues her story.

"I met him at the restaurant, and the date went fine. He wasn't bad looking, and we got on well enough, but there weren't any sparks either.

"Although he didn't do anything that repulsed me, or anything too bad, there were a few things during the date that raised a red flag for me. I can't remember specifics, but one of them was the way he treated the staff at the restaurant.

"The hostess was a younger girl, and he openly stared at her tits the whole time he spoke to her. Then the waiter who brought us our wine, he spoke to him like he was shit on the bottom of his shoe, looking down his nose at him the whole time.

"And finally, the waitress who served us for the evening, she was a little older, and he kept checking her out as well, making a few inappropriate comments.

"Nothing was really bad, but it was enough to register as red flags for me. That combined with us having very little in common meant that the conversation felt forced. He rarely asked about me, dominating the conversation the whole time with talk of himself, and his inflated ego.

"By the end of the meal, I'd had enough. We didn't get on... Well, I don't know if we would have got on as he didn't care enough to ask anything about me. It was all about him, and I'd seen enough to know that we weren't a match."

She pauses, dragging in a shuddered breath, and that's when I see a lone tear rolling down her cheek. I reach up with my thumb to wipe it away, and the look she gives me guts me.

"You don't have to tell me any more," I say, hoping she can hear how genuine I'm being.

For the longest time, I've needed to know her secret, and I still maintain for her own wellbeing, I should know it. But now the moment's here, I'm not sure I can hear it.

I meant what I said before, I'll never look at her differently, but it's quickly becoming apparent to me that I care about Chloe enough to feel her pain, and that scares me. I've never cared about any one else in that way before, except Miles and Jake.

She gives me a small smile as she says, "I do."

"Only if you're sure," I reply, and she nods her head, squeezing my hand tighter.

"When the date was over, we left the restaurant, and he asked me if I wanted to get a drink with him. I said I was going to head home, but remained polite as I thanked him for a lovely evening—lying through my fucking teeth.

"The moment I turned him down, his expression shifted. He insisted on giving me a ride home. Obviously, I tried to decline, but he said my parents wouldn't be happy with him if he didn't do the gentlemanly thing.

"I knew he was mentioning my parents as a threat, but I didn't know what else to do. So I got in the car with him."

Her voice cracks at the end, and the tears are now freely flowing down her cheeks. Her eyes look almost empty as she stares blankly, lost in the horrors of her past.

I don't say anything. Mostly, as I've no fucking clue what to say, but also to give her the time she needs. I keep my grip tight on her hand, letting her know that I'm still here.

"The next part is a little fuzzy, but without going into too much detail, he drugged me and took me to this room where he kept me prisoner for around two days."

My eyes spring wide open at that part, my brows shooting so high they disappear under my floppy fringe. "He fucking kidnapped you?"

She nods slowly, her eyes dropping back to the floor as she lets out a sob. "I'm sorry."

"What the fuck are you apologising for? Why the hell didn't I know you'd been kidnapped? Why didn't Jacob tell me? I'd have helped to find you."

I know I'm supposed to be staying calm, but I can't. Anger bubbles under the surface, making my skin itch as fire races through my veins. I'm so fucking furious right now, but then I hear her sob.

I look up to see her staring at me, tears rolling down her face as she shrinks away from me. She thinks I'm mad at her.

"I'm sorry, Chloe. I'm not mad at you, just the situation," I explain, pulling her close, so I can wrap my arm around her.

She lets out a sob, but leans into me. "Nobody knew," she whispers, so quietly I can barely hear.

"What?"

"Nobody knew I was missing. He texted my mother to say we were getting on so well that I was going to stay at his beach house for the weekend. Mother was just so pleased we were getting along, she didn't say anything.

"I'm not sure Dad or Jake even knew I was gone," she admits with a shrug of her shoulders, like that makes it better.

"Your mother is quickly making it to the top of my shit-list," I say through gritted teeth.

Chloe lets out a humourless laugh. "She's on mine too, but she'll never be at the top."

I sigh, knowing exactly what she's not saying. "Were you drugged the whole two days?" I ask, praying that she was.

It's pretty fucking bad when you're praying someone was drugged, just so they don't remember all of the horrors that were inflicted upon them.

"No," she says quietly. "I woke up in this room, tied to the bed, completely naked. Eventually, when I had proved I could be trusted, and wouldn't try to escape, he untied all of my limbs except one ankle. He kept that shackled on a long lead, so if by some miracle I managed to break out of the bedroom, I couldn't get far."

"Motherfucker!" I snap, letting my emotions get the better of me.

Chloe leans into my side harder, like she's the one comforting me, and once again I feel like an arsehole.

"It was the worst two days of my life. I hated every second, but most of all I despised the way he'd force my body to betray me. He took pleasure in making my body do whatever he wanted, even though I begged for it not to," she cries, her tears wetting the fabric of my shirt.

"What do you mean?"

She hesitates, taking a gulping breath as she buries her head further into my chest, hiding from me as she tells me why control is so important to her.

"He liked forcing me to orgasm, even though I wasn't enjoying myself. He said it was my body's way of telling me I liked it. Whenever I called it rape, he'd say it must be consensual as people don't come while they're being raped. It messed with my head in ways I can't explain."

Each word sends a torrent of different emotions swirling through my brain. The murderous rage I feel towards this unknown arsehole is like nothing I've ever felt before, but there's also shame, and that's all on me.

"I'm so sorry, Chloe. If I'd have known, I'd never have engaged in edging or orgasm denial play with you."

I hope she can tell just how genuinely sorry I really am.

Chloe pulls away from me until she's looking me in the eyes, her hard stare no longer vacant. Now, she's determined, though I can't ignore the silent tears that are still falling.

"Don't you dare fucking apologise. Everything that's happened between us is something I've wanted, and have fully consented to. But more than that, I've healed more in the last week with you than I have since it happened.

"You taught me that I can control my body, my orgasms, and I can choose who I give them to, which has given me power back that I thought I'd lost.

"Before you even knew what happened to me, you could see I was lost, that I was looking for help in all the wrong places.

"I thought that if I chose who I gave my body to, then it was my decision, whether I hated the experience or not. At least I got the option to consent. You saw what I was doing and made me see that I wasn't really helping myself at all.

"You once told me that being a slut isn't a bad thing, as long as there's consent and everyone is enjoying themselves, and you were right. Whenever I was with those other guys, being a slut felt dirty and wrong, but it's not like that with you.

"Somehow, you make me feel confident and sexy, and I want nothing more than to be a slut for you, as I know you won't ever abuse the trust I put in you.

"I've enjoyed everything we've done together so far, and I really hope there'll be more to come. After what happened, I never thought I'd want anyone to touch me ever again. I can't even bear to let Dad or Jake hug me. Yet, with you, it's like the past never happened. I need your touch like I need air, to make me feel alive."

The moment I do it, I know it's probably wrong but I can't stop myself. There's something about this girl that pulls me in like magic. I don't even hesitate as I lean over and press my lips to hers.

The feel of her soft lips against mine sends tingles through me, and I want nothing more than to deepen the kiss, but then I remember the situation, and I begrudgingly pull back.

Chloe looks startled as she brings her fingers up to touch her lips, like she can't quite believe what just happened. "You kissed me," she states, sounding a little bit dreamy.

I chuckle, the corner of my lip tilting into a smile. "I did."

"Why?"

"Because I'm starting to realise that I might want you too," I admit.

Now her eyes are almost comically wide, and she just sits there staring at me, looking stunned. I have to bite my lip to stop from chuckling.

"For sex?" she blurts out.

I freeze, not entirely sure what I'm supposed to say to that. Then I remember how honest Chloe has been with me, and I think I owe her the same in return.

Taking a deep breath, I give her a small smile as I do my best to explain.

"Honestly, I've never had a proper relationship. In fact, I rarely see women more than once, so I don't really know what it means to offer more than sex.

"Things are different with you, but I'm not really sure how yet. There's a lot of reasons why nothing can happen between us, but I'm very aware that at every available opportunity, I seem to be ignoring those reasons, barrelling ahead anyway."

Chloe laughs, and the sound is like music to my ears. "What are the reasons?"

"Your family and the treaty we have in place is a pretty big one. I love Blackthorn, and our city is finally in a stable place thanks to the treaty. If something were to happen between us, something more than sex, I'd be risking your family's wrath over that decision, and that could put the treaty in jeopardy," I explain, but Chloe's brow furrows like she's confused.

"How would it put the treaty in jeopardy?"

"Well, if your father says I can't be with you, and I refuse to follow his instruction, that would cause the power balance to shift. He'd most likely declare war on me for breaking the rules, so I'd have to be sure I'm willing to go to war before I go down that route, and that's a lot to put our city through just for me to be happy."

I try to make it sound simple, but it's really not.

Yes, I'm forbidden from dating Chloe, and I'd start a war if I did—that part is simple, but choosing between my happiness and a war is really not. Of course, I want to be happy, but I'm not sure I can risk the safety and wellbeing of my people for it.

"I had no idea it could start a war," Chloe says with a gulp, looking a little uncomfortable. "Maybe instead of jumping right into the deep end, we just take each day as it comes, and at the end of my time here, we can see where we are? If you get bored of me before then, we can just end it early."

I almost laugh out loud at the idea of being bored with her. After just one taste, I knew I'd never get enough of her. The problem isn't that I think it won't work between us, it's that I think it will.

I already see her as mine, and having her in my bed will only make that more pronounced. I'm not sure in the end that I'll be able to give her up, but the idea of pushing her away right now creates a hole in my heart.

I'm starting to see this is a lose-lose situation, so I may as well get some of what I want while I can. If I'm going to burn the world down, I may as well make her mine before everything turns to ash.

"I think we can do that. But first, I need you to do one more thing for me..."

After a few seconds of my silence, she asks, "What?"

"I want to know his name."

Her eyes widen and she pulls back, shaking her head vigorously. "No. Why?"

"I refuse to live in a world where he's allowed to draw breath. For all we know, he could be doing what he did to you to other women, and I can't allow that to happen," I say, trying to appeal to her caring nature.

Whilst I obviously care about the safety of the women in my city, and taking care of a predator will help with that, but we both know that's not my real motive.

I want revenge. I want to avenge Chloe, whether she wants me to or not.

"His family is powerful. It won't be that easy," she mutters, but I wave her off.

"There's no family more powerful than mine. Besides, I can always get our ruler, Bree's permission, if needed. Now, give me his name." I keep my tone light, but the force I intend for her to hear is there.

"What will you do to him?" she asks, chewing on her bottom lip.

I fix my gaze on her, trying to read her expression. "Do you really want to know?"

She nods. "Honestly, I've imagined punishing him in so many ways." She sounds almost ashamed to admit it, but fuck, if that doesn't make my cock twitch.

"Well, you tell me exactly what you want me to do to him, and I'll make it happen. As long as he suffers and is dead at the end of the two days, that's all that matters to me," I admit.

Her breath hitches. "Two days?"

"He tortured you for two days, I'm just returning the favour."

"Okay," she mumbles, her gaze dropping to the floor, like she's embarrassed to admit that's what she wants.

"Do you want to be a part of it? To face him? You can show him that you're not afraid of him any more, that you're taking back the control he stole from you."

She freezes, her eyes flicking up to meet mine, looking like a deer caught in headlights. "Face him? I don't know if I can."

"You absolutely don't have to, but the offer is there if you choose. If not, I'll just make him suffer in all the ways you've imagined. When he takes his last breath, he'll know he messed with the wrong girl."

Her lips tip up into a small smile. "Thank you," she whispers, before leaning over and pressing her lips to mine.

It's a short, chaste kiss, and it's over before it really starts, but my heart is pounding in my chest in a way that shows it was more than an innocent peck.

"Anything for you."

She leans in again, and I squeeze her hand to grab her attention as I pull my head away. Hurt flashes in her eyes, but I know I'm doing the right thing.

"I want nothing more than to kiss you right now, but we both know things will move quickly after that, and I don't think this is the right time. Your emotions are fresh, and I want your head to be clear when I fuck you. I'm not saying no, I'm just saying not now.

"Take the rest of the day, and we can revisit everything when you're ready. I want to be absolutely certain that you'll have no regrets when you agree to let me fuck you, as there will be no going back. Once I make you mine, that's it."

Her breath hitches, and I ignore the mixed messages I'm sending her. I mean she'll be mine while she's here with me, that's all. At least, I hope that's what I mean.

Fuck, focus, I shout in my head.

I quickly change the subject. "I'm not going to stop until I get his name."

She lets out a long sigh. "Fine, it's Frank Longoria. But I don't want you to do anything until I've decided if I want to be a part of it. Agreed?"

His name repeats over and over in my head. There's an element of familiarity, but I can't quite place how I know him. I'll have to ask Jacob when he comes over tomorrow, since Chloe seems to think he knew him and didn't like him.

I also have the overwhelming urge to ask Jacob how the fuck he didn't realise his sister had been kidnapped for two fucking days, or how he missed how messed up she'd become when she came back.

I know I can't ask him, as that would be breaking the trust Chloe placed in me, and I can't do that. Though Jake will need to face up to this sooner or later, and I suspect we'll see him spiral further when he finds out.

As shitty a person as Jake is right now, there's no denying how much he loves his sister. When he finds out just how much he failed to protect her, I think it'll kill him.

"I can agree to that. It'll take me time to come up with a good plan, anyway," I admit, my glare no doubt showing just how evil my ideas truly are.

I don't mention all the red tape I'll need to deal with in order to pull it off without repercussions. If he's as well connected as Chloe says, I'll need permission from people higher up to take him out without his family being able to retaliate.

Since he's not aligned with the Morellis, I'll need Santoro permission, and if I can't get that, I'll have no choice but to go to the big boss—Bree Doughty.

"Okay, and things between us just go back to normal?" She phrases it like a question, as though she's unsure of the answer.

"I believe what I said is that when you're truly sure it's what you want, when there's nothing else on your mind except me, then you can ask me to fuck you. Until then, we can go back to normal," I repeat, though I really hope it doesn't take her long to sort her shit out.

I know she has a lot on her plate, and I wouldn't blame her for taking her time, but I don't think my poor dick can take much more teasing.

"Right, well, I'll make dinner this evening then," she says as she stands from the sofa, her hand still in mine.

I stand with her, giving her a smile. I lean over and press a kiss to her cheek, the edge of my lips pressing against hers. "It's a date."

I hear her breath hitch as I let go of her hand and walk out of the room, my smile growing.

I have no idea what the fuck I'm doing, and I'm fairly sure I'm digging my own grave, but there's nothing in the world that will stop me now.

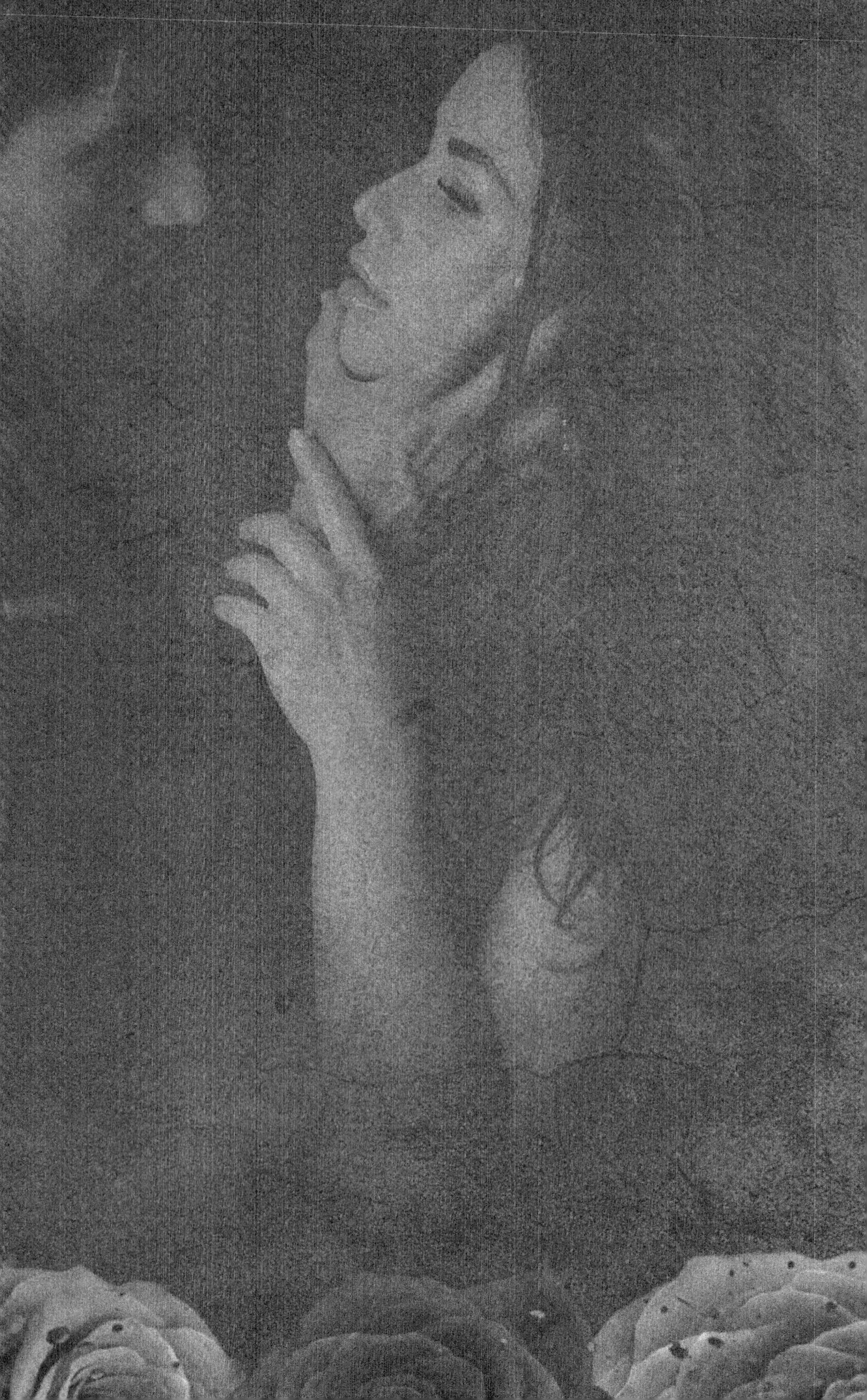

Chapter Seventeen
Chloe

Ever since I bared my soul to Marcus, and he basically put the ball in my court, I've been torn over what to do.

The part of me that's been obsessing over Marcus since I first discovered boys is screaming at me to get on with it, but then there's the rational side of me that seems to be holding back.

Telling him my secret wasn't half as bad as I thought it would be. I expected him to view me differently afterwards, and although I didn't go into too much detail, he still looks at me in the same way. I expected to see pity shining in those bright blue eyes of his, but that never came.

As I expected, he was furious on my behalf. I knew he'd be mad, and I sort of suspected he'd want to know his name, so he could punish him, but what Marcus is planning is so much worse than a punishment.

He wants to torture him, to make him endure pain and suffering for the same length of time that he held me captive, before eventually ending him.

I've never had someone want to fight my battles like that before, and I can't say his plans don't call to the darkness that lives inside of me.

Ever since Frank let me go, I've dreamed about all the different ways I could make him pay for what he did to me. But I've always known that's all they were—dreams.

Yet, now I have someone who wants to fight my battles for me, who wants to end Frank in whatever way I see fit, and I've never felt better.

One of my biggest fears is that I'll randomly bump into him in a club, and I'll have to pretend like I'm not standing face-to-face with the man who ruined my life.

For Marcus to offer me a world where my monster no longer exists, that's the best thing he could do.

So why the fuck haven't I jumped into bed with him?

He reacted much better than I planned. He didn't judge me, he wanted to help me, and he still wants to teach me to grow in sexual confidence, like I have been doing—so why haven't I asked him yet?

My mind is a mess, and while talking about Frank brought a lot of the nightmares back, I've also been focusing on the conversation I had with Marcus about us.

I don't know what on Earth possessed me to tell him how much I like him, but I was baring my soul, and it all just sort of came flooding out.

When he was honest with me in return, telling me he's never had a serious relationship—and has never wanted one—I was both shocked and a little concerned.

I knew Marcus had a reputation. I grew up with him, so I've seen the revolving door of girls that are in his life for a night and are never seen again, but it never really occurred to me why he doesn't want anyone serious.

It also never crossed my mind why me and Marcus might be off-limits. Of course, I know about the peace treaty between my family and Marcus'. It's the reason Blackthorn is no longer stuck in the middle of a civil war, caused by the battle for power that was raging for generations between our families.

The peace treaty only works because our families worked hard to make sure there was a balance of power. Each family is responsible for their side of the town, and they deal with loyalty shifts fairly, so that no family ever gains the majority.

It never occurred to me that if I were to be with Marcus, that would give him more power than the Santoros, putting the treaty on shaky ground.

I guess that's why my father always told him I was off-limits, and why Marcus spent the better part of our teen years either ignoring me or making it clear he didn't like me. He knew I liked him, but pushing me away was the safest option.

Although he's not willing to risk the peace treaty, or his friendship with

Jacob, he still wants to see what happens between us. But, for me, that's such a vague statement.

What if we spend the next few weeks together and realise, by some miracle, that we actually love each other? What then? Would he be willing to take a risk on me, or does everything have to end once the clock stops ticking, no matter what we feel?

That's the big problem for me. I know that spending more time with Marcus, handing over the trust that's needed for him to explore my body in the way he wants, that will change me.

It'll only strengthen what I feel for him, but I don't think anything will change for him. I suspect he will end things when the time is up, no matter what, and I don't know if my fragile heart can take that.

Which is exactly why I haven't walked into his room completely naked, begging for him to finally fuck me. And believe me, that thought has crossed my mind several times.

Instead, we're still being friendly with each other, having meals together, talking, getting to know one another, and it's nice... but fuck do I want more.

Thankfully, Jacob will be here in about ten minutes, which should give me some time to be in the same room as Marcus without picturing what he looked like on his knees when he was eating my pussy in the car.

I'm pacing around the living room, while Marcus sits in the comfy armchair, watching me with the ghost of a smile on his face. He thinks I'm nervous about Jacob coming over, which is part of it, but that cocky smirk of his isn't helping to stop me from thinking about other things that are getting me all hot and bothered.

Miles walks into the room and throws himself into the armchair opposite Marcus, leaning back with his arm over the top like he doesn't have a care in the world. "So, how are you going to do this intervention?"

I look over at Marcus, wincing at the thought of how much Jake would hate this being called an *intervention*. Marcus seems to have the same thought.

"We're not calling it that. We're just confronting him over his issues, as we're not really sure he's all that aware of them."

Miles rolls his eyes as he tuts. "No, he's barely aware of anything when he's off his face on drink and drugs. But what makes you think he's going to want to do anything about it?"

I freeze before turning to glare at Miles. "Why wouldn't he?"

Miles holds his hands up in a non-threatening manner as he speaks. "Well, he's been blacking out, waking up in puddles of his own vomit and piss for a while now, and if that's not enough to make him see he's hit rock bottom and needs to change, why will talking to you?"

Marcus lets out a groan and Miles' eyes go wide as he realises his mistake. "He's been getting so bad that he's passing out? Marcus, you knew he was that bad and you didn't tell me, or do anything?"

Marcus looks like he's about to reply, but Miles cuts in. "To be fair, you were going a bit wild yourself for a while, so I don't think telling you would have helped."

Both myself and Marcus shoot Miles matching glares, but he shrugs his shoulders like he doesn't care. Marcus turns back to me.

"Honestly, I haven't really known what to do or how to approach him. Even though he's my best friend, this crosses the line into telling him how to rule, and that's a very fine line."

I never thought of it that way. Although we're telling Jacob that he needs to get his shit together for his own health and wellbeing, the underlying reason is that we need him to be the leader we know he can be.

If he doesn't step up soon, Dad won't hesitate to find a replacement, and right now, that's Scott.

I can only imagine the war that will occur if Marcus is told he has to rule with Scott. It'll never happen, and the peace treaty will be a thing of the past. We need Jacob to get his head on straight, but I'm aware what we're asking is so much more than him just getting sober.

He's never wanted to rule, and I'm pretty sure he's acting out in this way to block out all the responsibility he suddenly finds is being thrust upon him. So asking him to embrace that, without the help of any substances, is going to be a tall fucking order.

"Yeah, I don't think he's going to take any of this well. I might need some time alone with him, just to sort of ease him into the idea before we hit him with the hard stuff.

"As siblings, we're used to falling out all the time, and we make up easily, but I don't want you to risk your relationship with him if he takes it badly," I say to Marcus, who nods in agreement.

Marcus fixes his gaze on mine, sending a shiver down my spine. "If he kicks off, you better call one of us. I won't let him treat you like shit."

"People who feel cornered will lash out," Miles adds, somewhat unhelpfully.

"Why are you here again?" I ask, sounding every bit as sarcastic as I intended to.

Miles glares at me as Marcus lets out a short laugh, before Miles turns to his friend, silencing him with just one stern look. Marcus holds up his hands.

"Hey, don't look at me like that. After the way Jake was with you the other day, I'm surprised you're here too. It's not like the two of you are even friends."

My brow furrows at this. "I thought you were all friends, and have been since school."

Miles' friendly expression turns blank, though he throws a glare at Marcus that is anything but friendly. "We all went to school together, but me and Jake only know each other because we're both friends with Marcus."

"I could have sworn you were all close when you were younger. I know you don't hang out that much anymore, but you used to do," I state in confusion, distinctly remembering the three of them hanging out when they were teenagers.

It wasn't just two people who were acquaintances because they share a mutual friend, I'm sure of it—so why is Miles lying?

"Look, it was a long time ago... Even if we used to get along, we don't any more. We've both changed a lot, and other than because of Marcus, we don't have any reason to see each other."

Miles sounds almost robotic, like he's reciting something he memorised just for occasions like this, yet there's no emotion in his voice. I don't believe a word he's saying, but the look Marcus is giving me tells me to drop the subject.

Naturally, I'm about to ignore him when the doorbell rings. *Saved by the bell*, I think to myself. Though I'm going to make sure this isn't the last time we have this conversation. Something happened between them that caused their friendship to end, and I fully intend on finding out what it is.

Marcus stands and goes to answer the door, startling me a little as I was sure Miles would go. He catches me looking and gives me a smirk that's not quite as effective as Marcus'.

"It's my day off. Marcus is pretty good at making sure I don't do anything that would be considered working when I should be off the clock."

Interesting. So he's not here in a work capacity. Just another piece of information to file away for a later date.

Marcus walks back into the living room with Jake trailing behind him. As soon as my brother is close enough, I spring up from my seat and rush over to him, pulling him into my arms.

"Jake, it's so good to see you. Thank you for agreeing to come," I say, squeezing him tighter.

Although he wraps his arms around me in return, he's oddly stiff, almost formal. I pull back just enough to get a good look at him, my hands still firmly on his shoulders so he can't move away.

His short, dirty-blonde hair that's usually styled into haphazard spikes has grown longer, and seems to be curling at the ends. His usually bright brown eyes are dull and sunken, surrounded by large dark circles.

Where I'd normally expect to see his rounded cheeks and dimples, his face is gaunt and pale, with patchy stubble splattered across his chin, giving off the appearance that he hasn't shaved in a few days.

Although my brother is wearing the designer jeans and T-shirt that I'd expect to see, they now look baggy on him. His once muscular frame is smaller, and I wonder how the hell I missed all this when I saw him just two days ago.

I guess I was so focused on him being wasted and behaving like an arse, I didn't look any further. If I'm being honest, that's probably what I've been doing for quite a while.

If I acknowledged that he really looked like this, I would've had to do something about it, and mentally, I wasn't in the right frame of mind to take on anyone else's problems.

Now I have Marcus to help me, so I finally allow myself to see just how bad things have really gotten for my big brother.

"Hey, Clo. You okay?" Jake asks, giving me a small smile that doesn't quite reach his eyes.

At least his pupils look normal, so he's not high right now, I think to myself.

"I'm good, thank you. Pleased to see you."

I give him another squeeze before taking a step back. Marcus is by my side and reaches his hand out towards Jake. "Glad you could come, Jake."

Jake looks down at his outstretched hand before flicking his gaze up to Marcus', glaring at him in a very unfriendly way. Somewhat reluctantly, he shakes Marcus' hand, but doesn't say anything.

As Marcus takes a seat in the armchair again, Jake looks around for where he's going to sit, his gaze landing on Miles, who is still lounging in his chair.

He's so relaxed, he's practically reclined, with his arm thrown over the back of the seat and his legs stretched out in front of him. Though the tense expression on his face tells a different story.

Jake's expression darkens, his nostrils flaring as he turns to face Miles. "Why the fuck are you here?"

Miles' lips turn up into a lazy smile that makes Jake clench his hands into fists. "It's my day off, so I'm just hanging out here," Miles says, sounding far more jovial than the situation calls for.

"You don't fucking live here, do you? So I don't see any reason for you to be here. You should get the fuck out," Jake snarls, taking a threatening step towards Miles, who doesn't even flinch.

"Jacob! Don't be so rude," I chastise, wondering where all this hatred has come from.

"Yeah, this isn't your house, and you aren't my boss, so you can't kick me out. Some of us can do whatever we want, we don't all have to do as Daddy tells us, Pretty Boy," Miles adds unhelpfully, and somewhat cryptically.

It's like he just added alcohol to a simmering flame, and Jacob's barely contained rage explodes.

"Fuck you. Who the fuck do you think you are talking to me like that?!" Jake yells, striding quickly towards Miles until he's towering over him threateningly.

Miles just rolls his eyes, like he's bored by Jake's outburst. Marcus rushes to my brother's side and grabs hold of his arm, which Jake quickly tries to pull away from.

"Calm down, Jake," Marcus says, his tone tinged with a warning.

Miles starts to stand up, and Jacob is forced to take a step back to give him room. Once Miles is at his full height, they're standing almost nose to nose, not much of a height difference between them, glaring at each other.

Marcus is hovering beside them, ready to intervene if needed.

"Jacob is too busy behaving like a spoiled teenager throwing a temper tantrum to calm down," Miles says to Marcus, before turning back to Jake. "Looks like you still haven't grown up enough to deal with your emotions like an adult."

Jake takes a step back on a gasp, like Miles slapped him. "Fuck you."

Miles shakes his head, looking more disappointed than anything. "Let me know when you decide to stop acting like a petulant child," he says, giving Jake a small smile before stepping away from him.

Both Marcus and Jake are looking at Miles with the same confused expression I'm sure is reflected on my face too. I have no idea what is going on between Miles and my brother, but he's not wrong. Jake is lashing out in all the wrong ways.

Just as Miles is about to leave, he turns to face me. "I'm out of here. Good luck. You're going to need it."

The door slams shut, leaving behind an awkward silence as we all just stand there, waiting for someone to be the first to speak. Marcus looks over at me, ignoring Jake as he sinks down onto the sofa.

"I'm going to go and check on Miles. Will you be okay for a moment?" Marcus asks, his intense gaze watching me to make sure I answer honestly.

"Of course. Go, make sure he's okay." I give him a reassuring smile, and he seems to like what he sees as he jogs over to the door, seeking out his friend.

As soon as the door closes, leaving me alone with my brother, I sit down on the opposite end of the sofa to him, giving him my best disappointed stare.

"Is this where you yell at me?" Jake asks, his eyes locked on where his fingers are picking at an imaginary piece of lint on his trousers.

"I mean, it probably should be. You were a real dick to Miles, when he's done nothing wrong that I can see."

I hate how old I sound when I'm telling him off, and I wince at the knowledge that it's only going to get worse from here.

"There's a lot you don't know."

"That may be true, but I still don't think that excuses your behaviour today."

Jacob lets out a long sigh as he drags his hand over his face. "I know."

"We both know this isn't just about your behaviour today, or the other day at dinner. You've been spiralling for a while, and it's only getting worse." I try not to sound judgemental, or as hypocritical as I feel, but it's clear in the way Jake's eyes narrow, he thinks I'm judging him.

"This isn't about me. I'm here to check on you. I need to know that you're okay here. I've been worried sick since that fucking awful poker night. I'm so sorry that I bet you, and that you're paying the price for my mistakes," he rushes out, guilt practically dripping from every word.

I can't help but chuckle, and Jake's eyes widen in confusion. "Jake, I'm happier here than I've ever been. You have nothing to apologise for. I want to be here."

"I'm confused. Are you and Marcus..."

I bite my lip as I shake my head, unsure how to explain what the hell is going on between us, but I settle for some version of the truth.

"No, we're not, but it's a bit of a long story."

"I've got time," he replies, fixing me with a stare that tells me it's not optional.

I let out a sigh, internally cursing Marcus for running away so I have to deal with this on my own. "Marcus made the bet with you because I asked him for his help."

"What?" Jake blurts out, interrupting me before I can finish.

"I don't want to marry Scott. I don't want any kind of arranged marriage, and yet nobody seems to give a shit about what I want. When I found out I was marrying him, I went to Caged and drank a lot.

"Marcus stopped me before I was about to do something stupid, and we, erm... We got talking, and he said he could help me get away for a bit. I was feeling suffocated, and although he couldn't get me out of the engagement, he said he could get me a few weeks of freedom, so I agreed.

"Honestly, I didn't really think much of the agreement, and I thought when the booze wore off the next day that it would be all talk. I had no idea what he was planning, so I was shocked when I found out about the bet. It wasn't Marcus' greatest plan, and I'm sorry you were hurt in the process, but I'm not sorry I'm here."

Jake shakes his head as he squeezes his eyes closed, using a thumb to rub circles into his temple like he's got a headache.

"So the bet wasn't real. You don't really belong to him? This was all just an elaborate plan to get you away from Scott, to delay your wedding for a few weeks?"

I reach over and take his hand in mine, squeezing until he opens his eyes. "I'm sorry."

"I'm so confused. Why didn't you come to me?" he asks, hurt dripping from every word.

"Honestly, you've not exactly been yourself recently, Jake. Whenever I talk to you, you're so off your face, you can barely string a full sentence together," I reply honestly, though I hate the way his face falls.

"I'm not that bad," he grumbles.

I squeeze his hand reassuringly again as I give him a sad smile. "Yes, you are, Jake. You have a problem—a big one. You need to go to rehab."

As soon as the word leaves my lips, he pulls his hand from mine and turns to glare at me, his face scrunched up in a way that makes his normally beautiful face appear ugly.

"Fuck you. I don't have a problem, and I don't need to go to rehab."

I don't know when Marcus came back into the apartment, or how long he's been standing in the hallway, giving me and Jacob some time together, but as soon as he hears Jake yell at me, he makes his presence known. He strides into the room, a fierce expression on his face.

"Do not talk to your sister like that!"

"Fuck you. I'm supposed to be your friend, and you lied to me," he snarls, shooting daggers at Marcus with his eyes.

Marcus ignores him and moves over to me, sitting next to me on the sofa. There's not much room between the sofa arm and me, but he lowers himself into the gap, pressing his side up against mine in a way that I shouldn't find both reassuring and incredibly sexy.

As always when he's this close to me, my body starts to heat. Luckily, Jacob's temper is enough to distract me.

"I *am* your friend, which is why I agreed to help your sister."

Marcus' words sting a lot more than they should. The idea that he's only helping me because of Jacob hurts, as I thought he was doing it for me.

"You should have told me and I would've helped her," he shouts.

Marcus lets out a harsh snort. "Help her? You can't even help yourself. You won't even admit you have a problem."

"I don't fucki—"

"STOP!" I yell, holding a hand out in front of both of them, stopping them from raising their voices any more. The tension in the room is growing, and if both of their egos expand anymore, we will get nowhere. "No more arguing with each other. You're both going to shut up, and I'm going to speak."

Jake looks suitably chastised and shrinks back in his seat, while Marcus' eyes flash dark, and I can tell he likes me standing up for myself. I wish he'd stop looking at me like that as it's making it really hard to focus.

I clear my throat and reluctantly drag my gaze away from his, so I don't get more distracted. I reach over and grab Jake's hand again, and although he looks like he's going to pull it back, he eventually lets me.

"Jake, the truth is, things have been so much worse recently than I think even you're aware of. You aren't doing your job properly, and although both Marcus and Dad are covering for you, it's not going unnoticed. People are starting to talk, and it's getting to the point where Dad can't ignore it anymore," I explain, trying to keep my tone as light as I can, so I don't come across as judgy. I want him to understand the seriousness of the situation.

"What do you mean?" Jake asks.

Marcus somehow manages to discreetly move his hand to my lower back, rubbing slow circles in a reassuring way, so when he begins to answer, I know he's calm enough that I don't stop him.

"People have been commenting about it for a while now, and I've been downplaying things. I tell people you play hard but you work hard too, often letting you take credit for things that I've done.

"But now things have changed, as not only is my father aware, so is yours. They've hinted on more than one occasion that they're not going to tolerate your behaviour any longer."

"So, what does that mean?" Jake asks, running his free hand down his face again, suddenly looking really exhausted.

Me and Marcus look at each other, silently trying to work out which of us is going to be the one to tell him. I know it needs to be me, so with a slight nod of my head, I let out a sigh.

"This is the reason I'm being forced to marry Scott so soon. Dad has decided that you're not fit to rule, and since you clearly don't want to, he's been looking for someone to replace you as his heir.

"As we have no other family who'd be eligible, the only option is for me to marry the person Dad wants to train as his heir. It would appear he's chosen Scott."

Jacob's eyes darken now in a way that reminds me of Marcus, anger flashing across his face. "He wants to fucking replace me with that arsehole?"

"Well, it's no secret that you've never wanted the role, and you've rebelled whenever he's tried to teach you, but Dad always believed you'd step up when the responsibility was handed to you—which you've not done, so now he's being forced to rethink."

"I-I... I mean, well, I..." Jake splutters, struggling to find the right words.

"Dad always thought the drinking and drugs were a phase that would pass, but it's only gotten worse. I think he's starting to realise that you're doing drugs and drinking too much to escape the world he's pushed onto you."

Jake shakes his head vehemently, looking a little sad. "I'm not going to lie and say I want the job, as I never have. But it's more about things being forced on me than the actual job itself.

"I was raised to become the person Dad expects of me, and there's no room for me to think for myself, or to do what I want to do. There's actually parts of the job that I enjoy, and I care about the people of Blackthorn, I just hate the lack of choice."

I let out a snort. "Now that's something I can relate to."

"Me too," Marcus adds. "But if you truly cared about the people of Blackthorn, you have to realise how much they'll suffer if things continue down this road."

"What's that supposed to mean?"

Marcus lets out a long sigh, his hand stilling against my lower back, and I lean in to his touch, giving him as much support as I can.

"You have to know that I'm never going to accept Scott as an equal replacement for you. If your father announces Scott as his heir, I'll have no choice but to tear up the peace treaty.

"Uniting your family with the Caprillos could potentially give him more power, and that would be a risk for me. I'd have to act straight away, to make it clear I won't ever see Scott as my equal."

"But that will start a war," Jake screeches, his eyes wide.

Marcus' mouth forms a tight line as he solemnly nods. "I wouldn't want to do it, but I'd be an idiot not to think Caprillo was a threat to me."

"I know putting off the wedding isn't a fix, but I figured it would buy us some time," I add.

"Time for what?" Jake asks, though I think he's already worked it out in his head, he just needs to hear the words out loud.

"Time for you to get your shit together," Marcus replies, taking a much harsher approach than I would have.

I glare at him, and he just rolls his eyes at me, his lips turning up into that cocky smirk that makes my stomach flutter. I turn away quickly and address Jake.

"We were hoping you'd use the time to go to rehab, to get better. This is about more than just stopping Scott from getting power. Marcus needs you to rule with him. The people of Blackthorn deserve the leader they think you are. But more than that, I'm sitting here, as your little sister, asking my big brother to help me.

"I don't want to marry Scott. I don't want to be forced into any marriage, and I know it's selfish of me to ask you to do a job that you hate just so that I won't be forced into the life I don't want, but I'm asking anyway."

Jake squeezes my hand, his chocolate eyes turning misty with unshed tears. This time when he speaks to me, his voice is small, barely above a whisper. "I'm scared. I don't know who I am without using as a crutch."

I shuffle closer to him so that I can throw my arms around him, pulling Jake into my chest, my heart breaking when I hear his small sob. "You don't have to be scared, Jake. You've got me, and I promise, I will be with you every step of the way. I know you can do this."

He pulls back, lifting his free hand to swipe away the rogue tears that are trailing down his cheeks. "I'm such a mess."

"It takes a lot to admit that," Marcus says, giving Jake a reassuring smile. "I think you're strong enough to handle this. I've seen you take on worse. Besides, I found that once I took over and proved myself to my father, I was able to move away from what he wanted and be who I want.

"I was raised the same way you were, with a shit tonne of expectations thrust on my shoulders from an early age. The pressure was crippling, and I hated the person my father wanted me to be.

"I could have rebelled the way you did, but I didn't. Instead, I did as I was told. I trained, I followed my father's every instruction, and I quickly became the heir he wanted me to be.

"Then, when he handed all the power over to me, there was nothing holding me back. I stopped doing what he expected of me, and I became my own leader. He's not pleased with how I handle certain things, but at this point, there's very little he can do about it.

"So my best piece of advice for you would be to play along for now, bide your time, and when you finally have his power, then you can step out from his shadow and be the person you want to be. At that point, he can't do shit about it anyway."

I can't help but laugh, and both guys turn to look at me, confused as to why I'd be laughing at such a tense moment.

"Sorry, it's just... We should have known you'd be playing the long game."

Marcus shrugs his shoulders. "I like having a plan."

I turn back to my brother, watching as he takes a deep breath to try and get control over his emotions again. "Are you okay?"

"Honestly, I don't know. But I know that I care about the people of

Blackthorn, and I don't ever want to let them down. I'd also do anything for my little sister.

"So, while the idea of rehab scares the shit out of me, and I'm not sure it will work, I'll give it a try—for you," he says, squeezing my hand at the end.

I shake my head, fixing him with a stern glare. "No, you need to do this for you. If you keep going the way you are, you could die. You need to get better because that's what's best for you."

Although his smile is small, it's genuine, and my heart soars. "Okay, I'll do it."

I turn to Marcus, a bright smile on my face, mixed with a little shock. Although I hoped Jake would agree, I didn't actually know if he would or not. Marcus was incredibly sceptical, but the smile on his face tells me he's just as pleased as I am with the outcome.

"Right," Marcus says as he stands, "I'm going to go and make some phone calls before you change your mind."

"What will we tell everyone?" Jake asks.

"We'll tell your dad the truth, and he'll cover for you with everyone else. He knows you've got a problem, and this will make him see you're serious about getting help. We need him to know you're doing this, so he reconsiders Scott," Marcus explains as he pulls out his phone, walking towards the hallway.

"That makes sense," Jake agrees.

"I'll make the calls in my office. I'll be back soon," he says, looking directly at me. I give him a smile, and what can only be described as an awkward wave, watching as he leaves.

When I turn back, Jake is looking at me with a fierce expression. "What's really going on with you two?"

I let out a long sigh. "It's complicated."

"What does that even mean?"

"Look, I know you're not going to want to hear this, but you asked me and it's the truth... I've liked Marcus for pretty much my whole life. He's never been interested, even going as far as to pick on me just so I'd hate him, but I never did," I confess, my cheeks heating up as I admit my feelings.

Jake lets out a short, sharp laugh that sounds suspiciously like a snort. "Please, I knew you liked him. You practically drooled whenever he was in the same room as you."

My eyes widen as my mouth flops open. "I did not!" I snap, though I have a sneaky suspicion he might be right.

Jake laughs, nodding his head. "You did. It was obvious you liked him. I was just never sure if he felt the same."

Well, that's not what I expected him to say. "He hated me in school."

Jake rolls his eyes at me before fixing me with an exacerbated look. "No, he pretended to hate you. He always looked out for you. I just couldn't work out if he was doing it because he saw you as a little sister, or if there was something more. I suspected it so much, I even made him promise that nothing would ever happen between you."

"Noooo. When?" I cry, my brows so high they're hidden in my hair.

"I think we were thirteen. I wasn't the only one to threaten him either. Dad made it clear you were off-limits too," Jake confesses, startling me.

"So that's why Marcus mentioned the treaty," I mutter to myself, not quite loud enough for Jacob to hear.

"What? Tell me, what's going on with you?" he says, more firmly this time.

"Look, I have no idea what it is. All I know is that I've liked him forever, and now he's offering me the chance to have just a little piece of him, so I'm going to take it. I don't know if he'll ever want more than this, but if there's even the slightest chance he will, I need to hold on to that. I'm always going to want him, and this is my chance."

My heart races as I finally voice the things I've only ever thought about in the darkness when I'm struggling to fall asleep. I like Marcus more than I should, which means I'll happily take whatever little piece of him he's willing to offer me, in the hope it becomes more.

Jake looks at me with a sad smile, pity written across his face and it makes my stomach sink. "Chloe, lovely, I'm not sure Marcus is capable of more—not just with you, but with anyone."

I shake my head defiantly. "No, he is. I know he doesn't do commitment, and that he's never had a real relationship, but that doesn't mean he won't ever have one, or that he can't. He's more scared of the situation than anything."

"What situation?"

"The treaty," I reply.

Jacob's brow furrows. "What about the treaty?"

"Apparently, Dad made it clear that I was off-limits from an early age, letting Marcus know that nothing could ever happen between us as it would disrupt the power balance, thereby voiding the treaty. Having me on his side would potentially make Marcus more powerful, depending on which of our followers remained loyal to me, and our family would never allow that. If Marcus chooses to be with me, he has to be prepared for the possibility that could start a war."

A dark expression crosses Jake's face as he scrunches his nose in a way I've always thought was cute, despite him trying to look angry. "I would never start a war against my best friend, or my sister, for that matter. I'm not saying I'd be ecstatic about the relationship, but I wouldn't go to war over it. As long as you are happy, and he does right by you, I'd be fine with it."

My shoulders feel a little lighter on hearing that, and I can't hold back my smile, before the situation hits me once again. My smile turns tight, as I remind Jake he's not in a position to make that kind of a promise.

"It's great that you say that, Jake, but right now, it really doesn't mean much. At the moment, you're not actually in power, Dad still is. While other people are making decisions instead of you, it will always be a possibility. Which is why I'm being forced to marry Scott."

Jake's silent for a moment, his body slumping as though all the energy is being drained out of him. "If I want to keep my family safe, and the people of Blackthorn, I don't really have a choice anymore. I have to become the leader they need me to be—that you need me to be."

I pull him in for a hug once more, wrapping my arms around him as he rests his head on my chest. "I'll go to rehab, and I'll get sober. I promise."

"Thank you," I mutter, pressing a kiss to his forehead.

"Promise me something," he asks, leaning back to make eye contact with me, so I can see how serious he is.

"What?"

"Just be careful with Marcus. I don't want you to get your heart broken, and by the sounds of it, you're deeper into this than he is."

I let out a groan, knowing he's correct. "You're right, but the problem is, I'm so far in now, I can't stop. I might get my heart broken, or I could get everything I've ever wanted since I was eight-years-old, so it's worth the risk."

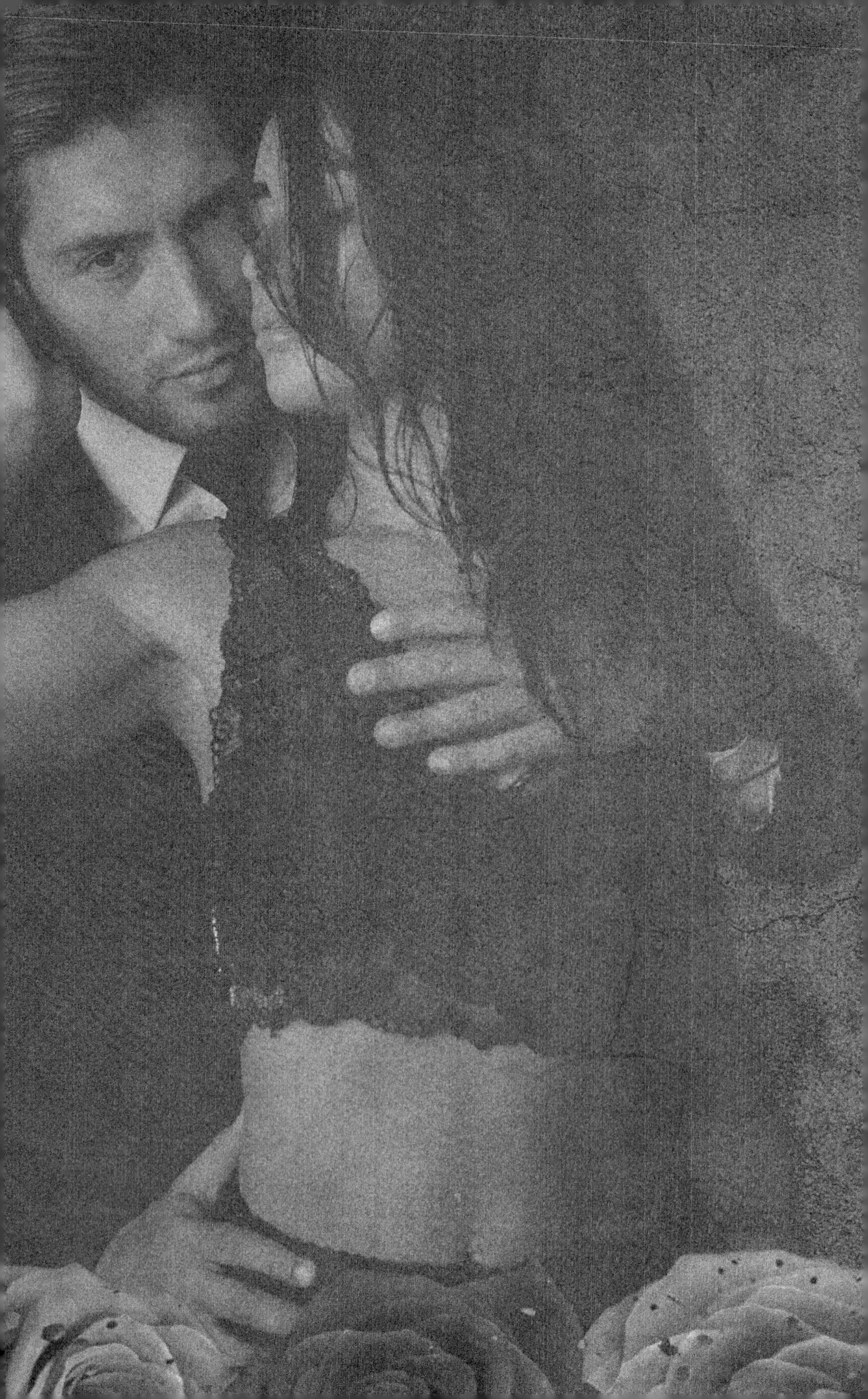

Chapter Eighteen
Marcus

Watching my best friend leave for rehab was much harder than I thought it would be, but seeing the pain on Chloe's face as he left was worse.

We both offered to take him, but he declined, shocking us when he said that Miles could drive him there.

When I told Miles, I expected him to kick off, after all the commotion from earlier in the day, so I was equally as surprised when he agreed without complaint.

I'm not even going to waste my mental capacity wondering what the hell is going on between them, as I don't think I can handle much more.

Things with Chloe, over the last couple of days, since Jake left, have been both easy and incredibly fucking hard. We've grown more comfortable in each other's presence, and have settled into a level of domesticity that I never saw coming.

I've lived alone for the last few years, with the exception of Miles crashing in the room he keeps here, and I like being on my own. I've always preferred having my own space, doing things when I want, not having to take anyone else into consideration.

It was one of the things I worried about the most when I agreed to let Chloe move in. I had no idea it would actually be the easiest part of living with her.

We just seem to move around each other with ease, like we've been doing it our whole lives. I make coffee and breakfast in the morning, as I'm usually awake before she is, and she returns the favour by making dinner in the evenings.

I've actually come to really enjoy the simplicity of our evenings together. We talk over dinner, sometimes sharing a glass of wine as we discuss our day. I've gotten to know her so much over the last few days, and she's not at all like I thought.

It's weird how you can know someone for most of your life without really knowing them at all. The more I've learnt, the more I like her. Though it's also increased the rage I feel towards her parents for forcing this charade on her all these years.

The person Chloe presents to the world is who her parents have shaped her to be. They've not taken into account who she really is, her personality, or even what Chloe truly wants. They don't care about any of that shit, only seeing her as a tool they can use to further their own games.

Now that she's here with me, that stops. I've been pushing her to separate the two versions of Chloe. She needs to get rid of anything that was created to please her parents, and focus solely on what she wants. I know this is something she's found difficult, but I'm proud of her for trying.

Watching the joy on her face when she comes home from another one of her baking classes is something else. She lights up the room, and she talks a million miles a minute as she tells me everything she learnt in the class, and how she plans to practise the techniques before using them.

Seeing her find something she's passionate about has made all the shit that happened with the bet worth it, as I've never seen her this happy. I also didn't realise that seeing her happy would make me feel good.

I've never really given a shit about other people before. Don't get me wrong, when Miles or Jake tell me good news, I'm pleased for them, but it doesn't really affect me.

Yet when Chloe tells me, I can feel my body lighting up, and the smile I give her is genuine.

That thought in itself should scare the shit out of me, but if I'm being honest, I've been so consumed by the negative side of Chloe being here, I've not had time to think about anything else.

I'm not even sure you could call it a negative side, but referring to it as hard is a bit too on the nose, as that's literally what it is.

Every moment I'm around her, my dick is in a constant state of excitement. I can't remember a time I was fully flaccid, and it's all because of her.

I knew when I had a taste of her, I'd never go back, yet I was stupid enough to pass the control to her. After everything she's been through, it seemed like the right thing to do. I want her to be one hundred percent certain when I fuck her that it's what she wants.

After our time in the car, I would have bet good money on her being ready, which is part of the reason I gave her the control. I thought she'd be begging me to fuck her after just a couple of days, yet we're almost a week later, and she's still not asked me.

I've no idea what to fucking do. All I know is that my hand isn't cutting it anymore, and I'm pretty sure my cock is going to burst if it doesn't get the attention it deserves soon.

I had to put my own needs aside, as I could see all throughout Saturday that the gorgeous, confident woman I've watched blossom in front of my eyes over the last few days, was starting to wilt. I didn't need to ask her what the matter was, we both knew.

As we sat down for our usual dinner, Chloe's glass of wine was larger than normal, and the silence between us was deafening. So when my phone rang, I breathed a sigh of relief.

I normally try not to answer the phone when I'm having a meal with her, but I decided to make an exception this time.

When I see Caleb Santoro's name flashing across my screen, I groan, swearing in Italian quite a lot in my head.

"Hello," I grind out, trying to remain the professional I'm supposed to be.

"Marcus," Caleb starts, not bothering with any pleasantries. "I'm calling to inform you that we're going away for a couple of weeks. We are in need of a holiday."

"Okay." I can hear the confusion in my voice, but I'm not entirely sure why they're letting me know.

"I just want to make sure that you will be okay on your own, with Jacob being indisposed at the moment," he replies, and I can't help the short humourless laugh that I let out.

"You mean while he's in rehab?"

"Erm...well, yes. Look, this whole business is very unpleasant. It's causing his mother a great deal of stress, and so I'm taking her away for a much needed break."

I don't point out that Fiona doesn't do anything other than attend posh events and go for spa days, and she certainly doesn't give a shit about Jacob, so I don't know why she's stressed. It's probably got more to do with how this is affecting her image than anything.

"No problem," I reply, managing to keep all the sarcasm from my voice.

"Obviously, since we will be out of town, Chloe won't be expected to attend Sunday lunch with the family, but when we return, she will be needed for a wedding planning session that is non-negotiable," he states firmly, but I just roll my eyes.

"We can discuss it on your return."

I hear him huff down the phone, clearly not appreciating my vague response. "I will be reachable by phone, if needed. You can always call Scott if I'm not available."

I snort, unable to stop myself, and out of the corner of my eye, I notice Chloe trying not to laugh at the awfully undignified noise. "That won't be happening," I snap.

Caleb growls, "He's joining my family, which means you'll need to start showing him respect."

I shake my head, even though he can't see me. "Until the day it's official, he remains inferior to me, and any respect will need to be earned, which I can assure you, at this point, it couldn't be further away."

"Fine, this can be another thing we discuss on my return."

"I look forward to it." This time, I allow the sarcasm to drip into every word, and Caleb hangs up the phone without saying anything further.

Chloe is staring at me, her brow furrowed. "You don't normally answer the phone at the table," she says, a hint of disapproval seeping into her tone.

"Sorry, but I figured it was important, and I was right."

"Is everything okay?"

I give her a nod and a smile. "Your father wanted to inform me that the stress of Jacob going into rehab has been too much for your mother to deal with, and as a result, they're going on holiday for a couple of weeks."

Chloe rolls her eyes. "Wow, it's hard for her?"

I chuckle. "You're missing the point. They won't be here for two weeks... So, no family lunches."

Her eyes light up, and I pointedly ignore the way my heart races at the beautiful smile that spreads across her face. She then lets out a high-pitched giggle, before leaning over and throwing her arms around my neck. "That's amazing news."

She pulls back a little, but I keep my arms around her, not letting her go. Although the corner of the table is in between us, making things a little uncomfortable, I don't care.

I don't even really know what the hell I'm doing. All I'm sure of is that I want to see Chloe smile at me like this a whole lot more.

What the fuck are you doing? This is supposed to be just about sex, and we're getting into feelings territory here, I think to myself, before quickly pushing the thoughts from my mind. Things are confusing enough, without overthinking too.

"I like seeing you smile like this," I admit.

Blush spreads across her cheeks as her expression turns shy, making my dick twitch once more.

"I can't remember the last time I smiled this much, if I'm being honest."

"I'm glad you're happy here." I leave off the *with me* part that I wanted to add at the end.

She nods her head, her breath fluttering over my cheek, enamouring me even more. "I'm shocked by how easy it's been. I like it here, though I'm a little worried how hard that will make things when it all has to come to an end."

My mood sours in an instant, and Chloe must be able to see it on my face as she pulls back, her brow furrowed. I let her move away this time, thinking a little space will make it easier for me to get my emotions under control.

The thought of her leaving, going back to that life, to *him*, sends me into a fucking rage, and I don't think logically when I'm like this. I know all the reasons why she has to return to her life.

I'm hoping that once Jake is sober, and he takes back control of his family, that he can stop her shit-show of a marriage to that dickhead, but until then, there's very little I can do.

The bet already pushed the boundaries of the treaty further than I should have, but the rules meant they had to be honoured. Anything else would be seen as me interfering in Santoro business, and I can't do that.

Chloe has her life that she has to go back to, and no matter how much I might not want her to leave, we both know our time together is a ticking time-bomb, and nothing we do can stop it.

"I can't promise that our time won't come to an end, as we know it has to, but I can do my best to make sure the life you go back to isn't as bad as it has been. When Jake's sober, he'll be able to help more too," I tell her, but the tight smile she gives me back tells me she doesn't believe me.

"I've always known what my life would be, Marcus. I'm just going to enjoy this time away from it while I can," she admits.

I let out a long sigh. "I wish I could do more."

She reaches over and grabs my hand, lacing our fingers together like we've done so many times before. "There's a few weeks before I have to leave, who knows what will happen by then."

I can tell she's just trying to cheer me up, saying what she thinks I want to hear, but she's not wrong. I may not have the answer for her now, but I've got plenty of time to come up with a plan.

My brain is ticking away when I'm pulled away by her squeezing my hand. "Shall we watch a movie? I made lemon meringue pie for dessert."

I groan, shaking my head as I pout. "No more making delicious puddings. I'm going to have to run for longer tomorrow now."

"But it'll be worth it," she says with a wink as she stands, clearing the empty plates from the table.

Fuck, that wink shouldn't have been so sexy, but everything about her turns me on at the moment.

I help her clean the table, and we settle onto the sofa, scrolling through the movies on Netflix until we find one we both want to watch. As soon as I taste the pie she made, my loud groan fills the room, and Chloe laughs.

"You really have found your calling," I tell her, shovelling more of the pie into my mouth when I've spoken.

"I like making desserts, but honestly, the thing I enjoy most is creating novelty birthday cakes. I've been practising the different design aspects, and I've made a few dummy cakes in class, and they've all turned out great. I have a way to go, but I'm picking things up quickly," she tells me, her eyes lighting up when she talks about it.

"I can't believe it's only been two weeks and you've found what you want to do with your life," I reply, not even bothering to hide the awe in my voice.

Chloe looks confused. "What do you mean? This is just for fun."

I shake my head at her. "Chloe, when you first came here, I told you to find what you are passionate about, to find what you'd do with your life if you got to choose. This may be something you're doing for fun now, but I get the feeling you're good enough to at least turn this into a small business, if you ever decided to."

Her brow furrows as her lips turn to a tight line. "I can't turn it into a business. That will never be an option for me. Hell, when I move back home, it'll be a fucking miracle if they even allow me to continue baking, since my mother thinks that's beneath me."

I reach over and place my hand on her thigh, squeezing it enough to stop the spiral I can see she's falling into.

"Stop! Like you said earlier, we'll deal with things when they happen. But I'm telling you, in an ideal future, this is the job you should be doing. Just think about it."

"Thinking about what I want and can't have is too hard," she replies, her silver eyes boring into mine. I get the feeling we're talking about more than just her cake business now, and I'm not entirely sure what to say.

"Chloe..."

"Let's watch the movie," she says, tucking her legs underneath her as she shuffles back on the sofa.

Before I know it, Chloe is leaning against my side as I throw my arm over her shoulder, her body tucked against mine. Slowly, her head droops until it's resting on my shoulder, and she curls her arm around my waist, pulling me against her more.

We're both wrapped up in each other, and I can't tell you anything that happens in the movie. I spend all my time watching Chloe. The rise and fall of her chest that slows as she begins to fall asleep. The way her breath fans the stray strands of her long brown hair that have fallen from her messy bun.

When she's tucked up against me, her arm wrapped around me, she feels so incredibly petite compared to me, and her body warmth heats me in the best way.

I stay like this long after the movie has ended, not wanting to wake her. Her mouth has fallen open into a little O, and her face looks serene. There's a ghost of a smile in her cheeks, making me hope I remember this moment.

It's not long until I feel sleep pulling at me, making my eyes heavy, and I war with myself over what to do. We'll both get a better, more restful sleep if we go to bed, but I can't bring myself to end this. So, against my better judgement, I let sleep pull me under.

An odd sensation wakes me up, and I slowly pry my eyelids apart, my brain struggling to catch up. I feel movement beside me, and that has me alert in no time.

Chloe is shuffling against my side, yawning as she stretches out her no doubt stiff limbs, though the arm that's wrapped around my waist doesn't move—thankfully.

She turns her body slightly to look up at me, still mostly tucked in against my side. She gives me a small, shy smile that I'm quick to return. "Looks like we fell asleep," she whispers.

I look over at the clock, noting it's just after two in the morning, which means I got about two hours of sleep here on the sofa, though my body seems to think it was longer.

I'm aching, desperate to stretch, yet there's no pain in the world that would make me move Chloe right now.

"Yes, looks like it," I add, not bothering to elaborate that it was my fault for allowing us to fall asleep like this.

Unfortunately, Chloe begins to sit up, removing her body from mine, making me feel colder than I was expecting, like I'm missing a part of me.

"We should get to bed," she says, as she stands from the sofa, reaching out her hand to me.

Is she inviting me into her bed?

My gaze flicks between Chloe's outstretched hand and her eyes, my body frozen. I see the exact moment she hears her own words in her head, as her eyes widen almost comically.

"Our own beds…I mean," she mumbles, the flush on her cheeks deepening as she looks away shyly.

I take hold of her hand, though I pull myself up. "I knew what you meant," I say, flashing her my best smirk.

She rolls her eyes at me, and I have to bite the inside of my cheek to stop from smiling. I love when she shows a little of her fiery side.

I pull her into the corridor, stopping outside of her bedroom door. The chemistry is fizzling between us, and I don't drop her hand, even though I know I should. I take a step towards her, which clearly startles Chloe as she steps backwards, until she hits the wall.

Now I see she's caged in between my body and the wall, I place my free hand flat above her head, leaning into her more. My lips are right beside her ear, my breath tickling across her cheek, and she shivers in response.

Her wide innocent eyes look up at me, but there's a heat in them that I know is in mine too. Her grip on my hand tightens, and it's the only thing stopping me from dragging it all over her body. But she still hasn't asked me to fuck her, so I can't.

That doesn't mean I can't get her a little hot in the process.

I close the already tiny gap between us, pressing my body against hers, and she gasps when she feels my hard length pressing against her stomach.

"I had a really lovely evening," I whisper into her ear.

She gives me a smile, and when she responds, her voice is hoarse. "Me too. Do you want to…"

She leaves the question unfinished, just hanging between us, but we both know what she was about to say.

I rock my hips in response, both of us groaning as my cock rubs against her. "I want to, but I don't think you're ready yet."

She shakes her head, and I'm inclined to agree with her.

What the fuck am I doing? I think to myself.

"I am ready," she argues.

"No, you're not. When you are ready, you'll know. It will be all you can think about. You'll be begging me, refusing to let me say no. You're almost there, and I can wait," I reply, though I'm not entirely sure I believe myself.

She gives me a nod and a small smile. "Thank you."

Without thinking, I lean down and capture her lips with mine. It was only supposed to be a small goodnight kiss, but as soon as I feel her soft, gentle lips beneath mine, I can't hold back.

I push myself against her as I deepen the kiss, pressing our lips together harder, swiping my tongue along her lower lip. I capture her moan in my mouth, using the moment to sweep my tongue inside, so I can taste her.

Our lips and tongues mesh together, kissing each other in a deep, sensual way as I rock my hips against hers. I feel her shuffling beneath me, widening her legs so I can slip my knee between them. She wastes no time grinding her fabric-covered pussy against my thigh.

I groan as I feel her rubbing against me, my cock hardening as it's trapped between us, the friction both maddening and amazing.

I want nothing more than to take this further, but it was only supposed to be a goodnight kiss, and now she's grinding her wet pussy on my thigh, and it's taking all my willpower not to remove my hand from hers, so I can touch her.

We both pull back from the kiss slightly, desperately pulling in some much needed air, and this seems to be enough space to allow the sex-induced fog to clear from my brain, and I groan in frustration.

"That was just supposed to be a goodnight kiss, not...more," I tell Chloe, which makes her laugh.

"Well, it was a hell of a night then," she replies, which makes me laugh too.

I press my lips against hers once more, hard and claiming, only this time I pull away before it can turn into more. She leans forward, chasing my mouth with hers, but I reluctantly pull back.

"I want nothing more than to keep kissing you, but instead, I'm going to say goodnight," I state, ignoring the way my cock is screaming at me.

Chloe's lip tips up into a smirk. "Who knew you'd be such a gentleman?"

I rock my hips into her, letting her feel all of my hard cock that's trying to burst free from my jeans, and her eyes widen.

"I'm not a gentleman, I'm just taking my time. I want to drive you crazy first. I want to be the only thing you think about, dream about.

"I want you to wish you could get yourself off to thoughts of me, knowing I won't give you permission to touch yourself. When I finally take you I want you dripping wet, needy, desperate for my cock.

"I want you begging me like you might die if I don't agree. I'm not a gentleman, Mio, I'm the wicked guy biding his time until he ruins you for all other men."

Her brows shoot into her hairline, and my devilish smirk grows at the sight of her wide, shocked eyes, but I can also see the need flashing in them too. She loves my dirty words, and she's not far off losing herself to the moment.

"I-I... You mean, I can't..." she mumbles incoherently, not able to finish her sentence, but I know what she's trying to say.

I lean in until I'm whispering in her ear, her body trembling beneath me. "No, you can't touch yourself, and you definitely can't come. I meant what I said, the next time I let you come, it'll be on my cock."

She shakes her head, looking a little alarmed. "I can't. I need to..."

"I will punish you, and it will be so much worse than before. Just be a bit more patient, and I promise, I'll make it worth it for you. You want to be a good little slut for me, don't you, Mio?"

Chloe nods her head, and I can't help but smile. "I want to be a good slut, but I'm so wet. I really need to come."

She's so quiet and shy as she admits it to me, I have to bite my lip to stop myself from moaning. I'm very aware I'm a bad influence on her, but that's not going to stop me.

"Get some sleep. I'll sleep well knowing your tight little cunt is wet and waiting for me," I growl, pressing my lips to her forehead before I finally step back.

Chloe almost slumps to the floor when she's not being held up between me and the wall, her legs wobbling as she holds onto my hand firmly. As she raises her head, the fierce glare she gives me reminds me of the phrase "if looks could kill," as I'd be six-feet under now.

My cocky smirk doesn't help, and she frowns at me. "I'm so frustrated right now," she groans.

"I know, Mio. Be a good girl, and I promise, it'll be worth it."

She shivers at the praise I give her, though her fierce look doesn't lessen. "Fine," she snaps, before her tone softens slightly when she adds, "Good night."

She presses a quick kiss on my lips and turns, slamming the door in my face before I even know what's happening. I bring my fingers up to my lips, wondering why I can still feel hers pressed against mine.

I quickly walk to my room, closing the door behind me before I fall back against it, my head banging off it as I do.

What the hell was I thinking? I could be balls deep in her tight pussy right now, but instead, I'm stuck with my hand again.

I know I'm doing the right thing, dragging it out until she's really sure it's what she wants, but fuck, if this burns any slower, my cock really might fall off.

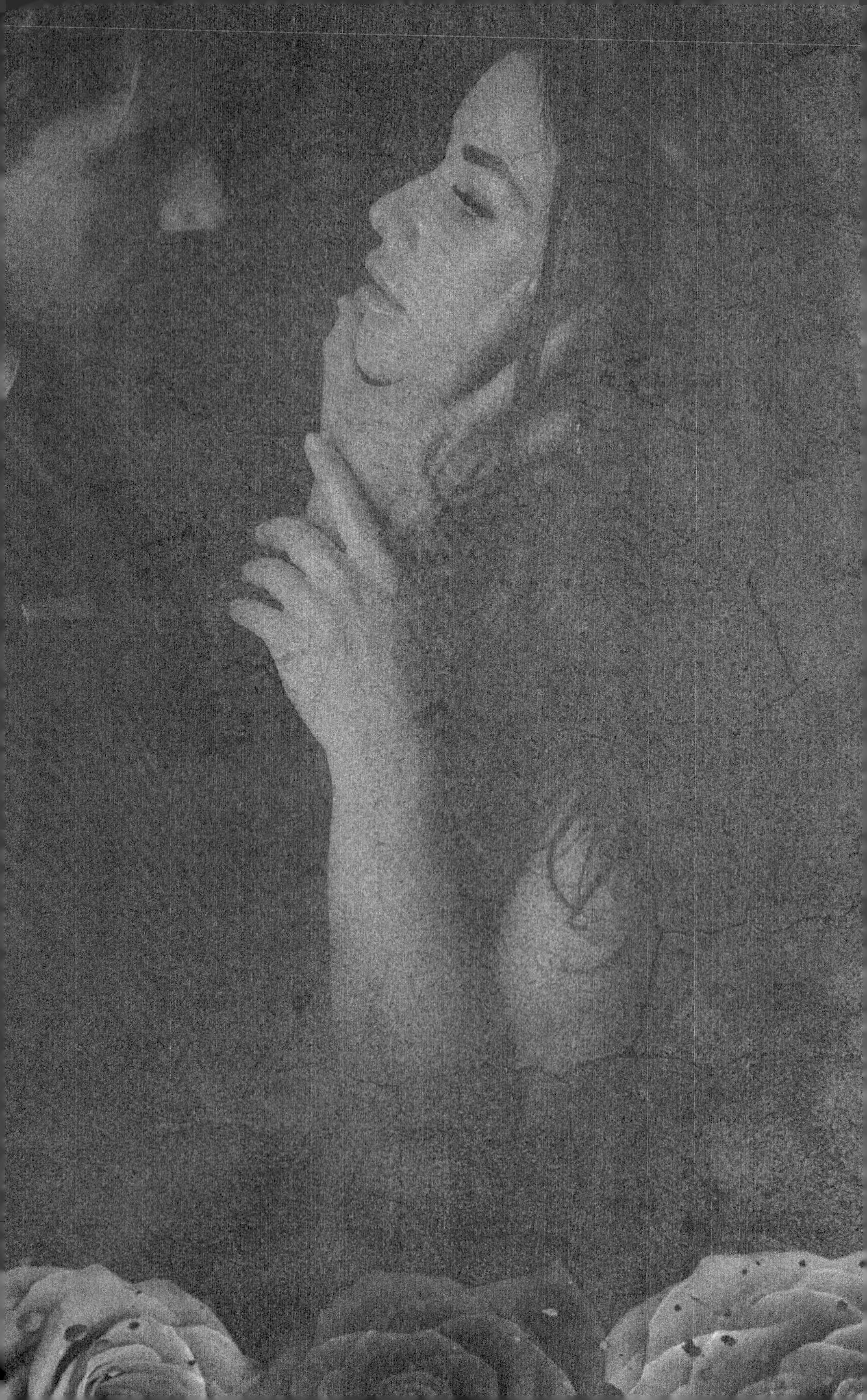

Chapter Nineteen
Chloe

It's been four whole days, and I'm still thinking about the kiss. I relive the moment constantly, whether I want to or not. Whenever my mind wanders, that's what I think about.

I've imagined so many alternate scenarios, and not one of them ends with me alone in bed, fucking frustrated and sizzling hot, to the point I can't sleep.

They all involve Marcus taking me, making me come. And let me tell you, they're a hell of a lot hotter than what actually fucking happened.

I'm still not done yelling at Past Chloe for her silence. I have no idea what the hell she was thinking, but she definitely didn't consider how bloody awful it's been for the last four days, living in a constantly horny state.

I wasn't even this bad when I was a teenager!

Realistically, Marcus wouldn't have any idea if I cheated—just a little. There's been more than one occasion when my fingers have drifted precariously close to my knickers before I've caught myself. Yet I still can't bring myself to break his rules.

The truth is, in every version of my fantasy, it's always his fingers that make me fall apart, never my own. Sometimes it's his mouth, or his cock, or all of the above, but it's never my own hand that I imagine.

So why the fuck am I still relying on fantasies instead of memories? I have no bloody clue, but for some reason, I just can't seem to ask him.

I don't know what the hell is going on with me, as there's nothing I want more, yet something is holding me back. *It's those pesky little things called feelings,* my brain helpfully reminds me.

I let out a sigh of frustration as the thought overwhelms me. I can pretend all I want, but deep down, I've not taken things further with Marcus because I'm scared.

I have feelings for him, and have since I was a kid, but he's been honest with me when he said he doesn't do relationships.

I'm always going to want more from him than he's willing to give. Yet, when he tells me I'm his, my heart races at the possibility there could be more.

Every girl wants to be the one to tame the bad boy, to make him want to settle down, and I can't stop that stupid notion when I think of Marcus. No matter how ridiculous it is, a girl can dream.

Tonight, I'm extra antsy, and not just because I'm incredibly sexually frustrated. Marcus has yet to come home, and this is the latest he's ever stayed out without letting me know.

There's times he needs to be at the club, or meeting with people late at night, but he always texts to let me know. Even when he's just working in his home office, taking late calls with people in different time zones, he lets me know.

I knew he was going to be out late with Miles, but they never specified where they were going, which, at the time, wasn't odd, since they don't always tell me about their work, but when Marcus didn't come home, or text me, I started to worry.

Watching the clock doesn't seem to be helping, time seems to be passing even slower now.

I've tried to sleep. It was three minutes past three when I fell asleep, and it was twenty-eight minutes past three when I woke up feeling worse than before.

I must have picked up my phone a million times, trying to decide whether I should text or call him, and each time I've thrown it down in a huff. I mean, I'm not sure I have any right to text him, demanding he lets me know he's safe. We're not together... We've barely just become friends, so I'm not sure I can make that sort of a demand on him.

Unfortunately, the longer my brain is allowed to run unchecked, the more outlandish the theories become. The most obvious one was that he's dead, and my heart hurt too much to even think that, so I quickly moved on to him being injured and in the hospital.

Granted, that didn't feel a whole lot better, but at least I could breathe normally, where thoughts of him being gone sent me into a hyperventilating panic.

Once I'd covered every option of him being injured, things quickly escalated. Maybe he'd fled the country in a private jet to avoid prosecution after the police started closing in.

I mean, it's unlikely to be that given he doesn't have a private jet, and the police of Blackthorn are very deeply in Marcus and my family's pocket.

I then went to the ridiculous, thinking maybe he'd accidentally got himself locked in a room, where he didn't have a signal, and he wasn't able to let anyone know he needed help.

Not a bad idea, but also a tad problematic as if nobody knows where he is, they won't be able to rescue him. Which, of course, led to very dark thoughts about him starving to death.

Then my brain takes a very dark turn when I wonder if he's gone home with another girl, since I haven't agreed to fuck him yet. Even though he doesn't do relationships, I assumed that while he's with me, he wouldn't be with anyone else.

Then again, he's not with me, since I've not asked him yet. So can I really blame him if he's found another girl to meet his needs?

I might not be able to blame him, but I can be very fucking mad at him.

I could ring or text Miles instead, I think to myself as the clock turns to forty three minutes past three, trying to distract from nightmares of Marcus with another woman.

It's not a bad plan, except, there's a good chance it would make me look even more insane than if I were to just reach out to Marcus. Then his friend would know I'm neurotic, and far too into him.

I reach over and grab my phone again, scrolling through social media in an attempt to distract me. I'm not at all looking to see if either of them have posted anything—which they haven't.

Six minutes later, the front door slams open loudly, grabbing my attention. Before I can even think it though, I spring out of my bed and rush into the hallway. It's empty, but I hear the sound of drawers banging in the kitchen, so I rush in there.

Marcus never makes this much noise when he knows I'm sleeping, so this, combined with his unexplained absence, has me really on edge. As soon as I get into the kitchen, I freeze, coldness washing over me as my stomach sinks.

The initial relief I felt, for just a fraction of a second, knowing he was alive and safe went flying out of the window when I see all the blood covering his suit.

At the sound of me entering the kitchen, Marcus spins around, his eyes wide as he brandishes a large knife. I take a small step back with a yelp, holding my hands up.

"It's just me, Marcus. Put the knife down," I tell him, my voice shaking about as much as my body.

He lets his wrist go limp, the knife dropping to the floor as his wide blue eyes remain fixed on me. I take a step forward, and he seems to tense more.

"Are you okay? Is that blood yours? Do I need to get you to a doctor?" I blurt out, each question coming out quicker than the one before.

He's silent for a moment, not even blinking.

"Marcus, tell me what to do. I'm scared," I whisper, my voice cracking at the end.

As soon as the last word leaves my lips, it's like Marcus is woken up with a jolt. He blinks rapidly, the darkness in his eyes receding as his bright blue colour starts to return.

This time when he looks at me, I know he's really seeing me, and my heart breaks for him as his face falls.

"I'm sorry. Please don't be scared of me," he whispers, sounding very unlike the Marcus I know.

I shake my head quickly, trying to stop the tears that are welling up from falling.

"I'm not scared of you, Marcus. I'm scared for you. Is that blood yours?" I say, pointing to his suit that is almost completely red.

He looks down, running his hand over his jacket, wincing as he moves his arm. "No, it's not all mine."

"Miles?" I squeak, bringing my hand up to my mouth to cover the sob.

Marcus takes a few steps forward, his arms out towards me, as if he's going to comfort me. Then he stops, looking down at his blood-covered body.

"No, Miles is safe. This is the blood of an enemy," he confirms, and I breathe a sigh of relief.

"Are you injured at all?"

Even though he's said the blood isn't all his, I still need to make sure he's not injured.

Marcus winces, like he was hoping not to answer that question. I fix him with a hard stare, making it clear I won't drop it until I get an answer.

"I have some injuries, but with all the blood, I'm not sure how bad they are."

My stomach sinks, and my heart races even faster, which I didn't think was possible. Without even thinking, I close the gap between us and take hold of his hand. Marcus looks down in shock at where I grab him, and we both choose to ignore the way someone else's blood stains my hand.

"What are you—"

I cut him off, dragging him behind me as I walk into the corridor. "Just come with me."

I pull him into the main bathroom, which neither of us use as we both have en-suites in our bedrooms. As it's the main bathroom in the apartment, it's large and luxurious, and when I spot the giant tub, I mentally chastise myself for not indulging in a soak in here.

The bathroom is decorated similarly to the other rooms in the house. Bright whites alongside a grey feature wall, with grey and white marble tiles covering the areas around the shower, bath, and sink. The grey wall is almost covered with a large mirror and the sink cabinet, which is big enough for a person to sit on.

There's a large walk-in shower, big enough for at least two people, with a bench seat along one side, and a large rainfall shower overhead. The bathtub is bigger than anything I've ever seen, and the little holes dotted around the side indicate it's a jacuzzi too.

I make a mental note to definitely come in here and enjoy a luxurious soak in the tub at a later date.

With one hand still holding onto Marcus, I open the door to the shower and lean in, turning on the water. I play around with the settings until I get it to the right temperature, not caring that I've just leaned under the water fully-clothed, and one half of my body is now soaked.

Since seeing Marcus covered in blood, knowing that he's hurt, I'll admit, I've not exactly been thinking clearly. I turn to face him, my breath hitching at the way his eyes are roaming over my body, fixating on the wet patches.

"We need to get the blood off you, so I can see what your injuries are," I tell him, but still he doesn't move.

Without thinking, I walk into the shower, pulling him with me. He stops just before he climbs in to kick off his shoes, but then he steps into the water, not taking his eyes off me.

Warm water cascades over me, drenching me completely, and I take a step back, pulling Marcus under the waterfall. As the water hits him, his dark hair flops down onto his face, some strands covering his eyes as it trickles over him.

Reaching over, as gently as I can, I swipe the wet strands away from his face, tucking the longer pieces behind his ears, while the others I just slick back, using the water to help me keep them in place.

His gaze remains locked on mine, but I see the way his breath hitches when I run my finger along his face.

I swipe my fingers over his cheek, washing away the small specks of blood that are dotted all over his face. When I get to those soft pink lips of his, I can't help but drag my thumb along his bottom one, loving the feel of how silky it is.

Marcus' bright blue eyes darken, and he looks down at me through hooded lashes, his chest rising and falling rapidly, confirming that he's just as affected by this as I am.

I'm so lost, just staring into his almost hypnotic eyes, I don't even see his mouth open, but I feel it under my touch. He pulls the tip of my thumb into his mouth, and my gaze drops to his lips instantly. He swirls his tongue around it before sucking gently.

A small gasp escapes, but it's drowned out by the loud pounding of the water. Given the way Marcus shudders, he heard the noise.

He somewhat reluctantly releases my thumb, and I'm a little upset about it. How the hell is he capable of turning me on with just his mouth on my thumb? Imagine what he could do with access to my whole body.

Focus, Chloe, I remind myself. *He might be injured, so focus on that, nothing else!*

Except, given the way he's staring at me, like he wants to devour me, it's hard to think of anything else. I take a deep breath as I try to steady my nerves, to help me focus on the task at hand.

I reach out with both hands and, as carefully as I can, I shuck the jacket off his shoulders before sliding each arm out. Despite being super gentle, he winces a lot, even going as far as a hiss and grimace when I move his left arm out of the jacket.

He allows me to manipulate his limbs, making it easier for me to pull his jacket off. I then throw it onto the floor in the far corner of the shower, silently praising whoever designed this place for adding a walk-in shower big enough to house several people comfortably.

Once I've removed his tie, discarding that alongside his jacket, I lower my gaze to assess as much as I can see. Given he's in a white shirt, which should be almost completely transparent by now because of the water, I was hoping I'd be able to get a clearer view of what injuries I'm dealing with without having to undress him further.

I should have known I'm not that lucky.

His once-white shirt is now completely covered in blood, and although the water has drenched it to the point it's sticking to his skin, it's done nothing to remove the blood stains.

I slowly lift my gaze to his, maintaining eye contact with him as I raise my hands towards his top button, making my intentions very clear. I move at a pace that would allow him to stop me if he didn't feel comfortable with me doing this, but he doesn't.

With slightly shaky hands, I begin unbuttoning his shirt. It's harder than it should be, but my trembling fingers, the water continuing to hit us, and the slickness of the buttons, thanks to the water, makes it a much more complicated task than it needs to be.

With each button I finally manage to open, the air in the shower cubical seems to crackle. Although it's the largest shower I've ever been in, the space begins to feel small with how close together we're standing, yet neither of us steps away. We allow the steam to fill the air around us as we just stare at each other.

Both of our chests begin to rise and fall quicker, and once I get to the buttons over his pecs, I can feel his heart beating beneath my touch.

I hold my hand there for longer than is necessary, but I find comfort in knowing his heart is racing for me. He's just as affected by this as I am, and that both thrills and scares me all at the same time.

As I reach the final button, I allow myself to ogle the perfect specimen of a man standing before me. He's lean with just the right amount of muscles, without being too big.

I watch as water droplets cascade over his smooth pecs, along the hard ridges of his abs—a perfect six pack, of course—until it reaches the trail of hair that disappears below his belt.

I don't even see the blood covering his pale skin, or the cut across his side straight away, as I'm too fixated on how annoyingly perfect he looks.

Once I slide his shirt off and he lets out a loud hiss, breaking the bubble I seem to have found myself in, I remember why we're doing this in the first place. I'm not undressing him so I can drool over him, I'm supposed to be making sure he's okay, and the wince of pain tells me he's not.

The shirt joins his jacket in the corner as the water around us runs crimson with blood. This time when I really look at Marcus, I see the way he's curling his right arm around his stomach, while trying not to move his left.

I take a small step back, just so I can get a better view. On the outside of his left arm, across his bicep, there's a slash wound with blood trickling from it.

I reach over and wrap my small hand around his right wrist, his eyes widening as I begin to gently pull his hand away. I wouldn't be able to move him if he didn't allow me to, so I give him a small reassuring smile when he does.

He hisses loudly. "Fuck," he mutters, breaking the tense silence that had been building between us.

Once his hand is out of the way, blood begins to ooze down his lower stomach, over his belt and trousers. I squat down slightly until I'm level with the wound, so I can get a better look, placing my hands on Marcus' hips for support.

It's definitely a knife wound, same as the one on his arm, though this looks worse. The slash across his bicep looks more superficial than anything, whereas this doesn't.

The wound seems to be around three inches long, but it's not a straightforward injury. It's almost like there are two wounds in one.

The outermost part nearest his side is long and shallow, similar to the slice on his arm, whereas the inner part, nearest his bellybutton, is deeper. About an inch of the wound looks to be very deep, like you'd expect to see in a stab wound.

I reach around Marcus and grab the flannel that's hanging on a hook on the wall, making sure to wet it under the shower-head first.

"What happened here?" I ask him as I scrunch the flannel into a ball.

"My meeting went to shit," he replies cryptically.

"I need to put pressure on this, to see if I can slow down the bleeding. It's coming out too quickly right now, but when I press, it might hurt," I tell him.

Feeling my shins start to burn from crouching for too long, I drop down onto my knees, so I can give his injuries my full attention, while not being distracted by my own body yelling at me.

He nods. "That's not a pr—holy fuck, that hurts," he yells, forgetting whatever he was about to say before I pressed the flannel against his deep wound.

It's not long until the light grey flannel is coated with blood, and I start to panic.

"Maybe you need a doctor. Should I take you to the hospital?"

Marcus shakes his head. "No doctors," he says through gritted teeth. "It's not as bad as it looks."

I roll my eyes at his stupid comment. "Really? Because it looks like you've got a fucking hole in you stomach."

He tries to give me that cocky smile of his, but it turns into a wince as I press the flannel harder, and I almost feel bad for just a second.

"The guy only managed to get the tip in before he was pulled away, which is why the wound looks weird. There's a stab wound where the tip went in, and then a slice from when he was dragged away from me."

"And your arm?" I ask, nodding towards the wound on his bicep, where the bleeding, thankfully, appears to be slowing down.

"The arsehole was waving his knife around like a lunatic and I got too close," he says casually, like getting stabbed is no big deal.

Prized Possession

"Do you have any other injuries?" I ask, fixing him with a stare that tells him to be honest with me.

He nods, grimacing as he does. "There's a small slice across my thigh."

He looks down at his right leg, pointing towards where his trousers have been cut open.

"Hold this," I instruct, moving his hand until he takes over holding the flannel, making sure he uses the correct amount of pressure, so we can try stopping the blood flow.

Once I'm sure he's got the pressure correct, I act on instinct. Reaching up, I begin unfastening his belt, sliding the zipper of his trousers down before popping the button.

I look up at Marcus to find him staring down at me through hooded eyes. His eyes are almost completely black, his pupils blown wide.

It's only then that I realise what this must look like to him. I'm soaked through, no doubt making my thin pyjama shorts and vest turn almost transparent, and I'm on my knees before him, unfastening his trousers.

He's clearly ignoring the stab wounds, the blood, and the look of sheer terror that I'm sure I'm not able to hide, but I don't blame him. Maybe this is a fantasy for him.

Great, now I'm frozen and my mind has gone to dirty places once more.

I must have been stuck there for longer than I should be, my fingers on his trouser button, without going further, as Marcus clears his throat before chuntering loud curse words when the movement hurts him.

Hearing him in pain is enough to snap me out of my lust-filled thoughts, and I waste no time removing his belt fully, so I can pull his trousers off, adding them to the growing pile of discarded clothes in the corner.

For just a moment, I'm grateful when I notice the water swirling around our feet is more pink now than red, which I'm hoping means we're managing to stop the bleeding a little.

As I look up at Marcus again, no matter how much I try not to look at his boxers, it's impossible not to notice the large tent sticking out in front of me.

I pull my lip between my teeth to stop myself from letting out a moan, trying to concentrate on what I'm supposed to be doing. I use my grip on his hips to turn him slightly so I can see his thigh.

The cut's about six inches long, but very thin, and the fact there's only a few droplets of blood leaking from the edges confirms it's most likely superficial.

I cup one of my hands until it's full of water, before tentatively placing my palm over the cut. I then gently swipe my fingers along all the edges of the wound, rubbing a little harder where needed to clean away all the dried blood.

Although it's only superficial, I make sure the injury is completely clean, to prevent any chance of infection.

"This one isn't too bad. It's the biggest, but it's mostly superficial. I've cleaned it well to prevent infection. If it's okay with you, I'll do the same with the other wounds too?

"They may need to be cleaned with antiseptic in the morning, but we can look at them again then," I tell him, concentrating on the wound so I don't have to look up at him again.

"Okay," he grinds out.

Don't do it, Chloe. Don't look up!

No matter how many times I repeat it in my head, I do it anyway. There's something in his voice that catches my attention, and I can't help myself. His jaw is tight, like he's grinding his teeth together, and he looks to be in more pain than he was before.

"Are you okay? Am I hurting you?" I rush out, my hands now back on his hips, though I try not to grasp too tightly in case I am hurting him.

"I'm fine." I hear the words, but his tone says he's very much not alright.

"You sound like you're in pain. You have to tell me. I can't help you if you don't—"

My words are cut off and quickly turn into a high-pitched squeal as Marcus, completely forgetting about his injuries, or the cloth he's supposed to be pressing against his side, reaches down, scoops his hands under my arms, and lifts me to my feet.

"The wounds aren't causing me fucking pain... You are," he snaps.

My eyes widen as my brow furrows in confusion. "What?"

Marcus reaches over and turns the shower off, then takes a menacing step towards me. Out of instinct, I step backwards until my back hits the glass of the shower door behind me.

Still, he keeps coming until he's right in front of me, with barely any space between us. His breath fans over my face as he reaches out and grabs hold of my hip, his grip hard enough to bruise.

"Every time I see you in these fucking sleep shorts, I'm in pain, but now they're fucking see-through and it's agony. Then, seeing you on your knees for me, your fingers trailing over my thighs in the most innocent bloody way, all while you look up at me with those big silver eyes, looking like every fantasy I've ever had—that's torture.

"No matter how many times that arsehole slashed or stabbed me, the pain of those wounds is nothing compared to being this close to you and not being able to fucking have you, Mio," he growls, his chest heaving from the intensity of his words.

My heart is pounding so hard, I can hear it echoing in my ears, and I'm breathing so quickly, I'm close to hyperventilating. I open my mouth, but I have no idea what to say.

The intensity in his gaze shatters me. I've never been looked at by anyone the way Marcus looks at me. Not just that he wants me, but like he might die if he doesn't have me, and that makes me feel like the sexiest woman in the world.

I pull in a sharp breath, before raising my chin just enough that I can look up at him. Once his gaze connects with mine, I say the only words I can think of at this moment. "You can have me."

I've barely finished my sentence when Marcus slams his lips against mine, claiming my mouth in the most delicious way. I wrap my arms around his neck, sliding my fingers into the hairs at the back of his neck, holding him close as I meet his kiss with my own.

This kiss is different from our others. It's deep, bruising, almost claiming, and I'm more than happy to get lost in him.

His tongue sweeps across my lip, and I let him in, melding mine against his. I whimper into his mouth as I taste him, my body heating up, burning from the inside out.

As soon as he hears the noise I make, Marcus rocks his hips, rubbing his boxer-covered hard cock against my stomach. When he does, he pulls his lips away, groaning in a very different way to before.

"Fuck," he mutters, taking a small step back, though my arms around his neck prevent him from going too far.

He looks down, his eyes widening as he does and I follow his gaze. Not only is there a small trail of blood running from the wound on his side, I'm completely covered in blood too. It most likely got there when I was helping him staunch the flow, or get undressed, but now it's hard to unsee.

"You need stitches in that wound. It's too deep to heal on its own," I tell him, and he nods in agreement.

"Let's get you cleaned up, and then I'll call my doctor to come and take a look," he says, glaring at the blood-soaked vest.

"Okay," I agree, before reaching down to grab hold of my shirt so I can pull it off.

I only make it as far as my belly button piercing before Marcus reaches out and grabs hold of my wrists. His jaw is tight, his eyes dark and fixed on my face.

"If you take your clothes off in front of me, my last bit of self-restraint will fly out of the window, and I will have to fuck you, no matter how much it hurts." His voice is deep and gravelly, and if I wasn't wet before, I sure as hell am now.

"Don't hurt yourself for me," I tell him, letting go of my shirt. "I'll help you clean your wounds, and you can get out while I wash. Sound good?"

He shakes his head. "No. Good would be me fucking you until you can't do anything except scream my name, but since we can't do that, we'll go with your plan."

I chuckle, reaching behind him to grab another cloth off the hook on the wall. I then direct the shower head away from us while I find the right temperature, before turning on the rainfall shower above us.

I try to keep my movements gentle but swift, knowing the longer I drag this out, the more torturous it'll be for us both.

Once I've washed all the blood off his body, I focus on his wounds, making sure they're as clean as can be. He winces, hisses, and occasionally swears, but that just tells me I'm doing a good job.

I'm not worried about the wounds on his arm or thigh, as they've both almost stopped bleeding already, but the one on his stomach is deeper and won't stop trickling.

It's not as bad as it was initially, but there's still enough blood for me to be concerned. Marcus also pulls away when I touch around it, which tells me it hurts much more than he's letting on.

"All done," I say when I finish cleaning the last bit of his body. "Well, except for your boxers and your hair. Do you want me to..."

I leave the sentence unfinished, just kind of hanging in the air. Marcus' eyes flutter closed as he takes a few deep breaths.

"Fuck, this is really testing me tonight, love. Can you pull off my boxers and I'll wash while you shampoo my hair? It will hurt my arm a lot less if you do it."

I give him a smile and a nod, my heart aching that he's allowing himself to be vulnerable enough to ask for my help. Now I just need to take his boxers off without groping him... Easy!

Ha, who am I kidding, it was so fucking hard—literally.

I tried to keep my eyes on Marcus' face, but it's incredibly difficult to remove someone's boxers when you can't see what you're doing, and it actually resulted in my hands brushing over areas I was trying to avoid. Marcus' loud groan made my core tighten, and I looked down, telling myself to focus.

I've seen his cock before, so this shouldn't have come as much of a shock, but last time I saw it, Marcus had his hand wrapped around the base as he came. Whereas now, it's bobbing free, it's full length on display, looking bigger than before.

I quickly crouch down, trying to ignore that I'm now at eye level with his rather large, hard cock as I pull his wet boxers down. As they're completely soaked, they are almost sticking to his skin, and it takes me longer than it should to get them down. If I believed in a higher power, I'd think they were definitely testing me right now.

As I manage to pull the waistband down over his arse, I feel my nails drag along his flesh, and the noise that comes from Marcus' throat is like music to my ears. When his cock bobs in front of me, I speed up until he steps out of them.

Once they're discarded along with the rest of his clothes, he turns so that his back is to me. This way I can reach his hair, and the spray is more directly over his front, so he can clean himself.

I reach over to the shelf by the shower controls and grab a small dollop of shampoo, before I stand on my tip-toes, lifting up my arms towards his hair. He must be able to tell I'm struggling, as he crouches down a little.

I take my time massaging the shampoo into his scalp, running my fingers through the longer strands afterwards. I tell myself I'm just doing a thorough job, when really I just love the feel of his silky hair between my fingers, and my imagination is running wild.

Before I can get lost in more dirty thoughts, I quickly rinse the shampoo out, making sure to massage his scalp as I make sure it's clean.

Each time I press into just the right spot, or gently rake my nails over his scalp, Marcus practically whimpers as he moans.

"Done," I tell him when I've finished, my voice deep and raspy from all the dirty thoughts.

Marcus turns off the shower and spins around so quickly, I find myself pressed against the shower wall again. "Did you mean it when you said I could have you?"

I nod. "Yes."

"I'm going to call the doctor and get stitched up. Meet me in my bed, Mio," he tells me as he climbs out of the shower, pulling a towel around his dripping body.

My heart pounds as I watch him leave, anticipation humming through my body as my mind spins. I quickly strip off my own clothes, taking care to wash all of the blood from my body as I do.

As I shampoo my own hair, my mind wanders to thoughts of what will happen next.

I told him he can have me, but can I have him?

All I know is that I've waited my whole life for him, I can't walk away now, just because there's a chance I might get my heart broken. This is one of those times when you have to risk your heart, and hope you win in the end.

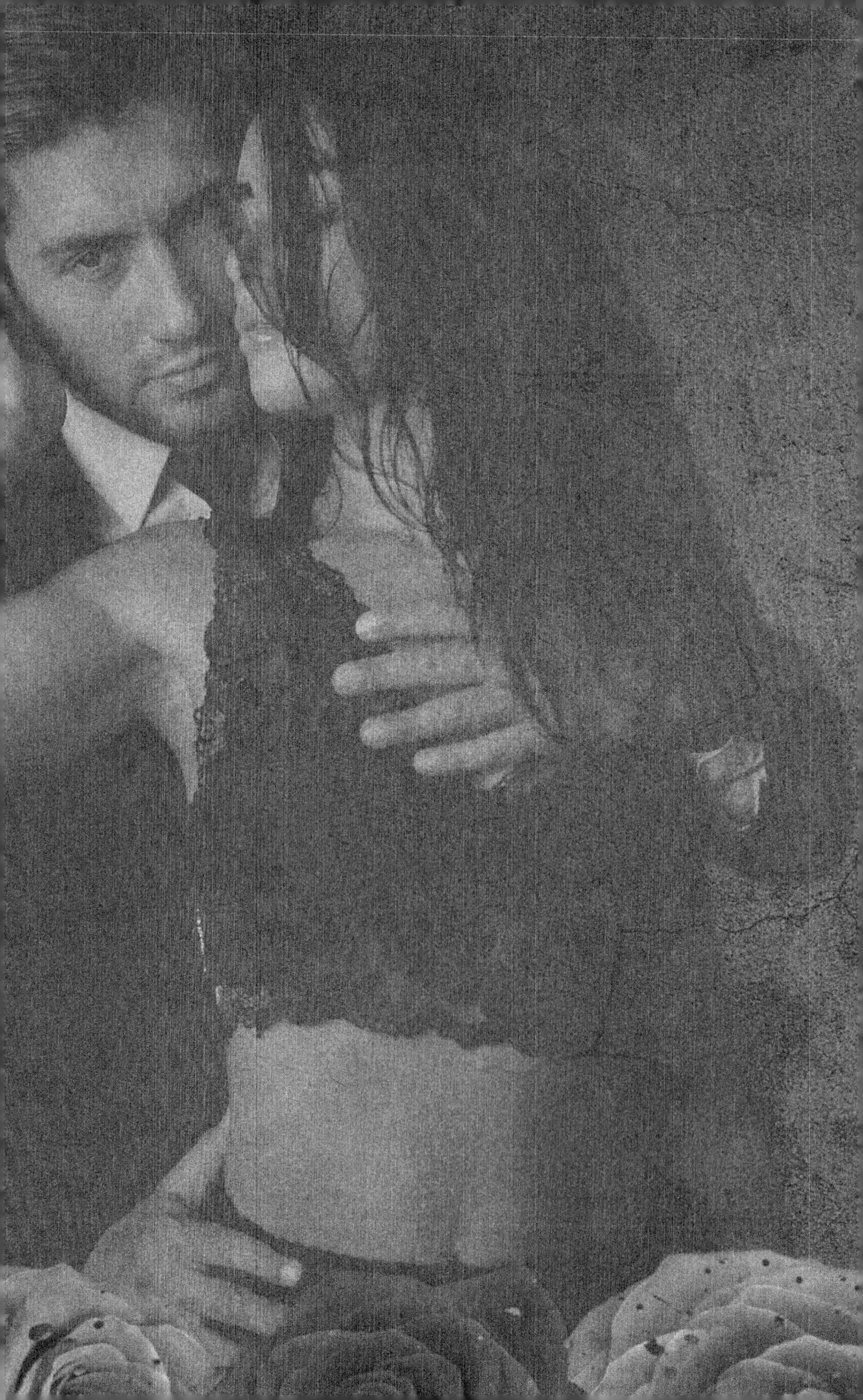

Chapter Twenty
Marcus

Getting stabbed wasn't exactly on my bingo card for today, but it became clear after being at the meeting for only a few minutes that things were going tits up.

We were meeting one of our suppliers, a gang called B23, who had recently been distributing a product that was clearly subpar. After a few emergency hospital admissions, I found out they were cutting their drugs with all manner of shit, which I don't tolerate.

Despite hating the drug industry with a passion, it makes me a lot of money, which I then invest back into Blackthorn, in an attempt to make it a decent place to live. Since I can't abolish the drug trade entirely, I made sure that rules were put in place to regulate it.

Nobody under the age of sixteen is involved in the business, no exceptions. They don't use kids to sell drugs, or to move them, and they sure as fuck don't sell to them. This is a firm rule, and everyone knows it.

All drugs that are sold in Blackthorn must be pure, and under the OD limit. I don't allow any product to be cut with other ingredients to bulk up the amount.

I'm aware that's how a lot of dealers make more money, but adding in random products is dangerous, and I don't allow the extra risk.

Finally, no fentanyl or ketamine. That shit kills people, and it's so easy to get the dosage wrong. There are enough illegal drugs on the market already, without adding more into the mix.

In exchange for my dealers following the rules, I allow them to keep a larger cut of the profits than is standard. But they all know that if they break my rules, they don't get a second chance.

I'd heard rumours that B23 were playing fast and loose with my rules, but after a couple of hospital admissions, I had the test results to prove it. I met with the gang's leader, Julian, and his second in command, Sue-Ann.

As soon as I showed them the evidence, things went south, quickly. In amongst the drama, Julian divulged that B23 were considering shifting their loyalties elsewhere, which shocked both me and Sue-Ann, who appeared to know nothing about this.

I politely reminded him that he could shift his loyalties to Jacob, as he has a right to do under the peace treaty, but this is one rule we're both in agreement on. So he won't get any better luck under the Santoro rule.

Imagine my shock when he laughed in my face and told me that the Morellis and the Santoros were not the only options.

Apparently, Scott Caprillo has been spreading the word that he's going to be taking over as leader soon, and he'll have a whole new way of working. One that will make everyone a lot more money.

My anger got the better of me, and it resulted in Julian pulling a knife, which he managed to slice me with twice, before stabbing me. Miles pulled him away, getting him a safe distance from me, before shooting him in the head.

Miles and I, along with my security team, then shot the six people that were with Julian as back-up. They fell to the floor in a matter of seconds, blood coating the room and us.

Sue-Ann was the only person we left alive, but only so that she could deliver my message. I will never work with Scott Caprillo, and he won't ever have any power.

Anyone seen to be supporting him, will be in direct violation of the peace treaty, and they will be taken down.

Sue-Ann quickly pledged her allegiance to me as she left, grateful that I didn't kill her too.

I barely remember Miles driving me home. He dropped me off at the door, letting me know that he needed to check in with his team, as well as getting word out about Scott's plans.

If I thought the knife wounds were painful, it was nothing compared to how much I fucking ached seeing Chloe dripping wet, taking care of me in the shower.

When I'd first arrived home, the look of concern on her face was something I wasn't used to. She had pulled me into the shower, taking her time to remove my clothes and all the blood, before cleaning my wounds.

Her soft fingers touched me so gently, as though she were afraid of hurting me, and the worry in her eyes made my heart ache. I've never had someone look at me the way she does, like she truly cares about me, and I have to admit, it was kinda nice.

Then she got on her knees, looking up at me with those big, innocent silver eyes, just waiting for me to corrupt her, and I couldn't control myself. I lifted her to her feet, even though it hurt like fuck, because I had to devour her right that second.

Then she'd told me I could have her, and all my restraint went out of the fucking window... Or it would have if the damn hole in my side wasn't holding me back.

Thankfully, the doctor I keep on retainer had already been notified about my injuries by Miles, and was on his way over. I'd just got out of the shower, dried off as best I could, before pulling on a pair of grey sweatpants, when the doorbell rang.

I clutched the towel against my side, as it was still bleeding a little, and made my way to the door. I opened it to find Mickey Young, my family doctor, leaning against the doorframe.

Mickey is in his late thirties, and although he hasn't worked with us for long, he's more than proved himself. He's actually the son of one of my father's advisors, and we paid for him to go to medical school, so that when he finished his training, he'd come to work for us.

The doctor he replaced had been with us for years, but wanted to retire. He stayed long enough for Mickey to undertake his training, and the extra years he needed to do in the emergency department at our local hospital, learning all the skills necessary to take care of us.

He still does the odd shift at the hospital, but mainly he takes care of me and Jacob, and our men. Everything from minor ailments to stab or gunshot wounds.

Mickey takes one look at me, rolls his eyes, and pushes his way into my apartment. I grit my teeth, taking a deep breath as I remind myself I'm not allowed to kill him.

Mickey might be the best doctor we've ever had, but he's a cocky arsehole, and he has no respect for authority. He will say what he wants, and he doesn't care who it offends.

"Well, you look like shit," he drawls, making his way into the kitchen.

He grabs a glass from the cabinet before pulling a can of Diet Coke from the fridge, looking like he owns the place.

"Help yourself to a drink," I reply sarcastically.

Mickey lets out a laugh. "You're hardly a great host. You'd never have offered me one."

"Well, I don't want you to feel welcome here," I snap, which just makes him laugh more.

"So, Miles tells me you got yourself stabbed."

I scowl at him, grinding my teeth together so hard, I'm surprised one hasn't snapped. "It's not like I did it on purpose."

"And yet, you still have a hole in your side."

He nods towards where I'm holding the towel, which is now stained red.

Although it's slowing down, I'm losing more than I'd like, which is probably why I'm starting to feel a little lightheaded. I must sway a little, as Mickey notices straightaway.

"Will you sit the fuck down before you collapse, please. I'm not picking your heavy arse up off the floor," Mickey snaps, pointing towards one of the dining chairs.

With a grumble, I shuffle over and take the chair he pointed to. "I see your bedside manner hasn't improved."

"You pay me to keep you alive, not to be nice to you," he retorts with a cheesy grin.

He places his medical bag on the table beside me, opening it up to rummage through for the supplies he needs.

"So, if I pay you more, will you stop acting like a dick?" I ask.

He pauses for a second, cocking his head to the side, making a big deal of showing that he's thinking about it, before quickly saying, "Nah. It's the only fun part of my job."

"Arsehole," I chunter, which makes him laugh again.

"Lie down on the dining table and let me take a look at these wounds," he says, moving his bag off the table onto one of the chairs.

"Do we have to do this on my table? It's where I eat," I grumble, but Mickey just shakes his head.

"Unless you have a medical gurney hidden away here, like I asked you to buy, this is the best place."

"What about the bed?" I ask, ignoring his obvious dig that I, in fact, did not buy the hospital equipment he requested.

Mickey shakes head. "It's too low down and soft. So unless you want to go to my clinic, where I have a proper gurney, and all the supplies I'll need, you'll have to make do here."

"Fine," I snap, wincing as I climb onto the table.

Mickey gets to work quickly. First, he assesses all of my body, cataloguing any injuries, and then he sets up a machine to monitor my observations. Once he has all the information he needs, he takes a better look at the wound on my side.

"This one is deep. It'll need stitches," he says, as I scrunch my eyes closed, trying to breathe through the pain that comes with him prodding the hole.

"That's what I said." My eyes fly open when I hear Chloe's soft voice from behind me.

I look around to see her leaning against the wall, staring at me with that same worried look on her face.

Her wet hair has been pulled up into a messy bun on the top of her head, and I take a moment to be grateful that she's wearing a pair of pyjama trousers instead of those shorts she usually teases me with.

"Well, who do we have here?" Mickey asks, wiggling his eyebrows as he stares at Chloe in a way that makes me want to stab him with his own scalpel.

"I'm Chloe," she says shyly, moving over to stand beside me. "How is he doing? He lost quite a lot of blood."

Her gaze roams over my body, stopping on my stomach wound, which Mickey is currently cleaning with antiseptic. Her eyes land on where my sweatpants are hanging low on my hips, showing off the trail of hair that leads below my waistband, and I see her gulp.

I have to think about the most boring things imaginable, recounting as many mind-numbing statistics as I can from my last finance meeting, just to stop myself from getting hard. Mickey will never let me live it down if I do.

"He's doing okay. I'll take a blood test from him before I leave, and depending on how much he's lost, he might need a blood transfusion, or just some iron tablets. We'll see," he replies whilst working on my wound, before he stops and turns to face Chloe again. "I'm Mickey, the mafia doctor. What's a pretty girl like you doing with an arsehole like him? I don't think I've ever seen a woman here before."

Don't stab him, don't stab him, I keep repeating to myself.

Chloe looks at me, her eyes wide as she struggles with what to say. I take pity on her and smack Mickey on the arm.

"Stop staring at her and do your damn job. It's none of your business. She's here…and will be for a while. So shut the fuck up and get me stitched up so you can get the fuck out."

"Someone is being an extra miserable bastard today," Mickey sings, grinning as he pours antiseptic on my wound.

"Motherfucker!" I yell, squirming to try and stop the burning sensation that feels like it's melting away the skin around my wound.

"Be nice to me or I won't use anaesthetic to stitch you up," Mickey says, wafting the needle in front of my face.

I keep quiet, except for the odd swear word as he sticks the needle into the sensitive skin around the edges of the wound. As the drug is pumped in, it stings and burns just as bad as the anti-septic, before the area goes numb.

As I'm wincing and trying to avoid how much the damn thing hurts, Chloe pulls up a chair next to my head, before reaching over and pulling my hand into hers. She laces our fingers together, and I turn my head to the side to see her giving me her fucking adorable smile.

"Squeeze my hand if it hurts too much," she whispers, gripping my hand a little tighter.

I stare into her bright silver eyes, watching as they occasionally flick down towards where Mickey is stitching me up, only for her to grimace and look back at me. Her face is a beautiful mix of concern and anguish, and it takes me a little while to realise that it upsets her seeing me in pain.

It's at that moment, I realise how much Chloe cares about me, and the damn monitor starts to alert when my heart begins to race. Mickey panics for a second, before he sees me looking at Chloe, then he quickly silences the machine with a roll of his eyes.

Chloe's eyes are wide as she stares at the machine. "Is he okay? Why did it start alarming like that?"

Mickey's lips spread into a shit-eating grin as I glare at him, silently telling him with my eyes that I will kill him. He turns to Chloe, and gives her a reassuring smile.

"It's a normal reaction, most likely from the pain. He's fine."

I nod my head, grateful that he covered for me, and now I don't have to kill him. Chloe looks over at me, her brow furrowed as she assesses me again.

"Are you sure?" She asks the question to Mickey, but her eyes never leave mine.

"I'm sure. In fact, I'm all done. I need to put a dressing over it, and put some steri-strips over the other two slashes, but then we're all done."

Both me and Chloe breathe a sigh of relief, and once all of my wounds are covered, she helps me to sit up on the table. I try to hide the sharp pain that sticks into my stomach, but she catches the grimace.

"What happens now? Is he going to be okay?" Chloe asks Mickey, who is clearing up his mess.

He gives her a reassuring nod. "I'm going to test his blood, and I'll be back this afternoon to check up on him." He then turns to me and says, "Just take it easy."

Yeah, that isn't going to happen, I think, as I look at Chloe.

"What will happen if I overexert myself?" I ask cryptically. By the way Mickey's eyes widen as he glances over at Chloe, I think he knows what I mean.

"You won't be exerting yourself," she snaps, her hand on her hip as she glares at me.

I shake my head, smiling at her bossiness. I turn back to Mickey, deciding I may as well embarrass her, since she's trying to tell me what to do.

"Ignore her, Mickey. She knows I plan to fuck her tonight, and no insignificant little stab wound is going to stop me. Give me some pain killers, so it won't hurt too much, and tell me what I need to do."

Chloe's cheeks turn a bright shade of red as Mickey bends over laughing. She glowers at me, looking like she's going to kill me, but I just shrug my shoulders.

Mickey clears his throat, trying to find his voice in between fits of laughter. "As your doctor, I have to recommend you not have sex for a couple of days, but as a man who can appreciate how fucking hot she is, I'll help you out."

"Call her hot again, or even look at her like that, and I'll jam that scalpel into your eye," I reply dangerously.

"Marcus!" Chloe chastises, but Mickey just keeps chuckling.

"I wouldn't let anyone near her either, Boss. Right, here's some pills that will take the pain away for a couple of hours. The anaesthetic won't wear off for a short time either, so that'll help. You'll get one round, and then you risk damage, so make it count.

"Try not to overexert and pop your stitches. If you do, put some of these steri-strips over where the stitch was, and I'll fix it when I call back this afternoon," he explains, handing over two small pills before laying all the wound dressings and extra steri-strips that we might need on the table.

"Thank you," Chloe mutters, unable to look Mickey in the eye as she grabs me a glass of water.

Once she hands it to me, I take the pills, hoping they kick in soon.

"Yeah, thanks for that," I tell Mickey, giving him a wink as he continues to laugh. "Now, get out of my house."

"Marcu—"

Chloe starts to shout at me for being rude, but Mickey puts his hand on her arm to stop her. I take a menacing step towards him and he quickly drops it.

"It's fine, Chloe. I'm finished, and I need sleep. It was lovely to meet you. I have no idea why you're with this possessive knobhead, but if he ever can't make you happy, you—"

"Get out!" I snap, interrupting whatever inappropriate proposition was about to leave his mouth, and Chloe chuckles.

"I'll show you out," she says, as Mickey picks up his bag and follows her to the door.

I can't hear what they say, but Chloe is extra red around the cheeks when she returns.

"Well, he's quite something, isn't he?" she laughs as I groan.

"If he wasn't the best, I'd have killed him years ago," I admit, though I'll never tell him that. His ego is big enough as it is.

Silence sits heavily between us, as Chloe runs her eyes over my body before stopping at the dressing on my side. "You should get some rest. I bet that hurts."

I shake my head as I take a step towards her. "Actually, the anaesthetic has made the whole area numb, and the painkillers will take away the last little ache that I can feel shortly."

She visibly gulps, her mouth popping as she thinks of what to say. "You must be tired. It's almost five in the morning."

"Adrenaline," I say, when I'm finally standing right in front of her.

She's so close, I can feel the heat from her body warming my own, as her breath flutters against my neck. I shudder at the sensation, wanting to close the minuscule gap between us.

I reach up and place my hand on her cheek, swiping my thumb across her flushed skin, before moving it until I'm holding the back of her neck. I place my other hand on her hip, making sure she can't go anywhere.

"I'm done waiting for you, Mio" I tell her, before pressing my lips against hers.

At first, Chloe seems hesitant, barely moving beneath my touch, but as I deepen the kiss, claiming her lips with mine, she melts against me.

She kisses me back with just as much passion as she had in the shower, and I'm very fucking grateful I'm off the heartrate monitor, as it'd definitely be alarming right now.

She reaches up and threads her fingers through my hair, tugging a little, creating a delicious sting on my scalp. I groan in response, pulling her body towards mine.

My hard length presses against her stomach, and just that little bit of friction makes me moan. But as soon as the sound leaves my lips, Chloe tries to pull away, but I keep my grip on her firm, so she can't go far.

"Are you okay? Did I hurt you?" she asks frantically, her eyes raking over my body in a clinical way, heading straight for the dressing on my side.

There's no indication of any blood seeping through, which is a good sign.

"Chloe, I'm fine," I tell her.

"But I heard you—"

I cut her off by capturing her lips with mine in a short kiss.

"You heard me moaning because my hard cock was rubbing against you. It was the good kind of moan, not a pain-filled one—though my dick is painfully hard."

She chuckles, looking down at the tent in my sweatpants, that's currently resting against her stomach.

"Are you sure this isn't going to hurt you?"

"Believe me, Mio, it'll be much more painful for me if we don't do this. Besides, I'd happily rip open every stitch if it means I get to fuck you," I tell her, rocking my hips against her as I do.

She leans in and kisses me, devouring me before she pulls away far too quickly.

"Are you worried we're going to cross a line we can't come back from?"

Without even stopping to think, I shake my head. "It's too late to worry about that now. You said I could have you, and I will. Now, are you going to be a good little slut and let me fuck you?"

A bright smile crosses her lips as she nods. She reaches down to the hand that's on her hip, taking hold of it and lacing our fingers together.

"Take me to your bedroom then. I want you to be comfortable when I show you how well I can suck your cock."

"Ohhh." A sound that's a mixture of both a moan and a groan leaves my lips as I let her pull me towards my bedroom. Once there, she pushes me to sit on the edge of the bed.

"Stay."

Even though I don't usually take instructions in the bedroom, I have no fucking intention of ever moving from here, so I do as she tells me.

My gaze stays locked on her as she slowly begins removing the baggy T-shirt she'd thrown on after the shower. As she pulls the tee off, showing me she isn't wearing a bra, my brain practically explodes.

I wanted to yell at her for being bra-less when that arsehole Mickey was around, but since I didn't even realise, I'm sure he didn't either.

Before I can shout at her, I'm distracted by how fucking perfect her tits are, and the way her nipples harden as the cool air hits them.

She slowly removes her sweatpants, and my heart almost stops when I see the lacey black knickers she's wearing.

She turns around, giving me a glimpse of what they look like from behind, and I bite the inside of my cheek to stop any more embarrassing noises from breaking free.

There's no denying, the way the lace knickers scoop over her arse, showing a plump swell of her cheeks peeking out beneath, it's one of the sexiest things I've ever seen.

When she looks over her shoulder at me, with that shy little smile on her face, I know I'm a goner.

"Take them off, Mio," I growl, palming my cock over my sweats, just enough to get some relief.

Chloe turns back around and wastes no time removing her knickers, throwing them to the side as she stands before me completely naked. Other than the way she pulls her lower lip in between her teeth, and the flush across her cheeks, you'd never know she wasn't as confident as she appears.

She begins walking towards me, but I shake my head and she stops.

"On your knees."

Her eyes widen, but she does as she's told, dropping to her knees. She arches her back in the perfect way as she crawls to me.

Once she's right in front of me, I spread my legs to make room for her, and she kneels between them, gazing up at me through her long lashes, looking like a fucking wet dream.

She places her hands on my thighs, and with her gaze still locked on mine, she grabs the waistband of my sweats. I lift up slightly to help her remove them, and she throws them over with her discarded clothes.

My cock bobs in front of her face, and she looks at it with both awe and apprehension, but when she licks her lips, I almost come right then.

She reaches out slowly, looking for me to stop her—like I fucking would—while she wraps her small hand around the base.

The feel of her squeezing my shaft makes me groan deeply, drops of pre-cum leaking from the tip. She looks at the drops of fluid gathering on the head, more joining as she pumps my shaft.

My eyes are fixed on her, like I'd ever look anywhere else, and I watch in amazement as she sticks out her tongue, flicking it over the tip to gather up all of the pre-cum before she swallows it down.

She looks up at me through hooded eyes, a mischievous smirk on her face as she leans forward and takes the head in her mouth. As her lips envelope me, she runs her tongue around the tip, driving me fucking crazy, before finally sucking me in deeper.

"Fuck," I grunt, watching in amazement as Chloe takes my cock into her mouth.

Each time she pulls back and bobs back down again, she gets a little deeper.

Whenever I hit the back of her throat, she makes sure to gulp, and the tight feeling of her throat contracting around my dick sends shivers down my spine, and my balls begin to ache.

She works my cock into a frenzy, alternating between pumping with her hands and using her mouth or her tongue, sucking and licking until she's driving me crazy.

I feel the tell-tale signs that I'm about to lose control, so I pull her off me, not wanting things to end just yet.

She looks up at me with big, innocent eyes, and I can see the hurt in them as I pull away.

"Did I do it wrong?"

I let out a humourless laugh, that most definitely was not a snort, as she appears even more confused.

"Love, there was absolutely nothing wrong with that. Quite the opposite. If you keep going like that, I was about to come in your throat."

"Oh," she says, dropping her shy gaze from mine before adding, "I wouldn't have minded."

I reach down and place a finger under her chin, lifting until she has no choice but to make eye contact with me.

"As much as I'd love that, and we will do that another time, I plan on filling you with my cum first."

She nods, that shy smile returning as she admits, "I think I'd like that."

"On your back on the bed," I tell her as I stand.

She quickly does as she's told and lays down in the middle of the bed. I grab hold of her ankles and pull her down a bit, until her arse is at the bottom of the bed.

I grimace as the muscles in my stomach burn slightly from the overexertion, but I push the pain away. It's barely noticeable now, thanks to the pills. I've just aggravated it.

Chloe must have caught the pain on my face, as when I go to kneel in between her legs, she sits up quickly, reaching out to stop me.

"No, don't do that. It'll hurt your stomach and side."

"It's fine, I'll rest later," I tell her, but she hits me with a glare that tells me this isn't negotiable.

I roll my eyes at her, pretending my cock doesn't twitch at the tone she uses on me.

"Fine, but I plan on eating out that pretty little cunt of yours, so decide how you want me."

"Er... I don't... I-I don't want to hurt you," she mutters.

"Fine, then I'll lay down and you can ride my face," I say with a shrug of my shoulders. As long as I get to feast on her pussy, I don't really care how we do it.

She shakes her head rapidly, the blush on her cheeks now spreading down over her chest.

"No. I've never... I'm too..."

She trails off, and it's a good thing she did or I would've interrupted her. I lay on the bed, fixing my eyes on hers.

"Either you climb on willingly, or I will reach over and pick you up. Now, be a good little whore and let me lick your pussy. I want to see how wet you are."

Her breath hitches at my words, but she moves towards me. Once she's kneeling beside me, she hesitates, clearly not knowing what to do.

I reach over and lift her leg, giving her no choice but to straddle my shoulders, her arse resting on my upper chest.

This is one hell of a view, and if I were to die now, I'd be a very happy man.

Her pussy is glistening in front of my face, and my mouth waters at the sight.

"I can see how wet you are from here, Mio. Did sucking my cock get you all wet?" I ask, and she nods her head.

"Yes," she mutters.

I run my fingers over her thighs, inhaling the sweet smell of her cunt as she wiggles around on top of me. I grab onto her hips, tight enough to bruise, forcing her to hold still.

"You're such a dirty little whore. Only fucksluts like you get turned on sucking cock. Do you want me to lick your pretty pussy to help ease some of the ache?"

"Yes, please." Her voice is barely a whisper, but my cock throbs at how innocent she sounds.

I reach out with my tongue, swiping it along her slit, groaning as I taste her juices. As I reach her clit, I slowly circle around it until she's squirming over me, before quickly flicking my tongue over her sensitive nub, making her cry out loudly.

As she loses herself in the sensations, she forgets all about her embarrassment, or how uncomfortable she initially was in this position, and she settles over my face. She's low enough down that I can breathe, but high enough that I'm able to devour her with my tongue.

She writhes around on top of me so much, I have to hold her down as I suck on her clit, devouring her as she begs me for more.

I alternate between low, lazy strokes with the flat of my tongue across her whole slit, even dipping into her entrance just enough to drive her crazy, before

Prized Possession

speeding up when I flick over her sensitive clit, only to finally suck it into my mouth, when I know she's close.

"Oh, fuck. I'm so close. Please, can I...can I come?" she asks, each word getting more high-pitched in between her moans.

I feel her impending release building. As she chases that high, her body becomes more frantic and less inhibited, and she's soon rocking her cunt against my face, taking what she needs from me.

As her orgasm builds, her body starts to tense. Her legs clamp tightly around my head, preventing me from moving, even just a little.

She reaches down with one of her hands and laces her fingers through my hair, pulling it just enough to sting. She uses her hold on my hair to direct my head exactly where she wants me, and I couldn't enjoy it any fucking more.

When I can tell she's right on the edge, I stop, just long enough to give her the permission she needs. "Come for me, slut."

I lick, suck, and flick at her pussy until her orgasm hits, and her body shudders above me. My lips are covered in her juices, and I happily lick them up, like I'm a death row inmate and this is my last meal.

I don't care that her cunt is suffocating me, or that she's pulling on my hair harder than I'd like. She's also slumped down onto my chest in such a way that makes it hard for me to draw breath, but I can't seem to care.

Watching Chloe take what she needs from me, as she comes all over my lips while calling my name, has made me lose all good sense.

Thankfully, Chloe comes around quickly, and climbs off just in time for me to draw in a big breath. I then lean over and capture her lips with mine, amazed when she drags her tongue over mine, tasting herself.

"That was amazing," she says with a laugh as soon as I release her lips.

"It's not over yet, love," I reply, while slowly dragging my fist over my hard length.

Chloe watches my movements, licking her lips as I swipe my thumb over the tip, spreading the droplets of pre-cum that built up during her orgasm.

"I need to fuck you," I tell her, my voice deep and gravelly as lust takes over.

She nods her head rapidly, before adding, "Only if you won't hurt yourself."

"I won't," I tell her, before saying, "Now get on your back and spread your legs wide like a good girl."

She does as she's told straight away, only looking a little shy as she parts her legs for me. I reach behind her and grab a cushion, instructing her to place it under her arse. It lifts her, tilting her pelvis in just the right way.

"I'm going to fuck you without a condom. Are you okay with that?" I don't know why I ask, as I don't want to stop.

"I've never done it without one before, but I have the contraceptive implant.

I got tested the last time I was with someone, and it was negative," she says, staring up at me with those big beautiful eyes.

"All my tests were fine too. But what I'm asking is if you want me to fuck you bare, to flood your cunt with my cum?"

She nods her head quickly. "Yes, please."

I flash the wicked smirk that I know she loves.

"You really are a dirty little whore. I'm going to turn you into my own little cum-dumpster, and fill you with my cum any chance I get. And you better say thank you every time I do," I warn her, loving the way her eyes flash with lust, even though she tries to hide it behind her shyness.

"I will."

I lean forward, lining up the head of my cock with her pussy before dragging it slowly through her slit. As her juices coat the head, I use my hand to spread it down the shaft, making sure I'm nice and wet for her.

When I press the tip against her clit, she moans loudly, bucking her hips, trying desperately to gain more friction. I grab hold of her hip with my free hand, pinning her in place as much as I can.

"Please," she begs, whimpering beneath me as my cock rubs against her clit.

I then move lower, lining up with her entrance before pushing in. I try to take my time, but the moment I feel her warm heat enveloping me, I almost lose control.

I drive forward, stopping only when I hear Chloe cry out, whimpering beneath me as her nails claw at my arms.

"Are you okay?" I hiss, and she nods.

"Yes. More. Please." She tries to rock her hips between each word, my dick slipping deeper until I finally bottom out.

As I hit a spot deep inside her, we both cry out. I hold still for a moment, leaning forward, so I can capture her lips with mine.

"You're doing so well, love. You're taking my dick so good, and you're so fucking tight."

She looks up at me, her smile bright from my praise.

"You can move now," she tells me, rocking her hips just a little for emphasis.

I pull back slowly, biting my lip at how fucking amazing she feels as she stretches her legs even wider for me. I then thrust back in, a quick sharp movement that hits deep, causing Chloe to scream out loud.

"Yes. Fuck. So good."

I do the same again; pulling back until just the tip remains inside before thrusting back in fast, hitting her hard and deep as her cries of pleasure take over.

Each time I push back in, she tilts her pelvis at just the right angle, so I hit her sweet spot, making her cling to me as she moans.

The feel of her tight cunt gripping my cock with each thrust is amazing, but hearing the noises Chloe makes, just for me, almost pushes me over the edge.

I continue fucking her, occasionally slowing down just enough to keep my release at bay, while still managing to drive her crazy. Her pussy is dripping wet, and I pepper kisses over her body, sucking and tasting wherever I can reach.

When I pull one of her nipples into my mouth, nibbling on it, her cunt tightens around me as she whimpers. Moving to her other nipple, I get the same response again, and I don't need Chloe to confirm it to know she's close.

"Fuck. Marcus, I'm so close. I'm going to... Please, can I come?" she begs, as I continue fucking into her, my balls slapping against her arse with each thrust.

I'm close myself, and it won't be long before I have to give in to the delicious ache in my balls, but I need to feel her first.

I lean closer, my lips pressing against her cheek as I whisper into her ear. "Why should I let you come, slut?"

Her eyes roll back as I thrust in deep at the same time, making it hard for her to find the words to respond.

While my cock is deep inside her, I keep it there, rocking against that sweet spot that drives her crazy.

"Oh, God," she cries, and I chuckle.

"It's not God, Mio. This is all me. Now, tell me, why do you deserve to come?" My voice is deep and husky, I'm just as lost as she is.

"I've been a good girl. I want to come for you. I want your cock to feel my tight cunt spasming around you. I only come like this for you. I'm your dirty little whore, and only you can make me fall apart."

I don't know where the dirty words come from, but they tumble out of Chloe's mouth, straight to my dick. Hearing her talk like that, looking so sweet and innocent with such a filthy mouth sends me over the edge, and my balls begin to tighten.

I reach down between us and place my fingers on her sensitive clit, rubbing it as she squirms and cries out beneath me.

"No, please. Don't... I'm going to, if you... Please, Marcus, please can I come? I'll be a good whore for you. Let me show you how good a slut I can be."

Her begging is like music to my ears, and I pound into her faster, rubbing hard against her clit.

Her body tenses, her legs tightening around me as she screws her eyes closed, thrashing around from side to side as her nails drag down my arms. She's trying to stop herself from coming, but her body is close to betraying her.

I don't want to set her recovery back, and I want to watch her fall apart, so this time when I thrust in deep, I say, "Come for me. Show me what a good little whore you are."

She cries out, her pussy spasming around me as her orgasm hits her. As it does, I tell her, "Eyes open, slut. I want to see you fall apart on my cock. I want to watch as I ruin you for all other men."

Her eyes roll, but she's quick to open them, and her silver gaze is fixed on me as she falls apart around me. Her cunt walls latch onto my cock, gripping me in a vice as she spasms.

Chloe's whole body trembles as she calls out my name. "Marcus. Oh fuck, I'm coming. Thank you, thank you. Thank you for letting your slut come," she cries, as she grabs hold of me tightly.

The feel of her pussy milking my cock, combined with her dirty words, tips me over the edge, and my orgasm hits just as hers begins to die down.

I rock my hips into her in short shallow thrusts, but it's just enough to have me shooting rope after rope of cum into her waiting cunt.

When I'm sure I've coated her walls completely, and we've both come down from our release, we flop onto the bed beside each other, gasping for air.

I pull Chloe against my non-injured side, feeling disappointed that my cock is no longer inside of her, but there's a little pride at knowing I've left a piece of me inside her, claiming her in the most primal way.

I lean down and kiss her. It's not frantic or needy like before, and we take our time just tasting each other, before we pull back, both with matching smiles.

"Are you okay?" she asks, trying to pull out of my arms, so she can check my side, but I don't let her. I keep her wrapped up beside me, her head on my chest.

"I'm fine. We can check it later. Right now, I just want to enjoy this moment with you," I tell her, feeling her smile against my chest.

After a few minutes of silence, I finally voice the thoughts that have been echoing on repeat since I watched her come on my cock.

"There's no going back after that. You belong to me now. You're definitely mine."

Chloe chuckles, lifting up on her elbow so she can meet my gaze.

"Marcus, I've belonged to you since we were kids, you just didn't know it." She then pauses for a second, a sad expression crossing her face. "I just wish you belonged to me in the same way."

"Chloe—"

I'm not entirely sure what I was about to say, but Chloe cuts me off, giving me a tight smile that doesn't quite reach her eyes.

"It's okay. I've wanted you for so long, I'll take whatever I can get, no matter how temporary it might be. I know I'm putting my heart on the line here, but I need to see this through."

I take a deep breath, warring with myself over whether I should stay quiet or show her the same level of vulnerability that she just showed me. After the amount of trust she's given me, honesty is the least she deserves.

"You're not the only one putting their heart on the line. I know there's a lot of reasons why we can't be together, but the more time I spend with you, the more I get to know the real Chloe, the easier it is for me to consider burning the whole world down, just so I can keep you."

Her breath hitches, and she looks at me with such emotion, my heart races.

"Really?" The hope in her voice almost guts me.

I nod my head. "You're mine now, and I will do whatever it takes to keep you."

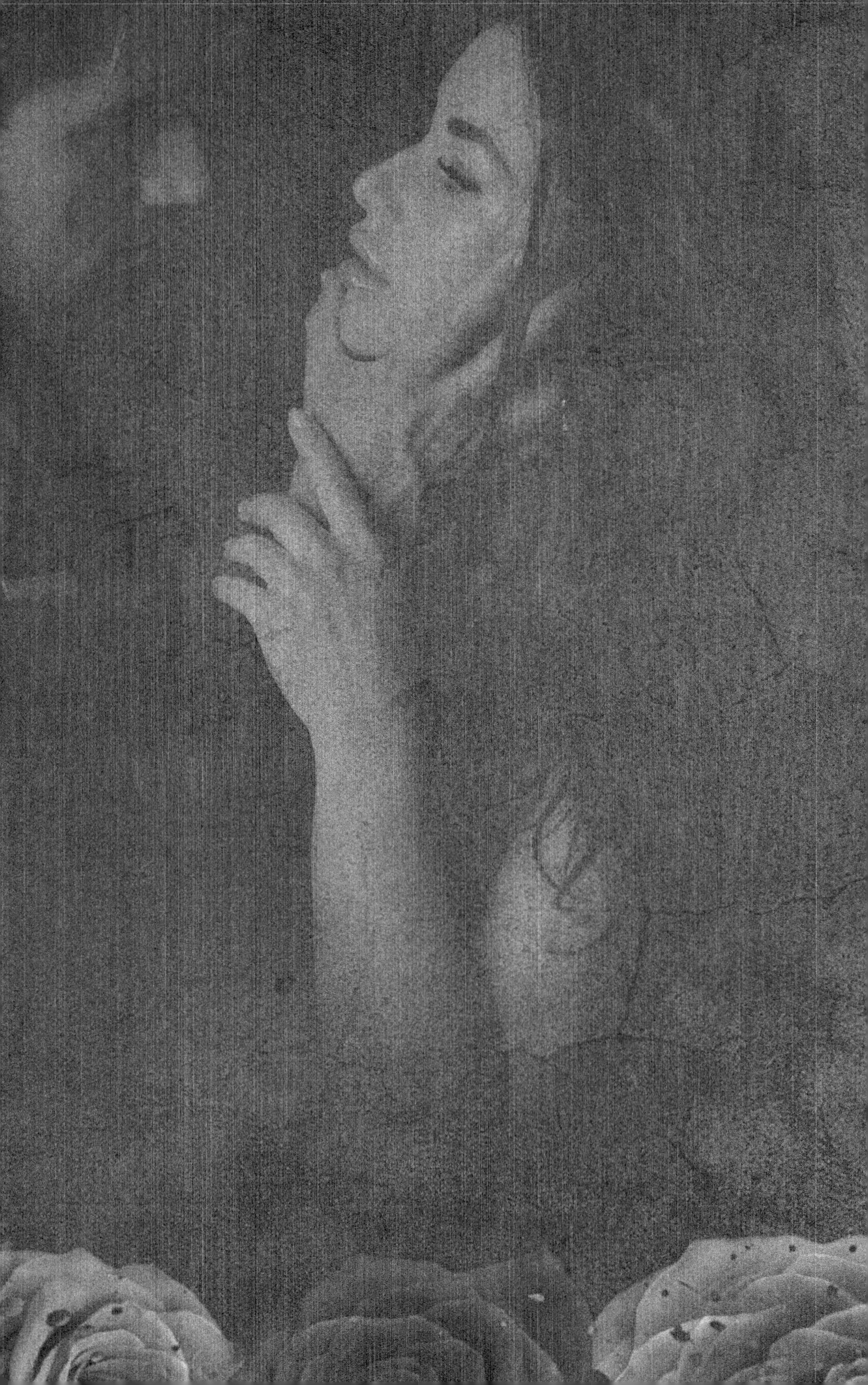

Chapter Twenty-One

Chloe

After that first time together, time seemed to fly by in the blink of an eye, and I'm not sure if that's a good or a bad thing. Marcus was true to his word, and once he'd fucked me, there was no going back. We couldn't keep our hands off each other, and no matter how many times we were together, it was never enough. We always wanted more, which is something we were both very happy to accommodate.

After putting my heart on the line, I had no idea what would happen.

Marcus was the first to fall asleep that morning, and given all the pills, sex, and stab wounds, that wasn't much of a surprise, but I spent the whole day just waiting for the other shoe to drop.

He'd said the most perfect things, yet I couldn't help worrying that maybe he was just caught up in the moment. I was living the dream I'd had since I was a child, and I didn't want to miss a single moment of it.

So, when Marcus finally did wake up a couple of hours later, I braced myself for his regret, but it never came. Instead, he kissed me with passion, and a smile that suggested he might quite like waking up next to me, which is a good thing as I've not been back to my own room since.

The first night after the sex, when we said goodnight to each other, I somewhat reluctantly headed towards my own room, and Marcus looked confused. I didn't know what to do, as we hadn't exactly given a label to whatever the confusing situation between us is.

Marcus simply laughed, threw me over his shoulder, and took me back to his room, all while I shouted at him for risking his stitches.

Since then, I've never even attempted to sleep alone, it just feels right to be with him.

It's more than just sex. Being next to him, talking to him, gives me more peace than I ever expected.

Somehow, the first weekend my parents returned, Marcus was able to get us out of going to lunch, stating he had to work, and he wasn't willing to let me go alone.

My dad argued, of course, but Marcus simply reminded him that he was amenable when he cancelled for two weeks to take my mother on holiday, so returning the favour is the least he can do.

Surprisingly, my dad backed down, and my nerves eased a little more.

While we are alone in the apartment, it's like we are in our own little bubble, completely unaware of the world around us.

I continue going to my classes, and baking at home to practise everything I've learnt, and Marcus still has his job to go to, but when we're at home, just the two of us, it's like we forget about the world outside.

One morning, at the start of my fifth week with Marcus, we're having our usual breakfast, just sitting together, grateful for each other's company, when Marcus turns to me, a serious look on his face.

"It just occurred to me, I've never taken you on a real date."

I can't help but laugh. "That's okay. We've spent lots of evenings having dinner together and then watching a movie, so we can class them as dates."

Marcus shakes his head, scowling at me. "Fuck, no. I can do much better than that."

"Is it...safe for us to go on a date?"

Although we're all over each other here in the apartment, on the rare occasions that we go outside together, we decided it'd be better if people don't know what's going on between us.

Marcus never specifically made any promises to my family at the time of the bet, but if people find out we're having sex, it would be a grey area where the bet is concerned, but with the peace treaty, there's no doubt it would be crossing a line.

We hadn't wanted to put too much pressure on our new relationship, so we kept our intimacy indoors.

"I'll pick somewhere that's safe. So, do you want to go on a date with me?" he asks, sounding a little shy.

I lean over and press my lips to his in a deep but quick kiss, pulling away with a smile on my face. "I would love to go on a date with you. When?"

He pauses for a second before saying, "How about tonight?"

I'm a little startled that he wants to do it so soon, but I don't even think before I blurt out, "Yes."

Marcus chuckles, his lips tipping up into his cocky smirk at how eager I sounded. "You don't have any classes?"

Shit, I do.

"No, it's fine. Nothing I can't miss," I tell him, and he stares at me, assessing to see if I'm being honest.

I roll my eyes at him, which makes him smile and he lets it go. "Okay, tonight it is. Shall we say six?"

"Perfect. Where are we going?" I ask, my heart racing like I'm a teenage girl all over again.

I rather depressingly realise that this will be the first date I've ever been on that I picked for myself. Every date I've had before was selected by one of my parents, which is an incredibly sad thought.

Marcus' smile turns mischievous, and I don't miss the glint in his bright blue eyes.

"I'm not telling you. It's a surprise."

Now I'm more than a little shocked. It almost sounds like he might have been thinking about this for a while, planning it, maybe?

"Okay, well, what should I wear?"

"Dress comfortably. So, jeans, no heels, with something warm on, like a hoodie," he adds, confusing me further.

"So I don't need to get all dressed up?"

Marcus shakes his head, before smirking at me once again. "No, but if you want to put on some sexy lingerie, I'm hoping to convince you to put out on the first date."

I can't help but laugh. "I'm not that kind of a girl," I tell him in my sweetest voice, though we both know there's no way I can resist this man, particularly if he turns on the charm on our date.

"Well, I'll have to see if you can be corrupted by the villain then, won't I?"

I flick my hair, giving him my best unaffected glare. "You are not the villain."

This time when he laughs, it's dark and dangerous.

"Oh, sweetheart, we both know I'm the villain. I'm not the hero who wants to save the world. I'd step on people as they lay dying, just to get to you. I'd let the whole world burn, as long as I managed to save you."

My heart races and my stomach rolls in the most pleasant way at his words.

"You might be the villain in everyone else's story, but that makes you my hero."

Before he has time to protest, I lean in and capture his mouth with mine. He wastes no time reaching over and lifting me from my seat, pulling me onto his lap, so I'm straddling him.

Once more, I'm grateful for the fantastic job Mickey did of patching Marcus up. He's been healing well, and thankfully, hasn't pulled any stitches—which given how often he fucks me, is a miracle.

The stitches have almost dissolved, and he doesn't need pain pills anymore. I've reached the point where I almost forget about the injury whenever I'm with him, though I'll never forget the awful feeling when I saw him covered in blood.

His hard length presses against me, silencing my thoughts, and I roll my hips into him, causing both of us to moan into each other's mouth.

We're so lost in devouring each other, we don't hear the door open.

"None of that at the bloody dinner table, please. Some of us eat here," Miles groans, grabbing a cup of coffee off the side, quickly pouring it into his to-go tumbler.

"Technically, she's not on the table, but that doesn't mean she hasn't been," Marcus replies cockily, which earns him a groan from Miles and a slap on the arm from me.

I try to climb off his lap, but Marcus' hold on my hips tightens. He's not paying any attention to his friend, he's just staring at me like he wants to devour me, whether his friend is here or not.

"Marcus, we have that meeting in twenty minutes. If we don't leave now, we'll be late," Miles states.

"Cockblocker," Marcus grumbles, as I kiss him on the lips before climbing off his lap.

I notice he discreetly rearranges himself in his trousers, though there's not a lot he can do with his very obvious erection.

"Keep staring and I won't be able to leave," he mutters, wiggling his eyebrows suggestively at me.

"Go, you don't want to be late," I say, as I take my own seat again. "Besides, I have class soon."

Marcus gets up, but not before glaring at his friend. He walks over to me and bends down until his lips are next to my ear.

"Don't forget about our date tonight, Mio."

He then presses a kiss against that sweet spot below my ear, sending a shiver down my spine, which only makes him chuckle.

"See you tonight," I reply, trying to keep the ridiculous grin from my face.

As they're leaving, I hear Miles ask, "What's tonight?"

"Mind your own fucking business," Marcus grumbles.

"Play nicely, boys," I shout after them, their laughter and swearing fading as the door slams behind them.

I love my classes, but I have an awful feeling today is really going to drag, and I'll spend the whole time wondering where we're going tonight. Not to mention, obsessing over what the hell to wear.

Even with the added anxiety, I can't quite believe I'm going on my first real date...and it's with the guy I've fantasised about for years. Young Chloe is having a massive party right now, that's for sure.

As I suspected, the day passed by slowly. I was able to throw myself into my class, learning all about creating figures out of fondant.

Initially, I was terrible at it, but by the end of the class, the animals I'd made actually looked like I intended.

Class ran late, which was a blessing in disguise as it meant I didn't have long to obsess over the date. Marcus had pretty much told me what to wear, I just picked the sexiest versions that I owned.

After showering and shaving my legs, grateful I'd had my waxing appointment just the other day, I start on my make-up. Marcus always says I don't need much, so I decide to keep it minimal, whilst also making it clear I've made an effort.

I use a bit of bronzer to add the colour my pale skin is missing, and blush to temper out my already red cheeks. I use the usual dark colours on my eyes, as the smokey effect makes my silver eyes pop, particularly when I add a little more black liner than usual.

To round it off, I add some deep red lipstick. It's a dark enough colour to look sexy, without standing out too much, and it makes my lips look soft and plump, which is what I was going for.

After blow-drying my hair, I pull the front parts back and secure them with a small clip, so they won't be in my face the whole night, but I leave the rest of my hair down.

Marcus has said, on more than one occasion, that he likes when I wear my hair down, and I often find him twirling one of my curls around his finger absentmindedly when we're laying together. So it was an easy choice, though I do put a hair tie and a clip into my bag, just in case we go somewhere that requires me having it up.

I pull on my black skinny jeans, the ones that are figure hugging enough to show off my curves, and add my favourite pair of Converse. When Marcus said comfy footwear, they were the first ones I thought of, and their black and white design fits with the rest of the outfit.

Since I want to look a little sexy, I opt for a black vest top that swoops just low enough to show a hint of cleavage. Well, it's actually more than a bit when I add my black lace push-up bra underneath, but Marcus will appreciate it.

I plan on wearing my black hoodie over the top, like he suggested, but I'll throw that on after he's seen me like this.

I know he'll like what he sees, as he's always telling me how much he likes my body, but he'll lose his mind when he sees the black lace knickers I have on underneath.

Marcus got home about an hour ago, but we both agreed to get ready in our own rooms. He wanted us to have that reveal that all first dates have, where you see what the person has chosen to wear. I teased him about him being an old romantic, but secretly, I was thrilled by the idea.

Even though I'm not getting as dressed up for him as I could, I still want to have that moment where I get to see what he thinks. And when we both walk into the living room at exactly six, I get the moment I was hoping for.

His mouth falls open, and he looks a little stunned, before he finally finds his voice.

"You look incredible. You know I think you're beautiful all the time, but I wasn't expecting you to take a casual dress code and make it so fucking sexy," he growls, his voice deep and husky as his eyes roam over my body in a way that makes me feel naked.

"You don't look too bad yourself," I reply, and that's a massive fucking understatement.

He's wearing dark jeans that hug his thighs, a tight black T-shirt that clings to all his muscles, and black biker boots that match the leather jacket he's thrown on over the top.

He looks dangerous and sexy, like sin personified, and my heart skips a beat at the thought that this gorgeous man is mine.

"Keep looking at me like that, love, and we'll never make our date," he growls, his dark eyes fixed on mine.

He reaches over and takes my hand, quickly pulling me forward, so that I'm right in front of him. He gives me a fierce kiss before pulling away far too soon.

"We should get going. We don't want to be late."

"Are you going to tell me where we're going?" I ask, as Marcus laces our fingers together, pulling me out of the apartment.

"No," he says, that cocky smirk on his face growing as I nag him the whole time we're in the lift.

Once we make it into the garage in the basement, I look around to where Miles usually has the car waiting, but it's not there. I glance over at Marcus, who begins walking towards the row of cars.

I've been in this garage more times than I can count, but I've never really paid much attention.

Miles has a car that he uses, and that's the car I'm used to going in whenever I go out with Marcus, but Kim also has her own car, which she uses to take me to my classes.

I just assumed that all of the other cars belonged to the people who live in the apartment block, but the way Marcus looks at them makes me wonder if that's true.

"Where's Miles and the car?" I ask.

"I gave him the night off. I don't really want my best mate coming on a date with me. We'll still have security following us, and I can't do anything about that, but if I drive, and it's just the two of us in the car, it's the best I could come up with to make it feel personal," he explains, wincing a little as he stares at me, almost like I might not be happy with his explanation.

"Marcus, I know you need to have security with you at all times. It's not a big deal. In fact, I rather like knowing they're around to keep you safe. But I do appreciate you trying to give us some privacy," I say with a smile, before adding, "You drive?"

Marcus chuckles. "It would be a waste, owning all of these cars if I can't drive them."

Even though he's only confirming my suspicions, I can't keep the shocked expression off my face.

"You own all of these?" I waft my arms around the large garage, signalling to the cars.

Marcus shakes his head with a laugh.

"No." I breathe a sigh of relief, before he adds, "I own all of the cars on the right. The ones on the left either belong to my staff or the people who live in the building."

My mouth literally flops open as I take in the cars on the right side of the garage. I may not know a lot about cars, but it's not hard to miss the differences between the two sides.

The cars on the left seem affordable, more practical, whereas the ones on the right are flashy and expensive, one sports car after another.

"I don't even know what to say. Do you need this many big flashy cars? If I didn't already know the answer, I'd ask if you were trying to make up for lacking in other areas."

Marcus throws his head back and laughs, a full belly laugh that I've never heard from him before, and it makes him look so much younger, lighter.

I decide in that moment that it's going to be my life's mission to make him laugh like this as often as I can. He needs a little bit more laughter in his intense life.

"Come on, I don't want us to be late. But I'm going to make a note to prove to you how much I'm not overcompensating when I get you naked later," he replies, pulling me towards a sleek black sports car.

He opens the door for me and I climb in, listening as he tells me all about what type of car it is.

Although the information goes in one ear and out the other, making zero sense to me, I smile at how passionate he is, talking about the car. It's clearly something he enjoys, and I'm grateful he's showing me another side to him.

We've not been driving for long, before he pulls into what looks to be an industrial area, confusing me further. Then, as he turns the corner, a bright sign lets me know exactly where we are.

"You brought me ice skating?" I ask, completely thrown by this.

Of all the dates I'd been imagining, this wasn't even on the list.

Marcus looks almost a little shy as he nods. "I don't know if you remember, but I used to play ice hockey when I was a teenager."

How the fuck could I forget?

Other than his skateboarding phase around age thirteen, I happen to think this was one of his sexiest hobbies. Since I can't say that, I just nod and he continues.

"I had to give it up when Father decided I needed to pay more attention to my role as his heir, instead of wasting my time with sports that did nothing more than distract me. I'm sure you can imagine his annoying voice saying that."

I laugh, because I can picture it. "I'm sure he loved you playing hockey."

"He hated me doing anything that wasn't related to this business, so I begrudgingly gave it up, despite it being something that I love. I've always missed skating, and then you burst into my life.

"You had the strength to ignore the person your parents wanted you to be, and you're doing what makes you happy. The night you took your first class, I came here. I've been skating regularly since then, and I thought I'd share it with you."

With each word, Marcus looks more and more vulnerable, and I fall harder and faster. This gorgeous man makes my heart race, and all I can do is pull his lips to mine and show him how I feel with a kiss. I'm breathless by the time we pull apart.

"Thank you for showing me this side of you, but I have to confess, I've never skated before."

He shrugs his shoulders and pulls me towards the entrance. "That doesn't matter, love, I've got you," he says, and I know he means it.

I'm shocked to find the rink is completely empty, until a sly-looking Marcus confesses to paying the company to close for an hour, so we can have the place to ourselves.

I want to shout at him for splashing out like that, but I'm too caught up in the moment to care.

Marcus walks me through the whole process of picking my skates and putting them on. I'm anxious to even step foot on the ice, and I want to be certain he won't let me fall.

So he tells me to take a seat ringside, and he then glides out onto the ice, showing me that he can definitely skate.

He moves so quickly I can barely keep up with him, gliding over the ice like he's been doing it his whole life. He changes direction with ease, and when he starts skating backwards, I smile at him showing off.

When he finally stops in front of me, a thin sheen of sweat across his brow, dampening the hair that's flopped onto his forehead, the grin on his face makes him look boyish and alive.

He's more than good enough to support me, and he'd never let anything happen to me.

As I predicted, as soon as I step foot on the ice, I look like Bambi learning to walk. My limbs go in different directions, and I'd have landed on my arse numerous times had Marcus not been there to catch me.

After a few quick instructions, we eventually get to the stage where I can stand on the ice, and Marcus takes hold of my hands, pulling me along with him. I'm not exactly skating, but it feels amazing.

Towards the end, I'm finally moving my own skates, propelling myself forward just a bit, even if I do cling onto Marcus like he's my life raft. For someone who's never stepped foot on the ice, I can't stop smiling.

As our time comes to an end, the owner signals that he's going to reopen the rink, and Marcus helps me off the ice.

It doesn't take long for the place to fill up with kids, who are all taking lessons. Figure skaters are on one side of the ice, and hockey players on the other.

Grumbling about the influx of people, Marcus picks up our things in one hand and grabs mine with his other.

With our skates still on, he pulls me towards one of the doors just off the rink. It reads *Private*, yet Marcus knows the code to unlock the door.

Once he pulls me inside, I look around to see we're in what appears to be a private changing room. Lockers line one wall, with benches in the centre, and a row of vanity desks and mirrors are on the other side. There's a door beside the mirror, which I'm assuming leads to a bathroom.

"What's this place?" I ask.

"It's a private VIP changing room. Not many people have access," he explains, and I roll my eyes at how posh he sounds.

"But you do?"

He simply nods, helping me to take a seat on the bench in the middle of the room. He takes off his own skates before kneeling down in front of me, so he can begin unlacing mine.

What starts as him simply removing my skates, soon becomes more. His gentle touch on my calves and my feet has my heart racing, but it's seeing him on his knees for me that really makes my head spin.

Marcus becomes aware of my shallow breathing straight away, completely in tune with me.

"Take your clothes off," he instructs, and my eyes go wide.

"Here? But anyone could walk in."

"Very few people have access to this room. Besides, the risk of getting caught will only make this more exciting," he growls.

I happen to agree with him, so why the fuck do I argue?

"But—"

He quickly cuts me off. "If you argue with me, I'll turn this into a punishment, and won't let you come."

My mouth flies open, the desire to reply growing, until that little voice in my head—that I suspect is ruled by my vagina—tells me to keep quiet.

Quicker than I'd like to admit, I remove all of my clothes.

I'd be bothered by the smirk on his face, if I wasn't distracted by the fact he's now naked too. He must have removed his clothes when I did, and my gaze is drawn to his hard cock.

"Sit," he snaps, pointing at the bench I was sitting on a moment before.

I do as I'm told, dropping down straight away, while Marcus lowers onto his knees before me, that devilish grin on his face growing as he pulls my arse to the edge, spreading my legs wide for him.

Before my brain can catch up, his lips are on my pussy, licking and sucking, devouring me in the best possible way. There's no teasing, no build up, he just goes straight in with his tongue, and it feels so fucking good.

A loud moan rips from my throat as he sucks my clit into his mouth, and he quickly pulls back, glaring at me with a smirk.

"You better be quiet, slut. You don't want someone to catch us, do you?"

He doesn't wait for a response, he dives back in, licking and sucking me like he's a dying man, and I'm the sustenance he needs to survive.

I have to use one hand to prop me up, grabbing hold of the bench behind me, so I don't fall backwards, but I slide my free fingers into his silky hair, grasping the strands as I hold his mouth against me. My eyes screw shut as I bite my lip, trying hard to keep quiet.

My body reacts under his expert tongue, and I arch my back, rocking my hips against him as much as I can with his arms wrapped around my legs, keeping me still. As one of his hands snakes across my stomach, pressing me down, he releases the other.

Before I have time to question it, his finger is probing at my entrance. It slides in with ease, thanks to how wet I am after his assault with his tongue, and he quickly adds a second.

I whimper, trying frantically to keep quiet as he slides his long fingers in and out, getting deeper with each thrust, while his mouth continues sucking and licking my clit.

With the pace he's going, it doesn't take long before my body responds, climbing closer and closer to the edge.

"I'm so close," I whisper-yell.

"Open your eyes, Mio. Look at me while I'm licking your cunt," Marcus growls against my clit, before biting down on it just enough to make me cry out.

My eyes fly open, and I look down at him as he kneels between my legs. He's staring up at me through hooded lashes, that have no business being so long, and his dark eyes make my core tighten.

I know he feels it around his fingers, as that smirk of his returns, and he keeps eye contact with me as he attacks my clit with his tongue.

"Fuck, fuck, fuck," I cry out, before quickly slapping my hand over my mouth.

Marcus chuckles and the vibration against my pussy sends a shiver through me. He then starts curving his fingers in the perfect way, rubbing against the exact spot that only he seems to be able to find, and my movements become frantic as pleasure threatens to overtake me.

"Shit. Fuck. I need... Can I... Please, Marcus," I beg, not able to form a proper sentence.

He chuckles again, and if I could risk taking the hand away from my mouth, I'd hit him with it.

"I don't hear a question, slut. Your cunt is getting so wet, you must be close. Tell me what you want, like a good little whore."

He blows against my clit, as he curls his fingers while they're deep inside of me, and I see fucking stars, my eyes practically rolling as I gasp for air.

"Please, can I come? I need to come? I'm going to... right now," I tell him, my begging becoming louder and more frantic as my orgasm draws closer.

Although I've learnt to control it to a certain extent, there are some times, like now, when the pleasure is just too intense, and I simply can't hold back.

In truth, I also don't want to. I want to feel how good this release will be as it crashes through me, and I'm starting to reach the stage where I'll happily take a punishment as long as I get to come.

Marcus must realise how close I am, as his eyes fix on mine, burning just as fiercely as my own.

"Come for me, slut, but keep your eyes on me. If you close them, you won't come for a week. I want to watch as my sexy little whore comes on my tongue."

No matter how much I might want to close my eyes, I keep them fixed on him. I let him see the moment I lose control, as my orgasm hits me like a truck.

I bite down on the hand over my mouth, which just about dampens the cries of pleasure that echo softly around the room.

My whole body shudders beneath Marcus' touch, and his fingers still as my pussy grabs hold of them, getting even wetter than I thought possible.

Marcus lavishes my clit with long, soft licks with the flat of his tongue, drawing out the feeling as my nub becomes even more sensitive than before.

I gasp for air as my body begins to relax, slowly coming down from my release. My brain feels like it's floating away, distantly aware of the sting I feel when Marcus removes his fingers.

Before I can even register what's happening, Marcus has lifted me up and spun me around, so that I'm bent over the bench I was sitting on just a second ago. My arse is in the air, my back arched, while Marcus uses his feet to nudge my legs wider.

The cool air hits my exposed sensitive pussy and I hiss, shivering from the sensations. Marcus leans over, covering my back with his body, passing on his warmth to me. I feel his hard cock pressing between my legs and I rock back into him.

I feel his breath against my cheek as he whispers in my ear. "Do you want me to fuck you now, Mio?"

I nod rapidly, turning my face just enough that I can capture his lips with mine.

"Yes, please."

Before I've even finished speaking, he pushes in.

He doesn't take his time, he thrusts quickly until I've taken his full length, pausing only when he's balls deep. I yelp at the sudden intrusion, which quickly turns into a groan as my pussy feels stretched and full, stinging just a little.

"So fucking tight," Marcus growls, his hands grabbing onto my hips to keep me in place.

His hold is bruising, but I don't care. I love seeing his marks on my body, but it's nothing compared to how he reacts when he sees them.

It's his way of claiming me, marking me as his, and I'd happily wear his bruises for the rest of my life.

"Please, fuck me," I tell him, when the stretching sting in my pussy turns into a desperate ache.

"Such a needy little whore," Marcus whispers into my ear, before sucking on the spot on my neck that makes me moan.

After a few seconds of holding still, he begins to move. He starts rocking slowly, pushing in a little deeper each time, and it's the start of a beautiful yet maddening rhythm.

He then begins to pull out more, though when he pushes in, he does it at such a slow pace, I can feel every inch of him as he spreads me open.

"More, please," I beg.

"More of what, slut? If you want something, be a good whore and tell me what it is."

"I need it faster."

Marcus chuckles at the desperation in my voice, but as always, he does as I ask.

He fucks into me quickly, jerking his hips as he hits deep inside, his balls rubbing against my clit in a maddening way. The sound of our skin slapping together mixes with my muffled cries, as I whisper-beg him for anything and everything.

"Such a good little fucktoy. You take my cock so well. Do you feel like a dirty little whore getting fucked in the changing room where anyone could walk in?" he asks, and I have to bite my hand harder to stop from moaning.

Almost as if they heard what he said, a loud bang on the door to the locker room has us both freezing. Marcus is balls deep inside of me, as we both turn to look at where the noise is coming from.

We can hear voices on the other side of the door, and it rattles like someone is trying to get in.

The handle goes up and down and my heart stops. Panic overwhelms me, and I try to move, but Marcus' hold on me, and his dick that's impaling me, prevents me from going anywhere.

Although the handle keeps going up and down, and the door shakes as the people on the other side try to get in, it thankfully doesn't open. We hear them pressing loudly on the keypad, before one of them shouts about the code being wrong.

I try to pull away again, knowing we're one correct code away from getting caught, but Marcus won't let me move. He leans over and whispers in my ear.

"Where do you think you're going, Mio?"

"We're about to get caught. We need to get dressed," I stress, my eyes going wide when he begins slowly moving inside me again, the head of his cock dragging over the spot deep inside that makes me see stars.

"We're not going anywhere until you've come on my cock, and I've filled your tight cunt full of my cum," he growls, pulling all the way out before thrusting in again.

"We'll get caught," I cry out, quickly covering my mouth with my hand again.

"Then you better make me come quickly, slut. I don't care if they get in. They can watch you begging me to come, like the good little whore you are."

My pussy flutters at his dirty words, and he chuckles.

"Didn't know you liked the idea of people watching," he says.

"I don't," I reply, but he shakes his head.

"Your cunt tightening around my cock says differently, love. Now, fuck me, hard," he instructs, as he pulls my hips back, slamming me onto his cock.

After that, his movements become more frantic. I rock back onto his cock as he pulls me onto him, hitting me deep and fast, before pulling back and repeating the same motion, getting quicker each time.

As he thrusts into me, the head of his cock scrapes against my magic spot, and it's not long until I'm on the edge again.

His balls slap against my clit, giving my overly-sensitive nub the attention it needs to help me reach my impending release quicker.

I can tell Marcus is close too, as his movements become more frantic, his breathing becoming ragged as he grunts and swears.

I'm distantly aware that someone is still trying to get into the locker room, but I'm so close to coming again that I can't seem to find enough energy to care.

"Marcus. Oh, fuck. I'm going to... Can I come?"

He takes one hand off my hip and reaches out to gather my hair into his fist. He then pulls on it hard, forcing me to lift my body off the bench, my back arched for him as he yanks my head back.

I place my hands on the bench, giving me enough support to lift up further, which changes the angle of his cock in my pussy, and he seems to get even deeper than before.

Both of our moans mingle together, and I'm certain we're being loud enough that the people on the other side of the door can hear, yet we don't stop.

Marcus continues to fuck me hard, and the intensity of his deep thrusts, paired with the stinging pain on my scalp, pushes me further into my pleasure.

"I can't stop it. I'm going to come. Please," I cry out, long past caring if people can hear.

"Look in front of you, slut," he instructs, and when I do as he tells me, I see us both in the mirror in front of us. He's staring at us with a fiery gaze as he fucks me with such power.

"Oh, fuck," is all I can say as I watch his face scrunch up, his abs tightening each time he fucks into me.

"I want you to watch as you come. Look at what a beautiful little slut you are, just for me. I want you to memorise the way you look, so you can dream about this. I want you to remember this moment forever," he tells me, and it takes all of my willpower not to fall apart at his words.

"I will, I promise."

I see the bright smile on his face in our reflection.

"Who do you belong to?"

"You," I breathe, not even pausing to think.

"Is this tight little cunt mine?" he growls.

"Yes! Please, fill it with your cum," I beg, needing desperately for him to give me my release.

"Fuck," he groans. "Come, now. Make sure you watch as I fill my cunt with cum, claiming you fully, slut."

Before he's even finished talking, my orgasm hits, and it's more intense than ever before.

My whole body goes rigid before shuddering through my release. I see stars, and if Marcus hadn't wrapped his arms around me, I'd have fallen face-first onto the bench.

As my pussy spasms around him, Marcus quickly finds his release right alongside my own. He presses in deep, roaring as his cum floods into my pussy.

As we both come down from the intensity of our orgasms, he presses little kisses along my spine.

We're so caught up in our own euphoric bubble, we'd forgotten about the people trying to get in. That is until there's a loud bang, like someone kicked the door, followed by yelling.

"Is someone in there? If you're stuck and need help, call out."

Marcus starts to chuckle, whereas I panic. "We need to get dressed."

Marcus rolls his eyes, but gently pulls out of me, making me hiss at his absence.

"Only because I don't want to kill anyone for seeing my girl in this state."

I try not to smile, but hearing him call me *his girl* makes my stomach flip in the best way.

"I'm going to clean up real quick," I say, pointing towards the bathroom, but Marcus grabs my arm, that mischievous look on his face again.

"No, you're not. You can put your knickers back on, but that's all. I want to know my cum is dripping from your pussy for the rest of the night," he states as he hands me my black lace knickers.

"But, I—"

"Don't argue or I'll punish you," he threatens.

I glare at him as I take my knickers, sliding them on. I make a good show of being annoyed, but I'm actually really fucking turned on by the idea.

We both dress quickly, and each time I move, I can feel the mixture of our wetness seeping from me.

Once we're dressed, Marcus pulls me in for a quick kiss.

"So, what do you think of our first date?"

I can't help but laugh at the smug expression on his face.

"I've had better," I tell him, though he knows I'm lying.

"Oh, now I really do have to punish you," he tells me, and I regret my decision instantly.

Marcus then pulls open the door, finding two people on the other side, with a member of staff who looks perplexed, unable to understand why the door wouldn't open.

As soon as they take one look at our dishevelled appearance, understanding dawns on them.

The man who had been trying to get in, and the male employee, both have matching amused expressions, but the female looks at me like I'm disgusting.

Although my cheeks flush redder, I refuse to feel shame. I hold my head high as I pull Marcus out of the room.

As I'm passing, I hear her mutter the word *slut* under her breath. I stop, leaning close enough so that just she can hear me.

"Don't be bitter because my guy knows how to fuck me just right."

Her startled expression makes my smile grow, and I let Marcus lead me out of the ice rink. He turns to me in the car park, awe clearly displayed on his face.

"I thought you might have been embarrassed, particularly when she called you a slut, but you handled it well."

I nod, feeling more confident than I have in a long time. "I don't care. I am a slut, but only for you. She's just jealous."

He chuckles, pulling me in for a hug. "She has every reason to be jealous. She's nothing compared to you. I'm a lucky guy that I get to call you mine."

As my heart pounds out of my chest, he claims my mouth with his, and everything else in the world fades away, leaving just me and Marcus, in our own little bubble of bliss.

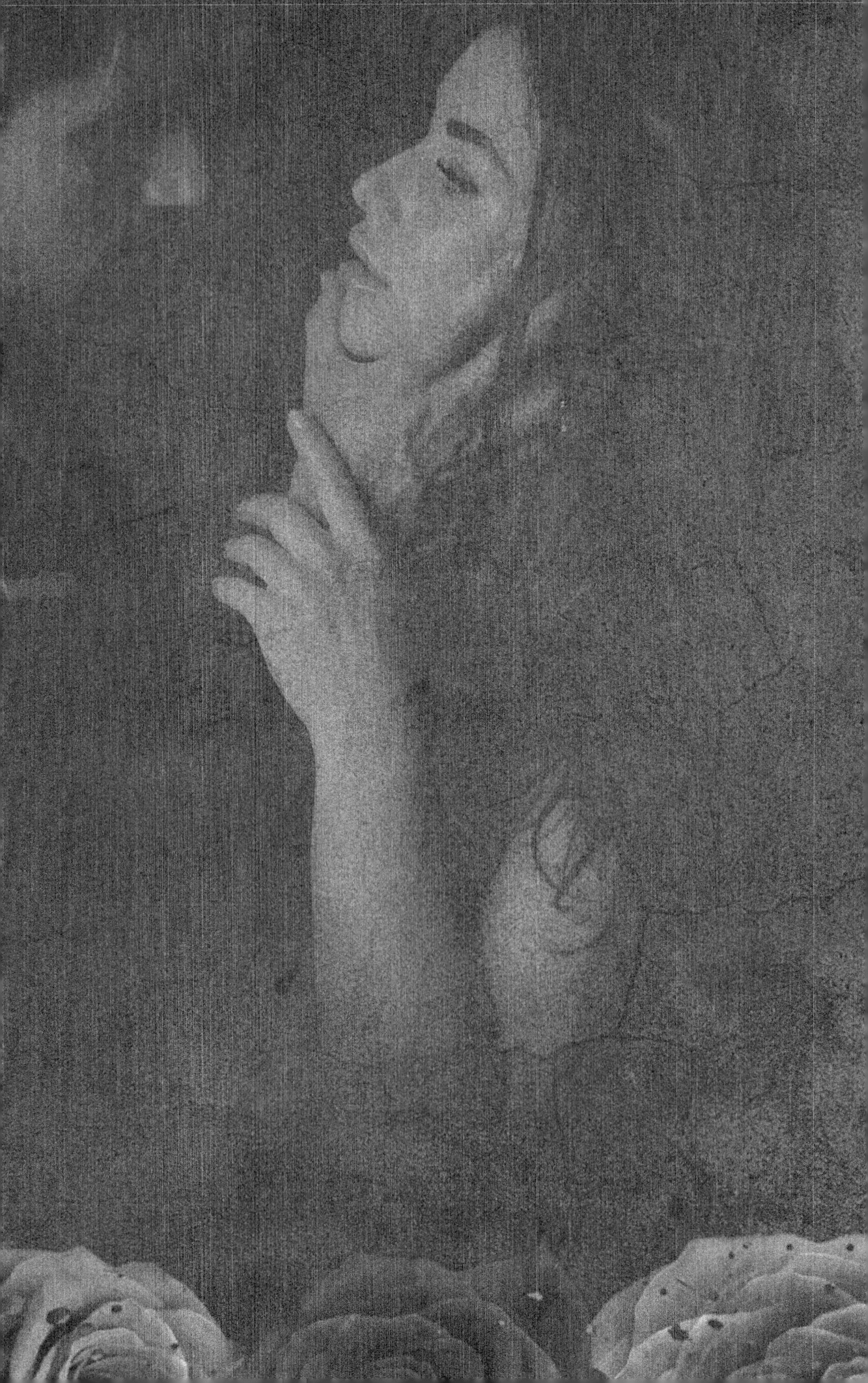

Chapter Twenty-Two

Chloe

After our first date, things between Marcus and I had definitely shifted. It was almost like he'd finally accepted that what he felt was more than just sex, even though neither of us had labelled it.

I knew what I felt... I was in love with Marcus Morelli.

Hell, I'd been infatuated with him for most of my life, and Teenage Chloe would have definitely called it love, even back then, but as I got older, I realised you can't love someone until you truly know them.

Living with Marcus means I've gotten to know him at a much faster rate than if we'd dated normally.

I know he can be grumpy in the morning if I talk to him before his coffee, or if he's not had much sleep. He moans about eating my baked goods, claiming he has to work-out more afterwards, but I've noticed several go missing overnight.

He secretly likes watching chick-flicks, though he'll deny that if anyone asks. Jacob and Miles are his only two friends, and he doesn't want more. He'd defend them with his life, and though they would do the same in return, he'd never want them to.

But the Marcus I've fallen in love with the most is the one I see when we climb into bed together after a long day. When we're both too exhausted to get lost in each other's bodies, so instead, he just pulls me close. He rests my head on his chest, while linking our legs together, throwing his arm over my stomach to hold me against him.

While I'm falling asleep, he strokes the hair out of my eyes, before running his fingers through my long dark strands, pressing a soft kiss to my temple. He tells me how beautiful I am, and how lucky he is to have me in his arms.

I listen to the sound of his heart racing, wondering if it's beating at the same rate as mine, because I feel like we're connected. As he wishes me sweet dreams, he makes promises to me for the future.

He talks about my dream business, about stopping my marriage to Scott, and making sure I stay here with him.

Each night, I fall asleep as he tells me about the future, and whilst it relaxes and calms me, giving me so much to hope for, there's also a bit of sadness there that I have to hide from him.

No matter how many promises he makes to me in the darkness when we're alone, faced with the harsh light of day, nothing is guaranteed.

To choose me would mean he'd have to burn a lot of bridges, and anger a lot of people. I want to believe he'll do it, so I can live a better life than the one my parents forced on me, but sometimes, hope hurts more than anything else.

Naturally, I haven't told Marcus about any of my fears, as he'd think I don't believe he'll keep his promises, and it's not that.

I guess, what it boils down to is…when the time comes, I don't believe he'll choose me. More than that, I'm not sure he should. I don't think I'm worth him starting a war over, but that self-doubt is something I have to live with.

I can bury it deep until our clock stops ticking and the decision has to be made. Until then, I plan to live in the moment, savouring every second I get to have with him, so if it does all end, at least I'll have the memories.

It's the Saturday evening of my fifth week here, and Marcus and I are having a Chinese take-out, since he's had a long day at work, and I've been in class all day.

We are joking and laughing with each other, sharing stories from our day when the front door bursts open and Miles stomps in.

He flops down onto one of the extra dining chairs and reaches over to grab a spring roll from one of the food containers in the middle of the table, groaning as he stuffs it into his mouth.

"I don't recall inviting you for dinner," Marcus states sarcastically, but Miles just ignores him, grabbing a prawn cracker next.

"Do you want me to get you a plate? There's plenty of food," I ask, earning me a glare from Marcus.

"Don't encourage him!"

I chuckle, rolling my eyes as Miles continues to stuff his face. Once he's swallowed what he has in his mouth, he turns to me.

"No thanks, I'm not staying. I just came in to tell you I'm sick of fielding calls and messages from your crazy family."

My brows furrow as I glance between both men. Noticing that Marcus looks a little sheepish, I fix my gaze on him.

"What?"

"Look, I didn't want you to have to deal with any of them, so I had all of their calls and texts diverted to another phone. Miles has been monitoring it and replying on your behalf where necessary," Marcus replies.

My mouth flops open, and I don't know whether to be angry with him or kiss him.

"As grateful as I am that you got them off my back, you should have told me."

Miles responds on his friends behalf. "He was worried you would say no, so I told him just to do it anyway. We saw how much they upset you at that first dinner, and we could only imagine what your text interactions were like. I have to say, we were completely correct. Your family treats you like shit."

I give him a sad nod as confirmation. Marcus, on the other hand, looks furious on my behalf.

"What? How are they treating her like shit? I'm going to kill them."

"Calm down, caveman," Miles laughs. "I've been dealing with them."

"I'm not a caveman, but I want to know what they've been saying to Chloe."

He bangs his fist on the table, not at all helping his argument that he's *not* a caveman.

"As much as I appreciate you both protecting me, I can look after myself," I state firmly, though I'm not entirely sure I believe it, and it's clear neither man does either.

Miles seems to ignore us both, and continues with his rant.

"Your mother, who is a bitch, by the way, keeps harassing you about the wedding. She has asked a million questions that she claims the planner needs to know, but even when I've replied for you, she doesn't seem to care about your response."

"You answered wedding planning questions for her?" Marcus asks, sounding a little amused.

"Look, there's a good chance she's not getting married anyway, so it doesn't matter. Besides, she asked whether you wanted a maroon or peach colour scheme, and since nobody looks good in peach, I thought it was the obvious answer," Miles replies, shrugging his shoulders dismissively.

"Peach?" I squeal. "She wants the colour scheme to be peach? Has she lost her damn mind?"

Miles chuckles, while Marcus flicks his gaze between the two of us.

"That's what I told her. She's an idiot thinking peach is a good idea," Miles laughs.

"What else?" Marcus grinds out, clearly trying to change the conversation.

I guess the idea of me getting married isn't something he wants to hear about. I can't help but wonder if it's just because I'm supposed to marry Scott, or the idea of marriage in general.

Don't get ahead of yourself, it's a bit early in...whatever the hell this is...to be thinking about marriage, I remind myself, whilst in the other part of my brain, I'm definitely thinking about whether Marcus would ever want to get married.

Miles winces as he says, "Scott has texted several times, and he's also tried calling a lot too."

"What does that shit-stain want?" Marcus growls.

"Pretty much the same as Fiona. He wants to finalise things for the wedding, but he also wants to discuss the 'rules for the marriage'."

On hearing Miles say the word *rules*, a shiver runs down my spine and I cringe.

"Him and those fucking rules."

"What rules?" Marcus asks, his gaze locked on me, looking concerned by my reaction.

"He has a very long list of things that he expects from me, as his wife. He told me about a few of them the very first time we met, but I told him, if they were that important, he should put them into a document for me to look over before the wedding. A bit like a contract, I guess.

"Honestly, I just wanted him to stop talking to me about them, so I made it up to delay the conversation."

I visibly shudder, thinking of the awful things I'm sure he's added to the list.

Marcus turns to Miles, fixing him with a hard stare. "Is it as bad as I'm thinking?"

Miles winces, his face scrunching as he squirms in his seat.

"He only brought up a few that he wanted to clarify with Chloe, but I can imagine the whole document isn't a great read."

"Motherfucker," Marcus snaps, hitting the table once more.

"I don't want to go to any meetings about this fucking sham of a wedding," I say, my voice low, giving away just how much it scares me that this might be my life some day soon.

"You don't have to," Marcus says, but Miles stops him.

"At some point, she may have to, so don't make promises we don't know for sure we can keep. We'll do our best to delay or minimise them, but as part of the bet, you agreed to a meeting, closer to the final weeks here."

Marcus glares at his best friend, who holds down his stare like it's nothing. I shift in my seat, feeling uncomfortable enough for us all.

"So what do we do right now?" I ask, trying to diffuse the tension in the room.

Marcus goes to respond, but Miles holds up his hand to stop him. For just a fraction of a second, Marcus looks like he might stab him in his hand with the knife on his plate, but he takes a deep breath and lets it go.

Miles gives him a tight smile before turning to me.

"You guys have managed to avoid it since your parents got back, but they've been very insistent. You have to attend Sunday lunch tomorrow, so I've suggested a two birds, one stone type scenario.

"I've said you'll talk about the wedding over lunch. It's not ideal, but you have to attend anyway, and at least this way you know both Marcus and myself will be there to support you."

I give him a smile as I nod. "Thank you. I guess, it's the best of a bad situation."

"Exactly," Miles says, grabbing another spring roll and a barbecue rib. "Anyway, I'm going to leave you to finish your meal in peace. I'll be here at twelve to drive us there for lunch tomorrow."

"You can stay, if you'd like," Marcus adds, shocking us both.

"Thanks, but I've got somewhere I need to be."

As he stands, Marcus glares at his friend, seemingly unhappy with his response.

"Where?"

Miles rolls his eyes. "None of your business. Enjoy your evening."

Before either of us can say anything, Miles has run down the hallway and he slams the door closed as he leaves. Marcus turns to me, his brow furrowed in confusion.

"He never keeps anything from me. Should I be worried? Maybe I should have someone follow him," he muses, pulling his phone out of his pocket.

I reach over and take the phone from his hand, placing it on the table. I then lace my fingers through his, squeezing just enough to distract him.

"No, you will not have him followed. Whatever Miles is doing, he'll tell you about it when he's ready. For all you know, he's seeing someone and wants to keep it private for now."

That doesn't seem to ease Marcus' worries, as he continues to shuffle, his from deepening.

"If he's seeing someone new, we'll need to run a thorough background check. He knows the rules. It's dangerous to go somewhere when nobody knows where you are."

"Marcus, relax," I tell him, stroking my thumb over the back of his hand in reassuring circles. "Miles knows all the safety rules, since he wrote most of them. He's not stupid. Besides, he has GPS tracking on both his phone and his car, so we can find him if we need to—though we won't need to."

Marcus' eyes light up, and I can't help but groan.

"That's a great idea, we can—"

I cut him off by placing a kiss on his lips.

"Enough! Finish your food. When we've eaten, I want to go and take a soak in the giant jacuzzi bath in the main bathroom. I've always wondered what it feels like to have sex underwater."

The fork he's just picked up clatters onto the plate, and his piercing blue eyes darken. "Let's go."

"Don't you want to finish eating?" I ask, pointing to his half-full plate.

He shakes his head. "We'll reheat it when we're done."

Without saying anything more, he stands, dragging me behind him into the bathroom. I smile the whole way, pleased my plan to distract him has worked. I hope Miles is grateful.

Then again, it's not exactly a hardship to let this gorgeous man ravish me in a jacuzzi, just to distract him from chasing down his friend. As plans go, this is one of my best ones.

When Miles shows up the next day to drive us to my parents house, Marcus is under strict instructions not to interrogate him.

I gave him a blowjob over breakfast, and promised he could do whatever he wanted with me when we return home, but in exchange, he couldn't mention anything about yesterday to Miles.

I knew from the minute we climbed into the car that Miles was preparing for an onslaught, and he was shocked when no questions came.

He threw a smile at me through the rearview mirror, having worked out that I'm the one responsible for Marcus' sudden character change.

It's not a big deal. Besides, he's been dealing with my family and Scott on my behalf, so I'm pretty sure he's got the shittier end of the stick.

The drive to my parents' house is annoyingly short, and by the time we arrive, my nerves are through the roof. My heart is racing so fast, there's barely a gap between the beats.

No matter how hard I try to concentrate on my breathing, what started as slow, deep breaths are now close to hyperventilating. I'm also pretty sure I'm sweating in places I didn't know I could sweat.

This time, I didn't need any encouragement from Marcus to wear whatever I want. Without hesitating, I pulled on my skinny, blue ripped jeans, and a tight black vest, which showed a little more cleavage than usual, so I threw a baggy red and black plaid shirt over the top.

I added my trusty black and white Converse, that my mother has tried to throw away on numerous occasions, and I did my make-up the way I prefer.

After brushing my hair and leaving it down, I was done. One look in the mirror confirmed that what I was wearing would likely give my mother a heart attack, but I didn't care.

I smiled when I saw Marcus dressed just as casually, his dark jeans and leather jacket making my breath catch in my throat.

Once we arrive at my family home, Marcus squeezes my hand. I hadn't even realised he was holding it.

"Are you okay?"

I can tell by the concerned look in his eyes, he already knows the answer.

"I'm nervous, that's all."

"I promise, I won't leave you alone with any of them. I'll be there the whole time."

At hearing his promise, I lean over and capture his lips with mine. It's a deep, passionate kiss that says more than words ever could.

Dropping my gaze, my heart aches as I admit what's on my mind.

"I hate that we have to pretend." My voice is small and insecure, which obviously saddens Marcus.

He reaches over and grabs my chin, lifting my head until I'm forced to meet his gaze.

"It's only temporary. One day, we'll tell them the truth."

I give him a small smile, trying to show that I believe him, when really my insecurities and doubt are overwhelming me.

"I know."

Marcus' gaze narrows, and I can tell he knows I'm lying, but thankfully, he doesn't say anything more. Miles cuts the growing tension between us by opening the car door for me, offering me his hand, so I can climb out.

From the moment we step inside, the dinner is just as awful as the last. The only difference is that Jake isn't here, which is both a blessing and a curse. Without him here, drunk off his arse, acting as a distraction, everyone is fixated on me.

With Jake's usual chair now free, Miles quickly sits in it, gesturing for me to take the seat he was in last time, so I'm between Marcus and him. Scott is still opposite me, a prime position for him to glare at me, but at least he's no longer in touching distance.

Mother insists I sit next to her, like last time, as she has so much wedding stuff to discuss with me. Thankfully, my dad insists that nobody move. He's hungry, and doesn't want to delay eating while people change seats, particularly when wedding talk can wait until afterwards.

I couldn't have been more grateful, even if he's thinking of his stomach rather than me.

The meal passes by relatively quickly, with Marcus and Miles doing a great job of distracting my mother and Scott whenever they try to talk about the wedding. Ewan and Dad are deep in conversation, so are none the wiser.

We try to leave as soon as the meal is over, but my parents wouldn't allow it this time. They insist on us joining them for a drink in the parlour room, and Marcus is just as annoyed by this as I am.

It quickly becomes clear this was their plan all along, as Dad tries to distract Marcus while Mother pulls out a wedding planning book. She's already filled in most of the pages, no doubt after ignoring all of the suggestions Miles made while he was pretending to be me.

I listen patiently as she goes through the book with me and Scott, but it's hard to ignore the way he keeps shuffling closer to me, pressing himself against my side.

When I shoot him a glare, he claims he can't see the book my mother is holding on the other side of me, but I know that's bollocks, especially when he puts his hand on my thigh—which is exactly why I wore jeans. At least I don't have to feel him on my bare flesh.

I grit my teeth and ignore the way he's rubbing circles into my leg. I don't need to look at Marcus to know he's staring at me, I can feel his eyes on me.

"When do you think you'll be free?" Mother asks, and I quickly realise I've missed most of what she's been saying.

In an attempt to block out Scott, and ignore her, I appear to have missed something important.

"Sorry, what?"

Mother glares at me before rolling her eyes, looking at me with disgust.

"Really, Chloe. Were you listening to me at all?"

"I was," I lie. "I just missed the question."

She grinds her teeth, clearly not believing me.

"I said, we're already cutting it fine as it is... You need to choose a wedding dress. I'm already going to have to pay a ridiculous rush fee, but if we leave it much later, you'll end up wearing something off the rack, and there's no way I could bear the humiliation of that."

Both Marcus and Miles, who must have been listening to our conversation, begin to chuckle, quickly hiding behind their hands as they make it look like they were talking to each other. I can't help but smile at them. My mother is being dramatic.

Had they not made me laugh, I would most likely be dissolving into a panic attack right now. The idea of picking out a wedding dress makes the whole thing seem so real, and I can't think about that.

"I'm sure we'll find something. You don't need to worry," I tell her, which only makes her glower at me more.

Scott chips in, supporting my mother. "Your dress is very important, Chloe. You need to look your best, as it's a reflection on both me and your family."

"Besides, I'm sure you'll love going dress shopping with your mother. You can even invite my mother and sister, they're very fashion forward, and would make sure you looked your best for me. Since you don't have any friends of your own, they'd be happy to step in."

Even though his words sound friendly and caring, the subtext is more than clear. Each insult hits me deeper than the last.

There's no way I'd enjoy dress shopping, especially if I'm with my mother. Adding his family in, who I've never met, would be even worse.

Then to point out my lack of friends... He may as well have cut me open and smiled as he watched me bleed.

I used to have friends, but I was made to stop seeing them, to concentrate on my role in this family. I hadn't realised how much it bothers me until this moment.

Feeling an overwhelming urge to burst into tears, I spring to my feet. "Will you excuse me, I need to use the bathroom."

I hear muttering around me, but I try to drown it out. Though when I hear a phone ring, I turn around to make sure it's not mine. Marcus pulls his phone from his jacket pocket and checks the screen.

Since it's not mine, I continue walking swiftly out of the room. I hear Marcus tell everyone he has to take the call, and I wonder for a moment what would be important enough for him to leave my family. Then another wave of emotions hit me, and the tears I've been trying to hold back break free, trickling down my face.

I keep moving down the hallway, but just before I reach the bathroom, someone grabs my arm and pulls me down one of the side corridors, until we reach the room at the end.

After my initial shock and yelp at being manhandled, I relax when I see it's Marcus who grabbed me. He closes the door behind us and walks me across the room, pushing me against another door on the opposite wall. He crowds over me, trapping me between his hard body and the wooden door.

"Do you know what's on the other side of this door?" he asks, his voice low and gravelly.

I blink away the tears before taking a look around the room, and after a few seconds, realisation hits.

"This is the sitting room that connects with our parlour room."

"So, what's behind this door?" he asks again.

"My family. It's where we're all having drinks."

He reaches up to cup my cheek, swiping his thumb under my eyes to wipe away the tears. It's an incredibly soft gesture, given how stern and dangerous he looks, his eyes almost black.

I can feel his barely restrained anger making his body vibrate, yet he touches me so gently.

"Don't cry, love. They're not worth your tears," he tells me, before pressing his lips against my cheek.

"I hate him." I try to fill the words with my hatred, but they come out like a sob.

"I know, so do I," he says, as he continues to pepper little kisses over my cheek, across my jaw, and down my neck.

Making sure to suck on the sweet spot over my pulse, he then moves down to my collarbone, his kisses light as a feather.

My body heats up quickly, my stomach fluttering with each kiss, and I wrap my arms around his neck, pulling him closer.

"Will you help me forget about them?"

He pulls back just far enough to make eye contact, and the way he stares at me makes me feel like he's trying to see into my soul.

"If we do this, we don't have time to be slow or gentle."

I nod my head rapidly. "I don't want that. I want you to show me how much you hate him."

His smile turns deadly as he attacks my lips with his, kissing me with fierce passion as he pulls off my shirt. He releases my lips just long enough to pull my vest and bra off, and then he's back on me.

He drags his lips over my neck, down to my breasts, while he reaches down and pops the button on my jeans, pulling the zipper down at the same time. As he takes one of my nipples into his mouth, grazing over it with his teeth, he pulls my jeans down to my ankles, and I quickly kick them off.

The more he pulls and bites my nipples, the harder it is for me to remain quiet. The rapid onslaught of sensations floods my senses, and I can't stop myself from moaning.

Marcus quickly spins me around, gently pushing me against the door until my tits and cheek are squashed into the wood.

"You need to be quiet, Mio. If you keep making noises, they'll know what I'm doing to you," he whispers into my ear, as one hand massages my arse cheek, while the other tugs at my peaked nipple.

"Can we... Can we go to the other side of the room?" I ask frantically as he presses against my lower back, forcing me to arch my back.

Once I do, my pussy is on display for him, and the cool air hitting my heated flesh sends goosebumps over my skin.

Marcus rocks his denim-covered cock against my exposed pussy as he leans over my back, his clothes feeling rough against my smooth skin. He grabs my ear lobe between his teeth, sucking it into his mouth.

"Not a chance, slut. I'm going to fuck you against this door, and you're going to be a good little whore and make sure we don't get caught."

"But what if they hear us," I gasp, my voice getting higher as panic sets in.

"You better make sure they don't."

As soon as he says the words, he presses two of his fingers into my pussy.

I wasn't expecting the sudden intrusion, and I gasp loudly, before quickly moving one of my hands to cover my mouth. After all those sweet little kisses, and the thought of us being caught, I'm more than ready for him.

"You're so wet already, slut. Is it all for me?" he growls, rubbing his thumb against my clit as he quickly thrusts his fingers in deeper.

His movements are fast and deep, hitting just the right places, and my head is spinning. I'm aware he just asked me a question, but my brain is too distracted to formulate a reply.

Marcus slaps my arse cheek, hard, causing me to yelp into my hand. Where he hit me stings, but I'm surprised by how much I liked adding that little bit of pain into my pleasure.

"Fuck, you liked that, didn't you, Mio? Your cunt tightened around my fingers and you got even wetter," he whispers into my ear, my eyes fluttering closed from all the stimulation. "Answer me, or I'll hit you again."

"Yes," I breathe. "I liked it."

Marcus chuckles against my ear, curling his fingers as he drags them over the spot that drives me crazy.

"And is it me that got you all hot and wet?"

I nod my head as best I can against the door with my hand over my mouth. "Yes. It's always all for you."

Marcus' smile widens as I feel my body building towards my release. I'm panting, rocking back against his fingers, chasing down that high.

Marcus reaches up with his free hand and pulls my hand away from my mouth. I look at him in panic, but he quickly places his own hand there instead.

I brace my hand against the door using it as momentum to help me push back against him, and it's not long until I'm whimpering into his hand.

Just as I feel my release approaching, he removes his fingers, leaving my pussy empty and throbbing.

"Please," I beg, my eyes wide open as I plead with him.

I don't need to beg for long. Before I even realise what he's doing, he replaces his fingers with his cock, sliding into me in one quick movement. I groan against his hand, feeling full and stretched open, aching at the speed of his intrusion.

Marcus pauses for just a second, and I hear him pulling in slow, deep breaths beside my ear. I smile at the thought that he's just as affected by this as I am, trying desperately not to lose control too quickly.

Unfortunately, we don't have the luxury of time. The longer we're in here, the higher chance we have of getting caught. Once I've gotten used to the fullness, I rock my hips, grinding against him in a way that pushes him deeper.

"Fuck me," I whisper.

"My pleasure, Mio," Marcus growls, before he begins his relentless thrusts.

Unlike usual, he doesn't start slow and build, teasing me to the point of frustration. We don't have time for that, so he moves straight to the deep, full strokes that speed up with each thrust.

It's not long until he's slamming into me relentlessly, his cock dragging against my walls as he drives me crazy.

His hand over my mouth covers some of the noises coming out of me, but I have to move my hands onto the wall on either side of the door, to push against, to stop my body from slamming into it too much.

Marcus is thrusting into me with such vigour, the door would be rattling off its hinges if I didn't stop it.

"Your tight little cunt fits around me like a glove, love. It's like you were made for me," Marcus says, pressing kisses across my shoulders and back.

"We were made for each other," I mumble back.

"We fucking were. Now I want you to show me how much of a whore you

Prized Possession

really are. Do you want to come with your family in the next room?" he asks, and I nod my head as best I can.

"Yes, please."

I'm close, but I'm not quite there yet, and I'm sure Marcus knows that, since he's become very in tune with my body over the last few weeks.

With the hand that's covering my lips, he slowly slides one of his fingers into my mouth, and I don't hesitate to suck on it like I'd do his cock. His groan vibrates through me, and I suck harder.

He kisses the spot on my neck that drives me crazy, while his thumb circles my clit, and I'm so distracted, I almost miss the cold, wet sensation on my arse. Though, I don't miss him taking his hand off my mouth, pulling his finger out.

I turn my head a little more and see him dribbling spit down into the crack of my arse. Before I can ask him about it, he parts my arse cheeks with his hand.

I watch, completely mesmerised, as he runs the finger that is wet from being in my mouth, over my arsehole.

My eyes widen and my body tenses when I realise what he's about to do.

"Relax. Trust me."

As soon as he says that, I try to release all of the tension in my muscles. I do trust him, and I know he'd never hurt me.

Besides, I've said this is something I'm open to trying, I just didn't picture this scenario for my first time.

He spreads my own spit with his, making sure my puckered hole is wet, before he begins pressing one finger in. His cock slows, pushing into my pussy in slow, deep thrusts as he works his finger into my arse.

"Relax, love," he reminds me again, before reaching underneath me, pressing on my clit.

That's all I need to get lost in the sensations, and as soon as I relax enough, Marcus presses his finger all the way in. I feel so incredibly full, and all of the stimulation happening at once quickly becomes overwhelming.

Marcus only gives me a second to get used to his finger, before he leans over and whispers in my ear again.

"Use a hand to cover your mouth, or everyone will hear you. I'm going to show you what a dirty whore you really are. I'm going to make you come with a cock deep in your cunt and a finger in your arse."

I shudder at his words, and he begins his relentless onslaught, manipulating my body to his will.

His cock ploughs into me over and over, hitting me deep inside each time, while his balls bounce off my clit, sending shivers of pleasure through me each time.

His finger in my arse eventually stops stinging and starts to feel fucking amazing, enhancing the full feeling his cock gives me. I bounce back against him, loving the way he presses into me, claiming both my holes.

It doesn't take long at this speed for me to feel my orgasm approaching.

"Can I come?" I mutter beneath my hand.

"Yes," Marcus groans. "Come with my finger in your arse, slut."

His filthy words have their usual effect, and my orgasm hits me. It's like fire rushes through my veins, heating me up as my body tenses, shuddering as the pleasure ripples through me.

"Marcus," I cry out, louder than I intended, even with my hand in place.

As soon as my pussy stops clinging to him, he begins his long, quick strokes, and he only needs a couple before he's grunting against my back, his cum spilling into me.

"Fuck. Take my cum, slut. Do you like when I come in your tight little cunt? Claiming you as mine?"

I nod my head, pressing my arse back against him, keeping him deep inside me for as long as I can.

"Yes. I need your cum."

We both stay there, panting desperately as Marcus practically holds me up, my legs having turned to jello moments before. As we both catch our breath, he pulls his finger slowly out of my arse, before doing the same with his cock.

I feel his cum seeping out, dripping down my thighs. Marcus must notice it too as he reaches down and scoops it up, gathering his cum on his fingers before he gently presses them back into my sensitive pussy. I whimper, and he rubs my arse reassuringly.

"I don't want you wasting any of my cum. Put your knickers on quickly. I want to know when that fucker, Scott, is talking to you that your dirty cunt is covered with my cum."

He keeps a hand on me until he's sure I'm sturdy enough to stand on my own. He helps me dress, making sure all his cum is where it should be.

Once we're dressed, looking as presentable as we can with kiss-stung lips and rosy cheeks, we head towards the door we came in through—not the one I just came on!

I take a deep breath, not wanting to bring up a subject I know will piss him off, but I have to say it.

"Just in case you didn't know, I don't want to talk about the wedding with them."

Marcus gives me a tight smile. "I know. Every time one of them talked about you trying on wedding dresses, it made me want to pull my gun and shoot them. I hate the idea of you trying on a wedding dress."

I drop my gaze, my heart sinking. "White's not really my colour."

He reaches out and puts his finger under my chin, forcing me to look at him again.

"That's not it, Chloe. I don't want to think about you choosing a dress that you'll wear walking down the aisle to Scott, or any other man, for that matter. The only time you're going to put on a wedding dress is if I'm the one at the end of the aisle."

My breath catches at the intensity of his words, my heart beating so hard I'm surprised it's not broken out of my chest. I try to find the words for such a momentous statement, but before I can, Marcus gives me a short yet passionate kiss.

"We better get back. I'll go first, you follow in a couple of minutes."

I nod my head in agreement, needing to use the time after he's gone to compose myself.

Did he just imply he wants to marry me one day? Or was it just another of his possessive statements?

The little girl that's been dreaming about becoming Mrs Morelli since the age of eight, when she first put a pillowcase on her head, pretending it was a veil, knows which she's hoping for.

Once I've pulled myself together, I go back into the parlour room. Mother glares at me, but everyone else is deep in conversation, barely having noticed my absence. Scott must have grown bored with Mother and is now brown-nosing with my dad.

Thankfully, not long after my return, Marcus announces it's time for us to leave. Just as I'm almost free and out of the door, my mother stops me, grabbing me by the arm.

"Since you haven't given me a firm date, I've looked at my diary and chosen for you. I will make an appointment for Wednesday morning for us to go dress shopping."

I look down at where she's gripping my arm, glaring at her until she has the good sense to remove it. I feel Marcus place his hand against my lower back, and it's just what I need to draw strength from.

"I can't do that day, I have class."

"What class?" Mother stutters, both Dad and Scott looking equally as confused.

"I've started taking baking and cake decorating classes. I've gotten quite good, and I really enjoy it," I tell them, holding my head high with pride as I admit that it's something I'm skilled in.

Scott looks furious. "Why on Earth are you wasting your time with stuff like that?"

I roll my eyes. "Because I enjoy it. I'm thinking of starting my own celebration cake business."

Scott lets out a dark laugh, as my mother dramatically gasps.

"I can't stop you from wasting your time right now, but I can assure you, when we are married, you won't be messing around with such ridiculous notions."

"Why would you need to start a business, Chloe? Scott will provide for you," my mother cries, holding her hand to her chest dramatically.

"Well, I think it's a great idea," Miles cheerfully chimes in, breaking the growing tension.

"We should be going," I add quickly, before anyone else can give me tips about my life.

"This isn't over, Chloe. We will need to discuss this," Scott snarls.

Marcus steps towards him, but I grab his arm, pulling him away. I shout goodbye over my shoulder, rushing to get into the car. I can feel the rage vibrating off Marcus, and I'm barely holding it together myself.

The drive home is awkward and silent, neither of us wanting to be the first to speak. Once Miles pulls into our garage, we mutter our goodbyes to him and head inside. As soon as the door is closed, Marcus takes my hand and pulls me into the kitchen.

He goes over to one of the drawers that we rarely use and pulls out an envelope, which he places on the kitchen island before sliding it over to me. As I go to pick it up, Marcus breaks the silence.

"Open it."

"What is it?" I ask, looking at the blank envelope with intrigue and a little nerves.

"What Scott said pissed me off so much, but I was more proud that you finally told your family about your baking. I've watched you fall in love with it, but you've never said you wanted to make a career out of it, until today," he explains.

I shrug my shoulders and give him a tight smile. "I've never really believed I could choose this as something for me."

Marcus' smile widens. "I've always believed... Open it."

I quickly open the envelope and pull out a cheque. It's for a thousand pounds, and it's made out to Chloe's Charming Cakes. But the bit that really has me choked up is the date in the corner.

"You wrote this cheque over a month ago?"

He nods. "After your first cake class. I knew this was what you were supposed to be doing with your life, I was just waiting for you to realise."

I throw myself at Marcus, who quickly catches me, letting me wrap my legs around his waist as I attack his mouth. I kiss him with everything I have.

When I pull back, letting him see the tears that are building, I smile for him.

"Thank you. You don't have to give me money. Just knowing you believe in me is enough."

He kisses me again. "This is me investing in you. Take the money and buy what you need to build your business. Consider me a silent partner. You don't have to keep the name, it's just the first thing I could think of," he admits, his cheeks flushing in a way that almost makes me blurt out those three little words, but we're not ready for that yet.

"I love the name." It's not quite what I wanted to say, but close enough. "You can be a partner in my business, as long as you promise to be my partner in life too."

I don't know where that came from. I was so busy trying not to tell him I love him, I say that instead.

We've been saying we belong to each other, and Marcus has said he doesn't want this to end, but we've never talked about the reasons why we can't be together. Marcus has said he thinks I'm worth the risk, but we've never labelled anything.

After he mentioned marriage today, I couldn't hold back. I expect him to freak out, to put me down and walk away, but he doesn't. He places a sweet kiss on my forehead, giving me that smile that makes my legs go weak.

"I'm yours for as long as you'll have me," he says, and I can't stop my eyes from going wide.

"Really? What about the peace treaty, and the arrangement with Scott?"

He shrugs his shoulders as best he can with me wrapped around him.

"I don't really give a fuck. I will take on anyone who tries to stop us from being together."

"I'm yours too, for as long as you want me," I tell him, and he captures my lips with his, walking us towards his bedroom—*our* bedroom.

Although his kisses are distracting me, I allow myself a giddy moment to truly be happy. I've got the guy, and he's willing to do whatever it takes to be with me.

I just hope we can deal with whatever comes our way, as once people find out about us, it's not going to be an easy road. But at least we can deal with it together.

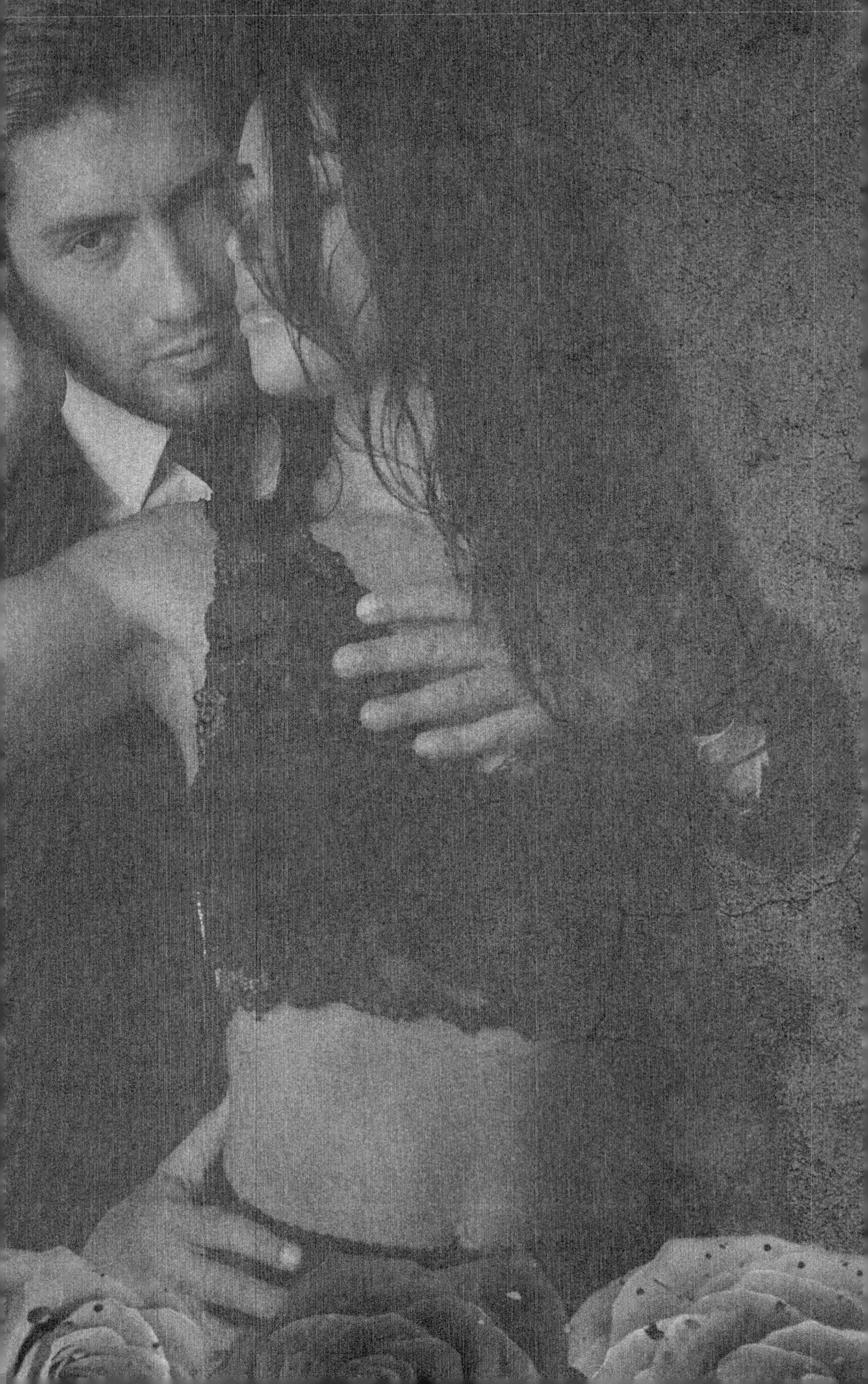

Chapter Twenty-Three
Marcus

Things with Chloe seem to be going from strength to strength, and in an effort not to sound like a love-sick teenage girl, I really couldn't be happier.

When it's just the two of us, in our own little bubble, everything is surprisingly easy. Gone are the days where I worried about how I'd cope sharing my space with someone else. Living with Chloe is simple, almost like we've been doing it forever.

The issues start whenever we're forced to leave our bubble and confront the harshness of reality.

I'm very aware that I've created this little fantasy world with her where everything is great, and we can ride off into the sunset without any issues, but it's a fucking fantasy. Reality is much harder.

Whenever we're forced to interact with her family, and I have to pretend she means nothing to me, it drives me crazy.

To hear her family plan her wedding to another man makes my blood run cold, and the urge to murder people grows with each passing second.

I also hate what it does to Chloe. The whole time she's been with me, I've watched her grow. I've chipped away at the carefully constructed facade her parents helped mould, and I've watched her slowly find the real Chloe.

She laughs more now than ever before, and when she smiles, there's nothing fake about it. I love being the one to put that smile on her face, and in return, she makes me feel lighter and freer than I have in a long time.

We were both raised with heavy responsibilities on our shoulders. I've always known ruling would be my end game, and I spent my whole life training for it, even though it wasn't necessarily my choice. My father raised me to follow in his footsteps, and that included believing that all his decisions were the correct ones.

Whereas, Chloe knew her role would be to strengthen her family's connections through marriage, and her parents have raised her to be the perfect wife and mother to a person of their choosing. Her right to make her own decisions was taken from her at birth, and she didn't think she could question it.

While I forced Chloe to think about what she wanted, in turn, it made me do the same. Maintaining the peace treaty and ruling Blackthorn to the best of my abilities has been my only goal in life, and it took me far too long to realise my father created that goal for me.

Of course, I want to keep Blackthorn safe. They're the people that I rule, and I care about their safety and wellbeing, but I didn't realise until I fell for Chloe how much I've given up to make that happen.

Since I asked her to look deeper, I did the same.

That's when I realised I was faced with an awful dilemma. If I choose to be with Chloe, I put the people I'm duty-bound to protect at risk, as the peace treaty would be in jeopardy, and that could lead to war. But if I choose the people instead, I'd have to give up the only thing I've ever really chosen for myself—Chloe.

I may not have told her yet, but it's strikingly obvious to me that I'm falling in love with her. I probably have been for a while.

I knew when we started having sex that it'd be a slippery slope, but there's a good chance I was in too deep before I even touched her.

She's all I want, and now that I've had her, I don't want to let her go—I can't. So now I just need to find a way to stop the world from going to shit.

I managed to get us both out of going to the next two family dinners. After the stress of the last one, I didn't want to put Chloe, or myself, through that again.

Naturally, her parents were pissed, and her father tried to argue with me, stating I was breaking the rules of the bet. I was quick to point out he didn't care much for the rules when he whisked his wife away on holiday and missed two weeks.

I made up a lie that I was extra busy with work, since I am doing the job of two while Jake is in rehab.

Pulling on his guilt helped, though I did feel bad about using Jake as an excuse. But it worked as I intended, and they reluctantly agreed to us missing the lunches.

However, since I'm not that lucky, I had to agree to Chloe doing two short check-ins via video call. Chloe wasn't happy about this, but since she knew she could hang up on them if things got to be too much, she agreed.

I made sure to stress that the check-ins would be with her parents only. If I got word of Scott trying to use them to contact Chloe—which is in breach of the bet, I reminded them—I would end the call. They agreed, and we didn't hear from the shit-stain for two blissful weeks.

As the weekend of our seventh week approached, I could tell Chloe was becoming more anxious. I've stopped looking at us as being on the clock, as I know when the sixty days are up, I won't be giving her back. I've told Chloe as much, and even though she smiles and tells me she believes me, I can see her hesitancy.

It's not that she doesn't trust me, it's that she believes something will go wrong. She wants to stay here with me, and she's said as much, but there's a part of her that's waiting for everything to go to shit, forcing her back to her old life.

I've stopped telling her that won't happen, I'm just going to show her. There's no way I'm letting her go without a fight, and nobody will want to take me on. A man fighting for the only important thing in his life is the most dangerous of all, as he knows what he's got to lose.

When Miles strolls in on Saturday morning with a strange look on his face, I'm on edge. He sits down with us for breakfast, and we both know something is off, he's being far too quiet.

I take the approach that always seems to work—I wait.

After about ten minutes, Miles lets out a long dramatic sigh.

"Are you both busy today?"

Chloe looks at me, trying to see if I know what's wrong with Miles, and I shrug my shoulders.

"I've got some work to catch up on, and Chloe's practising her cake decorating. Why?"

His face scrunches into a wince. "It's family day at Jacob's rehab, and he's allowed visitors. He initially said he didn't want to see anyone just yet, but now he's changed his mind, and he'd like to see you both."

Chloe and I have matching looks of shock on our faces, and I'm the one to voice what I'm sure we're both thinking. "You've stayed in contact with Jake?"

Miles nods his head, refusing to make eye contact.

"When I dropped him off, the doctor said he would be cut off from the outside world, as that's usually the best way to handle the initial detox. But they always ask for a family contact person. Initially, it's just the doctor who keeps them updated, but when the patient is well enough, they can call their contact too, but only them.

"Jacob wasn't sure who to put as his contact person. He thought of you, Chloe, but he didn't want you to see him at his worst. Same goes for you, Marcus. He couldn't bear the thought of talking to his parents, for obvious reasons. So, in the end, he asked if he could put me down."

"And you said yes?"

Obviously he did, but I can't help phrasing it as a question.

Miles nods, the hint of a smile on his face now. "I didn't want to at first, but Jacob can be quite insistent. He wanted someone he knew could handle seeing him at his worst, but who wouldn't cave to his demands, and he had a lot of them," Miles laughs, before continuing.

"When he was going through his roughest patch, he'd call me several times a day. Mostly begging me to break him out, or to bring him things he was sure he needed. When I refused, he'd call just to shout, swear, and get angry at me, but then things changed. I could hear him starting to get better."

A rogue tear slides down Chloe's cheek and she tries to swipe it away, but I saw it.

"He's better?" she asks, her voice thick with emotion.

Miles raises his gaze to meet hers, giving her a small smile. "He's better than he was. He still has a way to go, but he's over the worst of it. He could come home and start a community program, but he's volunteered to stay there a little longer. Just until he feels strong enough to deal with the real world."

"But he's well enough to see us?" I ask.

Miles nods. "I think so. The doctor agrees. Jacob is a little more hesitant, but that's just because he has a lot to work through, and some of that involves the two of you. But as both me and his doctor reminded him, he won't know if he's capable of doing it unless he tries. So, can you both come?"

I look over at Chloe, who is already nodding her head rapidly. She then glances over at me, her eyes pleading.

"Can you spare the time away from work to come?"

I reach over and grab her hand, giving it a reassuring squeeze. "Of course. Nothing is more important than this."

Just over half an hour later, we're in the car, making the journey to Jake's rehab centre. It's a small, private facility out in the countryside, so we have to drive for close to an hour to get there.

I use the time to mentally prepare for what we might be walking into, whereas Chloe uses the drive to get more and more anxious.

She fidgets constantly, drumming her hand on her thigh, shuffling in her seat, not able to sit still. Eventually, when she's almost driven me mad, I reach over, unfasten her seat belt, and pull her over to me. She curls up by my side, resting her head on my chest as I wrap my arms around her.

We don't say anything, as I know she doesn't want to hear false platitudes, so I just stroke her hair and comfort her the best way I can. I just hope like hell Miles has read the situation correctly and we're not visiting him too soon.

From the small amount of research I've done, people can detox in a month, but the road to true recovery is much longer. Getting free of the substances is almost the easy part.

Looking at why people use in the first place, and making enough changes to stop them from using again when they're back in their real life, that's the hard part.

Jacob has never spoken to me about the catalyst that made him fall off the deep end. I'm not even sure if there was just one, or if it was a series of things that snowballed. I've tried looking back, to see if I could tell when he started becoming wilder, but I honestly can't pinpoint any specific time.

Maybe he's just been losing control for so long, I can't remember a time when he didn't drink or do drugs?

Then again, he wasn't like this when we were teenagers, so something must have changed. The more I think about it, the worse I feel about myself. What kind of shit friend doesn't notice their best friend slowly falling into the darkness?

Don't make this about you, arsehole, I remind myself. *This is about Jake, you can berate yourself another time.*

Fuck, my mind really can be brutal sometimes, but it's not wrong. I'm here for Jake, and to support Chloe. It's time for me to be the friend I should have been all along.

As we arrive at the facility, with the exception of all the security we have to pass, I'm shocked by how normal the place looks. It's a large manor house, and seems more like a home than a healthcare facility. Though if you look closely, there are a few giveaways.

The old-fashioned windows have bars over them, painted white so as to not detract from their beauty. All of the doors have locks on them, along with magnetic strips that appear to be for key cards.

It's eerily quiet, and we don't see another person until after Miles has parked the car, and he takes us to what looks to be a white security hut. There's a glass window with a two-way speaker in the middle, and behind the person who is sitting waiting for us, I can see several security monitors showing the various CCTV streams.

Miles steps towards the microphone. "Hello, Doris. It's lovely to see you again. Are you having a good day?" he says, far more chirpy than he was in the car.

The older lady with tight curls all over her head gives him a bright smile. "My day always gets better when I see you."

Miles laughs, winking at her as her cheeks flush.

"You flatter me. I'm here to see Jacob, and I've got the two visitors with me that I told you about."

Doris turns her attention to me and Chloe, and she's much less friendly with us. Her assessing gaze turns into more of a glare when she gets to me. Although she's staring at me, she talks to Miles.

"Have you made them aware of the security protocols?"

"Of course, Doris. You know me."

Miles went over the very extensive rules that the place has when we were in the car. We both listened intently, making sure we do right by Jake.

"Do they have anything that will need to be stored?" she asks.

"Our electronics. Marcus is wearing a belt, and Chloe will give over her bag too," Miles states, pointing to us as he does.

Doris glares at me, her gaze dropping to my jeans, and for just a second, I worry she's staring at my junk, until Miles elbows me.

"Take off your damn belt."

"Oh shit, sorry."

I'd literally just heard him say that, but clearly my brain isn't functioning correctly.

We had to agree to hand over all electronic devices, and anything that could be seen as a weapon, or could be used by someone to harm themselves.

Doris opens a large hatch beneath the window. "Slide everything into the hatch."

Miles grabs Chloe's bag from her, and I hand over my phone, wallet, and belt. Miles adds his own things into the hatch, as he says, "Done."

Doris glares at each of us again, though her expression does soften more for Chloe and Miles. She then does a quick double take back to Chloe.

"Turn around."

When Chloe doesn't move straight away, Miles gently pushes her to spin around. As soon as her back is to Doris, she shouts for her to stop.

"I'll need the hair grip."

Chloe turns around, looking confused. "What?"

Doris rolls her eyes, growing inpatient. "The clip that's in your hair. I will need to take it."

Chloe shakes her head. "How the hell can a hair clip be used as a weapon?"

"You'd be amazed by what I've seen," Doris replies.

Before Chloe can reply, Miles reaches up and unclips her hair. "Just hand it over, then we can get in and see Jake."

At the mention of her brother, Chloe backs down, though I can see she's not thrilled with Doris' less than friendly approach. Doris turns back to Miles and slides a clipboard into the hatch.

"Fill in the paperwork as always."

Miles quickly fills it in, adding both mine and Chloe's information, so we don't have to. He slides the clipboard back to Doris, who inspects the paperwork closely. After a few minutes of silence, a loud buzzer sounds and the side gate slowly begins to open.

"Follow the rules, or you're out. Give Jacob my best, Miles," she adds, in a much more friendly tone than the stern one she initially used.

Miles blows her a kiss as he practically pushes us through the door.

"Well, she's a treat," I grumble, earning a laugh from Miles.

"She's actually fairly sweet, when you get to know her."

I'm about to argue when Miles drags us both towards the entrance to the large house, where we're greeted by a middle aged woman in a nurse uniform. She has a kind smile, and she waves at Miles, calling him over.

"Good to see you again, Miles. How have you been?"

Miles reaches out and shakes her hand, giving her a bright smile back. "Same old, Jane. Thanks for asking. I brought Chloe and Marcus, as discussed. How's Jake doing?"

Jane smiles at us both, holding her hand out for both Chloe and myself to shake in turn.

"I'm so glad you could both be here. Jacob will be pleased to see you. He's doing good, if not a little nervous."

"How's he getting on with the new nausea medication?" Miles asks, and both Chloe and I look at each other in bewilderment.

It's very clear Miles has been here a lot, and more than that, he knows enough about Jake's treatment plan to ask questions about the side effects of his medications.

It fucking obvious Miles has been keeping a lot from me, from us both, and I very much intend on quizzing him about this later. For now, he gets a pass while we visit Jake.

"He's actually not needing any nausea meds anymore, which is great," Jane replies, before turning to face me and Chloe again. "Before I take you to see Jacob, do you have any questions?"

I look over at Chloe, who looks just as startled by the question as I am.

"Should we have some?" I ask pensively.

Jane chuckles. "No, not at all. Some people are apprehensive the first time they visit someone here. They have questions about what they should or shouldn't say, things like that. Miles spent almost an hour with me on his first visit, making sure he wouldn't say or do the wrong thing to set Jacob back in his progress. I'm assuming he's filled you in on all that, so you don't have the same worries."

I look over at my friend, his cheeks turning a bright shade of pink as he purposely tries to avoid meeting my gaze. Chloe shuffles from one foot to the other, looking more nervous as she replies to Jane.

"Is there anything specific we should avoid saying to him?"

Jane shakes her head. "What we usually say is just let Jacob guide the conversation. Don't ask too many questions, and if he doesn't choose to answer one you ask him, please respect that. He's working through a lot of psychological treatments, but he still has a way to go. We've talked extensively about what he'd like to say to you both today, so I suspect, if you let him lead the conversation, you will be fine."

"Thank you," Chloe says, letting out a breath as she does.

"Miles, can you lead the way, or would you like me to escort you?"

"I'll take us. Thank you, Jane," Miles replies, and Jane waves as she walks away.

As we walk down the corridor, Chloe takes hold of my hand. "I'm nervous. What if seeing us does more harm than good?"

"It won't," both Miles and I reply at the same time.

Miles stops in front of a door that says *Family Room* on the tag.

"I know this feels weird, and Jane has already told you how hard I found the first visit, but it's still the same Jake. Let him lead, and it'll be fine. If he's not happy, he'll ask you to leave."

I narrow my gaze at my friend. "Has he kicked you out before?"

Miles chuckles, a mischievous smile spreading across his face. "A fair few times. So you have nothing to worry about."

Without saying anything more, Miles opens the door and steps inside. I give Chloe's hand a squeeze before letting go, ushering her into the room before me.

While the room has a clinical feel to it, with white walls and the sterile smell you associate with hospitals, they've added a few personal touches to make it seem homely.

To the left of the room there's a long wooden table with six chairs around it, a water jug and empty plastic cups in the centre. Along the right wall there's a bright green sofa, with two matching arm chairs arranged beside it, making it into a U shape, with a low coffee table in the middle.

Other than a couple of landscape paintings on the wall, what looks to be a coffee machine against the wall beside me, and a TV in the corner, the room is almost empty.

Jake is sitting on one of the six chairs around the table, his fingers tapping on the surface until he sees us walk in. At first, he looks a little nervous, but as soon as his gaze lands on Chloe, he brightens up, smiling at her.

I don't know what I expected, but he looks better than I've seen him in a long time. Although he's a little pale, and appears to have lost some weight, he has regained some of his muscle definition.

His brown hair looks clean and soft again, and there's no dark circles under his eyes.

I can't remember the last time I saw him and he didn't have sunken cheeks and hauntingly blank eyes. Now his face has rounded out, and there's life in his chocolate eyes again.

I can't help but smile at how much he looks like the friend I remember.

"Thank you for coming," Jake says softly as he stands.

Chloe sniffles, and I don't have to look at her to know she's crying.

"Can I hug you?" she whimpers.

When Jake holds his arms open, she launches herself at him, wrapping her arms tightly around him as he catches her. Chloe sobs loudly as she tells her brother how much she's missed him, and I see the tears sliding down Jake's face too.

I almost feel like I'm invading a personal moment between them, so when Miles goes over to the coffee machine, I join him. Although I don't help him or speak, having my back to them, giving them the alone time they clearly need, makes me feel better.

When Miles has made coffee for us all, we turn back to the dining table, taking two cups each. Jake and Chloe pull apart as we put the cups down on the table.

Jake and Chloe take their seats at one side, her hand still firmly in his, and Miles and I take two seats opposite.

We each take sips of our drinks, silence filling the room, all of us waiting for someone to be the first to speak. I'm surprised when it's Miles who addresses Jake first.

"How've you been? Jane says the nausea has gone."

Jake nods, giving Miles a bright smile. "I'm good. So fucking glad the nausea has finally gone, I can eat a bit more now."

"Anything special you want me to bring now you can eat more?"

Jake's eyes widen as he nods, looking like a kid in a sweet shop.

"Nutella. I've been craving it, but the thought of eating any sort of chocolate has made me sick. Now that's gone, I want to try it."

"I can do that. I'll bring you some next time."

"Thank you," Jacob replies, his gaze fixed on Miles in a way I've not seen before, and he almost seems shy about it.

"I've missed you," Chloe says, breaking the tension that seems to have been growing as Miles and Jake look at each other.

Jake turns to his sister, a sad smile on his face.

"I've missed you too. It's been really rough in here, I'm not going to lie. For a long time I hated it, and I hated all of you for making me be here."

"I didn't want to get better, far from it, but I think if I hadn't come here, I wouldn't have lived for very long."

"Don't say that," Chloe sobs, and Jake pulls her into his side, wrapping his arm around her in comfort.

"It's not nice to hear, but it's the truth. Being here has forced me to look at my life in a way I never have before. The drink and the drugs were what I turned to so that I could block out the bigger issues. They were my crutch, and without them, I had to confront the reasons that made me use in the first place," Jake explains, taking a sip of his coffee as Chloe pulls out of his hug.

"I bet that's hard."

I can hear what Chloe isn't saying—she knows better than anyone what it means to hide from her demons, acting out as a way to avoid dealing.

"It is. Identifying what my issues are was tough, but actually working through them has been harder. Part of healing involves facing the people who have been hurt through my addiction, and that's why I wanted you both to come today."

"You didn't hurt—"

Before Chloe can finish, he raises his hand to cut her off.

"Please, just listen to me. My addiction may have hurt me physically and emotionally, but it would be selfish of me not to acknowledge the way it's affected all of you. The person I was, whilst under the influence, was not great. I wasn't a good brother, or a good friend."

Jake looks at me and Miles as he says the word friend, and when neither of us challenge him, he gives us a tight smile.

He then turns in his seat to face Chloe, and I feel Miles stiffen beside me, like he knows what's about to happen. I lean forward, on edge, ready to protect Chloe if she needs me.

"Chloe, while I've been doing my therapy sessions, they've been forcing me to look at my behaviour, and how I was around others. I knew you'd started acting out, drinking more, sleeping around, generally displaying destructive behaviour, but I was too caught up in my own issues to care.

"I remember thinking, I wonder why you're behaving like that, but then I'd take drugs and forget all about it. I know that makes me the shittest brother in the world, and I want you to know how sorry I am."

A tear rolls down Jake's cheek as he apologises, and Chloe leans over to wipe it away with her thumb.

"You don't need to apologise. You had your own stuff to worry about," she says, but he shakes his head, giving her a fierce glare.

"That's not an excuse. You clearly had stuff going on, but still found the time to take care of me."

"It's in the past," Chloe replies, waving her hand dismissively.

Jake's expression turns sad. "It's not in the past, but you do seem better lately," he says, looking over at me. "I guess, I have you to thank for that."

I smile at my friend, not really sure what to say.

"She's doing much better than she was." It's the truth, but it doesn't betray any of the trust Chloe placed in me.

Jake turns back to his sister, grabbing her other hand now too. "I want to be a better brother, so when the time comes that you feel comfortable enough to tell me what happened, I'll be here to listen. I'll do whatever it takes to prove you can trust me."

"It's not about trust, Jake," Chloe says, sounding so lost and sad.

I want nothing more than to reach over and pull her onto my lap, but she needs to do this with Jake. I can hold her later.

"It is, Chloe. It's about you trusting me with your secret, knowing I won't be selfish, and will help you."

Chloe turns to me, and I can see the confusion on her face, but there's longing there too. She wants to trust her brother, to believe all the things he's saying.

"You don't know until you try," I tell her, reminding her that she has to give people a chance to be there for her.

Chloe lets out a long sigh and looks down at the table. I can see her trembling from across the table, but Jake keeps hold of her hand, supporting her.

As Chloe opens up, telling Jacob her biggest secret, I watch it play out over the table.

She starts with the date she went on, and when Jacob finds out who she means, the rage in his eyes is barely controlled. It worsens when she tells him about the days he kept her kidnapped.

Although she glosses over the details of what happened in those two days, like she did with me, she uses the word *rape*, and I feel like I've been stabbed in the gut, so I can only imagine how Jake feels.

He keeps hold of her hands, giving her his full attention, even when they both have tears streaming down their faces. And when she finishes, he pulls her in for a hug that seems to last for ages, but they both need it.

As the siblings hold each other, Miles leans over to me, whispering in my ear, so that only I can hear. "Did you know about all of that?"

I turn and give him a stern nod, trying to keep my expression as neutral as I can.

"She told me a while ago, before anything happened between us."

"I'm assuming we're killing him?" he growls, looking just as furious as I feel.

I'm sure the sadistic grin that spreads across my face is almost maniacal, but I don't care.

"He'll be wishing for death when we're done with him."

Miles' sadistic smile matches mine, reminding me why we've been friends for so long. "I'm in."

I give him a short laugh. "I assumed you would be."

Whilst Miles appears friendly and easy going, and often has a smile on his face compared to my scowl, if you've wronged him, or anyone he cares about, he's a sadistic son of a bitch, and won't hesitate to get his hands dirty to get his revenge.

I hear my name being mentioned by Jake as he talks to Chloe, and it pulls me back to their conversation.

"We don't have long left in this visit, and I'd really like to talk to Marcus about work stuff. Are you okay giving us five minutes alone? Miles can show you around a little, if you'd like?"

Chloe nods and smiles at her brother, looking lighter than before she came in here.

"Of course. Do you promise you're going to be okay? I don't want what I've told you to set you back."

Jake shakes his head vigorously. "No, I promise you, that won't happen. I'm stronger now, and I'm glad you told me. I'm just sorry you couldn't tell me before."

"It's okay."

Her voice is small, and we all know she doesn't mean it, but it's nice of her to say that to Jake. Knowing him, he'll have to live with the guilt of not protecting his sister for a long time, but being in therapy should help.

Miles stands and gestures to Chloe. "Come on, I'll show you around and tell you all the gossip I've learnt about the staff here."

Chloe links her arm through Miles as he leads her to the exit. She turns to face me, giving me a soft smile. "I'll see you soon."

As soon as the door closes behind them, I turn to see the solemn face of my friend.

"Did you know?" he asks, his voice thick with emotion.

I shake my head. "No. I knew something was going on with her, but it took her a while to open up to me."

"You better be able to tell me the arsehole is dead already," he snarls, balling his hands into fists on the table.

I let out a long sigh. "Sadly, no. I have a plan, but executing it has not been easy. His family is protected by yours, and while your father is in charge, in your absence, there's not much I can do.

"I asked Caleb for permission to punish him, but without going into details about his crime, which I can't do as Chloe asked me not to tell anyone, he refused.

"If I were to take him out, without Santoro permission, it would be in breech of the peace treaty," I explain, sounding just as fucking frustrated as I feel.

Jacob bangs his fist on the table.

"Fuck my father. You have my permission. You won't be breaking the treaty, just deal with him."

"I wish it were that simple, Jake, but until you get out of here, Caleb is calling the shots, and he's made that very fucking clear to both me and my father."

"I don't give a shit. I'll back you up with my father, if it comes to that. I just can't bear knowing he's breathing for another day," Jake pleads, his voice breaking at the end.

"Okay, we'll take care of it. But it won't be a quick or easy death. He made her suffer for two days, and I intend on repaying that back to him," I snarl, anger coursing through my veins at the thought of what the sick bastard put my girl through.

"Good." Jake smiles. "Now, tell me what's going on with you and Chloe."

I groan, running my hand over my face. "You've had a lot of information thrown at you today. I'm not sure this is the best time to have this discussion."

"So there is a discussion to be had?" he probes, glaring at me with his brows raised.

"Jake," I warn him.

If he keeps tugging on this thread, I'm not sure he's going to like what he finds on the other end.

Jake lets out a loud sigh, running his fingers through his hair, making it stick up at all angles.

"Look, I'm not an idiot. I see the way she looks at you, how she's always looked at you.

"I may have been high most of the time, but I noticed there was something going on with her, even if I ignored it. I've also seen a change in her since she came to live with you... A change for the better, and I can't deny that."

"I know there's a lot of reasons why we shouldn't, my friendship with you being one of them, but we are together."

My chest almost feels lighter now I've admitted it. I think this might be the first time I've said the words aloud, and it feels right.

"Together, together? As in, it's more than just...sex?" He shivers at the last part, cringing as he asks about his sister's sex life.

I chuckle. "I really like her, Jake. It's not just about sex. I know you're going to say we can't be together—a lot of people will say that—but I don't care. I really like her, and I'm not giving her up. She's mine, and I'll do whatever it takes to keep her."

His chocolate eyes narrow as he assesses me, the silence between us growing more tense until he finally sighs.

"I've never seen you be serious about a girl. I can't even remember the last time you had a relationship."

"I've never had one. I've never wanted one before, then Chloe happened," I admit, unable to keep the smile off my face when I think about her.

"Look, I'm not thrilled by the idea, but I'm not against it. I see how happy you make her, and there's nobody I trust to protect her more than you. So, not that you need it, but you have my blessing."

"Thank you," I say, hoping my voice shows just how grateful I am for his words. "I'm just not sure your blessing will be enough."

Jake's brow furrows as my smile turns to a scowl. "What do you mean?"

"When people find out about us, it's not going to go down well. Your parents will be furious, as will Scott and the Caprillos. What I've done goes against the rules set out in our bet, but more than that, I'm in breach of the peace treaty. By choosing Chloe, I could start a war between our two families."

As I voice the worry that's been on my mind since I first decided I was going to keep Chloe, Jacob grows more pensive and then angry.

"Look, I can't say exactly what will happen if the news gets out while I'm still in here, but if you can hold off telling anyone until I'm out, then I'll support you. There's no way I'd allow our families to go to war over this. I'll stand by you as much as I can."

"I knew you'd be a good leader one day," I tell him, and he waves his hand at me, not wanting to hear the compliment.

"Promise me, you'll look after her," Jake says as he stands and rounds the table towards me.

"With my life," I reply, pulling him in for a hug.

"I'm glad you have each other. You both deserve to be happy," he tells me, patting me on the back.

I pull away, fixing him with a look that he can't turn away from.

"So do you. I'm proud of you for taking care of yourself. You deserve happiness too."

He lets out a small sigh as he nods. "I'm starting to finally believe that."

We head out of the family room and find Miles and Chloe waiting nearby. We all say our goodbyes, and it feels sad to leave Jake behind, but he's clearly in the right place.

Miles says he'll meet us at the car after he's walked Jake back to his room, so Chloe and I make our way outside, choosing not to comment on how much their friendship seems to have changed recently. I'm glad they're finally becoming friends again.

Once we get to the car, I spin Chloe around, pinning her against the door with my body. I lean down to capture her lips with mine, kissing her the way I've wanted to for the last hour.

As I pull back, I give her a bright smile as I keep my gaze on her.

"I'm so proud of you. I know today wasn't easy, seeing Jake here like this, or telling him your secret, but you were really brave."

She reaches up to wipe a stray tear off her cheek. "I'm worried I overloaded him with information at a time when he's fragile. What if I set his healing back?"

I reach up and take both her cheeks in my hand, smoothing my thumbs under her eyes.

"I spoke to him afterwards, remember? You haven't set his healing back. If anything, you've made him stronger. He said that if we keep our relationship a secret until he's out of here, then when he's back as the Santoro leader, he'll support us."

Her eyes widen as her mouth falls open. "Does that mean I won't have to marry Scott?"

I smile and nod. "Exactly, but there's so much more. If he condones our relationship, it means I'm not breaching the peace treaty, or breaking the terms of the bet. I won't have to start a war to keep you.

"If his leader has backed our relationship, Scott isn't allowed to retaliate. Our relationship would be official, and we wouldn't have to hurt anyone or start a war for it."

Chloe squeals and jumps into my arms, wrapping her legs around my waist when I catch her. She threads her fingers through the hairs at the nape of my neck and presses her lips against mine.

She kisses me with passion and my heart races as she claims me with her mouth, our tongues mingling as one. I meet her kiss, showing her just how much she means to me.

When she pulls back to draw a breath, her smile brightens up her beautiful face. "I can't believe I finally get to live the life I want, the life I choose."

"And what do you choose?" I ask, needing to hear the words.

"I choose you. And I couldn't be happier with my choice."

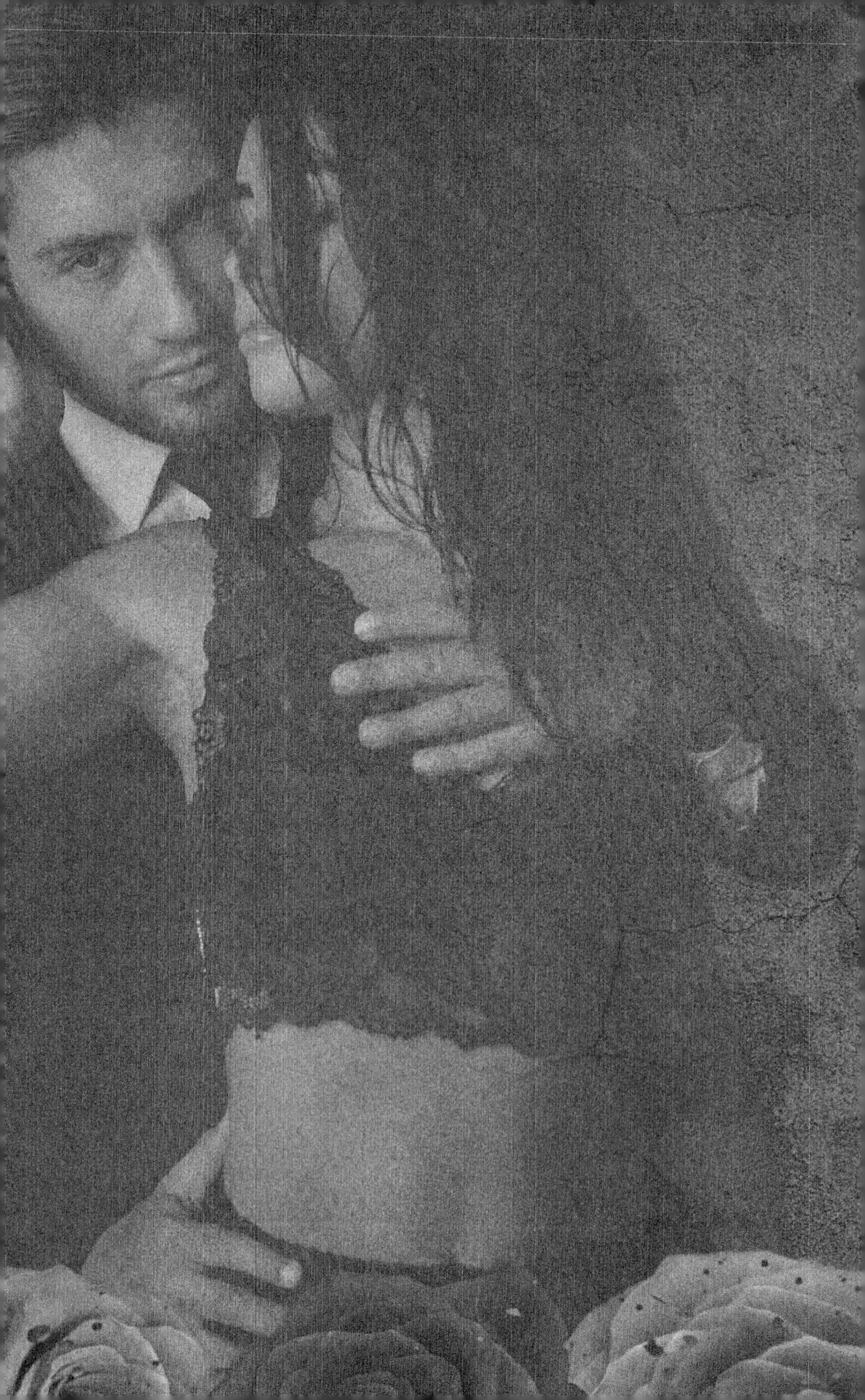

Chapter Twenty-Four

Marcus

When I woke up the following morning, with Chloe curled up beside me, her long hair fanning in my face as she breathed softly, I felt a peace I wasn't expecting.

Telling Jake about us was more of a relief than I expected it to be. I knew he wouldn't be happy that I'm seeing his sister, but to know he'll stand by us and support our decision means a lot. Not just on a professional level to avoid starting a war, but on a personal one.

He's my best friend, and Chloe's brother, and although we don't need his approval to continue seeing each other, having it means more than either of us thought.

We fell into each other's arms as soon as we got home, and fucked well into the night, which is why I'm not surprise to find it's almost eleven in the morning when I start rousing.

Chloe is still fast asleep beside me, and whilst I don't want to disturb her, I also don't want to leave. I'm not going all soppy and watching her while she sleeps, but I enjoy the feeling of having her close, and I don't want that to end quite yet.

Instead, I reach over to the nightstand and pick up my phone, choosing to work here as much as I can. With one arm wrapped around Chloe, rubbing light yet soothing circles into the smooth skin of her back, I navigate my phone with the other.

I do this for around twenty minutes before it starts to loudly vibrate in my hand, Caleb's name flashing up on my screen. I quickly decline the call, but the noise is enough to disturb Chloe.

She groans from beside me, shuffling around as she stretches before opening her eyes, a small smile on her face when she sees me looking down at her.

"Morning," I say, leaning down to press a kiss against her forehead.

"Good morning. How long have you been awake? You could have woken me," she replies, her voice thick with sleep.

I stroke the hair away from her face as I shake my head.

"Only about twenty minutes. I had no reason to wake you. You can go back to sleep, if you'd like?"

She sits up a little, the duvet cover slipping just enough to give me a distracting glimpse of her bare tits, and she clears her throat when she catches me looking.

"Didn't I just hear the phone?"

As if by magic, my phone starts ringing again, Caleb's number flashing up for a second time.

"It's your dad. I declined the call last time. He can wait."

Chloe's eyes narrow, and she's just as curious as to why he's calling as I am. He knows we're busy today, as we already cancelled our Sunday lunch with him, after I told him I had urgent business, so he has no reason to call.

"You should answer, find out what he wants," Chloe says, as the call rings off, no doubt going to my voicemail.

"He knows I'm busy," I tell her, pulling her against me as I lean down and kiss her.

We're just about to deepen the kiss when my phone vibrates again, this time indicating a text. I mumble under my breath about Caleb cock blocking me, as I pull up the message.

CALEB SANTORO

666 Blackthorn

As soon as I see the message, I moan loudly, pulling away from Chloe.

"Motherfucker."

"Is everything okay?" Chloe asks worriedly.

"He's going to call again and I have to answer. He's used our emergency work code. If either a Morelli or a Santoro use that code, it means whatever the emergency is, it trumps whatever we have going on right now," I explain, rolling out of the bed and pulling on a pair of sweatpants.

Chloe looks even more concerned now, but I don't have time to comfort her as my phone rings. This time, I answer, "Yes?"

"Did you get my message?" Caleb asks, forgoing all the pleasantries, as I did.

"I did. What's the emergency?"

Caleb sighs. "I'd prefer not to discuss it over the phone. I need you to come down to my office straight away."

"Caleb—"

Before I can even try to fob him off, Caleb interrupts.

"You know the rules if we use the code word, Marcus. I expect you here within the next thirty minutes...and bring Chloe."

"Why do I need to bring Chloe? I thought you said this was work-related."

"It is. Just bring her and I'll explain everything," he states, and my anxiety begins to spike.

"If you're misusing the code to get to your daughter, there will be consequences."

I make sure he can hear the unspoken threat in my voice.

"I'm not misusing the code. Get here, now."

He hangs up before I have a chance to say anything further, and it takes all of my willpower to keep the phone in my hand, instead of throwing it at the nearest wall.

Chloe is perched on the end of the bed, staring at me. She's fiddling with her fingers, looking anxious, and I know she heard me mention her name.

"Is everything okay?"

I let out a long sigh as I reach over and cup her cheek, rubbing my thumb over it softly. She leans into my touch, giving me a small smile.

"We need to go to your father's house, now. He didn't give me any other information, but I need you to come with me."

Her eyes widen in shock. "Me? Why me? Didn't you say the code was for business?"

I give her a nod, trying to keep all of the anxiety and anger from my expression.

"I don't know why he wants you there. He used the work code, and he wouldn't do that unless it was urgent. Nothing good ever follows us using the damn code."

Chloe begins to tremble beneath my touch, looking terrified.

"I promise, whatever it is, I will keep you safe, Mio. I need to call Miles, so can you get ready quickly, please?"

Chloe nods, and I lean down to give her a kiss. It's not the way I want to kiss her this morning, but it's all I have time for.

After twenty minutes, we're down in the garage, waiting for the car to arrive. My back-up driver Leo opens the door.

"Where's Miles?" Chloe asks once we're inside.

"He's busy and wouldn't have been able to get here in time, so I called Leo. He's my reserve driver," I reply, trying to ignore how nervous I feel at not having my best friend by my side.

In next to no time, myself, Chloe, and Leo are pulling up outside of the Santoro house. A member of Caleb's security greets us, performing the usual safety checks on us all.

As we go to make our way inside, he blocks our path.

"Mr Santoro has requested that your driver wait with the car, since he's not your usual security, and doesn't have the same level of security clearance."

I freeze, my brain working a million miles a minute to try and think of a way to refuse, but he's right. Although Leo is trained in security, none of my staff—other than Miles—have the security clearance to be part of Blackthorn Council meetings, which this clearly is.

I don't like the idea of having no back-up by my side, particularly when I have no idea what I'm walking into, but on this occasion, I have no choice.

I turn to Leo. "Wait by the car, but be alert for my signal."

He gives me a nod of understanding, before turning to stand by the car.

Once he's gone, I turn back to the man who is showing us inside. Only now the look on his face is of extreme caution, and I'm instantly worried.

"Thank you. Mr Santoro has also requested that Miss Santoro wait in the living room, since she has no reason to be part of Council business."

As soon as he's finished, he visibly tenses, no doubt waiting for me to kick off.

Anger ripples just beneath the surface, threatening to break free at any moment, as my grip of Chloe's hand tightens. She looks confused and scared, and that makes my decision for me.

"Absolutely fucking not. You can tell Caleb that I'm not leaving her on her own. Either Chloe attends the meeting with me, or neither of us do."

"Please, stay here, I'll be back," he squeaks, scrambling away to Caleb's office.

"This is bad, isn't it?" Chloe whispers, her grip on my hand tightening.

"You don't have anything to be afraid of, love. I'll take care of you," I tell her, stroking my thumb over the back of her hand.

I want to pull her into my arms, to hold her, to kiss her, to reassure her as best I can, but we both know I can't do that here. Holding her hand is pushing things, but her family have seen us do it before, so I'm not too worried. I just can't push it any further.

The man rushes back, looking flustered. "Mr Santoro said I can bring you both in."

I don't say a word, keeping my grip on Chloe's hand as I lead us towards Caleb's office. As soon as I step inside, I know Chloe was right. This isn't good.

Caleb is sitting behind his large desk, an unreadable expression on his face, though when he sees Chloe beside me, I think I see a flash of concern, but he's quick to hide it.

To the left of the door, sitting on two chairs, are Scott and Ewan Caprillo, matching expressions of disgust and anger on their faces. When Scott sees Chloe, he glowers at her, his face turning almost murderous when he catches our intertwined fingers.

I'm surprised to see my father on the right, sitting beside two empty seats. He looks far more laid back than I'd expect, in what is clearly a very tense and volatile situation.

My father stands and approaches us, speaking before anyone else can. "Lovely to see you again, Chloe. Why don't you both have a seat here with me?"

He holds out the chair in the middle for Chloe, indicating she should sit between us, which instantly has me on edge.

Under normal circumstances, I'd always sit by my father's side, as his heir. It's how things have always been done, to show hierarchy. So for him to throw custom out of the window, it suggests there's a reason Chloe might need both of our protection.

My heart is racing so fast, and I have to focus on my breathing to not give away how truly terrified I am right now.

I make sure my face displays the perfect arrogant sneer I'm known for, making it seem like I don't give a shit about anything, and I definitely don't want to be here.

"Why are we here?" I ask, trying to remain as professional as I can, despite being able to feel Chloe's hand trembling in mine.

Caleb leans over his desk, picking up a brown envelope. He then lays out a series of photographs, and as soon as I see the first one, my heart sinks.

Chloe freezes beside me, letting out a small gasp when she recognises the images.

The photographs are all of me and Chloe.

The first few were taken just yesterday, outside of Jake's rehab centre. They show me kissing her against the car, her jumping into my arms with her legs around my waist, and us both looking at each other with the biggest smiles on our faces.

The next set of photos were taken from our date the other day, at the ice rink. They show me holding her hands to glide her around the ice, me on my knees in front of her as I help to put her skates on, and us kissing on the ice.

But the photo that makes my blood boil the most is the one Caleb throws down at the end. It's very poor quality, no doubt from a distance away with a long-angled lens, and as it's taken through a window, there's glare around the edges.

There's enough clarity to make out my living room, though the blinds were closing from either side. It was a lucky shot, and the photographer had managed to get it at just the right time.

I was shirtless, wearing just my grey sweatpants, and Chloe was in her underwear. She was on her tip-toes, wrapping her arms around my neck as she pulled me in for a kiss.

The silence in the room is deafening as we all take in the photos. Without saying a word, I reach across and turn over the photo of Chloe in her underwear, not wanting anyone to see her like that.

"Aren't you going to fucking say anything?" Scott shouts, his face turning red with anger.

Ewan lays a hand on his arm, but he shrugs it off.

I ignore his outburst and turn to Caleb. "If this is a Council meeting, as your emergency message suggested, why are you including people without the correct security clearance?"

I keep my voice as impassive as I can, which does the job of winding Scott up further.

"Fuck security clearance. I have a right to be here, you're fucking my fiancée. I should kill you right now," he screams.

I can't help but laugh at his ridiculous behaviour, which, not surprisingly, seems to wind him up more. I'm more shocked when my father speaks up.

"No matter the circumstances, we are your leaders. You just made a threat against my son's life, which I take very seriously. So unless you want me to shoot you on the spot, I suggest you calm your temper and behave like an adult."

Scott goes to speak, but Ewan stops him.

"I'm sorry, my son didn't mean what he said. He's just very emotional right now, as this is a huge display of disrespect."

"I understand that, but threats will not be tolerated," my father snaps, making it clear that will be his only warning.

Ewan nods his head, a sombre expression on his face as he keeps a grip on his son's arm. He then turns to Caleb, trying to sound as respectful as he can.

"As our loyalty is with you, Mr Santoro, as is our marriage deal, we'd like to formally escalate this matter."

Caleb looks more than a little annoyed, but it's not clear if it's at the situation or the Caprillos. He turns to my father, wincing as they glare at each other.

"The rules in this situation are clear."

He shuffles around behind his desk, making a point not to make eye contact with his daughter, who is tense and unmoving beside me. I stroke my thumb over the back of her hand, but still her grip remains tight.

Caleb then turns his attention to me. "Marcus, these photos are evidence enough that you have clearly broken, not only the arrangement made at the time of this stupid bet, but also the treaty between our two families.

"As per the bet, you we're not to touch Chloe, and you made a point of saying that you weren't interested in sex—"

I cut him off, deciding now would be a good time to correct him.

"Actually the terms of the bet were rather vague. I said the bet wasn't sexually motivated, but I didn't agree never to get involved with her. I specified that if Chloe was interested, she'd need to be the one to make the first move.

"I also clearly pointed out that when you made the marriage contract with the Caprillos, they knew Chloe wasn't a virgin, and there was no arrangement in place stating she had to remain celibate until her wedding. So, us entering into a relationship neither broke the agreement of the bet, nor your marriage contract with the Caprillos."

"Like hell it fucking didn't," Scott shouts, trying to jump to his feet, only for his father to grab him and pull him back down.

"Silence," Caleb yells, making Chloe gasp beside me.

I turn to look at her for the first time since we entered the room, and she looks visibly terrified. Tears are filling her eyes, but she's trying her hardest not to let them fall. She's pulled her lower lip between her teeth, and I'd be surprised if she's not drawn blood.

What scares me the most is the almost vacant look in her beautiful silver eyes. She's staring at a spot above her father's head, making it look like she's paying attention, but I can tell she's not. She's not blinking, just staring out into the abyss, no doubt as a way of protecting herself from whatever is about to happen.

The fact these arseholes are making my girl so terrified makes my blood boil, and I grind my teeth together to prevent myself from lashing out.

Caleb glances between us and the Caprillos, looking more annoyed each time. He stops on me again, attempting to intimidate me with his icy cold stare.

"Even if you get away with the bet, on a technicality, it doesn't change the fact you've broken the peace treaty between us."

Chloe takes in a shuddered breath, and I feel her eyes on me. She's no longer trying to zone out. Now, she's very much aware of the shit situation we're in, and my heart breaks at seeing how devastated she looks.

"However, I'm willing to give you a chance to make this right," Caleb adds, and both mine and Chloe's gaze flicks over to him.

Chloe looks hopeful, and I want to tell her that this won't be the reprieve she thinks it is. Whatever Caleb is about to offer, it's not going to be good, but I nod for him to present his case all the same.

"You will end the bet right now. Chloe will move home and marry Scott, as agreed, and after you've paid a fine to the Caprillos for offending them, we can put this whole mess behind us. I think it's more than a fair deal," Caleb explains, his chin in the air as he tries to make himself seem magnanimous.

I'm about to unleash my anger on him for such a stupid fucking request when Chloe drops my hand, my flesh tingling from her absence.

I look over to see she's staring at the floor, tears trailing down her face. She looks defeated, and my heart cracks open.

She thinks I'm going to hand her over to Scott, and pretend like the last six weeks together didn't happen.

I cast a glance over to my father, expecting to see a mixture of shame and anger glaring back at me, so I almost fall off my chair when I see pride.

He looks between me and Chloe, giving me a smile as he nods. I don't need him to say anything to know he's telling me to do the right thing.

I reach down and grab hold of Chloe's hand. She gasps, her gaze flicking up to meet mine, and as I smile at her, her eyes grow wide. I reach out and wipe the tears from her eyes, ignoring whatever Scott is saying on the other side of the room.

With our fingers firmly laced together, I turn back to Caleb, who now looks confused.

"Thank you for your offer, but I'm going to have to decline. Chloe and I are together, and nothing will change that. I don't care if it breaches the treaty, or if it means we have to go to war. I'm choosing Chloe, and I'm hoping she chooses me."

As soon as I look over at my girl, she gives me her brightest smile, nodding her head as her tears fall even harder now. "Yes, I choose you, too."

The kerfuffle on the other side of the room grows louder, and Scott's chair smashes to the ground as he fights off his father's hold and rushes forward. He pulls out a gun and aims it at me.

Without thinking, I stand and position myself between Scott and Chloe, pulling out my gun at the same time. Even though he's aiming at me, my instinct is to protect her.

Shouting echoes around the room as Ewan tries to pull back his son. Before I know it, both my father and Caleb have drawn their guns and they're aiming at Scott too.

Everyone is shouting, and I'm not sure who is saying what.

"Put your gun down."

"Let's all calm down."

"I'm going to fucking kill you."

Well, that last one was clearly Scott shouting at me, but other than that, I couldn't make out much.

When the door to the room slams open, we all fall silent. None of us wants to take our eyes off the people pointing guns, so we go quiet to hear who just came in.

"Looks like the party started without us," Jacob says.

"I hate when that happens," Miles sarcastically agrees with him.

I turn to face the door, shocked to see Jake and Miles casually walking into the room like they're just running a little late.

"What did I miss?" Jake asks, throwing a wink at me.

"What are you doing here, Jacob?"

Caleb is staring at his son with both shock and apprehension, his gaze dragging over him in an assessing way.

He's clearly trying to work out if his son is sober, which he obviously is. It's the brightest I've seen Jake's chocolate eyes in a long time.

"I heard there was an emergency Council meeting. It sounded important, so I thought I better not miss it," he replies, somewhat smugly, not even reacting to us pointing guns at each other.

Scott turns to Jacob, sneering at him like he's disgusted to see him here.

"I thought you were in rehab? You're not even on the Council anymore, and once I marry your sister, you won't ever be."

Jacob laughs at Scott, which only seems to make him more irate. Normally, that's something I'd like to see, but as he's pointing a gun at me, and his rage is making his hand shake, it has me a bit on edge.

"Well, as you can see, I'm here, and I'm healthy. It's my right, as the Santoro heir, so I'll be taking back my position on the Council. I'm also declaring that I approve of Chloe and Marcus' relationship, meaning there is no breach of the treaty, as far as I'm concerned. We will not be going to war with the man who makes my sister happy."

He then turns to his father, fixing him with a stare.

"If you respect me, Dad, you'll support me on this. If not, you can find yourself another heir. Though I'd suggest picking one a little more mentally stable, as Scott here looks like he's about to burst a blood vessel."

Miles chuckles from beside him, and Jake turns to smile at him. He then looks back to his father, who has turned very quiet.

Caleb looks between Jake and Scott, before finally casting his gaze over to Chloe. She's poking her head around me, and he looks down to see our hands are still firmly interlocked. He lets out a sigh as he lowers his gun.

Caleb pulls his back straight and lifts his head high as he turns to Scott and Ewan, a stern, powerful expression on his face.

"Jacob is my heir, and I honour his position as the ruler of the Santoro family. His decision is final."

"You can't fucking do that," Scott snarls, lowering his gun just enough for his father to take it from him.

"Shut up, Scott," Ewan whisper-yells as he puts the safety on the gun before placing it back in his pocket.

"I will not shut up. Promises were made, and now they think they can fuck us over and go back on their word. I will not be disrespected like this."

Jacob clears his throat loudly, interrupting Scott's rant.

"Since you feel so slighted by us, my ruling shouldn't bother you too much. I hereby declare, officially, that the Caprillo family are exiled from Blackthorn.

"You and your family have twenty-four hours to get out of our town. If you even think about returning, I will kill every last person in your family. Do I make myself clear?"

Both Scott and Ewan's faces fall, looking distraught, but it's clear Jake isn't playing around. Ewan grabs hold of his son and bows respectfully at Jacob.

"We understand. We'll leave now."

Jake nods to the door, a polite way of telling them to fuck off. Ewan is dragging Scott behind him, who looks to be in a daze.

Just when I think they're going to make it out of the room without incident, Scott glares at Chloe as he passes us, and decides to open his big mouth.

"I didn't want to marry a dirty whore like you anyway," he snarls at Chloe, who takes a step back under the weight of his hateful sneer.

Without even hesitating, I raise my gun and shoot him in the leg.

"Oops, it looks like my gun went off as I was trying to put it away," I deadpan, not at all sounding sorry.

Jacob and Miles chuckle, and I'm pretty sure I hear my father laughing too. Scott is swearing loudly, all his words jumbling into one.

I turn to Miles. "Can you make sure this sack of shit gets off the property and out of town, please?"

Miles steps forward and grabs Scott's arm, gripping it hard, but he doesn't say anything.

"It would be my pleasure."

He then pulls a bleeding Scott from the room, his distraught father following behind him. Once the Caprillos have left, and the tension starts to die down, we all put our guns away.

Chloe walks over to her brother and pulls him into a hug.

"Thank you for what you just did, Jake."

He wipes the tears from her eyes, giving her a smile. "You don't ever need to thank me for looking out for you."

Caleb clears his throat, looking more than a little uncomfortable. "So, you two..."

He pauses, clearly not quite knowing what to say, so I finish for him.

"We're together."

Chloe looks at her father, pulling her shoulders back to stare at him with the confidence I've seen grow in her over the last few weeks.

"If he'll have me, I plan on staying with Marcus from now on."

I chuckle, shaking my head at her. "There's no way I'm ever letting you leave."

Jake groans beside us, but there's a smile on his face. Caleb turns to my father.

"And you're okay with this?"

My father shrugs his shoulders, throwing a small smile my way. "As long as Marcus is happy, that's all that matters."

For a moment I'm stunned, having never heard my father say anything like that before. I didn't think he gave a shit about what makes me happy, having forced me into a life I didn't choose.

But when it counts, when my heart is on the line, he's by my side, and I can't thank him enough for that.

"We're happy together. This is just the start of our forever."

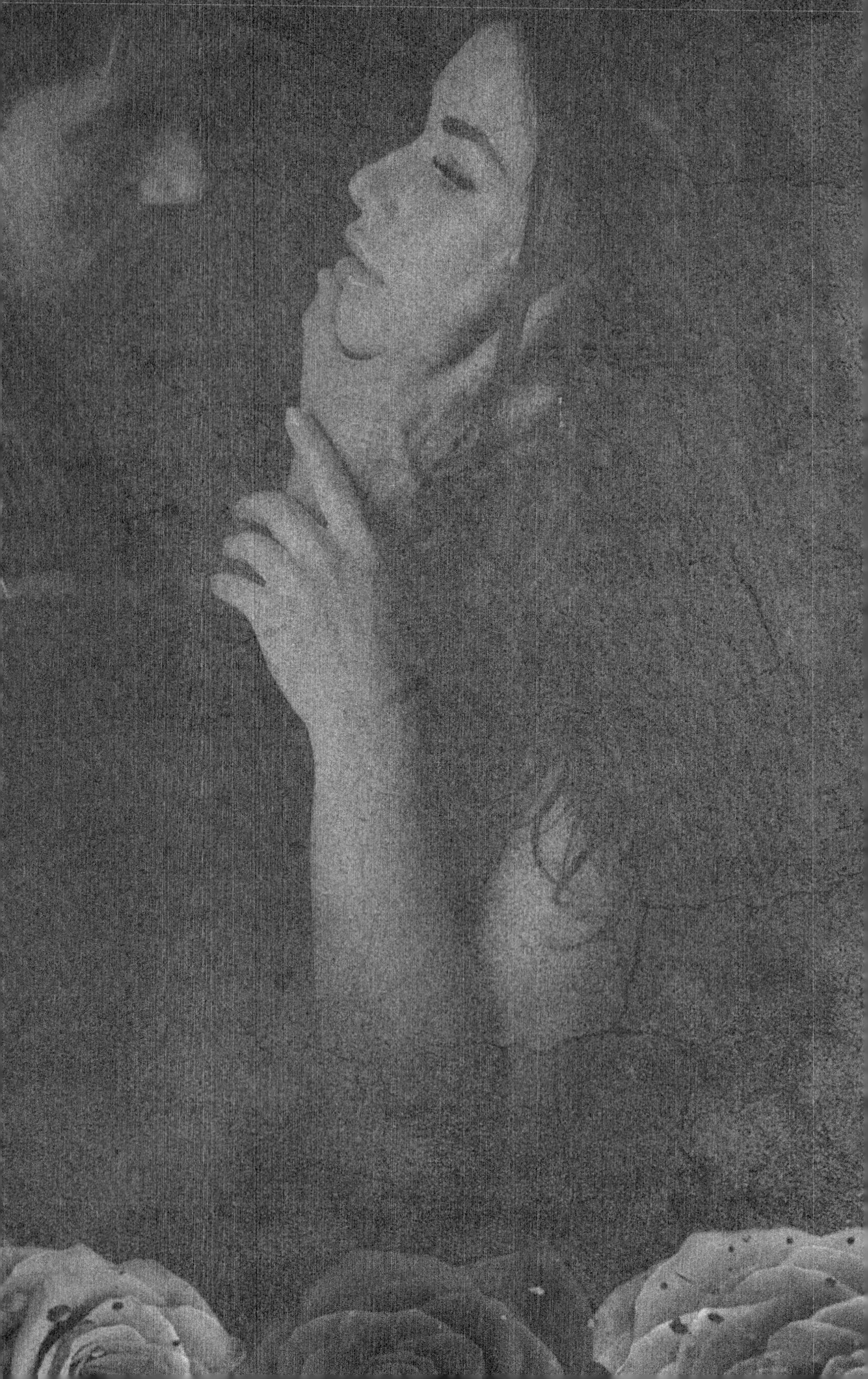

Chapter Twenty-Five
Chloe

As soon as I climb in the car, my body almost sags. I'm in this weird state of disbelief. Over the course of about ninety minutes, I've been through a wide range of emotions, and I'm mentally drained.

For a moment, in my father's office, when I let go of Marcus' hand, I thought reality was finally catching up with me.

I've spent the last few weeks living my dream, getting a taste of what my life could really be like, and despite Marcus' reassurances, there's a part of me that's been waiting for the other shoe to drop, for it to be snatched away from me. I thought today was that moment.

I looked over at Scott, snarling and swearing, glaring at me like I was a piece of shit on the bottom of his shoe, and I had no idea why he was fighting so hard to marry me.

Then I realised it was nothing to do with me at all, he just wanted the power that came with me. He didn't want me, quite the opposite actually…he was stuck with me. But it was worth it as he got the power he craved.

Then Marcus said he'd willingly break the treaty, take any punishment thrown his way, as long as he got to keep me—I was literally stunned.

It was one of those movie-type moments where you see it play out, but when things don't happen the way you expect, you worry it was your imagination, and reality would kick in any minute.

Yet, this was reality. Marcus Morelli was fighting for me, and my heart doubled in size.

Even when guns were drawn, he put himself between me and the weapons, determined to protect me, even if it was with his own body. I was both annoyed and happy, all at the same time.

As Leo starts the car to take us home, I reach and grab Marcus' hand, squeezing just enough to grab his attention. He looks over at me, and I give him my best glare, letting him know I'm about to start my lecture.

"You do know that you're not a human shield, right?"

Marcus chuckles. "What?"

"When the guns were flying around in there, you put yourself in front of me," I deadpan.

Marcus tilts his head to the side, looking confused. "Yeah, so?"

"So?" I repeat, sounding as exacerbated as I feel. "You are not a shield. Had that fucker shot you, you'd be dead."

"Yes, but you wouldn't be," he states, matter-of-factly.

I shake my head in frustration. "You can't take a bullet for me."

He lets out a short, humourless laugh. "I absolutely can, and I will. Every. Fucking. Time."

"Marcus! Obviously, I don't *want* to get shot, but do you know how I'd feel if you took a bullet that was meant for me?" I ask.

"I expect it'd feel a whole lot better than a bullet wound would," he replies sarcastically.

I slap him on the arm, which just makes him laugh again.

"I'm serious."

He reaches over, unfastens my seatbelt, and lifts me onto his lap. I shuffle around until I'm straddling him, a knee on either side of his thighs. He places his hands on my cheeks, tilting my head down so I meet his gaze.

"I'm serious too. From now until the end, I'll take every bullet that's intended for you, and you won't change my mind on that."

Before I can argue, he presses his soft lips against mine. The kiss is gentle and slow, as he roams his hands over my body, taking his time with me.

I rock against him, feeling his hardness grow beneath me with each kiss and touch. I run my fingers through his hair, gently pulling at the strands as I try to deepen the kiss. Just a little taste of him makes me crave more.

Just as Marcus begins *really* kissing me, the car comes to a stop and the engine is turned off. I groan as he pulls his lips away, and his cocky smirk after hearing it makes me roll my eyes.

I try to climb off his lap, but he keeps hold of me.

"What are you doing?" I ask, as Leo pulls the car door open.

Without responding, Marcus begins climbing out of the car, with me still on his lap. As he stands, I wrap my arms and legs around him tightly, so he doesn't drop me.

"Put me down. I can walk," I grumble, but he just tuts, walking us towards the lift.

After jostling me just a tad, he's able to press the button to call the lift, and thankfully, the doors open straight away.

Once we're inside and the doors are closed, he backs me up against the wall and begins kissing me again. This time it's not slow, it's hard and fast, just what I need.

In between devouring my mouth, he makes sure to kiss along my jaw, down my neck, over my collarbone, up my throat, before sucking on that sweet spot over my pulse point.

We're in the lift for no more than a couple of minutes, and that's all he needs to get me hot and bothered. He carries me into the house with ease, like I weigh nothing, kissing me the whole time.

Once Marcus gets me into the dining room, he places me on the table and I open my legs for him to slot in between them. Our kisses become a bit more frantic as we roam our hands over one another's bodies, and it's not long before we begin stripping each other.

When Marcus has removed my shirt and bra, he leans down and pulls my nipple into his mouth, using his finger and thumb to roll the other one at the same time. I throw my head back, arching into him as I rock my hips against his hard length.

As his tongue circles my nipple, his teeth graze over the hard bud, making me moan, while on the other side, he nips and pulls, adding a little pain in with my pleasure. My whimpers grow louder as I grip his hair, holding him in place.

He swaps sides, using his tongue to lavish the nipple that is stinging after all the tugging, and the ache in my core grows. My pussy is dripping wet, and I rock against Marcus, desperately trying to create any sort of friction to help ease my growing need.

As soon as he releases my nipple, he kisses down my stomach, over my belly button piercing, until he gets to the waistband of my jeans. With a bit of wiggling on my part, he soon has my jeans off. I go to take my knickers off at the same time, but he keeps them in place, silently telling me I can't take them off.

I watch with fascination as he drops to his knees, looking up at me through his lashes, a wicked smile on his face.

With a hand on each thigh, he spreads my legs further apart, so he can fit his wide shoulders in easier. He then hooks his arms around my upper legs and pulls me down until my arse is on the edge of the table.

My fabric-covered pussy is right in front of his face, and I watch intently as he drags the flat of his tongue through my slit, over the top of my knickers.

When I first realised that's what he was going to do, I wanted to whine and complain, as I thought I'd barely be able to feel anything, and it definitely wouldn't be the same as without my underwear.

Fuck, was I wrong.

Well, it's not as good as if he were licking my bare flesh, but it's still intense.

The roughness of my knickers combined with the warm heat of his tongue is the perfect combination, and I can't stop the moan that rips from my throat.

With each stroke of his tongue, the fire in my stomach grows, my knickers becoming drenched from both sides. He then pulls at the fabric, wiggling it in just the right way that it bunches together between my lips, rubbing against my clit.

"Fuck," I cry out, rocking against my knickers.

"You're so fucking wet, love," Marcus tells me, running his tongue through my slit again, whilst rubbing the fabric against my clit.

I drag in a ragged breath, my body on edge as I crave more of his touch.

"More. Please," I beg, my eyes closed as I throw my head back, lost in the sensations.

I feel him move my knickers to one side, so his warm, wet tongue makes direct contact with my pussy, and it's just what I need. Then he adds two fingers, thrusting inside me deep until I'm quivering.

"So good," I cry, tilting my hips to meet his hand.

"You are so tight and wet for me. Are you ready to show me what a good little slut you are for me?" he growls, flicking his tongue over my clit, so I struggle to form coherent sentences.

"Yes! Oh, fuck, yes."

I look down at him, letting him see the effect he has on me.

Marcus chuckles with a wicked smirk on his face as he speeds up his fingers, hooking them to drag them along my front wall until my legs are trembling.

He licks, sucks, even blows on my clit, until my whole body is on fire.

"I'm so close," I tell him, sounding low and breathy.

"Such a needy cunt, rocking against my hand, soaking my fingers."

Marcus' low gravelly tone combined with his dirty words make me shudder.

"Can I come, please?" I beg.

When Marcus doesn't reply, but continues his assault on my pussy, I start to panic. I try to focus on anything except the fucking overwhelming sensations that are rippling over my body, all while begging him to let me come.

I tense up, trying to think of something to distract myself, but all I can think about is Marcus hitting that sweet spot deep inside, and how fucking amazing it feels.

"I can't... I need... Please, Marcus... Can I..." My words are frantic and disjointed, almost incoherent babble, but the purpose is the same.

I need to fucking come, right now, and I won't be able to hold it for much longer.

My body starts to tense, and I'm reaching the point of no return, my legs shaking from the intensity of trying to hold it back. Yet, just as my orgasm is about to hit, Marcus pulls away, both his fingers and his tongue leaving me feeling empty.

I cry out loudly as my pussy throbs and aches, the build up of my impending orgasm beginning to fade away with each second he's no longer touching me.

I rock my hips, desperately trying to alleviate that growing ache, but there's nothing to create friction.

"Noooo. Marcus, what?" I cry out, my legs turning to jello as he drags his nails down my thighs, making me shiver.

"What's the matter? Does my needy little whore want something?"

I nod my head frantically, reaching down to rub my fingers over my pulsating clit, but Marcus grabs my hand, forcing it to my side.

"I was so close. I need to come."

"Do you think you've been a good enough girl to come, Mio?" he asks, and I nod my head.

"I have. I've been a really good girl."

"If you come, what do I get?"

His voice is a low growl, and I can see the predatory gaze he has me locked in. I just walked into his trap, and I don't care.

"Anything. I'll do anything," I tell him, meaning every word.

"Take off your knickers, get down on your knees, and show me how much you want to come," he says calmly.

I waste no time jumping off the table, sliding my knickers off, before falling to my knees.

While I'm getting into position, Marcus removes all of his clothes, his hard cock standing to attention in front of my eyes. I stick my tits out, curving my spine as I lock my hands behind my back, presenting myself in the way I know he loves.

"Open your mouth, slut."

I obey, sticking out my tongue as I do.

He drags the tip of his dick over my tongue, and I can taste the salty droplets of pre-cum as he wipes them over me. He slides his shaft over too, soaking it with my saliva.

"Are you going to suck my cock like a good whore?"

I nod, smiling around his dick as it rests on my tongue.

He edges in slowly as I close my mouth around his length, running my tongue along his smooth skin. Marcus takes his time, pushing until he hits the back of my throat, making me gag around him.

"You can take more, can't you?"

I nod again, pulling in a breath through my nose as he works his cock back in, a little faster this time. When he reaches the back of my throat, I try to swallow, pulling him in further, while the squeezing sensation causes Marcus to groan.

After that, his actions become more frantic and desperate. He pulls out before thrusting in, getting deeper with each stroke, hitting the back of my throat as I suck him down.

I hollow out my mouth, sucking hard as I swirl my tongue around his soft flesh, feeling the pulsing of blood along the underside of his shaft. Each time he hits the back of my throat, making me gag and splutter, he moans with pleasure.

His hand on the back of my head tightens, and it's not long until he's fucking deep into my throat. Even though he's making me gag, he never pushes me further than I can handle.

"You take my cock so well, love," he praises me, and I moan around his dick, making him shiver.

It's not long before I feel him getting even bigger in my mouth, and I concentrate my efforts on making him come down my throat, but just as he's getting close, he pulls me off him.

He reaches down and grabs me, and before I know it, I'm bent over the dining table. My chest and cheek are pressed against the wood as Marcus shuffles my legs wider, tilting my hips. With my back arched in just the right way, my pussy is on full view for him.

SLAP!

A loud strike ripples over my arse cheek as he spanks my left side, quickly doing the same on the right. My arse stings, but as Marcus rubs his warm hands over my tingling flesh—that I'm sure is bright red from his handprint—it soothes the pain.

"Put your hands out and take hold of each side of the table," Marcus instructs firmly, slapping my arse cheek again when I don't do as I'm told fast enough.

I yelp as he spanks the other side too, evening up the redness. Once I have the table firmly in my grasp, he begins dragging his nails down my spine, making me shiver as goosebumps erupt over my flesh.

"Do you want me to fuck you, Mio?" he asks, nipping at my ear as he presses kisses against my cheek, followed by my neck, and across my back.

"Yes, please," I beg, tilting my arse a little more, presenting my pussy to him.

This time when he spanks me, it's directly on my clit, and I cry out, more from shock than pain. It leaves behind a deep stinging ache that feels fucking amazing.

If it wasn't for the risk of receiving a punishment, I'd be rubbing my pussy against this table, desperately craving my release.

I feel his large cock pressing at my entrance, stretching me open. A loud groan rips from me as he holds my hips in place, stopping me from rocking onto him.

"If you move, I'll punish you," he growls.

I look over my shoulder at him. His intense blue eyes are dark and sexy, and I believe him. I just haven't decided if I want the punishment enough yet or not.

"Yes, sir," I reply, watching as his eyes grow wide, before darkening with lust.

"What did you call me?" he asks through gritted teeth.

"Sir?"

It comes out as a question, because I'm not sure if he's mad about it or not.

"Fuck, I like that," Marcus growls as he pushes his full length into me in one powerful stroke, stopping only when he bottoms out.

We both moan loudly, my pussy aching and stinging from the sudden intrusion, while also being relieved at finally getting what I need. Marcus holds me there for a moment, his grip on my hips becoming tight enough to bruise.

He leans down and captures my shoulder between his teeth, sucking and nibbling at the flesh until I'm panting, trying my hardest not to writhe around. He is definitely marking me.

"Please, sir. Please, fuck me," I beg, hoping the use of his new nickname will be enough to get him moving.

"Shit, I love when you call me sir," he growls, pulling back at such a slow pace, it's almost painful.

He pulls out until only the tip remains, stretching me out in the most delicious way, before pressing back inside. He continues thrusting until he finds his rhythm. Drawing back slowly before pounding in fast, hitting the spot deep inside that makes me cry out.

I was already overly sensitive from him edging me before, so it's not long until my pussy is aching and throbbing, desperate for release. It takes every ounce of strength I have to remain still, to not rock back, or roll my hips in the way I know drives him crazy.

I just have to lay there, letting him fuck me into the table—not that I'm complaining!

As my release approaches, I cry out to let him know, begging him to let me come this time. All the time I'm begging to come, he talks dirty to me, telling me what a good slut I am, how wet I am, like a good whore. He degrades me and praises me, making my head swim with desire, just as much as my body is.

"I can't hold back. Please, sir, please, let me come," I shout, knowing my body will betray me soon if he doesn't give me permission.

Without responding, he presses a finger into my arse, roughly stretching me, making me feel so incredibly full, as well as a little naughty.

"Come, slut. Come like the dirty little whore you are, with a cock filling your cunt and a finger in your arse," he shouts, pressing his finger in as he pulls his cock out, then vice versa.

It only takes a couple of thrusts, and his permission, to tip me over the edge, my release hitting me like a brick wall.

My cries of pleasure echo around the room as my whole body stiffens, before my legs start to tremble. My pussy shudders, clamped around his dick.

"I'm coming, Marcus," I cry out, my hold on the table becoming so hard, I'm surprised it hasn't snapped.

He rocks into me as my head swims, dark spots flicking into the edges of my vision as I gasp for air, riding through the after effects. Marcus fucks into me a couple more times, his movements becoming more frantic as his own release draws near.

"Where do you want my cum, slut?" he asks, not slowing down his thrusts.

"My pussy," I reply, almost dreamily.

"You want me to fill your cunt with my cum?"

I nod. "Yes, please."

"I'm going to fill your cunt, marking you as mine. I want to see my cum dripping from your tight little hole," he whispers against my ear, making me tremble.

Almost straight away, Marcus grunts as he spills his load into my pussy, his grip on my hips tightening as my walls milk him dry.

"So fucking good, Mio," he mumbles, and I chuckle.

He flops over me, gasping for air as all of his energy seems to deplete following his orgasm. As he pulls out, I wince at the sting, but also at how empty I feel. I can't help but smile as I feel his warm cum dribbling down my leg.

Marcus picks me up and carries me over to the sofa, pulling the blanket over us that's normally draped over the back. I snuggle against his side, unable to keep the smile off my face.

I ignore the mess between my legs, since it clearly doesn't bother him. In fact, I think he quite likes knowing I'm messy thanks to his cum.

"Today feels a bit unreal. I can't believe everyone knows," I admit.

I still feel like this is a dream, and I'm going to wake up to find I'm actually living the hell I've been trying to avoid.

"This is the start of our future," he tells me, pressing a kiss against my forehead.

"Yeah, and I start working on my very first customer cake tomorrow," I tell him, his eyes growing wide at the news.

"Really?"

I nod with a bright smile on my face. "Yeah, it's actually for Leo. It's his daughter's birthday. He saw me practising, and after talking, he asked if I'd make her cake. I'll start making it tomorrow, ready for him to collect it the day after.

"He wanted to pay me, but I said I'd do it for free, in exchange for a review and being able to use the pictures on social media, to help build the business. He agreed, though he was somewhat anxious about not paying."

"I'm so proud of you, love," Marcus beams, kissing me on the lips.

"Thank you."

Marcus pauses for a second, looking a bit unsure about whether he should carry on or not. I wait, knowing he'll speak when he's ready.

After a deep breath, he fixes me with a tight yet comforting look, before speaking.

"Me, Jake, and Miles have actually made some progress. We're in a situation where we can finally take out Frank, and we're going to be putting the plan into motion tomorrow."

I freeze as soon as I hear *his* name, my breath catching in my throat as nausea ripples through my stomach. Marcus strokes his hand down my arm reassuringly, pressing a kiss to my forehead.

"Breathe, love. I'm only telling you because you have a right to know. I don't have to tell you anymore, if you don't want me to. But if you want to face him, to see him get the punishment he deserves, then I can absolutely help you with that."

Once I've got my heart rate down, and I'm breathing normally again, I give

Marcus a tight smile. When I find my voice, I hate how small and weak it sounds, just at the mention of that monster.

"I think I need to see him, but only when he's in a weakened state. I want to see him as scared as he made me. Then maybe I can get some closure, and bury his ghost for good."

Marcus places his hand on my cheek, stroking me softly. "I'm so fucking proud of you, love. You are stronger than you know. But once we've taken him down, he'll never haunt you again."

I smile, knowing he's the final hurdle I need to overcome, before we can truly start our lives together.

Marcus was right, this is the first day of our future, and for once, it's entirely of my choosing. I'm finally living the life I want, with the man I choose, and I won't let anyone take that from me.

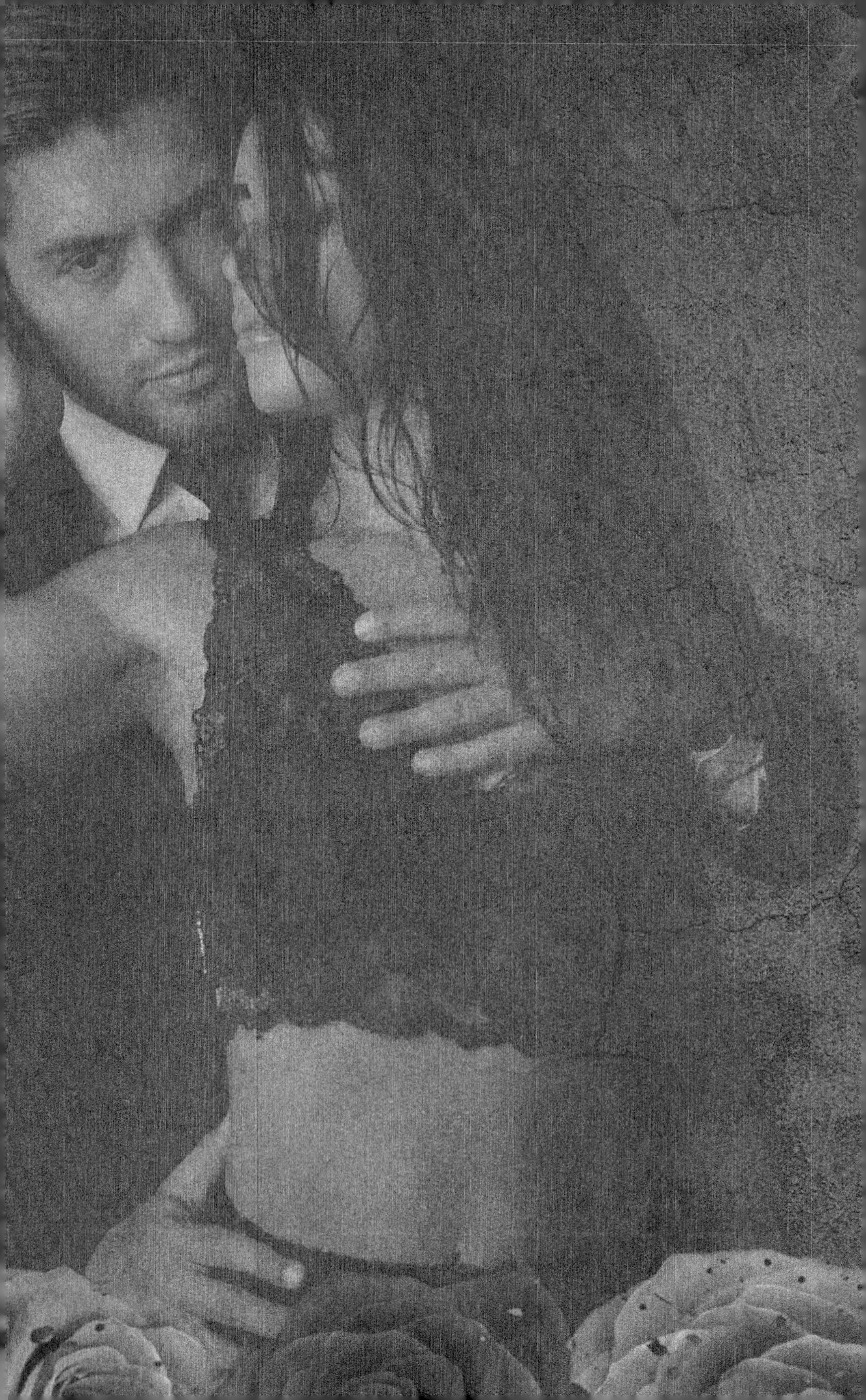

Chapter Twenty-Six
Marcus

Waking up with Chloe in my arms the next morning felt like a dream. Although she's been sleeping with me every night since our first time, it feels different now that everyone knows.

What we're doing isn't secret or forbidden anymore, it's out in the open. I know Chloe was worried I'd lose interest when the danger element was gone.

She thought I enjoyed sneaking around, being with someone who I wasn't supposed to be, breaking the rules, but that couldn't be further from the truth.

If anything, worrying about all of those things made it more stressful. Having to choose between the woman I was falling for and the role I've been training for my whole life—not to mention possibly starting a war with my best friend and her family at the same time—was terrifying.

I didn't think, no matter which option I chose, there'd be a good outcome. Yet here we are.

Today feels different, like the first day of the rest of our lives, and I intend to start it with a bang.

As Chloe sleeps beside me, her head resting on my chest, her leg thrown over mine, I keep my arm wrapped around her, despite having lost feeling in it a while ago. With my free hand, I grab my phone and send a text to Miles.

MARCUS
Are we all set?

MILES
Yes, I sent you the address.

MARCUS
Good. I'm very excited.

MILES
Jacob has just arrived. It'll take all of my effort to hold him back, so don't take too long.

MARCUS
Why is he there so early?

MILES
Excitement. It's been a while since I've seen him look forward to something this much.

MARCUS
I have to admit, I can't wait.

MILES
Well…get here quicker then.

MARCUS
Can't. Chloe is still asleep.

MILES
You've become such a sap. Why do you have to wait for her to get up?

MARCUS
She's asleep on me and I'm not waking her. Besides, I'm not missing out on morning sex because you and Jake are impatient.

MILES
I don't need to hear about your sex life.

MARCUS
You're just jealous because you don't currently have a sex life. Tell me…has your virginity grown back yet?

MILES
Fuck off, arsehole. Don't make me trigger the security alarm in the house to wake Chloe up.

Prized Possession

> **MARCUS**
> Don't you fucking dare.

> **MILES**
> Then grow a pair and get here soon!

I throw the phone down with a huff, not wanting to argue with my friend anymore. I hear it vibrate twice, and I feel sure without looking that Jacob has started texting too.

I'm not sure I like this new-found friendship they have going on, particularly when they gang up on me.

Chloe shuffles beneath me, blinking a couple of times before she opens her eyes fully, a bright smile on her face as she looks up at me.

"Morning," she says, her voice thick with sleep.

I lean down and press a kiss to her forehead. "Morning, love. I didn't wake you, did I?"

"No, but you could have." She looks at her watch, before glancing back at me, apprehension on her face. "Don't you have somewhere you need to be right now?"

"I do, but it can wait. I like waking up with you," I tell her, this time capturing her lips for a kiss.

Before I know it, she's sitting on my lap, straddling my thighs as we kiss. I know she can feel me growing harder the longer she rocks against me. Her naked pussy rubs against my growing length, and I groan when I feel how wet she is.

As I press kisses over her cheeks and neck, I reach down and slide my fingers between us, dragging one through her slit.

"You're so fucking wet, Mio," I tell her, my voice sounding breathy.

"I'm ready," she whispers, rocking against me, coating my dick with her juices.

She lifts up slightly and reaches down, grabbing the base of my cock. Once she has it lined up with her entrance, she sinks down, not stopping until she has all of me inside of her.

She arches her back as a groan of pleasure rips from her throat, pushing her tits into my face. With my hands on her hips to keep her steady, I pull one of her nipples into my mouth, nipping and sucking as she rolls her pelvis, my cock still buried deep inside.

"Fuck me. Take what you need from me, love," I tell her, and her eyes roll as she begins to rub her fingers against her clit.

She then starts to move, slow and a little unsure at first, but once she finds a comfortable position, she takes what she needs.

My beautiful girl bounces up and down on my cock, rubbing her clit as I devour her nipples with my mouth, swapping from one to the other.

She lifts all the way off and sinks down, getting faster and more forceful each time. When her movements become more uncoordinated, her breathing ragged, I grasp her hips tighter and rock my pelvis to meet her thrusts.

As she drops down onto me, I push upwards, hitting her deeper than before. Her cries turn to whimpers as she tells me how close she is.

"I'm going to... Fuck, I'm so close. Keep fucking me."

I do as I'm told, using my hands on her hips to pull her down onto me while pushing my cock deeper. I can feel her tightening around me, her pussy getting wetter each time I hit a spot that makes her cry out.

"Can I—"

Before she can ask, I cut her off. "Come for me, love."

Her fingers rub against her clit frantically as I push into her, hard and deep, and it's not long before her orgasm hits. Her moans turn to her crying out my name as she falls apart above me.

Her pussy clamps around my cock while I'm impaled deep inside, and she shudders around me, her head thrown back as she rides the wave of her release.

I sit there just staring at her, my hands still on her hips to keep her steady, watching with amazement at how fucking gorgeous she is when she lets go.

As she catches her breath, she begins moving again and winces. I quickly lift her off my cock.

"Are you okay? Did I hurt you?" I ask frantically, cursing myself for not doing more foreplay before fucking her so hard.

She shakes her head, a dreamy look on her face. "No, you didn't hurt me. I'm just a little sensitive, and maybe a bit sore. We've fucked a lot the last few days —not that I'm complaining."

I laugh at her adding that on the end, whilst still being a bit annoyed at myself for not checking with her sooner.

"Okay, well, you can have a long soak in the bath after I've gone. There's some bath salts in there that I use for aching muscles, which might help. We can take it easy."

She looks down at my hard cock, bobbing against my stomach, glistening with her juices.

"No, you still need to—"

I cut her off again. "Forget about me. I can have a quick shower."

Not to mention a fucking amazing wank in the shower, but I leave that unsaid.

Her eyes narrow as she glares at me, looking very unimpressed with my suggestion.

"Just because I'm resting my pussy doesn't mean I can't get you off."

Before I even have time to process what she said, she grabs hold of the base of my cock until it's pointing upwards, and lowers her mouth around me.

She's on her hands and knees, bent over my cock, when she looks up at me, watching for my reaction as she twirls her tongue around the head, licking off her own juices.

I moan loudly and almost blow my load at that sight alone.

"Fuck, such a dirty girl. Do you like licking your juices off my cock?"

She hums her approval around my dick, sending a shiver down my spine. I watch in amazement as she takes the head in her mouth, sucking hard as she pumps her hand along the base.

She keeps eye contact with me the whole time, staring at me through hooded lashes, watching as she takes me apart with her mouth. Although I rest my hand on her head, holding her hair back so I can see everything, I don't control her movements.

This whole morning hasn't been about power or control, it's been about both of us letting ourselves go enough to fall apart with each other.

I hate the term, but it does feel more like we're making love than fucking, and I never thought I'd enjoy this more relaxed style of sex, but I actually do.

As Chloe stares at me, learning what actions have the most impact, teaching herself how to give me the maximum amount of pleasure, I can't help but feel proud of her. She's not only confident enough in her own body to ride me, to take the orgasm she needed, but now she's taking the lead to make me fall apart.

Gone is the shy girl who hated her body and didn't know what she wanted. Now she's in tune enough with what she wants that she doesn't even have to ask, she knows how to take it from me.

And whilst I'll never stop wanting to control her, to turn her into my dirty little slut when we fuck, I'll also give her times like this.

I think we both need it. To feel closer to each other, not just taking what we need from the other's body.

Watching my beautiful girl take control, and feel confident in herself, makes me so fucking proud.

As she presses most of my length into the back of her throat, the tip bobbing against the back of her throat, I know I'm not going to last much longer. My balls are aching, tingling, ready for release.

"I'm going to come, love. Where do you want it?"

She doesn't pull my cock out of her mouth to reply. Instead, she sucks me deeper, massaging her tongue against my shaft, her throat tightening just enough to push me over the edge.

I try to pull her off slightly, but Chloe holds firm, making her wishes clear, and I'm not fucking going to argue. With a grunt and a moan, my orgasm hits me and I blow my load into the back of her throat.

As the first load hits, she swallows, sending a shiver down my spine as I grunt with pleasure. She then pulls her head back a little, using her hand to pump the base of my shaft, dragging out the next few shots of cum, which land perfectly on her tongue.

My cum pools in her mouth as ropes of it hit the back of her throat and her tongue. She keeps her eyes locked on mine as she milks the last few drops from me.

I watch with rapt attention as she shows me the cum on her tongue, before swallowing it down.

Fuck, if I hadn't just come, I might be getting hard again right now.

"That's the hottest thing I've ever seen," I tell her, my voice deep and raspy.

With a devilish smile on her face, she drags her tongue over the head of my cock, making sure to clean up the last few drops that we're pooled there. She then licks all over my shaft, making sure she doesn't miss anything.

When she finally sits back, she's no longer looking as confident. Her cheeks are flushed and she gives me a shy smile.

"Was that okay?" she whispers, looking down at the bed.

I reach over and tilt her chin up so she has to meet my gaze. "That was fucking amazing, Chloe. Why would you ever think it wasn't?"

"Well, it was a little different from the way we normally do things. I didn't realise I'd been in charge until after, I was just lost in the moment."

I can't help but chuckle, which makes her look confused.

"Chloe, I don't have to be in charge every time. We also don't have to fuck hard and fast each time.

"Now that we're together, it's only natural to have more slow, sensual sex when the occasion calls for it, which I think it did here. I happen to find you taking what you need from me very fucking sexy."

Her eyes widen a little with hope. "So we can do a bit of both? I love when you dominate me, and I'm your slut. That sort of sex is fucking amazing, but this was different. More intense, in a way."

"I think it's important we do both. The sex where I call you a slut and you call me sir, that's more about us taking on the roles we enjoy in sex, but this, what we did this morning, that wasn't roleplaying. It was just us, and that's what made it more intimate," I explain, relaxing when I see her finally let out the breath she's holding.

"So both have their rightful place," she repeats, and I nod.

"Absolutely."

"Good, because I enjoy both in different ways," she admits, the flush on her cheeks becoming redder with her confession.

I have to admit, I wasn't sure I'd enjoy sex without the control and dominance element, but I did. I know what she means when she says she enjoys both.

"As much as I hate to leave this bed while you're still naked, I better get going. Miles and Jake are already moaning that I'm late," I tell her, hating how she tenses when I avoid mentioning where I'm going.

"Yes, and I have a cake to make."

As she says that, her face brightens up.

"I think we're both going to have a very good day," I tell her, capturing her lips for another kiss.

"Enough of that or we'll never start our great day," she jokes, slapping my arm playfully.

With regret, and a lot of moaning, I climb out of bed and head for the shower, getting ready for what I know will be a fucking fantastic day.

I ARRIVE AT THE WAREHOUSE MILES GAVE ME THE ADDRESS FOR ABOUT FORTY MINUTES later, which is apparently far longer than either Miles or Jake is happy about. They both have matching annoyed expressions on their faces, but I dismiss them both.

"Good morning," I say chirpily, loving the confused looks that spread over their faces.

Miles turns to Jake. "Did he just say good morning? Like a normal person, in a happy, cheerful voice?"

Jake visibly shudders. "This is the most animated I've ever seen him...and it's freaking me out. What happened to Mr Dark, Broody, and Miserable?"

"He started the day with an amazing blowjob, which I highly recommend," I point out.

Jake makes gagging noises, pretending to vomit, while Miles laughs.

"Yeah, that'll do it," Miles adds.

Jake glowers at him. "Don't encourage the arsehole. He's talking about my fucking sister."

"You wouldn't be as uptight if you started the day with a blowjob?" I rather unhelpfully point out.

Jake takes a menacing step towards me, glaring at me, but I just roll my eyes, while Miles holds out his arm between us.

"Enough," Miles says firmly. "We're all going to have a great day when we get in this room."

The reminder of why we're all here is enough to straighten us all out. We pull on the professional masks we've spent years perfecting, looking like cocky, dangerous arseholes as we get ready to play out the plan we've been perfecting over the last few days.

Initially, Miles and I were worried about involving Jake. Although he left rehab to help us, knowing he'd need to take his place as ruler if we were to avoid conflict, it doesn't mean he was ready to leave.

He'd finished his mandatory detox period, but both him and the healthcare professionals felt he needed more time to work on his issues.

Choosing to put Chloe and us before his own wellbeing means a lot to me, and I know it's just another of many sacrifices we've all made for this job, but that doesn't stop me worrying about him.

He's still seeing his psychologist and rehab support worker on an outpatient basis, but one of the things they warned him about is stepping back into the life that pushed him towards substances in the first place. It's easy to fall off the wagon when you've not long been on it.

Miles has been helping him stay sober, going with him to meetings, and generally being there for him, but we both worry about putting Jake under too much pressure too soon. This is something we could do without him, but he was adamant he wanted to be here.

This guy not only assaulted his sister, he lied to Jake's family, and disrespected them. He's here for both Chloe and his family name, but really, he wants closure.

He had suspicions about Frank, and didn't trust him, yet he never stopped his parents from forcing Chloe to date him.

That guilt will be with Jake for a long time, and this is his way of righting the wrongs he made when he was more focused on substances than his family.

Miles opens the door, and I see Frank is tied to a chair in the middle of the room. The chair has been bolted to the tiled floor. He's wearing nothing but his boxer shorts, just as we planned.

Other than a bloody lip, Frank looks fine, though I do cast a glance over at Miles, raising my brows enough that he knows I'm silently asking about the blood. He was supposed to bring him here unharmed.

"He put up a fight," Miles mutters with a shrug of his shoulders, as Jake chuckles.

I know from my research that Frank is about our age, though his receding hairline and thinning bald spot on the top of his head make him look older.

He's thinner than I was expecting, with very few muscles, other than his barely noticeable biceps, which stick out on his small frame.

I imagine, if he were to stand up, he'd be a little taller than me, making him look lanky. With his pale skin, he's one pair of glasses away from looking like a science geek.

For a fraction of a second, I wonder how the hell anyone could ever be scared of this guy, then I remember that he uses drugs to overpower them, and once he's made sure they're not a threat to him, then he's safe to abuse them. My rage grows the longer I think about it.

I pull up a chair and put it a few feet away from him. Jake does the same beside me, while Miles remains standing, hovering behind us. Once we're seated, we remain silent, letting the tension grow as we simply stare at him, loving the way he squirms under our gaze.

He has the good sense not to speak, though he looks like he might a few times, his mouth opening, but no words fall out.

After a few tense, silent minutes, I clear my throat, making him jump.

"Do you know why you're here?" I ask, sounding deep and dangerous.

He shakes his head rapidly. "No, I don't."

I look over at Jake, then back to him. "Do you know who we are?"

"Yes," he mutters, looking terrified now.

"Do you know which of us you've wronged?" I ask, watching as he flicks his gaze between the two of us, his eyes widening as panic starts to set in.

"No, I don't. I think you might have the wrong person," he blurts out.

I pull out my phone, scrolling until I find a recent picture of Chloe. She's smiling at the camera, looking at me with those bright silver eyes of hers, and I almost hesitate.

I don't want him to see her at all, but I need him to see how happy she is, despite what he did to her.

I turn the phone, showing him her picture. I see the moment realisation hits, and all of the colour drains from his already pale face.

"Do you know who this is?"

He shakes his head in denial, but he doesn't say a word.

Jake's anger takes over, forcing him to chip in, and the sheer venom in his tone has Frank shaking in his boots.

"So my parents didn't arrange for you to take her out? You didn't go on a date with her?"

"I-I remember now," he splutters, panic and fear making his voice strained.

"We went on a date a long time ago, but we didn't really get on too well, so it ended quickly."

The lie tumbles out of his mouth quickly, his gaze flicking between me and Jake, and it looks like he's holding his breath, no doubt praying we believe him—which we don't.

"That's not the way I remember it," Jake replies calmly, and the rapid change in his mood has Frank even more on edge.

His arms are moving behind his back, as he no doubt tries to remove the bindings that he stands no chance of escaping from. I guess, in this escalating situation, he has to feel like he's doing something.

"Chloe was gone for two days. She texted to tell us that she was with you, as you'd got on so well. Are you saying my sister was lying? Or are you lying?" Jake asks, sounding more dangerous at the end.

Frank shakes his head, looking around the room like he's trying to find an escape plan. The room is empty, except for us.

"I-I... I'm not lying. I just... I didn't want to talk to you about the intimate relationship I had with your sister. Nobody wants to hear about their sister's sex life."

Hearing him say the word sex, like what happened was consensual, is like lava flooding my veins, and I have to bite my lower lip to stop myself from ruining the plan before we've even started.

Jake tenses beside me, no doubt feeling just as much rage as I am.

"What do you mean?" Jake grinds out.

"I didn't want you to be mad at me for sleeping with your sister, even though I knew we didn't have a future together. She was a nice girl, but I wouldn't ever want to marry her, which is what your parents wanted, but we weren't a good match."

The lies fall out of his mouth in a rush, my nausea growing with each new thing he says.

"We both agreed we didn't have a future, but we decided to have some fun together anyway."

Seeing the way he tries to hide a smile as he says the word *fun*, it sends me over the edge.

Fuck the plan, I think as I stand up and punch him on the nose.

Blood spurts out as he cries out. "Fuck, what the—"

I cut him off, squeezing his shoulder to get his attention.

"For every lie you tell me, I will hurt you. Now, let's try again."

Jake continues to ask Frank questions, and he carries on lying. So each time he tells a lie, I kick him, punch him, nip him, twist his arm...whatever form of pain I can think of.

Eventually, when Frank is a bloody, battered mess, sobbing uncontrollably, he begs for me to stop.

"Are you going to tell the truth? You have one final chance to answer Jacob's questions honestly, or I'm moving on to the knife."

I pull out my large carving knife, allowing the sharp blade to glisten under the harsh lights of the room. His eyes widen, fear glistening in amongst the tears.

"What happened between you and Chloe?" Jacob asks, sounding bored of repeating the same question over and over.

When Frank hesitates, I move my knife closer to him, which has him frantically telling me to stop.

"Okay, okay. I'll tell the truth, but you won't like it. Remember, you asked me to tell you this," he starts, snot and tears flying everywhere as he blubbers.

"Get on with it," Jacob snaps, his patience wearing thin.

"Chloe told me about her fantasy, and she asked me if I'd help her bring it to life. She said she's always had a non-con kink, and so I drugged her and tied her up before having sex with her for the weekend. It was all her idea. I was just trying to help her live out her fantasy."

As he talks, a red mist descends over me, and I struggle to remain calm. My heart is racing, and my blood is boiling.

As soon as he finishes, he looks at us, assessing whether we believe him.

Without hesitation, I stab the knife down into his thigh, causing him to scream and shout, thrashing against his binds. I kneel down, so that I'm face-to-face with him, waiting for the fucker to calm down enough.

Once his gaze is locked on mine, and I can see the fear in his eyes, I reach out and grab hold of the handle. As I speak, I turn the knife, rotating the blade as I remove it from his flesh at an agonisingly slow pace.

"You are a liar. We know what you did. You raped and tortured Chloe for two days, tormenting her and terrifying her. What you did almost destroyed her, and now we plan to return the favour. You will stay here for two whole days, and we'll give you a taste of your own medicine."

Jake stands and walks to my side, as Miles goes to unlock Frank's bindings. He struggles against us, but he's weak, and doesn't stand a chance against the three of us. We move him over to the table that's tucked into the back corner of the room.

Bending him over the table, we secure an ankle to each leg, his chest and cheek pressing against the cool surface. Miles pulls Frank's hands over his head, and ties one to each of the legs on the opposite end, spreading him out like a starfish.

"What are you doing?" Frank asks frantically, trying to move around on the table.

Miles reaches over and secures a long belt over his lower back, pulling it tight enough that he can't move any part of his body, which makes Frank panic more.

"What's the matter? Does this position make you feel vulnerable?" I ask, taunting him.

He keeps quiet, other than his whimpers. I use my blade to slice through his boxers, exposing his pale arse to the world, which makes his eyes widen as he thrashes harder. When he starts to scream, Jake places a piece of duct tape over his lips.

"What about now?" I ask, chucking when he starts to cry.

Miles walks back over after gathering what we need from the bag in the corner, Jake's eyes growing wide when he sees the very large dildo Miles is holding. It's about eight inches long, and a decent girth too.

Miles hands the dildo to Jake, who looks just as startled as Frank, holding it like it's a fucking bomb that might go off at any second. Miles chuckles at his expression, as he quickly runs out of the room, returning a few seconds later with a machine that he pushes in.

Jake leans down to Frank's level, the dildo hovering between them almost comically.

"This is a fucking machine. We're going to attach this dildo to it, and we're going to sit back and watch it fuck you. We're not going to use any lube, as we don't want you to enjoy it too much. But we are going to make sure it fucks you until you love it."

Frank tries to shake his head, muffled screams hitting the duct tape as he tries to protest, but they fall on deaf ears.

Miles preps the machine, putting a small amount of lube on the dildo that Frank doesn't see, just so we don't rip his arsehole open too early on. We want to make this last.

Miles looks between me and Jake once the machine is ready, grimacing. "Are you sure neither of you wants the honour?"

As I shake my head rapidly, Jake chuckles. "Fuck, no. Besides, we won, fair and square. We get to watch while you get your hands dirty...so to speak."

I have to bite my bottom lip to keep from laughing at the look of disgust on Miles' face, needing to keep my stern mask in place for Frank.

When we came up with this plan, this moment right here has always been an issue. Although we all agreed it's a suitable punishment, neither of us wanted to be the one to put the dildo in.

Prized Possession

I still laugh whenever I remember the conversation we had, sitting around my kitchen table.

Jake laughs, the evil glint in his eyes twinkling as he approves of my suggestion.

"I think raping him with a massive fucking dildo for two days is the least he deserves. I'm sure we can even buy one of those fucking machines to make it easier."

Miles' eyes narrow on Jake, looking confused. "What's a fucking machine?"

"Haven't you ever seen porn where they attach a large dildo to this machine, which then does a kind of thrusting movement to fuck the girl? You can change speeds, vary between going slow then fast, you can even control how deep the damn thing goes," Jake explains.

"You clearly watch too much porn," Miles retorts. "Besides, where the hell would we get one in real life? I'm guessing you can't buy them on Amazon?"

"I suspect it's more of a specialist purchase," I add, after I've taken a sip of my beer, pleased the guys have taken my suggestion and ran with it.

"Fine," Miles snaps. "Say we manage to get this weird sex machine... Then what? Someone still has to... You know?"

Jake's brow lifts in question. "Has to, what?"

Miles groans, and I can't help but chuckle. I think I know what he's trying to say, but it seems to be annoying him enough that I'd rather watch this play out than help him.

"Someone has to put the damn thing in his arse," Miles groans, running his fingers through his hair as he takes a drink of his beer.

"Not it!" Jake shouts, slamming his Coke can down.

We offered not to drink beer in front of him, but he refused, saying he'd be fine. He wants things to be as normal as possible, so we reluctantly agreed.

"You can't fucking call it like that. We're not teenagers any more," Miles snaps at him.

They both turn to look at me, hoping I'll act as peacekeeper, but I just take another swig from my bottle.

"None of us wants to do it, but one of us will have to. Besides, the touching will be minimal. It's not like we're going to prep the guy."

Miles chokes on the mouthful of beer he'd just taken, slapping his hand over his mouth, so he doesn't spit it everywhere.

"Fuck, I hadn't even thought about prep," he blurts out.

Jake leans towards Miles, their gaze fixed on each other as Jake says, "You should always think about prep when you're going to fuck someone's arse. You'd want it to be pleasurable, wouldn't you?"

Miles gulps, and the tension in the air quickly grows. I look between them, not entirely sure what I'm witnessing, but it feels like something I shouldn't be a part of.

When neither of them says anything, I clear my throat awkwardly, and that's enough for them to both spring apart, looking a little uncomfortable.

"We don't want it to be pleasurable," I say, just because the silence was becoming too fucking deafening.

"I know that," Jake snaps, glaring at me.

"So, what? It's just a case of parting the guy's cheeks and letting the machine do the rest?" Miles asks, and we both look to Jake, since he's the one who knows the most about the machines.

Jake shrugs his shoulders.

"Honestly, I've got no fucking clue. Porn doesn't really show a lot of the prep work. I'd assume we need to get him into position, hold his arse cheeks open, and then ease the head of the dildo in. Then the machine can do its job after. Getting the head in will be the hard bit."

Me and Miles look at him with disbelief on our faces, and he flips us off.

"It's common sense. I've fucked girls in the arse before, and getting the head in is always the hardest bit. Once it's in, everything is fine after that. With this guy, it will be even tougher, as he's not exactly going to be cooperative and do all the things we tell girls to do when we're pushing in," he adds.

I nod as I take another swig. "He's right. Getting his arse to loosen up enough to let the head in isn't going to be easy. If we were doing it to a girl for fun, we'd prep her fully, stretch her out with our fingers, and she'd do as we say when we tell her to push back against us and relax as we first enter. None of that counts here."

"Thank fuck," Miles says, breathing a sigh of relief. "I thought one of us was going to have to stretch his arsehole, and that did not appeal."

"So you don't like having your fingers in someone's arse?" Jake asks, his tone much more flirty than it should be.

"Erm...I-I... I mean... I have, it's just—"

I take pity on Miles trying to splutter out a response and cut him off.

"He just means he doesn't want to do it on this fucker, not that he never has or wouldn't. Now, shut the fuck up, stop annoying each other, and help me come up with a plan.

"If we rip this guys arsehole open too early, we won't get as much satisfaction out of this. We need it to be pleasurable for him."

"So we use lube," Jake says with a shrug of his shoulders, before an evil smirk spreads across his face as he adds, "We just don't tell him."

"Someone still has to get the dildo into his arse though," Miles adds, and we all grimace.

"I think, if it's lubed up, the person could just spread his arse cheeks and push slowly, wiggling it around a bit if he tries to resist," I state, looking between my friends.

"So, how do we decide who gets the honour?" Jake asks, sarcasm dripping from his words.

"Let's do it how we always do. We'll play a round of poker. Losing hand has to do it," I suggest, and both my friends agree. Though we're all quick to point out that none of us actually want to do it.

After a very intense game, we're ready to show our cards. Each of us slowly turns them over, and my heart is beating out of my chest. I don't have the greatest hand, but I'm hoping it's enough.

Once all of the cards are down, I breathe a sigh of relief as Miles groans loudly. I only just beat him, but it's still a win.

"Motherfucker," he snaps, slamming his hand down over the cards.

Jake chuckles. "Don't worry. Think of this as a good thing. Learning how to be gentle as you fuck someone's arse will come in useful in the future, I'm sure."

Miles looks like he's about to throw his bottle at Jake, so I cut in.

"So, we're agreed on the plan?"

They both mutter their agreements, no matter how unhappy Miles is, and as we finish our drinks, we look forward to putting the plan in place.

I'M PULLED OUT OF MY DAYDREAM BY MILES SWEARING AND CHUNTERING UNDER HIS breath. Just because Jake thought it would be funny, Miles is wearing a pair of bright yellow cleaning gloves as he parts Frank's arse cheeks just enough for Jake to push the machine in closer.

When Frank feels the tip of the dildo at his hole, he freaks out even more, screaming into the tape, trying as much as he can to thrash around, even though he can't move at all.

I kneel down beside his head, making sure he can see me through the tears that are streaming down his face, mingling with snot and sweat.

"Make sure you relax. It really does help if you push against the cock. It'll slide in much easier. You don't want us to rip your arse this early on.

"Even if you're bleeding, the fuck machine will continue, it'll just be fucking excruciating for you. So, do yourself a favour, be a good fucking whore and let the dick in."

I make my voice as taunting as I can, knowing whatever he said to Chloe would have been so much worse.

Jake chuckles as he loudly says, "What a fucking cock whore, he's letting the dick in. I bet he's done this before."

I open my eyes wide, making an exaggerated gesture just for Frank. "Is that true? Have you had a big dick in your arse before? Is that why you rape women, because secretly you wish you could fuck guys instead?"

Frank tries to shake his head, but the tip of the dildo must have finally breached his rim as he lets out a scream.

"Stop," he mumbles beneath the tape. It's the only word I can clearly make out.

"How many times did Chloe ask you to stop? How many times did you ignore her?" I snarl, watching as Jake moves the machine, pushing the dildo further into Frank, who groans.

"It's in," Miles announces.

"Now for the fun part," I tell Frank, before nodding to Jake to turn on the machine.

It starts slowly, rocking back and forth, no more than an inch, letting him get used to the feeling of being stretched out, which is more than he deserves, but we have a plan.

Jake then increases the speed, adjusting the settings, so that the dildo now pulls almost all the way out before thrusting back in, hitting Frank deep. Each time it does, he's pressed against the table, his dick getting squashed against the edge.

After a few minutes like this, we see the moment it stops being painful for Frank, and the dildo begins dragging over his prostate, giving him pleasure. His eyes widen and his cries of pain turn to whimpers of enjoyment, which was our plan all along.

"Are you enjoying this? Does it feel good having a cock deep in your arse?" I ask tauntingly.

"I bet his tiny dick is rock hard. The little cock slut clearly loves having his arse filled," Jake adds.

Miles chuckles. "Now he finally knows what a real man's dick feels like. I bet if we were to remove his gag, he'll be begging for more."

We deliberately set the machine so he'd enjoy it, but it's not going fast enough or deep enough to get him off. It's just touching his prostate, not massaging it the way he no doubt wants it to.

The company we bought the machine from gave us a lot of help with this, no matter how embarrassed the three of us were when we asked about how to use it.

"Shall we take the gag off?" Jake asks.

I lean in closer to Frank. "Listen to me, cockslut. If I take this gag off, and you complain once, I'll replace the dildo you have now with one twice the size. Do I make myself clear?"

Frank nods, and out of the corner of my eye, I see Miles' brow raise in question. We don't have a bigger dildo, but Frank doesn't need to know that.

Jake reaches over and yanks the tape off, making sure it hurts. Frank screams before quickly clamping his mouth shut, biting on his lip as his eyes roll, and I know he's trying to stop himself from making any noise.

"You don't need to keep quiet, cockslut. We want to hear how much you're enjoying having your arse raped," I taunt, a devilish smirk on my face.

"Tell us, does it feel good? Are you becoming a filthy whore for cock?" Jake asks, his voice just as mocking.

"Yes," Frank whispers, making all three of us laugh.

"Is it making your little dick hard?" Miles asks.

Frank moans, closing his eyes as he gets lost in the sensations. "Yes, but it hurts as it's trapped against the table. Will you..."

His words trail off, replaced by a loud groan when the machine hits a particularly deep part of him.

"Will we, what? What do you want, you dirty cock whore?" Jake snarls.

"To come," he mutters, his cheeks flushing red as tears of shame trickle down his face.

All three of us start laughing, and he looks completely humiliated.

"Fuck, no. We're not going to make this good for you. If you come, we want it to hurt, so you feel every drop of humiliation that Chloe felt when you forced her body to betray her," I snarl, stepping away from him when my anger builds to the point I want to stab him again, ending our fun before it begins.

Instead, I take my seat again, watching with amusement as Miles turns up the power on the machine, while Jake taunts Frank mercilessly.

They degrade him, call him names, and mentally torment him over his reaction to being fucked.

It's not long until he comes for the first time, his cock spurting against the table, as Frank cries with a mix of pleasure, pain, and shame.

Jake makes sure to point out that now he's come, it can't be rape. That he clearly enjoys it, since he blew his load everywhere, and Frank's humiliation is there for all to see.

Still, we continue fucking him, the machine never letting up, even as he continues to come. After he's blown his load for the fourth time, it's too much for Frank, and he becomes almost incoherent. Screaming and begging for it to end, whilst admitting how much he loves it.

In the end, he willingly admits he's a whore for cock, and he even offers to suck us off or let us fuck him, as long as we turn off the machine for a bit.

The more we laugh and taunt him, the more humiliated he gets, yet he doesn't stop begging. All he can think about is getting us to turn off the machine.

When he comes for a fifth time, he actually blacks out for a moment. The intensity of the situation clearly became too much for him, and as I look at my friends, we're all silently in agreement.

Miles slaps him around the face, bringing him back to consciousness, while Jake humiliates him further.

"Wow, you must really be a whore for cock. You love it so much you passed out from the intensity. Do you like the feeling of having your dirty hole stretched with a dick so much bigger than yours?"

"Yes," Frank sobs.

"And if we bring a string of men in here and tell you to suck their cocks, what would you do?"

"I'd suck them off."

Franks drops his gaze to the table, looking ashamed of himself, which only makes me smile.

"You'd swallow all their loads like a fucking dirty cum dumpster, wouldn't you?" Jake laughs, sounding a little manic.

"Yes, I would."

Miles kneels down beside Jake, making sure Frank can see him. "If we turn off the machine, will you beg for a real cock?"

"Yes, I'll do anything," he pleads, his eyes widening in hope.

"If you don't, this punishment will seem like a walk in the fucking park. Do we make ourselves clear?" Miles' tone takes on a threatening edge that has Frank agreeing instantly.

As Miles turns off the machine, not bothering to be gentle when he pulls the dildo out, Frank cries and thanks us relentlessly. Jake unties him from the table, making sure to leave one ankle connected, so he can't move too far.

We leave him there, sobbing uncontrollably, his dick hard and covered in dried cum, his arsehole gaping in a way he won't ever recover from, as tears stream down his face. He curls up into a ball on the floor as we walk towards the door.

"We'll be back soon for more fun," we tell him as we leave, his sobs growing louder before we slam the door behind us, locking him in.

I turn to my friends, who both have matching satisfied expressions.

"Well, that was a good day. I'm going home to my girl... I'll see you in the morning."

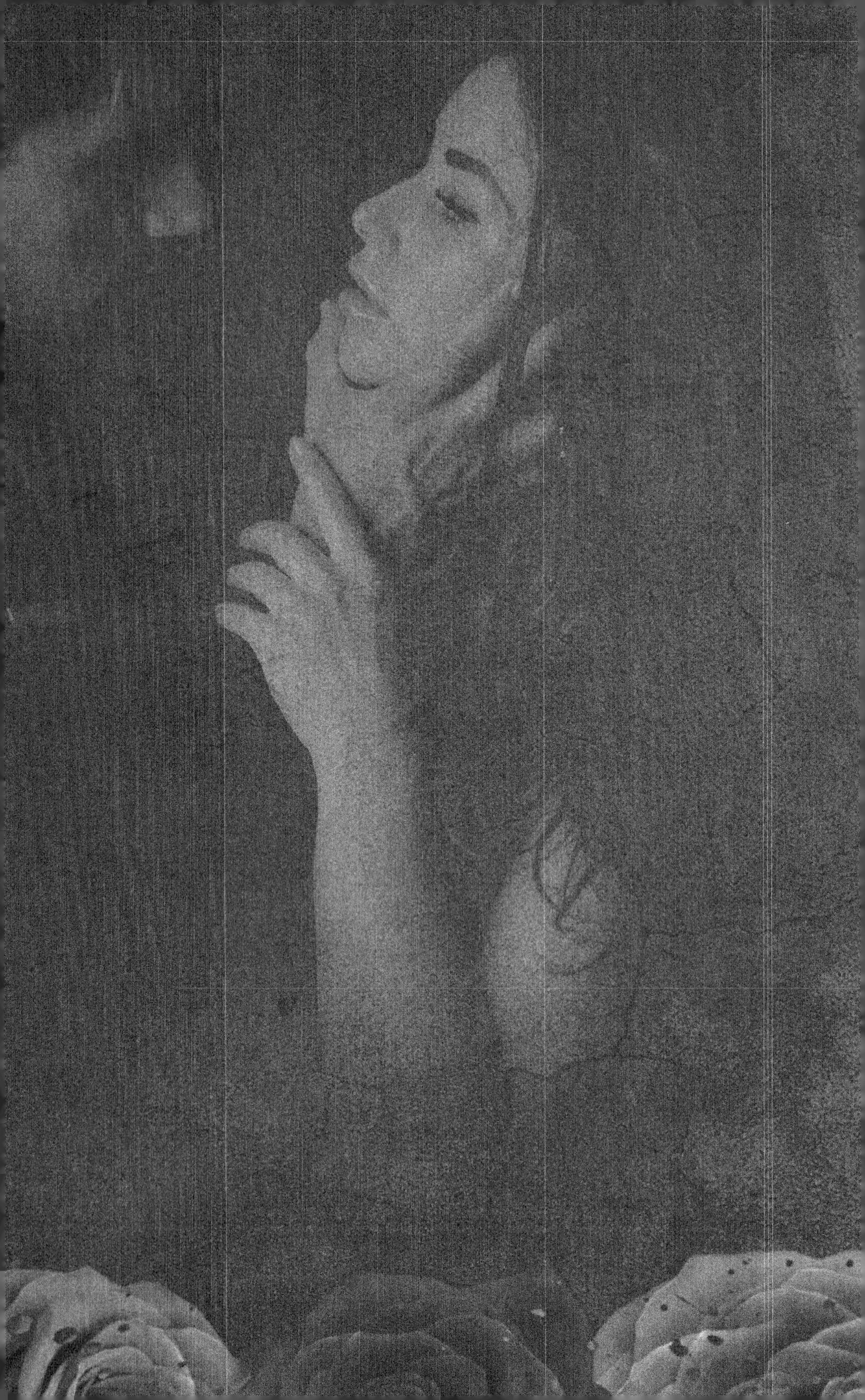

Chapter Twenty-Seven

Chloe

As my eyes flutter open, I'm shocked to find I'm the first to wake up. Normally, Marcus is wide awake, watching me as I sleep, but this morning, he's still fast asleep.

I roll back slightly, trying my best not to disturb him, but I want to take advantage of this moment the way he does. I've never understood what he gets out of watching me sleep, but as I lean back just enough to look at him, it suddenly makes sense.

He looks so young and peaceful, all the harsh lines of his face that he uses to create the dark, angry vibe he has going on have softened, making him look almost serene.

His mouth has fallen open a little, and he lets out the softest snore I've ever heard. It's closer to a rough exhale than a snore, but that's not what I'll tell him.

His arm is wrapped around me the way it always is, and once I've moved my head into the crook of his shoulder, instead of laying on his chest, it allows me to get a better view of his body.

Don't get me wrong, over the last few weeks, I've had more than enough opportunities to take in the firm lines of his body, having kissed almost every bit of it, but that doesn't mean I'm not going to look.

He's all kinds of perfect, and for just a moment, I do a little happy dance in my head, struggling to believe this is really my life. If you'd have told ten-year-old me that one day this would be my life, I'd probably have passed out with excitement.

I'd only just discovered boys, but already I knew which one I wanted. Even when he tried to make me hate him, all that did was make him hotter.

Girl world is hard to understand, but the idea of wanting what we can't have isn't a new concept. Not to mention, he was a bad boy, and all girls want to tame the bad boy—I just never thought I'd be the one to do it.

I look over at the clock on the nightstand, seeing it's almost seven in the morning, and my stomach lurches as I remember why my nerves have woken me up so early.

It's cake day!

Marcus opens his eyes to find me smiling to myself, and blush spreads across my cheeks as he stares at me.

"What's got you so excited? Were you checking me out?"

He throws me a cheeky wink that makes my stomach flutter, but I roll my eyes at him, trying to look cool.

"Of course, I was checking you out. But I'm excited—and fucking terrified—as it's cake day. In fact, I really have to get up now and get to work."

As if to reinforce my statement, the alarm on my phone begins to gently vibrate when the clock turns to seven, letting me know I have to get up.

Marcus completely ignores me and pulls me in for a kiss, which quickly deepens and makes my toes curl. Reluctantly, I push away from him.

"I want nothing more than to stay in bed with you, but this is really important," I tell him, and Marcus gives me an encouraging smile.

"I know it is, and I'm so fucking proud of you, love. You go and finish your cake, and we can say you owe me," he smirks.

I lean down and kiss him one more time, pulling away before either of us can get caught up.

"I look forward to it," I tell him. After taking a deep breath, with my voice as sincere as I can make it, I say, "Thank you."

He shakes his head as he gives me a bright smile. "You don't ever have to thank me, love. This is all you."

"You believing in me means more than you know," I admit, and the look he gives me in return makes me think maybe he does know.

He stays in bed as I rush into the bathroom. When I return, I quickly pull on my leggings and T-shirt, before heading into the kitchen.

Pulling out my notepad, I make a step-by-step list of everything I have left to do for the cake, and once I'm organised, I get to work.

Time flies while I'm in my own little bubble, flicking between my to-do list and the cake. Marcus comes into the kitchen for breakfast, making sure I stop for just a few minutes to eat something, which I'm grateful for.

Same again when he comes in and forces a coffee on me, whispering words of encouragement before he goes back to his office, leaving me in peace.

As the clock ticks on, my nerves begin to grow. I'm incredibly happy with the cake, but there were a few things that didn't go according to plan, making me pivot in my design more than once.

I didn't factor those mistakes into the schedule, which was stupid of me, so I'm cutting it close to get this cake ready on time.

Around fifteen minutes before the scheduled pick-up time, I take a step back and just look at the cake. I've been assessing every little detail for the last hour, making minor tweaks to get it looking perfect, but now's the time to step back and look at it as a whole.

When I do, my eyes fill with tears as I'm overcome with emotion. I look at the beautiful creation in front of me and I'm filled with a sense of pride I've never felt before. I made this—it was all me, my hard work, and it looks amazing. I just hope Leo and his daughter like it.

It's at that point the nerves become overwhelming, and I start to panic. I tip-toe towards Marcus' office, listening at the door to see if he's on the phone, or busy with something important. When I don't hear anything, I softly knock.

Within seconds, it springs open, Marcus' concerned gaze scanning over me.

"Is everything okay? Why did you knock?"

I place my hand on his chest to reassure him. "Everything is fine. I'm sorry if I worried you. I knocked because I didn't want to disturb you if you were working."

Marcus lets out a sigh, pulling me into a hug. "You don't ever need to knock, love. I'm never too busy for you."

I wrap my arms around him, burying my face into his chest as I breathe in his warm comforting smell. "Thank you."

"Are you okay? How's the cake?" he asks, and I can hear the concern in his voice.

I let out a sigh as I pull back to look at him. "I think it's good, but I'm so nervous. Do you want to come and see it?"

"Of course," he replies eagerly, pulling me towards the kitchen.

I hold my breath the whole way there, my heart racing as Marcus takes in the cake but remains silent. I'm about to have a nervous breakdown when he turns to me with a look that could only be described as awe on his face.

"You actually made this? It's fucking incredible, Chloe."

I let out the breath I was holding and smile, relief flooding through my veins.

I quickly box the cake back up, not wanting anything bad to possibly happen to it, even though it won't be long until collection. It's always better to keep it wrapped and protected, as you never know.

"I just hope Leo and his daughter like it."

As soon as the words are out of my mouth, the doorbell rings. I practically sprint to the door, Marcus following behind me. I open it to find Leo standing there with the cutest little girl.

She's got curly blonde hair that falls to her shoulders, and bright chubby pink cheeks that make the green of her eyes stand out. She's wearing a puffy pink princess dress with a large badge that says *Six Today* on it.

"Morning," Leo says, before looking at his watch and adding, "Well, it's closer to lunch, actually."

We agreed the cake would be ready for collecting at eleven thirty in the morning, and they're only a couple of minutes late.

"Morning," I reply, before bending down to greet the little princes. "And happy birthday to you. I'm Chloe."

She holds her hand out to mine, a bright smile on her face. "I'm Penny, and it's my birthday."

"I can see that. You look so pretty," I tell her as I shake her hand.

She turns her attention to Marcus, who is standing behind me, her eyes taking on an almost dreamy edge as she stares at him, her mouth open. "Who are you?"

Leo groans as Marcus chuckles. "I'm Marcus. Happy birthday, Penny. I love your dress."

Her cheeks turn red as her smile grows. She grabs the edges of her dress and twirls, watching him as she does.

"It's my princess dress."

"It definitely is," Marcus agrees, his face soft as he smiles at her.

"Shall we see the cake?" Leo asks, breaking Penny out of her growing infatuation with Marcus.

"Yes, yes, yes," she shouts, bouncing on the tips of her toes as she throws her arms around.

"Come on in then," I tell them, leading the way into the kitchen.

I hear Leo politely address Marcus, who tells him there's no need for formalities when it's his day off.

Leo apologises for Penny being so hyper, telling him she's not even had any sugar yet, this is all just the excitement of her birthday, which makes Marcus laugh.

I almost want to turn around and look, as I don't get to see him truly laugh as much as I'd like to. He always looks so relaxed and carefree when he does, and I wonder if Leo is a little thrown by this side of his boss.

If he is, he doesn't say anything that I hear, though Penny is pulling me alongside her, muttering about all of the things she got for her birthday.

Once we get into the kitchen, she spots the big white box instantly, bouncing around in excitement. Leo quickly grabs hold of her, picking her up and settling her onto his hip.

"Are you going to close your eyes?" I ask her, and she nods.

Penny makes a big deal about squeezing them shut, but she's clearly just squinting, so she can still see. Marcus moves closer to her.

"Why don't I cover them, so you can't peep?" he asks, and she nods excitedly, making Leo laugh.

When Marcus wraps his hands over her eyes, she giggles excitedly, placing her hands over his.

I think someone has an admirer.

As I lift off the middle section of the box, and pop open the bottom, the sides fall away to reveal the cake. Leo's eyes widen as he gasps. Penny must have heard him as she begins pulling on Marcus' hands.

"Let me see. Let me see," she chants, full of energy.

Marcus looks to me, and when I give the nod of approval, he removes his hands. Penny's eyes grow wide and full of wonder as she takes in the cake, her face almost frozen as she stares at it.

The longer she's silent and unmoving, the more anxious I become. My heart is pounding and my hands are clammy, and I'm seconds away from hyperventilating.

"Ohhh, that's so beautiful," Penny eventually cries out, and I finally breathe a sigh of relief.

She leans forward to get a closer look, taking in all the details of the large castle cake.

Although Leo didn't need a lot of cake, he wanted something special for his princess. This is her first birthday without her mum, who passed away ten months ago, and he wanted to make it special.

So the large bottom tier of the cake is fake, made of polystyrene, but covered in white fondant that I've made to look like marbled brick.

The next layer is a chocolate fudge cake, just what the birthday girl requested. It's also got the same white brick effect, and around the top of both cakes, I've made it look like the turrets of a castle.

On each side of the cakes, I've added two towers, the larger ones at the back, with the smaller at the front, using ice cream cones to create the spikes of the tower.

The four towers have the white brick effect, but the spikes have been covered in pink fondant, to give it a princess vibe.

Around the base board, I added green fondant, as well as lettering that reads Happy Birthday Penny. Then after adding some windows and flowers, to make it look really pretty, I put on the final finishing touches.

Three Disney Princess figurines were placed on the cake, and she'll be able to keep them afterwards. I added bright pink flags to the top of the tower spikes, with the number six on each of them.

I then covered the cake in glitter, making the white castle sparkle. Before finally, on top of the cake, I placed a pink number six candle.

"Do you like it?" I ask, trying not to sound too desperate for praise.

Penny turns towards me, lets go of her father, despite still being on his hip, and throws her arms around me, pulling me into a hug.

"I love it so so much. It's so pretty. It's the perfect princess castle, and it looks just like the one I want to live in when I'm all grown up."

Marcus chuckles as Leo smiles at me, his eyes becoming misty. "It's fantastic. I can't thank you enough for this."

"It was my pleasure. I had a lot of fun making it," I tell him, as Penny lets go of me to take another look at her cake.

"I know you said you didn't want payment, but you have to let me pay you for this. It's more than I was imagining when I asked for a princess cake," Leo tells me, setting Penny down on the floor as he reaches for his wallet.

I put my hand on his arm to stop him.

"Absolutely not. We had a deal. As long as you tell people about the cake, and it's okay for me to put the pictures I've taken online, then I'm more than happy."

Leo nods and smiles, grabbing hold of Penny's hand when she reaches out to touch the cake.

"When we get it all set up at her party, I'll send you some more pictures you can use, and I will let everyone know who made it. I'm sure it'll taste as great as it looks, but I can send you some pictures after we've cut it too."

"That would be great," I tell him as I begin reboxing the cake, much to Penny's annoyance.

As I get to work, Marcus distracts her. He gives her some money from his wallet, and tells her she can go with her daddy to buy something that she really wants. Her eyes light up, and she looks at Marcus like she might be in love.

Get in line, kid.

Leo glances at his boss, looking a little shy. "You didn't have to do that."

"She's a great kid, it's the least I can do. She deserves to be spoiled, after everything you've been through," Marcus says kindly.

Although Leo didn't tell me much about his story, Marcus told me enough. His wife was ill for a few months before she passed from cervical cancer.

She had lots of operations and treatments in a short space of time, but just seemed to get worse not better.

Leo found it hard juggling work, and looking after his sick wife and Penny, so Marcus gave him the time off, making sure he got paid extra during that time too.

The kindness he showed Leo and his family made me fall harder for him, but it was the humble way he said he was just doing the right thing that blew me away.

The mask Marcus presents to the world is literally just that—an act. If you're lucky enough to have earnt Marcus' respect, or have him care for you, he will show you a different side to himself, and it's a beautiful thing to witness.

He cares about his staff, and he treats them well, which is why they'd protect him with their lives.

"This is the best birthday ever," Penny cheers, waving the cash in the air.

Her father quickly takes it from her, putting it in his pocket for safe keeping, earning him a glare from his daughter. I quickly pull their attention away, as Penny looks like she might shout.

"This is all ready. All of the instructions are on the box, including which parts aren't edible. It's quite heavy, do you want help carrying it to the car?"

Before Leo can respond, Marcus reaches over and tells him he's carrying the cake for him. Once we've got it secured in the backseat of the car, and Penny is in her car seat, Leo pulls me in for a hug, thanking me once more.

Just as he's about to close the door, Penny shouts to me. "Will you make my birthday cake every year from now on?"

I look over at her father, who nods.

"I can do that," I tell her proudly.

Her smile grows as she waves goodbye to both of us, looking a little too long at Marcus. As the car drives away, I turn to him. "Looks like I have a little competition."

He laughs and wraps his arms around me, nuzzling my nose with his. "As cute as she is, there's only one girl for me."

He presses his lips to mine, his kiss sending shivers down my spine. He leads me back into the apartment, looking at me in amazement.

"I'm so fucking proud of you, Mio. That cake was fantastic. I think this is going to be the start of something great for you."

And within an hour, I'd gotten two texts from people who work with Leo, asking if they could meet to discuss cakes. I was practically bouncing when I told Marcus. He just smiled, kissed me, and told me he knew I could do it.

"I want to celebrate," I tell him.

Marcus looks a little hesitant, before saying, "I do have a way for you to celebrate, but it's not exactly traditional."

"What do you mean?"

"Well, before we can truly celebrate this new start, I think we have to say goodbye to the last pieces of the old Chloe. To do that, you need to exorcise the demon that haunts your past."

I don't need him to say his name to know what he means. "You have him?"

A vicious smile crosses his face, making him look more dangerous than I've ever seen him.

"I spent all day yesterday torturing and humiliating him. Miles and Jake have been with him this morning. They think he's broken enough for you to face him."

"I'm scared," I whisper, my voice breaking as I admit how I feel.

Marcus pulls me into his arms. "You have nothing to be afraid of, and you'll be sure of that the minute you see him. You are stronger than you know, Mio."

I pull back a little, giving him a tight smile. "Are you ever going to tell me what Mio means?"

"You've never looked it up?" he asks, his brow furrowed.

I shake my head, fixing his gaze with mine. "No, I figured you'd tell me when you wanted me to know."

He lets out a laugh. "It means 'mine'."

My eyes widen in shock. "You've been calling me that this whole time, even before we got together. In fact, you called me it when we were growing up, whenever we argued."

His lip tips up into that cocky smirk of his that makes me melt. "I was an arsehole, held back by the thought that I was doing the right thing, but I always knew you were mine, even when you couldn't be."

I lean over and capture his lips with mine, pulling him in for a deep bruising kiss.

"I've always been yours," I tell him, before taking a deep breath to steady my nerves. "I'm ready."

Prized Possession

Marcus drives us to an old warehouse, though I don't really pay much attention to where we are, or how long it took to get here. The drive felt long, and we sat in silence.

Marcus seemed to know I needed time to gather my strength. He just placed his hand on my thigh, letting me draw strength from him as he drove.

As I climb out of the car, Marcus laces our fingers together and I pull my shoulders back, drawing in a deep breath. I try to school my face into a mask similar to Marcus', but I can't hide the way my hands are trembling.

Marcus squeezes my hand, giving me a reassuring smile. "Are you sure you want to do this?" he asks when we get to the entrance.

I pause for a moment, trying to slow down my racing heart, before I say, "I need to do this. I'm strong enough, now. I need him to know he didn't break me."

Marcus presses a kiss to my forehead, looking at me with nothing but love.

"I'm so fucking proud of you, and I'm right by your side."

As we get to the room, Marcus tells me he's just on the other side of the metal door we're standing in front of. I pause to take a few deep breaths and gather my composure.

"You ready?"

I nod, and he opens the door for me to step inside. As soon as I take in the scene before me, I breathe a sigh of relief.

Frank is on the floor, completely naked, curled up into a ball. He looks to be silently sobbing, while Jake and Miles sit nearby, just watching the shell of a man.

He looks completely broken, though he doesn't appear to have been beaten as much as I was expecting.

Sure, he has cuts and bruises, with dried blood across his legs and chest, but the injuries don't seem to be what's caused Frank to break like this.

As I stare at the broken, sobbing man, I know now why Marcus said I shouldn't be afraid. When I look at him, I feel nothing but pity.

At hearing us enter the room, Frank looks up, his eyes widening as his body trembles when he realises it's me. He quickly rolls onto his knees, not bothered that he's completely naked, and begins bowing low in front of me.

Jake and Miles chuckle, watching this unfold like it's a show for their amusement.

"He follows instructions well now," Jake comments, and Miles quickly agrees.

"What do you have to say to her?" Miles shouts, making Frank jump.

He continues bowing in front of me, his voice small and shaky as he speaks.

"I want to apologise to you. I can't tell you how sorry I am for all the pain I caused you.

"You did nothing to deserve it, and I'm sorry. I'm begging you to accept my apology and let me go. I'll leave Blackthorn and never return."

I look between Marcus, Jake, and Miles, silently asking them what the hell I'm supposed to say to that. Marcus just nods towards him, letting me know it's up to me.

"I have a question for you, and I expect you to be honest with me," I tell him, and he quickly sits up, making eye contact with me through the tears.

I expect to shy away under his gaze, but he's the one to drop his eyes to the floor first, looking terrified. Marcus chuckles beside me.

"He wouldn't dare lie to you, love. Would you, cocksucker?"

Frank shakes his head vigorously, his words tumbling out. "No. No, I'd never lie to you. I only tell the truth now."

I'm frozen at the absurdity of this moment, glancing between the guys, who are looking incredibly smug right now. I have no idea what they did to break him, but it seems to have worked.

"I need to know if you did to other women what you did to me?"

Frank freezes, remaining totally silent as the last bit of colour drains from his already pale face. If I thought he looked terrified before, it's nothing compared to now.

Jake clears his throat, startling Frank. "I don't hear you answering."

"Yes," he replies, barely above a whisper, his body deflating as the word comes out.

"How many?" I ask through gritted teeth.

Frank looks over at Marcus, but whatever he sees on my guy's face must be scary enough for him to talk. With his eyes fixed on the floor, his trembling voice says the words that guts me in a way I wasn't expecting.

"Twenty-six, including you."

I gasp loudly and Marcus steps forward, punching Frank on his nose. Blood spurts out while he falls backwards, sobs racking his body as he curls into a ball on his side.

Miles stands behind him and grabs his hair, dragging him back onto his knees. I take a small step forward, Marcus' hand in mine.

"You need to pay for what you've done." I then look at the three guys. "Is there any way to get him to hand over every penny he owns, along with the names of his victims, so they can be reimbursed for what he did to them? Money won't take away the horror of what he did, but it'll help."

"I think that's a great idea, Clo," Jake says, pressing a soft kiss against my temple.

Miles pulls Frank onto the chair in the middle of the room, not needing to tie him down as he just stays there, sobbing as he holds his nose.

"I'm going to get you a pen and paper, and you're going to write down the names of every one of your victims. Can you do that?" Miles asks him.

Frank nods his head slowly, almost like he's given up.

"How will we get his money?" Jake asks.

Frank clears his throat, spitting blood out of his mouth. "If you get me a laptop, I can transfer the money online."

"Why are you volunteering to do that?" I ask, suspicious as to why he's giving in so easily.

Frank lets out a sigh. "I'll do whatever it takes to get out of here. I don't want to die."

Miles tells us he'll be back in a minute, and we wait in silence for his return. It's not long before he's back with a pad and pen, and his laptop.

Jake pulls a small dirty table over and places it in front of Frank. I don't miss the way he cringes when he sees it, and I wonder once again what the hell they've done to him.

As Frank starts making a list of names, with as much detail as he can remember, to help us identify the girls, Miles works on getting a bank account set up for him to transfer the money into.

Once Miles is ready, he grabs Frank's attention. "Right, the login page is open. What next?"

"I can log you in," Frank says, holding his hand out for the laptop.

Miles shakes his head. "You're not touching it. Just tell me what to do."

With a resigned sigh, Frank gives Miles step-by-step instructions on how to log in. Just a few minutes later, the new account he just set up is almost thirteen million pounds richer.

Miles shows Frank his almost empty bank account.

"Don't worry, I left you with four pounds and twenty nine pence. We're not total monsters," he jokes, earning dark chuckles from Jake and Marcus.

As Miles collects the list, I give him an appreciative smile. "Can you make sure the girls get an even share of the money?"

"Of course," he says, squeezing my arm in comfort.

With one last look at Frank, who appears completely broken and lost, I take a deep breath. Feeling stronger than I have in a long time, I turn to Marcus, whose bright blue eyes are quietly watching over me.

"I'm done."

Frank hears what I say to Marcus, and his eyes widen. "Does that mean I can go now?" he asks hopefully.

I can't help but laugh at how weak and desperate he sounds.

"No, I meant that I'm done. After today, I'm never going to think of you or what you did to me ever again.

"For a long time, I thought you ruined my life, but now I know that I had to break into little pieces so that this man could build me back up again, and now I'm stronger than I ever was before.

"I'm going to make sure that every girl you hurt knows that she never has to think of you again either. None of them will fear you again after today.

"But the only way to be sure you're not a threat to me, those girls, or any woman ever again, is to eliminate the risk."

I pause, and Frank looks confused, like he's not really following what I'm saying.

I turn to Marcus, holding my head high as I tell him, "It's time to end this, for good."

Without saying another word, I turn and walk out of the door, Miles following behind me. As soon as the door slams shut, I hear whimpering that's quickly silenced by several loud gunshots, before everything descends into silence.

I lean against the wall, surprised by how calm I feel. Marcus walks out of the room, scanning his gaze over me, no doubt looking for signs I'm about to crack.

I see a few specks of blood over his shirt and trousers, but give him a reassuring smile. He quickly pulls me in for a hug, wrapping his arms around me as he presses his lips to my temple.

"I'm so fucking proud of you, Mio."

I lean back and stare at his beautiful blue eyes, wondering once more how I got this lucky, to have a man who'd go to these lengths to protect me.

"I don't know how to thank you for this," I tell him.

Marcus cups my cheek with his hand, running his thumb over it in a comforting gesture. He gives me the smile he reserves just for me and my heart aches.

"You never have to thank me. The world is a better place without that fucker in it. You're the one who battled her demon and won, I just helped."

I chuckle as I reach up and kiss his lips. My heart races but I know there's no better time to tell him.

"I love you, Marcus."

The words rush out and Marcus freezes, his hand on my cheek stops completely as he just stares at me. Panic starts to set in, and I wonder if I've ruined things by saying it too soon.

When Marcus finally breaks his silence, his voice is thick and husky. "Say that again."

I shake my head. "Sorry, I didn't mean to blurt—"

Marcus cuts me off by placing his finger over my lips. "Say it again."

"I love you, Marcus."

This time, even though I say it in a shy, somewhat uncertain way, Marcus' face lights up, his bright smile growing as his blue eyes sparkle.

"I love you too, Chloe."

Hearing him say the words back to me makes my heart almost double in size, and I can't stop the girly giggle from breaking free.

He presses his lips against mine, looking at me like I'm the most important person in the world. I've never felt more alive, more loved, and it's all because of Marcus.

I need to lose myself in this man right now.

"Take me home."

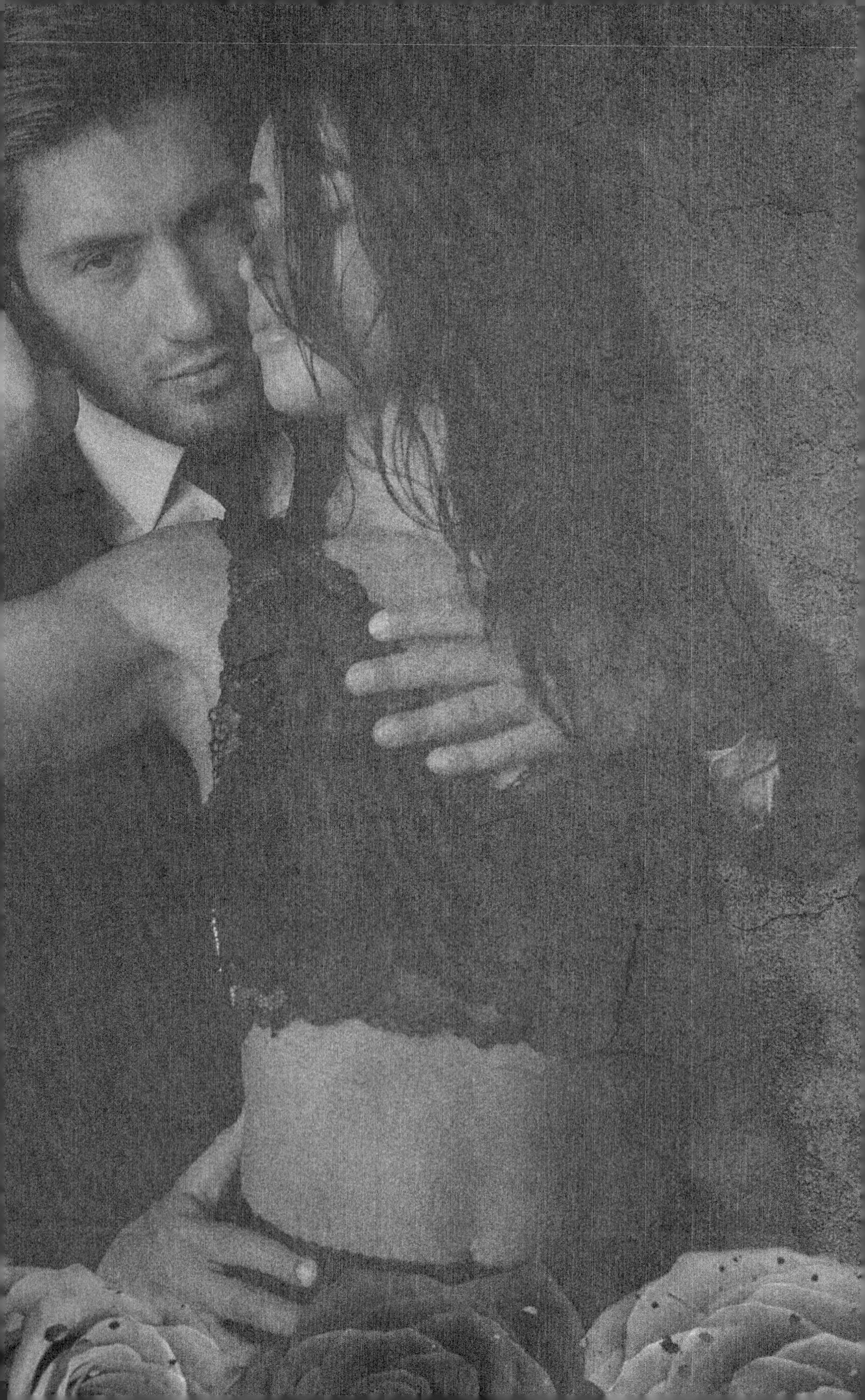

Epilogue
Marcus

It's been just over six months since we disposed of that shit-stain, Frank, and my life just seems to have gotten better and better, which is definitely not something I ever expected.

Chloe's cake business took off, and what started with just my employees getting cakes from her, soon expanded, and she's always fully booked.

She put her pictures on social media, and with a little help from word of mouth, the requests for cakes flooded in.

She's selective over how many she books in each week, as she never wants to compromise on quality, and spends a long time putting all her love and attention into each cake.

She also makes sure we still have time together, particularly on an evening when we curl up on the sofa together watching movies or crime shows.

It's not just her business that's blossomed, I've loved watching Chloe become the woman she wants to be.

She's confident, feisty, and so incredibly kind. I still have no idea why she's with a miserable bastard like me, but I thank whoever is listening every day that she chose me.

Although we usually enjoy a quiet life, tonight we've opted for a night out, since it's Chloe's birthday tomorrow. Initially, Chloe was reluctant to go to a club because of her brother's sobriety, but Jake reassured her that he'd be fine.

He's come a long way over the last six months too. He's still sober, and sees his outpatient treatment physicians regularly to help him stay that way.

He's also stepped up to be the leader I've always known he could be, and he's surprised himself with how much he's actually enjoying it now that he's trying. Doing things his own way, instead of simply obeying his father is helping too.

Miles has even agreed to take the night off to celebrate with us, though he'll have several members of security dotted around the club, watching over us.

As soon as we arrive, Jake and Miles are already seated in a booth to the right of the bar. They're leaning in close to each other, talking.

Chloe and I still haven't worked out what happened between them to stop their arguing, but they seem to be getting on well now, so we're trying not to jinx it.

They both stand and wish Chloe a happy birthday once they spot us, pulling her in for hugs. Before Chloe can sit down, I grab hold of her arm and guide her towards me. Miles and Jake look confused, but I give them my best cocky smirk.

"We'll be back soon."

Jake looks like he's about to argue when Miles grabs his arm, pulling him down into the booth. I ignore them both and drag Chloe through the club.

As always, the people part for me, some of them saying hello as I pass.

I greet everyone politely, while keeping my strides firm, not slowing at all. I'm aware Chloe is shouting something at me, but I can't hear her.

Once we reach the door to the back delivery alley, I punch in the employee code and the security door swings open.

I pull Chloe out into the alley, dragging her down to the wall at the end, just like I did all those months ago on the start of our journey. I press her back against the bricks, crowding her body with mine and she smiles at me.

"This feels oddly familiar," she laughs.

"Hard to believe this was over eight months ago now," I reply, pressing a kiss against her neck.

"I was so fucking mad at you for leaving me the way you did," she growls, rolling her eyes at me when I chuckle.

"I had a plan. I was supposed to make you hate me, so nothing would happen between us," I confess, which makes her laugh.

"It's not the best plan in the world, I don't think."

PRIZED POSSESSION

I lean in so that my breath is fluttering over her ear. "I stood no chance against you, love. As soon as I tasted you, I knew I'd lost."

"You should have fucked me then. That's what I wanted that night," she replies, pulling my ear lobe into her mouth, making me moan.

"I'll just have to fuck you tonight to make up for it."

She pushes me, a determined look in her eyes, so I step back. A mischievous grin spreads across her face as she reaches up to the neckline of the red silk mini-dress she's wearing.

In a smooth motion, she slips the thin spaghetti straps off her shoulders and shuffles it down until her tits are free.

I move towards her, licking my lips as my eyes flare with passion, but she holds out a hand to stop me. Once she's sure I'm not going to move, that cocky smirk is back, and it almost rivals my own.

I watch with rapt amusement as she slides her fingers over her nipple, giving them a small tug before she trails her hands down her hips.

When she reaches the hem of her dress, which sits a little too high up on her thigh for my liking when we're in public, that smirk of hers turns devilishly sexy.

With her gaze locked on mine, she lifts the dress until it's bunched around her waist, and she opens her legs wider, to prevent it from falling down.

I'm so caught up in how fucking sexy she looks that it takes me a couple of seconds to realise she's not wearing any fucking knickers.

I'd worked out by the way her nipples poked through the red silk in the cold air that she didn't have a bra on, but I had no idea she didn't have any knickers on either.

Her bare pink pussy seems to shine under the moonlight, and my cock springs to life. I reach down and grasp my length through my jeans, squeezing just enough to help ease the throbbing ache that comes with my dick desperately wanting to be free.

"You seem to have lost your knickers, Mio," I joke, my voice thick with desire.

"Oh, I didn't lose them. I purposely didn't put them on," she replies cockily.

"Is that so I'd get easy access?" I ask, taking a small predatory step towards her.

"That, and I knew it'd drive you mad."

"You wanted to drive me mad?" I growl, pressing my body against hers once more.

Her smile doesn't falter. "I wanted to get you wound up enough that you'd fuck me the way I wanted you to all those months ago."

My dick twitches in my boxers. "And how would that be?"

She lets out a sigh, her face relaxed as she meets my gaze.

"For ages afterwards, I dreamt about what would've happened if you hadn't walked away. I woke up crying out your name, my fingers between my legs, wishing they were yours. I dreamt of you finishing it in so many ways, but there was always one that I came back to."

"Tell me," I rasp, grabbing hold of her hair, so I can move her head to the side, giving me better access to nibble along her neck.

"I wanted it fast and rough, as we didn't have much time before someone noticed we were missing. You pushed me against the wall, making my curve my back and present my pussy to you. You plunged into my pussy without any build up, knowing I was dripping wet for you already, as you'd checked with your fingers.

"When I was about to come, you pulled out, saying I hadn't been good enough to come. You then told me you wanted to find out how much of a slut I could be, and you took my arse.

"I told you it was my first time, and you were slow and gentle at first, making sure I enjoyed it, and once I was used to being stretched open, you pounded me hard. As I came, you told me that only good sluts come with a cock in their arse."

"Fuck," I mutter, suddenly feeling very fucking overheated. "That's hot."

"It is," she smiles cheekily.

"Is anal something you want to try? I know we've played a little, and you've said you're open to trying, but you've never specifically asked for it."

She nods slowly, suddenly looking shy again.

"I think I can make that happen, love," I say, spinning her around, pushing her face against the wall.

I don't have to tell her, she arches her spine, presenting herself to me. Something sparkly catches my eye, and I look down to see something shiny in her arse. I crouch down to get a better look.

Once I'm at eye-level with her pussy, I find Chloe looking at me, assessing me with her eyes.

"I've been practising, getting myself ready for you," she whispers, reaching back with both hands to spread her arse cheeks open.

The butt plug is on full display now, the fake gem glistening at me in the place of her puckered hole. A shiver of pleasure runs through me, and I feel my last strands of control beginning to snap.

"How long have you been wearing that?" I ask, dragging my hand over the smooth skin of her arse, my finger trailing around the toy.

"Since we left the house."

Her voice is thick, and she's looking at me with those innocent silver eyes, challenging me to see what I'll do next.

As I drag my finger around the toy, a shiver runs up her spine, and I take hold of the jewelled end, pulling it just a little. The small movement makes Chloe gasp, and my cock twitches at the sound.

"Do you like having this in your arse? Did it make you feel dirty, walking around the club with it in, knowing nobody else knows what a nasty little slut you are?"

She nods her head, groaning as I pull the toy out more. Once the widest part of the plug is spreading her ring, I keep it there, loving the way she's stretched out for me.

"Yes, I love it," she says, sounding breathy and desperate.

With my other hand, I reach beneath the toy, sliding my finger through her slit, biting my lower lip when I feel how wet she is.

"You're fucking dripping, Mio."

"I need you so bad," she cries.

Hearing how much she wants me is the biggest ego boost, and I don't want to draw this out any longer. My already fragile control is hanging by a thread, and I really want to let go.

As I circle her clit, while wiggling the butt plug that's still stretching her at the widest part, she rocks against me, begging for me to take her.

"Please, Marcus. Don't tease me. I need you, right now."

Since it's her birthday, and there's a risk of getting caught, I give her what she wants. It's not at all because my cock is straining so much it's fucking painful.

As I continue teasing her arse with the buttplug, I press my fingers into her pussy, finding her wet and ready for me, just as I expected. I thrust my fingers in fast and deep, loving the way she rocks back against me, fucking herself on my hand.

Her moans turn to whimpers when I pull my hand away, but before he can protest, I slam my cock into her pussy, not stopping until I'm balls deep. Both of us cry out when I bottom out, and I grab her hip tight to hold her against me.

As she's getting used to me, I use my other hand to press the buttplug back in, until it disappears, leaving just the jewelled end behind. I can feel the wide plug through her thin wall, pushing against my cock, making her feel even tighter.

"Fuck, I'm so full," she groans, her eyes blown wide with lust.

"Mio, you're so fucking tight," I tell her, taking several deep breaths to stop myself from losing control too soon.

Chloe lets out a soft breath before looking over at me, a blissed out expression on her face. "You can fuck me now."

I don't need to be told twice. With my finger on the jewel of the toy, to keep it in place, I slowly begin fucking her pussy with my cock. If I thought she was tight before, it's nothing compared to how she feels now that she's so full.

It's a weird sensation, but I can feel the outline of the plug as I drag my cock over her cunt walls, and I'm surprised by how amazing it feels. I pull out slowly, savouring the unique feeling, before slamming back in, loving the way Chloe hisses when I hit deep.

I keep my thrusting hard and deep, speeding up as Chloe begins rocking back to meet me each time, pressing herself onto me further. Her moans are like music to my ears, and the way her walls tighten around me makes me tremble.

As her whimpers become more desperate, and her walls start to tighten, I know she's close. She's not told me yet, but it won't be long till she's begging me.

Sure enough, just a couple of thrusts later, Chloe starts pleading to come. "I'm so close. Please, please, can I come?"

Instead of responding, I quickly pull my cock out, removing the buttplug at the same time. Chloe's legs almost give way as she cries out in frustration, no doubt feeling incredibly empty after being stretched and full.

"Nooo. No, please..." she cries, her fingers sticking into her flesh so much, I'm surprised she's not drawn blood, but still she keeps her arse spread for me.

Before she can finish her complaint, I place the buttplug in my pocket and press the wet head of my cock against her stretched arsehole. She looks over her shoulders at me, her eyes wide when she realises what I'm about to do.

I stare at her for a second, waiting to see if she's changed her mind, but when she gives me a smile as she nods her head, I take that as consent.

I take my time pressing into her, stretching her tight hole wider than ever before. Although she's been prepping herself, which has helped a lot, I doubt she's taken anything as large as me, and so take my time with her.

Her eyes flutter closed as she concentrates on breathing, forcing her muscles to relax. When I get to the hardest part, I feel her tense, but before I can instruct her, the muscles around my cock start to push, and I know Chloe's letting me in.

As the head pops in, we both groan loudly. I lean over and place my forehead against her back, taking deep breaths, so I don't end this too soon.

"You're going to be the fucking death of me, love," I groan.

When she chuckles in response, her arse clamps around my cock until I'm shouting out a string of expletives. I spank her, which earns me a yelp. But as she's startled, she presses back onto my cock further—a happy accident.

With one hand on her hip, to steady her movements, I press the other against her lower back, helping her to keep that perfect arch to her spine.

Once we've both caught our breaths, and I'm fairly sure I'm not going to come straight away, I begin pressing in again slowly.

After rocking and advancing a few times, I finally bottom out, and Chloe breathes a sigh of relief when I tell her she's taken all of me.

"Open your eyes, Mio. I want to watch as you fall apart with my cock in your arse."

Her lids fly open straight away, revealing molten silver eyes that are almost black, heavy with lust. Her mouth is wide, and she looks so relaxed, lost in the feeling.

"You're so deep," she breathes.

"Are you ready for me to fuck you now?" I ask, rubbing my hand over her back.

She nods her head as best she can with it against the wall. "Yes."

As much as I want to slam into her, taking her as rough and hard as I know she loves, I take my time, letting her arse get used to me. I keep my movements slow as I pull back, thrusting back in a little quicker each time.

After a few thrusts like this, her fierce gaze locks with mine. "Fuck me harder, please. I can take it."

As if to prove her point, she slams her hips back against mine rapidly, forcing my cock to hit her deep, dragging a ragged cry from both our lips.

Determined to give my girl what she wants, I follow her lead, thrusting into her hard and fast. I move my other hand to her hip, so I can use both to control her while I slam my cock into her, pulling her back against me, hitting a spot deep in her arse that drives her crazy.

Chloe's cries and whimpers turn louder and more frantic. She moves one of her hands from where she was spreading her arse, and slides her fingers over her clit.

"Oh fuck, fuck, fucking fuck," she cries as her fingers rub against her sensitive nub.

I have to use my hands on her hips to keep my thrusts coordinated, because as soon as Chloe begins playing with her clit, her actions turn frantic and desperate, her cries a jumbled mess of words and sounds.

As her release approaches, her arse grips my cock tighter than before, making my balls twitch and ache the way they always do when I'm not far from shooting my load.

"You're so fucking sexy like this," I mutter, rocking into her at a bruising pace.

"Shit, I'm going to... Please, can I..."

She closes her eyes, her fingers rubbing circles around her clit as she rocks her hips back against me, chasing the pleasure she desperately seeks.

"Open your eyes, Mio," I tell her, and she obeys instantly. "Does my beautiful whore want to come with a cock in her arse?"

"Yes, please."

"Where do you want me to come?" I grind out, knowing I won't be able to hold it for long after she falls apart.

"In...in my arse," she cries out.

"If I come in your arse, I'm going to put the toy back in, so I know my cum is plugged inside you for the rest of the evening. Do you want that, slut?"

Her eyes widen before they flutter, a soft smile gracing her lips.

"Yes. I want you to fill me with your cum. I want your cum inside of me."

I groan at how fucking sexy she is when she says things like that to me. I'm so lost in the moment, I don't even think before I speak.

"If I come in your arse now, when we get home, I'm going to come in your pussy. I want to fill your cunt with my cum, claiming you as mine, while making you round with my baby."

Her eyes widen in shock, and she stares at me, but doesn't falter on her movements. She continues meeting my thrusts, pressing me deep into her as her orgasm draws closer.

"You want to have a baby with me?" she rushes out, followed by a loud moan as the head of my cock hits her deep.

"Fuck, one day, I do. You're mine forever," I tell her.

There's a distant part of my brain that's aware this isn't the best scenario to be having this conversation, or the most romantic way, but it's not like I can take it back.

"I-I... I want that too...someday," she cries. "Please, can I come?" Her desperation quickly puts an end to the discussion.

I lean over and place a kiss on her neck, nibbling on her ear as I say, "Come for me, slut."

As she falls apart around me, I bite down on her neck, sucking at the spot I've marked with my teeth, claiming her in the most primal, possessive way.

Her arse clamps down on my cock, and I can feel the walls of her cunt fluttering as her orgasm hits.

She trembles as she holds her position, my cock deep inside as her orgasm rips through her body. She cries out my name as she stops frantically rubbing at her clit, moving to circle it lazily instead, as she draws out the last bits of her release.

As hers dies down, and her walls relax enough for me to move, I take what I need from her body as I chase my own orgasm. Only a few hard, deep thrusts later and I'm grunting my release, shooting row after row of cum deep into her arse.

Her walls tremble as she feels me painting her insides with my cum, while I desperately try to catch my breath. I slump over her body, resting my cheek on her back as I hold her tight.

When we've both caught our breath, I lean back a little, my heart aching at the beautiful shy smile she throws at me. Her eyes track my movements as I pull the plug from my pocket.

I bring it up to my mouth, sucking and licking it until it's covered in my saliva. Her eyes widen as she watches me taste her on the used plug.

I give her a cocky smirk as I slowly pull my limp cock from her arse. She hisses loudly once I'm all the way out, but she's distracted from the sting by watching me scoop up the cum that's trying to slide free.

I use it to get the plug extra wet, before gently pressing it inside her gaping, used hole, making sure the rest of my seed stays where it belongs.

She hisses and moans as the widest part of the plug stretches her already stinging hole, but once it's in, she breathes a sigh of relief. I slide my fingers around the jewelled end that's on display, where her puckered hole should be, making sure any evidence of our sex session is gone.

Once I'm happy, I take a step back, keeping a hand on Chloe, as her legs are still a bit wobbly. She turns around, pulling her dress back into position, so she's no longer on display, while I tuck my cock back into my boxers, and fasten my jeans.

When Chloe stands up straight, her mouth falls into an O as she shuffles from one foot to another.

"Are you okay?" I ask.

She smiles and nods, placing her hand on my chest. "I can feel your cum deep in my arse. I thought the plug would be too much for my sensitive, stretched arse, but it's really not. It feels good, sending little shivers of pleasure to my clit."

"Fuck, if you keep saying things like that, I'm going to want to fuck you again, love," I growl, stealing a kiss.

"Well, we better go and be sociable for an acceptable amount of time, then you can take me home and fuck me all night," she replies, wiggling her eyebrows at me suggestively.

I chuckle, looking at my watch as I say, "Is ten minutes acceptable?"

She playfully slaps my chest. "No, but maybe we can have a dance instead? When I grind against you, you'll be able to feel the jewel."

"You're going to be the death of me, love," I tell her with a groan, kissing her again.

I will never get bored of this. Each time I kiss her, the taste of her makes me tingle like it's the first time.

"It's a good way to die," she laughs.

I pull her closer, wrapping my arms around her as she looks up at me, her beautiful silver eyes locked with mine as she smiles.

"I don't know how the hell I got so lucky. You're the best thing that has ever happened to me, and I'm just sorry I wasted all that time pushing you away, when we could have been together."

She quickly shakes her head. "I think we needed to go through what we did to bring us here, to make us the people we are now. We weren't ready for each other before, but we are now."

My heart races as I smile at her. "I love you so fucking much, you know that, right?"

This isn't the first time I've told her I love her. I've been telling her for months, but each time feels just as momentous as the first. My love for her grows each day, and I want her to know that, to feel it.

"I know. And you know how much I love you. You saved me, and gave me the life I've always wanted, and I can never repay you for that. But I can spend forever loving you," she replies, kissing my cheek.

"That's more than enough, Mio."

I take hold of her hand as she steps away, getting ready to go back into the club, but she stops, looking at me with that shy smile that makes my dick twitch.

"Did you mean what you said before? Or was it just in the heat of the moment?"

She doesn't have to elaborate for me to know what she's referring to.

"I meant it. I probably shouldn't have brought it up when I did, since I was caught in the moment, but it doesn't change how I feel.

"I don't mean right now, but someday, I'd like to have children with you. If that's what you want?"

She nods her head, giving me a smile as her eyes start to mist over. Her grip on my hand tightens. "I want that too, but..."

She trails off, looking embarrassed again.

"But, what?" I prompt.

"Only if we're married," she rushes out.

My cocky smirk grows as I watch her cheeks flush. "Oh, we will be married. You just have to wait for me to propose."

"You want to propose?" she asks, sounding shocked.

A short laugh rips from my throat and she narrows her gaze at me. "Love, I've had a ring for months. I'm just waiting for the right moment."

"You have? Since when?"

I look down at the floor, suddenly feeling a little shy myself. She reaches up and places her hand on my cheek, forcing me to look at her.

"After the first night we had sex. I knew I'd never let you go after that."

"That long?" she blurts out, and I chuckle.

"That long. You're mine, and I knew I wanted forever with you."

She gives me a bright smile as she stands on her tip-toes, giving her just enough height to lean into my ear.

"I want forever with you too. So, whenever you ask me, just know that I'll say yes in a heartbeat."

She kisses my cheek before pulling back, not aware of how fast my heart is beating after that.

"Well, that's a pretty big spoiler," I joke, making her laugh.

"Come on, we better get back inside to make sure Jake's not breaking your rules," she says, pulling me towards the door.

We go back to the booth to find Jacob is by himself. "Where's Miles?" I ask.

"He said there was something he needed to check on, and he went into the office a few minutes ago," Jake replies.

A few minutes after we slide into the booth, one of the VIP waitresses walks over to us. I recognise her as the new girl, Indie. I hired her about three weeks ago, and she's been fitting in well ever since.

She's a couple of years younger than me with long blonde hair that falls down to her waist in waves. Her bright green eyes glisten, and she wears bright red lipstick to emphasise her already plump lips.

She's got curves in all the right places, and she wears clothes to emphasise them—no doubt so she can get more tips. But the real draw she has to my customers is her shy personality.

She's quiet and timid, which doesn't seem to match with the way she dresses or does her make-up. She's an enigma, and men love those.

Sadly, from the moment she comes over to our table, Jacob is enamoured with her.

"Hey, can I get you guys a drink?" Indie asks, her voice soft, yet loud enough to be heard over the music.

I give her a polite smile. "Hi, Indie, how are you getting on?" I ask, my boss hat taking over.

"It's going well, thank you, sir. I'm really enjoying working here," she replies.

Chloe squeezes my hand suggestively and I remember my manners.

"Sorry, Indie, this is my girlfriend, Chloe," I tell her, before turning to Chloe.

"Indie started her about three weeks ago. She's just moved here, but has been fitting in well."

Chloe gives her a wave. "It's nice to meet you, Indie. How are you liking Blackthorn?"

Indie shuffles from one foot to the other, looking a little uncomfortable. "Honestly, I've not seen too much of it. I've just been working and trying to get settled into my new flat. Besides, I've been here before, but it was a while ago, and I didn't stay long."

Jacob shifts closer to Chloe, holding his hand out to get Indie's attention.

"Well, if you need someone to show you around, I can help with that. I'm Jacob, but most people call me Jake. It's a pleasure to meet someone as beautiful as you, Indie."

I throw a glare at Jake as Chloe rolls her eyes. Indie just stares at his hand before somewhat reluctantly reaching out to shake it.

"It's nice to meet you too."

"I can give you my number, if you want, and we can arrange something?" Jake adds, pushing his luck just a little more.

I fix him with a glare that he ignores. Indie's eyes go wide and she looks terrified. "Oh, I... Well, I'm not sure—"

Chloe takes pity on Indie and steps in. "Jake, you know you aren't supposed to ask out the girls who work here."

Jake glares at his sister, while Indie shifts uncomfortably.

"I was just offering as she looks like she could use a friend in town, nothing more."

I let out a snort, which earns a death glare from Jake. Indie's gaze flicks around the booth, before settling on Jake. She's silent for a moment, then when she speaks, it's so low and timid, we can barely hear her.

"I don't mind, if it's just as friends. Nothing more," she tells him, and I'm shocked that Jake doesn't seem deterred by this.

Just as they're about to swap numbers, much to my annoyance, Miles walks back over to the booth. He greets us as he slides in next to Jake, then he notices Indie, and turns to look at her, only to freeze.

My best friend is frozen on the spot, all of the colour draining from his face as he stares at Indie, and she has a matching expression. Miles then seems to break out of his trance and snaps at Indie, using a tone I've never heard him use towards anyone.

"What the hell are you doing here?"

We all look between Miles and Indie, who seem to just be staring at each other. Jake breaks the uncomfortable tension by asking, "You two know each other?"

Miles turns to look at me, and the expression on his face makes my stomach drop. I've never seen him look so lost. Even though Jake asked the question, he replies directly to me.

"This is Dee."

As soon as I hear the name, a flash of recognition hits me, and I wince on his behalf.

"The girl from the summer after uni?"

Miles nods, and Indie looks like she might be sick. Jake chimes in again, "How do you know each other?"

Miles gives me a look that tells me I can explain the basics.

"Remember that summer after university when we went on a bender and Miles went to stay with his family, before starting work for me afterwards?"

"Yes?" Jake draws out, encouraging me to continue.

"He had a fling with a girl called Dee. He fell for her hard, and then she left, breaking his heart."

I look over at Indie, seeing the desolate look on her face as tears well in her eyes.

"It wasn't like that," she whispers, her eyes cast down at the floor.

Miles shuffles out of the booth and jumps to his feet, the sneer he gives her as he does makes Indie shrink back.

"I don't give a fuck what you have to say. I can't be around you."

Miles storms off, but I catch the way his face falls as he does. My heart breaks for him.

I look up and see tears streaming down Indie's face. She glances over at me as she wipes them away. "I'm guessing you're going to fire me now?"

Before I can respond, Jake jumps in. He climbs out of the booth and places his hand on her arm.

"He's not going to fire you. Everyone has a past."

I shake my head at Jake, but my glare is ignored.

"He's right, I'm not going to fire you. I'll speak to Miles. Take a break and get yourself together. As long as your work isn't affected, we can continue."

She breathes a sigh of relief. "Thank you, sir. I won't let it affect my work, I promise."

"Go and take a break, I'll sort out our drinks," Chloe says, giving her a reassuring smile.

As Indie walks away with thanks, Jake trails behind her. I look over at Chloe, shaking my head like I can't quite believe what I just witnessed.

"Now I can see why you have a 'no fucking the staff' rule," Chloe jokes.

"So much fucking drama," I chunter as she laughs.

"I have a feeling this is only the start of that particular shit-show."

I groan loudly, running my fingers through my hair. "I just want an easy life."

"Well, since our friends are clearly busy, why don't you take me home?" she asks, wiggling her eyebrows suggestively.

I take her hand, dragging her out of the booth. "Burying my head in your sweet cunt is just what I need to help me ignore the rest of this fucking world."

"Fine by me," she says, pressing a kiss to my lips.

As I drag her out to the car, I can't help but think how fucking lucky I am.

I have the girl of my dreams. I'm in love, but most importantly, I'll never again have to deal with dating drama, like Jake and Miles are right now.

That thought makes me smile as Chloe kisses me once more, reminding me just how lucky I am.

The End

Want to find out what happens between Jake, Miles, and Indie?
Pre-Order Mutual Obsession Now!
https://geni.us/RoB-MO

Acknowledgements

There are so many people I have to thanks for helping me finish this book. As most of you will know, I fractured my wrist just before I started writing Prized Possession, and once I was out of the splint, I still had a lot of pain. Pushing through that, to get back to writing, was incredibly difficult, but I missed writing so much.

After a lot of encouragement, I finally sat down and once I started writing, Marcus and Chloe's story came easily. I'd had the idea from the moment I saw the model on the cover design, and I couldn't wait to write it. I'm so pleased with how it turned out, and I hope you've all enjoyed it too.

Here are just some of the people I need to thank for helping me get this book done...

JAMIE LUNA - You've have been with me through every book, helping me with names and design ideas. You encouraged me to write the book, to find a new way of working around my painful wrist, and I couldn't be more grateful. You're my partner in crime, and I love you!

MY BETA - KERRIE - I can't thank you enough for helping me with this book, and for working on it, even when you were ill. Thank you for all your love and support!

AMBER NICOLE - MY EDITOR - Thank you for all your hard work on this book, and for loving my characters as much as you do!

ABRIANNA DENAE - MY PROOFREADER - Not only am I incredibly lucky to have you as my proofreader, making my words shine, you're also my friend. I can't thank you enough for everything you do!

RJ CREATIVES - MY COVER DESIGNER - Thank you for creating the cover that sparked the whole idea for this book, and the series as a whole. And then for creating the gorgeous discreet cover to go with it. I can't wait to see what you do with the rest of the series.

SHALEY AT PRETTY LITTLE IMAGES - Thank you for creating the most beautiful teasers and countdown graphics, as always. I'm also pleased you let me push you out of your comfort zone, to create the interior images used in the paperback chapters. You've made my book even more stunning, and I couldn't be more grateful to you!

MY MUM (MOMMA LUNA) - Not only are you my mum, you're also my best friend. You listen to all the mini-meltdowns I had when I thought this book would never get started. You always believe in me, and I love you for that!

TO MY LUNATICS - You are the reason I get to keep doing what I love. I'm so incredibly humbled every time a reader tells me they've read my book and fell in love with the characters. While there are people out there who love my books, and care about my characters, I will keep writing. I can't wait for you to see what I write next! Thank you!

About
Emma Luna

Emma Luna is a USA Today Bestselling dark romance author from the UK. In a previous life she was a Midwife and a Lecturer, but now she listens to the voices in her head and puts pen to paper to bring their stories to life. In her spare time, when she should be sleeping, she also loves to edit, proofread, and format books for other amazing authors.

Emma's books are dark, dangerous, and devilishly sexy. She loves writing about strong, feisty, but underestimated women, and the cocky, dirty-mouthed men they bring to their knees.

When Emma isn't writing, promoting, or editing books she can be found napping, colouring in adult colouring books, and collecting novelty notebooks. She also enjoys coffee and gossiping with her mum, playing or having hugs with her gorgeous nephew, who is the light of her life, and curling up on the sofa to watch a film with Mr Luna. Oh and for those of you that don't know, Emma is a hardcore Harry Potter fan—Team Ravenclaw!!

Thank you for taking a chance on a crazy Brit and the voices inside her head. That makes you a true LUNAtic now too!

Follow
Emma Luna

I absolutely love chatting and catching up with readers. I love letting you know what books I'm working on, what I have coming up next, and my new releases. So, don't be afraid to come and say hi, or drop me an email. If you love my characters, tell me!!

If you want to find out all things Emma Luna before anyone else, you can join my newsletter here:

https://www.emmalunaauthor.com

If you have facebook, you can join my reader group for exclusive news and giveaways:

https://www.facebook.com/groups/emmaslunatics

If you would like to check out any of Emma's other books or stalk her in more places, you can find everything you need here:

https://www.linktr.ee/emmaluna

- facebook.com/EmmaLunaAuthor
- instagram.com/emmalunaauthor
- amazon.com/Emma--Luna/e/B082GNYLM4
- bookbub.com/profile/emma-luna
- goodreads.com/emmaluna
- tiktok.com/@emmalunaauthor

Also By
Emma Luna

BEAUTIFULLY BRUTAL SERIES COMPLETE BOX SET

Beautifully Brutal Series: Part One
(Contains Black Wedding, Trust In Me, and Fighting To Be Free)
https://geni.us/BB-BoxSet-Part1

Beautifully Brutal Series: Part Two
(Contains The Time Is Now, The Lies That Shatter, and Together We Reign)
https://geni.us/BB-BoxSet-Part2

BEAUTIFULLY BRUTAL SERIES

Black Wedding - Bree and Liam's Story
https://geni.us/BW-BB

Dangerously Deceptive - Kellan's Prequel
https://geni.us/DD-BB

Trust In Me - Kellan and Mia's Story
https://geni.us/TiM-BB

The Ties We Break - Declan and Belle's Prequel
http://Geni.us/TTWB-BB

Fighting To Be Free - Kian and Freya's Story
http://Geni.us/FTBF-BB

The Time Is Now - Ryleigh and Shane's Story
https://geni.us/TTIN-BB

The Lies That Shatter - Finn and McKenna's Story
https://geni.us/TLTS-BB

Together We Reign - Evan and Teigan's Story
https://geni.us/TWR-BB

.

BEAUTIFULLY BRUTAL ORIGINS

Beautiful Beginnings - Desmond and Siobhan's Prequel
FREE TO DOWNLOAD
https://geni.us/BB-BB

.

RIVALS OF BLACKTHORN

Prized Possession
https://geni.us/RoB-PP

Mutual Obsession
https://geni.us/RoB-MO

.

STANDALONES

Under the Cover of Darkness
https://geni.us/TL8-UtCoD

.

I Was Always Yours

http://Geni.us/IWasAlwaysYours

.

WILLOWMEAD ACADEMY - CO-WRITE WITH MADDISON COLE

Life Lessons

https://geni.us/WA-LifeLessons

.

SINS OF OUR FATHERS SERIES

Broken

https://geni.us/SouF-Broken

.

MANAGING MISCHIEF

Piper

https://geni.us/MM-Piper